THE
PUSHCART PRIZE, X:
BEST OF THE
SMALL PRESSES
1985-86 Edition

THE PUSHCART PRIZE X:

BEST OF THE SMALL PRESSES

BEST OF THE SMALL PRESSES

. . . WITH AN INDEX TO THE FIRST TEN VOLUMES

An annual small press reader

EDITED BY BILL HENDERSON

with The Pushcart Prize editors

Introduction by George Plimpton

Poetry Editors: Stanley Plumly, William Stafford

published by THE PUSHCART PRESS
1985-86 Edition

THE PUSHCART PRIZE, X:

Note: nominations for this series are invited from any small, independent, literary book press or magazine in the world. Up to six nominations—tear sheets or copies selected from work published in that calendar year—are accepted by our October 15 deadline each year. Write to Pushcart Press, P.O. Box 380, Wainscott, N.Y. 11975 if you need more information.

Pushcart Press sends special thanks to The Helen Foundation of Salt Lake City for its generous awards to the authors of our lead short story, poem, and essay.

Library of Congress Card number: 76-58675
ISBN 0-916366-37-5
ISSN: 0149-7863

First printing, July 1985
Manufactured in The United States of America
by Ray Freiman and Co., Stamford, Connecticut

Acknowledgments

The following works are reprinted by permission of the publisher and author:

"Agriculture" © 1984 Confluence Press
"Whiskey, Whiskey, Gin, Gin, Gin" © 1984 Quarterly West
"Quantum Jumps" © 1984 Ploughshares
"Turning Out" © 1984 TriQuarterly
"The Secret Lion" © 1984 Blue Moon and Confluence Press
"Sarah Cole: A Type of Love Story" © 1984 Russell Banks
"Heaven and Earth" © 1984 New England Review and Bread Loaf Quarterly
"The Easter We Lived in Detroit" © 1984 Paris Review
"Sundays" © 1984 Stuart Wright, Publisher
"The Hector Quesadilla Story" © 1984 Paris Review
"Hot Day On The Gold Coast" © 1984 Black Warrior Review
"Greenbaum, O'Reilly & Stephens" © 1984 Conjunctions
"Heart Leaves" © 1984 Crescent Review
"Death's Midwives" © 1984 The Ontario Review
from "The Cripple Liberation Front Marching Band Blues" © 1984 Mho & Mho Works
"Hot Ice" © 1984 Antaeus
"The Art of Seeing With One's Own Eyes" © 1984 New England Review and Bread Loaf Quarterly
from "The Great Pretender" © 1984 Triquarterly
"Big Brother Is You, Watching" © 1984 Georgia Review
"The Circumcision Rites of The Toronto Stock Exchange" © 1984 Charnel House
"Under Another Name" © 1984 Granta
"Hemingway's Wound—And Its Consequences for American Literature" © 1984 Georgia Review
"Bohemia Revisited; Malcolm Cowley, Jack Kerouac and *On The Road*" © 1984 Georgia Review
"Wilderness" © 1984 Brown Journal of the Arts
"Kodiak Widow" © 1984 Orca
"To Future Eleanors" © 1984 Stuart Wright, Publisher
"Why I'm In Favor of A Nuclear Freeze" © 1984 Christopher Buckley
"Cranes" © 1984 Telescope
"The Fundamental Project of Technology" © 1984 American Poetry Review
"Cloud Painter" © 1984 Poetry
"Dickinson" © 1984 Virginia Quarterly Review
"A Setting" © 1984 The Antioch Review
"Grasmere" © 1984 Paris Review
"A Poem With No Ending" © 1984 Paris Review
"Sorrow and Rapture" © 1984 Telescope
"Rain Country" © 1984 New England Review and Bread Loaf Quarterly
"Rondo" © 1984 Sonora Review
"For Starr Atkinson, Who Designed Books" © 1984 Barnwood Press
"The Elect" © 1984 Ohio Review
"Child's Grave, Hale County, Alabama" © 1984 Kansas Quarterly
"Dog Fight" © 1984 Wormwood Review
"Dinosaurs of the Hollywood Delta" © 1984 Gerald Costanzo
"Vesper Sparrows" © 1984 Antaeus
"The Objects of Immortality" © 1984 Amelia
"Exodus" © 1984 Antaeus
"Shooting" © 1984 Epoch
"Birthday Star Atlas" © 1984 Missouri Review
"The Librarian of Alexandria" © 1984 Salmagundi
"Ledge" © 1984 Grand Street
"Where We Are" © 1984 Bluefish
"Season's Greetings" © 1984 Cedar Rock
"Pier" © 1984 Poetry
"The Meal" © 1984 Alice James Books
"Mute" Wesley McNair © 1984 Poetry
"The Consolation of Touch" © 1984 Georgia Review

*In Celebration
of Our Tenth Anniversary
This Edition Is Dedicated to
The Founding Editors
of The Pushcart Prize Series*

THE
PEOPLE WHO HELPED

FOUNDING EDITORS—*Anaïs Nin (1903-1977), Buckminster Fuller (1895-1983), Charles Newman, Daniel Halpern, Gordon Lish, Harry Smith, Hugh Fox, Ishmael Reed, Joyce Carol Oates, Len Fulton, Leonard Randolph, Leslie Fiedler, Nona Balakian, Paul Bowles, Paul Engle, Ralph Ellison, Reynolds Price, Rhoda Schwartz, Richard Morris, Ted Wilentz, Tom Montag, William Phillips. Poetry editor: H. L. Van Brunt.*

EDITORS—*Walter Abish, Ai, Elliott Anderson, John Ashbery, Robert Bly, Robert Boyers, Harold Brodkey, Joseph Brodsky, Wesley Brown, Hayden Carruth, Raymond Carver, Malcolm Cowley, Paula Deitz, Steve Dixon, M. D. Elevitch, Loris Essary, Ellen Ferber, Carolyn Forché, Stuart Friebert, Jon Galassi, Tess Gallagher, Louis Gallo, George Garrett, Jack Gilbert, Louise Glück, David Godine, Jorie Graham, Linda Gregg, Barbara Grossman, Michael Harper, DeWitt Henry, J. R. Humphreys, David Ignatow, John Irving, June Jordan, Karen Kennerly, Galway Kinnell, Carolyn Kizer, Jerzy Kosinski, Richard Kostelanetz, Seymour Krim, Maxine Kumin, Stanley Kunitz, James Laughlin, Seymour Lawrence, Naomi Lazard, Herb Leibowitz, Denise Levertov, Philip Levine, Stanley Lindberg, Thomas Lux, Mary MacArthur, Daniel Menaker, Frederick Morgan, Howard Moss, Cynthia Ozick, Jayne Anne Phillips, Robert Phillips, George Plimpton, Stanley Plumly, Eugene Redmond, Ed Sanders, Teo Savory, Grace Schulman, Harvey Shapiro, Leslie Silko, Charles Simic, Dave Smith, William Stafford, Gerald Stern, David St. John, Bill and Pat Strachan, Ron Sukenick, Barry Targan, Anne Tyler, John Updike, Samuel Vaughan, David Wagoner, Derek Walcott, Ellen Wilbur, David Wilk, Yvonne, Bill Zavatsky.*

CONTRIBUTING EDITORS FOR THIS EDITION—*John Allman, Philip Appleman, John Balaban, Bo Ball, Jim Barnes, Charles Baxter, Barbara Bedway, Gina Berriault, Clark Blaise, Michael Blumenthal, Philip Booth, David Bosworth, T. Coraghessan Boyle, David Bromige,*

Michael Dennis Browne, Richard Burgin, Frederick Busch, Kelly Cherry, Amy Clampitt, Naomi Clark, Marvin Cohen, Stephen Corey, Christopher Jane Corkery, Henri Coulette, Douglas Crase, Robert Creeley, Art Cuelho, Phil Dacey, Michael Daley, John Daniel, Lydia Davis, Susan Strayer Deal, Terrence Des Pres, Sharon Doubiago, Rita Dove, Andre Dubus, Richard Eberhart, Susan Engberg, Raymond Federman, Michael Finley, Jane Flanders, H. E. Francis, Celia Gilbert, Patrick Worth Gray, Donald Hall, James Baker Hall, Yuki Hartman, Don Hendrie Jr., Brenda Hillman, Edward Hoagland, Andrew Hudgins, Elizabeth Inness-Brown, Josephine Jacobsen, Laura Jensen, Rodney Jones, Edmund Keeley, Ted Kooser, Marilyn Krysl, Naomi Lazard, Gerry Locklin, David Madden, Bobbie Ann Mason, Dan Masterson, Cleopatra Mathis, Robert McBrearty, Michael McFee, Thomas McGrath, Heather McHugh, Joe Anne McLaughlin, Sandra McPherson, Paul Metcalf, Barbara Milton, Susan Minot, Susan Mitchell, Judy Moffett, Mary Morris, Jennifer Moyer, Lisel Mueller, Joan Murray, Naomi Shihab Nye, Sharon Olds, Mary Oliver, Alicia Ostriker, Linda Pastan, Jonathan Penner, Mary Peterson, Joe Ashby Porter, Tony Quagliano, Pattiann Rogers, Thomas Russell, Michael Ryan, Reg Saner, Sherod Santos, Philip Schultz, Steven Schutzman, James Scully, Hugh Seidman, Beth T. Shannon, Gary Soto, Marcia Southwick, Elizabeth Spencer, Elizabeth Spires, Ann Stanford, Maura Stanton, Timothy Steele, Felix Stefanile, Pamela Stewart, Elizabeth Tallent, Mary Tallmountain, Elizabeth Thomas, Barbara Thompson, Sara Vogan, Ellen Bryant Voigt, Michael Waters, Bruce Weigl, Kate Wheeler, Richard Wilbur, Harold Witt, David Wojahn, Christina Zawadiwsky, Patricia Zelver.

DESIGN AND PRODUCTION—*Ray Freiman*

EUROPEAN EDITOR—*Kathy Callaway*

MANAGING EDITOR—*Helen Handley*

ROVING EDITORS—*Anthony Brandt, Gene Chipps, Lily Francis, Kirby and Liz Williams*

POETRY EDITORS—*Stanley Plumly, William Stafford*

EDITOR AND PUBLISHER—*Bill Henderson*

PRESSES FEATURED IN THE PUSHCART PRIZE EDITIONS

Agni Review
Ahsahta Press
Ailanthus Press
Alcheringa/Ethnopoetics
Alice James Books
Amelia
American Literature
American PEN
American Poetry Review
Amnesty International
Anaesthesia Review
Antaeus
Antioch Review
Apalachee Quarterly
Aphra
The Ark
Ascent
Aspen Leaves
Aspen Poetry Anthology
Assembling
Barlenmir House
Barnwood Press
The Bellingham Review
Beloit Poetry Journal
Bilingual Review

Black American Literature Forum
Black Rooster
Black Scholar
Black Sparrow
Black Warrior Review
Blackwells Press
Blue Cloud Quarterly
Blue Wind Press
Bluefish
BOA Editions
Bookslinger Editions
Boxspring
Brown Journal of the Arts
Burning Deck Press
Caliban
California Quarterly
Calliopea Press
Canto
Capra Press
Cedar Rock
Center
Chariton Review
Charnel House
Chelsea
Chicago Review

Chouteau Review
Chowder Review
Cimarron Review
Cincinnati Poetry Review
City Lights Books
Clown War
CoEvolution Quarterly
Cold Mountain Press
Columbia: A Magazine of Poetry
    and Prose
Confluence Press
Confrontation
Conjunctions
Copper Canyon Press
Cosmic Information Agency
Crawl Out Your Window
Crazy Horse
Crescent Review
Cross Cultural Communications
Cross Currents
Cumberland Poetry Review
Curbstone Press
Cutbank
Dacotah Territory
Daedalus
Decatur House
December
Dragon Gate Inc.
Domestic Crude
Dreamworks
Dryad Press
Duck Down Press
Durak
East River Anthology
Empty Bowl
Epoch
Fiction
Fiction Collective
Fiction International
Field
Firelands Art Review
Five Trees Press
Frontiers: A Journal of Women
    Studies

Gallimaufry
Genre
The Georgia Review
Ghost Dance
Goddard Journal
David Godine, Publisher
Graham House Press
Grand Street
Granta
Graywolf Press
Greenfield Review
Greensboro Review
Hard Pressed
Hills
Holmgangers Press
Holy Cow!
Home Planet News
Hudson Review
Icarus
Iguana Press
Indiana Writes
Intermedia
Intro
Invisible City
Inwood Press
Iowa Review
Ironwood
The Kanchenjuga Press
Kansas Quarterly
Kayak
Kenyon Review
Latitudes Press
L'Epervier Press
Liberation
Linquis
The Little Magazine
Living Hand Press
Living Poets Press
Logbridge-Rhodes
Lowlands Review
Lucille
Lynx House Press
Manroot
Magic Circle Press

Malahat Review
Massachusetts Review
Michigan Quarterly
Milk Quarterly
Missouri Review
Montana Gothic
Montana Review
Mho & Mho Works
Micah Publications
Mississippi Review
Missouri Review
Montemora
Mr. Cogito Press
MSS
Mulch Press
Nada Press
New America
New England Review and Bread
    Loaf Quaterly
New Letters
North American Review
North Atlantic Books
North Point Press
Northwest Review
O. ARS
Obsidian
Oconee Review
October
Ohio Review
Ontario Review
Open Places
Orca Press
Oyez Press
Painted Bride Quarterly
Paris Review
Parnassus: Poetry In Review
Partisan Review
Penca Books
Pentagram
Penumbra Press
Pequod
Persea: An International Review
Pipedream Press
Pitcairn Press

Ploughshares
Poet and Critic
Poetry
Poetry Northwest
Poetry Now
Prairie Schooner
Prescott Street Press
Promise of Learnings
Quarry West
Quarterly West
Rainbow Press
Raritan: A Quarterly Review
Red Cedar Review
Red Clay Books
Red Earth Press
Release Press
Revista Chicano-Riquena
River Styx
Rowan Tree Press
Russian *Samizdat*
Salmagundi
San Marcos Press
Seamark Press
Seattle Review
Second Coming Press
The Seventies Press
Shankpainter
Shantih
Shenandoah
A Shout In The Street
Sibyl-Child Press
Small Moon
The Smith
Some
The Sonora Review
Southern Poetry Review
Southern Review
Southwestern Review
Spectrum
The Spirit That Moves Us
St. Andrews Press
Story Quarterly
Stuart Wright, Publisher
Sun & Moon Press

Sun Press
Sunstone
Tar River Poetry
Telephone Books
Telescope
Tendril
Texas Slough
13th Moon
THIS
Threepenny Review
Thorp Springs Press
Three Rivers Press
Thunder City Press
Thunder's Mouth Press
Toothpaste Press
Transatlantic Review
TriQuarterly
Truck Press
Tuumba Press
Undine
Unicorn Press

Unmuzzled Ox
Unspeakable Visions of the
    Individual
Vagabond
Virginia Quarterly
Wampeter Press
Washington Writers Workshop
Water Table
Western Humanities Review
Westigan Review
Wickwire Press
Willmore City
Word Beat Press
Word-Smith
Wormwood Review
Writers Forum
Xanadu
Yale Review
Yardbird Reader
Y'Bird

CONTENTS

INTRODUCTION

by GEORGE A. PLIMPTON

I would imagine that one of the more intense pleasures in life is to receive the news that one's work has been selected to appear in an anthology. Raymond Carver was so pleased when he got his copy of *The Best American Short Stories* annual, which included his "Will You Please be Quiet, Please?", that he took the volume to bed with him and slept with it.

The Pushcart Press with its annual anthology, *The Pushcart Prize: Best of the Small Presses* has been providing similar rushes of pleasure and exhaltation for a decade. The present volume is the tenth in a series which has been almost universally praised, not only for the concept (an anthology of material from small-circulation publications) but for the importance of the contents themselves.

Naturally, there have been dissenting voices. Last year, *The New Criterion* ran a long, polished piece—ostensibly a review of *Pushcart Prize VIII*, but really a dissection of the motives of Bill Henderson, the founder of the Pushcart Press, to decipher why anyone should absorb himself in such an enterprise. In brief, based largely on information from Henderson's own essays (whose self-mocking tone seems to have been missed entirely) the article traces Henderson's unsuccessful struggle to get published, his disaffection with the commercial publishing houses, and the eventual private publication, among other works, of a volume entitled *The Publish-It-Yourself Handbook: Literary Tradition and How-To*—the success of which (it sold 40,000 copies), allegedly led him full-circle back into the commercial fold. *The New Criterion* article concludes that the reason behind this familiar progression from disillusioned revolutionary was that the editor of the Pushcart

Prize series was striving to fulfill "a keen desire for a permanent niche in the New York literary establishment."

Reading this critique brought back to mind my own experiences editing a literary magazine anthology and especially the animus that seems to rise from just about all quarters during the process of doing such a thing. The volumes ran to three numbers; a fourth was in the works but was abandoned for lack of funds. It was called *The American Literary Anthology,* an annual program supported by a grant from the National Endowment for the Arts and Humanities. The aims of the Anthology were very much what Bill Henderson's are with the *Pushcart Prize*—"through wide distribution . . . to give greater circulation to work that has appeared in magazines with limited circulation."

A considerable difference was that money was involved, since a second aim of the Anthology program was "to supplement the small payments made to authors by such magazines—paying grants of $1000 for prose material, $500 for each poem, and to reward editors who had the perspicacity to publish the selections with grants for use in the development of their magazines." It seemed such a basic concept—a simple way of fulfilling what writers hope to get from their labors . . . recognition, distribution, and compensation.

Alas, it was not the success it should have been. The administration of the program was clumsy. Various factions felt they were not sufficiently represented in the volumes. The constituency was very hard to please. The distribution of the taxpayers' money compounded the problems; merit, at times, seemed the least of considerations. Leonard Fulton, the editor of *Small Press Review* and a powerful voice for the smaller magazines, wrote, "The making of an anthology should begin not with just a desire to have an anthology and then seeing what's around to put into it, but rather with a knowledge of what *is* around and attempting to get a fair representation of *that*."

It was a principle to which we tried in some parts to adhere—to the point that the *judges* began objecting. Anthony Hecht resigned as a poetry judge for the third volume, upset at being sent piles of what he termed "the careless and militantly third-rate" submitted for a "cultural Poverty Program for Underprivileged Poets."

What led to the finish of the Anthology was a one word calligraphic poem by Aram Saroyan ("lighght") which was published in

Volume II. Its brevity caught (and held!) the eye of Congressman William Scherle of Iowa. An arch-critic of the National Endowment and its programs, Scherle found the fact that the American taxpayers had paid $500 for Saroyan's effort, and $250 to the editor of the *Chicago Review* where the poem appeared, a perfect whipping boy for his views. He flailed away on the floor of the Congress. Editorial and letters columns had a field day. Among other things, the furor caused the Endowment to take a much closer look at the contents scheduled for Volume III. There, to their dismay, they discovered an essay by Ed Sanders on the Peace-Eye Bookstore in the East Village, an avant-garde establishment which had on its shelves a number of "literary" artifacts. Among these Sanders had described a half-used Vaseline jar which had once belonged to Allen Ginsberg with a legend affixed describing what it had been used for. Eyes popping, the Endowment people read this, and decided that if the description ever fell into the hands of Congressman William Scherle he could very well use it to bring down the entire National Endowment for the Arts and the Humanities. They asked me to remove the piece. It was not a question of censorship; it was a question of saving the program!

In retrospect, it seems doubtful that Allen Ginsberg's Vaseline jar could have brought down the whole structure, but at the time the jar was talked about as if its contents contained the ingredients of a terrible plague. I finally succumbed to all this. I agreed to postpone the Ed Sanders essay from Volume III on the condition that the Endowment would find some way to subsidize the fourth volume. The Endowment reneged on its promise. The fourth volume was never published.

It was a disturbing time. I was under fire from the literary community for knuckling under to official pressure. The Coordinating Council of Literary Magazines passed a motion of censure. The National Endowment was down on me for scaring the bejabbers out of their people for selecting material jeopardizing their relationships with the Congress. But especially galling was that I found myself officiating over the collapse of a project that seemed to offer such benefits to an important segment of the literary community . . . for those who tend to practice the dictum from the opening manifesto in *transistion* "the reader be damned" or more politely stated by Margaret Anderson of the *Little Review* who spoke of her contributors as those "who make no compromise with public taste." About the only good that came of it all was that I was so outraged by Congressman Scherle's personal attacks on me on the floor of the Congress that I went to Iowa to campaign for a candidate I knew nothing about (nor did many other people) except that he was in the race against Scherle, who was supposedly solidly entrenched. He turned out to be quite a politician. Tom Harkin. My own contribution was miniscule, but Harkin beat Scherle in the race and has gone on to become the junior senator from Iowa!

Bill Henderson tells me that he was unaware of *The American Literary Anthology* when he started the *Pushcart Prize: Best of the Small Presses*. All to the good! Perhaps he would have had second thoughts. But I doubt it.

I know something about Bill Henderson. He was in Paris in the 60s, an aspiring writer, very short of funds, and living across from the Sorbonne near the Musée de Cluny. I never knew him personally. Apparently he submitted a story to *The Paris Review*. He told me (many years later) that it had been rejected with a note addressed to a "Mr. Sonnabend." "Dear Mr. Sonnabend," the note read, "We'd like to see more of your things." He remembered being put off not only by the magazine getting his name wrong but also referring to his work as "things".

The story was called "The Kid Who Could"—a faintly autobiographical account of a youngster disillusioned in a world he had been led to believe could be his oyster. It was a story that over the next six years Henderson expanded into a novel and then—the commercial publishers having rejected it—he published it himself. Henderson's experiences with his own book provided, of course, the basis and background for the subsequent publication of *The Publish-It-Yourself Handbook*.

Henderson was unsure what to do with the income derived from the *Handbook*. He once told me: "I didn't know whether to put the money into a cabin on Long Island, or into a book." What he decided, of course, was to do the *Pushcart Prize*—which with its first volume in 1976 became an instant publishing success. "I didn't know," Henderson said, "there was going to be such feeling for it."

I have not thought to ask Bill Henderson what his personal motives might have been in engaging himself in what Terry Southern once mockingly called "The Quality Lit Game". Such causations tend to be rather obscure. Jay Laughlin's absorption with *New Directions* appears to be in a part a compensation for a bookless and antiseptically non-intellectual childhood. I remember Princess Caetini, the editor and publisher of *Botteghe Oscure*, telling me that much of the impetus that kept her publishing that remarkable journal was hearing the thump of the mailbag outside her apartment door and appreciating that it might possibly contain an interesting manuscript.

Even the manifestos that so bravely pronounce a literary magazine's purpose are not always reliable or lasting. *Prairie Schooner* was originally founded (in 1927) to promote the work of "local (Lincoln, Nebraska) poets and writers". *Partisan,* founded in 1934, "as an organ of the John Reed club" was almost from its inception rent by political convulsion. *The Paris Review* in its first number promised never to use the word "zeitgeist" and has several times since.

But Henderson has been remarkably consistent. He wrote some years ago that he started the Pushcart series "to preserve and promote" literature from the small presses and literary magazines that might otherwise be overlooked. He has kept to that simple determination. The Index of the *Pushcart Prize* series indicates that work by over 500 writers—the great majority of them unknown—from over two hundred different presses has been reprinted.

Whether Henderson is doing all this to seek a permanent niche in the New York literary establishment is beside the point. Working, as he does, out of a garage a hundred miles from the city seems an odd way to achieve that particular goal. One thing, though, is for certain. His volumes have earned their place in a *literary niche*. They are now a welcome part of the literary landscape. Their continuation seems assured. Their appearance each year is a noteworthy event. Their contents reflect the best of what is being done by that part of the literary community which Henderson seeks to serve. That is ultimately what is gratifying and important.

THE
PUSHCART PRIZE X:
BEST OF THE
SMALL PRESSES
(1985-86 edition)

QUANTUM JUMPS

fiction by TIM O'BRIEN

from PLOUGHSHARES

1.

Am I crazy?

It's after midnight, and I kiss my wife's cheek and quietly slide out of bed. No lights, no alarm. Blue jeans and work boots and a flannel shirt, then out to the backyard. I pick a spot near the toolshed. Crazy, you think? Maybe, maybe not, but listen. This is the hour of mass murder. Hear it? The sound of physics. The soft, breathless whir of now.

Just listen.

Close your eyes, pay attention: an electron, wouldn't you say? And the clickity-clack of photons, protons, the steady hum of a balanced equation.

I use a garden spade. High over the Sweetheart Mountains, a pale dwarf moon gives light to work by, and the air is chilly, and there is the feel of a dream that may last forever. "So do it," I murmur, and I begin digging.

Turn the first spadeful. Then bend down and squeeze the soil and let it sift through the fingers. Already there's a new sense of security. Crazy? Not likely, not yet.

It won't be easy, but I'll persevere.

At the age of forty-five, after a lifetime of insomnia and midnight peril, the hour has come for seizing control. It isn't madness or paranoia. It isn't a lapse of common sense. Prudence, that's all it is.

Balance of power, balance of mind. A tightrope act, isn't it? And where's the net? Infinity could split itself at any instant.

3

Crazy, my ass.

Grab the spade and go to work.

Muscle and resolve, signs of sanity. Arms and legs and spine and willpower. I won't quit. This mountain soil is stubborn, but so am I. Go ahead, mock me. Lift those eyebrows. It doesn't matter. I'm a man of my age, and it's an age of extraordinary jeopardy. *Who's crazy? Me? Or is it you?* The deaf and dumb. The smug, the faithful, the ignorant, the deep sleepers of our species. You poor, pitiful animals. You cocktail-sippers and Sominex-swallowers. Listen: Kansas is on fire. What choice do I have? You do your sleeping, I'll do my digging. Just dig and dig. Keep at it. Find the rhythm. Think about Custer and Kissinger. Think about Noah. Think about those silos deep in fields of winter wheat. No metaphor, the bombs are real.

I keep at it for a solid hour. And later, when the moon goes under, I slip into the toolshed and find a string of outdoor Christmas lights—reds and blues and greens—rigging them up in trees and shrubs, hitting the switch, then returning to the job.

Silent night, for Christ sake. There's a failure of faith. When the back door opens, I'm whistling the age-old carol.

"Daddy!" Melinda calls.

Now it starts.

In pajamas and slippers, ponytailed, my daughter trots out to the excavation site. She shivers and hugs herself and whispers, "What's happening? What the heck's going *on?*"

"Nothing," I tell her, but my throat tickles. Am I blushing? "Nothing, princess. Just digging."

"Digging," she says.

"Right."

"Digging what?"

I swallow and smile. A sensible question, of course, but the answer carries all kinds of complications. "A hole," I say. "What else?"

"Oh, sure."

"Just a hole. Simple, isn't it? Hustle on back to bed now. School tomorrow."

"Hole," Melinda mutters.

She folds her arms and looks at me with an expression that is at once stern and forgiving. A strange child. Twelve years old, but very wise and very tough: too wise, too tough. Like her mother, Melinda sometimes gives me the willies.

"Okay," she says, then pauses, then gently nibbles her lower lip. "Okay, but what *kind* of hole?"

"A deep one."

"I know, but—"

"Look, angel, I'm serious. Back inside. Pronto."

Melinda squints, first at my spade, next at the Christmas lights, then at me. I feel some discomfort. It's a mixture of guilt and foreboding, perhaps a touch of embarrassment. That mature gaze of hers, it makes me squirm.

"Come on," she demands. "What's it *for?*"

"A long story."

She nods. "A dumb story, I'll bet."

"Not really."

"And goofy, too."

"No."

"Daddy!"

I drop the spade and kneel down, patting her tiny rump. An awkward gesture, almost beggarly, as if to ask for pardon. I make authoritative noises. I tell her it's not important. Just a hole, I say. For fun. No real purpose. But it doesn't work. She's a skeptic, a believer in point-blank truth; Santa Claus never meant a thing to her.

What can I do?

I look at the mountains and tell her the facts. The world is in danger, bad things can happen, we need a safety valve, a net, a place to hide. "Like an insurance policy," I say softly. "Like . . . like with gophers or rabbits, a place where they can be safe."

Melinda smiles.

"You want to *live* there?" she says. "In a gopher hole?"

"No, baby. It's only a—"

"God."

"Don't swear."

"Wow," she says.

Her nose wiggles. She's not impressed, I can tell. There's suspicion in that stiff posture, in the way she slowly cocks her head and shrugs and backs away from me.

Kansas is on fire.

5

How do you explain that to a child?

"Well," she sighs, "it's goofy, all right. One thing for sure—Mommy'll hit the ceiling."

"Probably."

"God, she'll *divorce* you."

"We'll work it out."

"I bet she'll say it's stupid, I bet she will. Who wants to live in the *ground?*"

"You don't understand."

"No kidding, I don't."

"Safety," I tell her.

Her smile is not compassionate. She wags her head and kicks at the hole.

"Poop," she says.

"Let's go now. To bed."

I try to lift her up, but she wiggles away, telling me I'm sweaty, so I lead her inside by the hand. The house smells of Windex and wax. My wife is meticulous about such things; she's a poet, the creative type; she believes in clean metaphors and clean language, tidiness of structure, things in their place. Holes aren't clean. Safety can be very messy. Oh, yes, Melinda's right, I'm in for some domestic difficulties—a war of nerves, no doubt about it—and if this project is to succeed, as it must, it will require the exercise of enormous tact and cunning.

Begin now.

I march Melinda to her bedroom. I tuck her between the all-cotton sheets. I brush a smudge of soil from her forehead, offer a kiss, tell her to sleep tight. All this is done tenderly, yet with authority.

"Daddy?" she says.

"Yes."

"Nothing."

"No," I say bravely, "go ahead."

She shakes her head. "You'll get mad."

"I won't."

"Bet you *will*."

"Try me, kiddo."

"Nothing," she mumbles. "Except."

"Yes?"

"Except you're pretty nutto, aren't you? Nutto-buggo."

I don't say a word. I smile and close the door.

In the kitchen, however, my fingers curl into fists. Nutto? What's nutto about survival? I pour myself a glass of grape Kool-Aid and then stand at the big window that looks out on the backyard. Was Noah nutto? Custer? It's late, and my head hurts, but I make myself think things through rationally, step by step. Mid-April now. I can get it dug by June. Or July. Which leaves three months for finishing touches. A nice deep hole, then I'll line the walls with concrete, put on a roof of solid steel. No skimping or cutting corners. Install a water tank. And a generator. Wall-to-wall carpeting. A family room, a pine-paneled den, two bedrooms, lots of closet space, maybe a greenhouse bathed in artificial sunlight, maybe a Ping-Pong table and a piano, the very latest appliances, track lighting and a microwave oven and all those little extras that make for comfort and tranquillity. It'll be cozy, by God. What's a shelter if it isn't home? What's a home if it isn't shelter? I'll put in a word processor for Bobbi, a game room for Melinda, a giant freezer stocked with shrimp and caviar and . . . Nutto? I'm a father, a husband. I have responsibilities—an obligation to provide and protect. It isn't as if I enjoy any of this. I hate it; I fear it. I would prefer the glory of God and peace everlasting, world without end, a normal household in an era of abiding normalcy.

It just isn't possible.

I finish the Kool-Aid and rinse the glass and then plod out to the hole. I'm exhausted, yes, and a bit groggy, but I find the spade and resume digging.

I'm not crazy.

I'm normal.

Eccentric, maybe. But who wouldn't be? These headaches and cramped bowels. How long since my last decent shit? A full night's sleep? My belly hurts, I've got bacteria in the brain. Clogged up, frazzled, a little dizzy. But not crazy. Fully sane, in fact.

So dig.

Patience and tenacity. An inch here, an inch there. It's a game of inches. Beat the Clock. Dig and dream.

A rough life, that's my only excuse. I've been around. I've seen lava flowing down the streets of Chicago, Kansas on fire, the violet twinkle of eternity—I've *been* there, an eyewitness. No poetic metaphor. It's real. Ask the microorganisms in Nevada. Ask the rattlesnakes and butterflies on that dusty plateau at Los Alamos.

7

Ask the wall shadows at Hiroshima. Ask this question: Am I crazy? And then listen. You'll get one hell of an answer: the soft drip of a meltdown, the ping-ping-ping of sonar, the molecular cooings of radioactive decay, the half-life of your own heart. What's to lose? Try it. Take a trip to Bikini. Bring your friends. A picnic lunch, a quick swim, then sit on the beach and take a deep breath and just *listen*. Let's consider it a dare. I'll pay for the goddamned ticket, we'll see who's crazy. We'll see who blinks. We'll go eyeball to eyeball and we'll . . . Sure, I'll admit it—a rough life. Ten years on the run, dodging danger, dodging the feds, hopping from hideout to hideout like a common criminal. I was a wanted man. My face decorated the covers of *Time* and *Newsweek*. Listen, I was sought after; I was hounded by Interpol and Defense Intelligence and the FBI; I was almost ambushed by the Puerto Rican National Guard; I was a celebrity; I was a mover and shaker in the deep under-ground; I could've been another Rubin or Hoffman; I could've been a superstar. But it's all over now. No more crusades. We're late in the century, and the streets are full of tumbleweed, and it's every man for himself. Times change. People change. Take a good look. Where's Mama Cass? What happened to Brezhnev and Lester Maddox and Clean Gene? No heroes, no villains. And who cares? We've forgotten the lyrics to all the old folk songs. I hear they're drafting people for the Peace Corps. And me . . . I'm middle-aged and middle-classed. A property owner. A blond wife and a blond daughter, and expensive Persian rugs, and a lovely ranch house in the Sweetheart Mountains. I'm established, thank you. Who isn't? Call it what you want—surrender, copping out, dropping out, numbness, the loss of outrage, simple fatigue. I've retired. Time to retrench. Time to dig in. Safety first.

2.

Don't quit, just dig.

Two weeks on the job, and my hole is nearly four feet deep, seven yards square. She's a beauty—I'm damned proud—but I've paid a terrible price. My daughter says I'm nutto. My wife won't speak to me. Won't look at me, won't sleep with me. Crazy, isn't it? She thinks I'm crazy. And dangerous. She refuses to discuss the matter. All day long, while I'm busy saving her life, Bobbi hides in

8

the bedroom and quietly cranks out an endless ooze of odes and sonnets. She uses silence like a blackjack; she withholds the ordinary courtesies of love and conversation. It hurts. I won't deny it. Those fucking poems. Christ, she's baiting me. This one:

> *The Mole In His Hole*
> Down, shy of light,
> down to that quilted
> bedrock
> where we sleep like
> reptiles, dreaming
> starry skies and ash
> and molten seams of coal
> and silver nuggets
> that hold no currency
> in a life misspent.
> Down, a digger,
> blind and bold,
> through folds of granite
> layered like the centuries
> to that brightly lighted
> chamber: fool's gold.

I don't get it. Meanings, I mean. What's the point? Why this preference for metaphor over the real thing, this insatiable appetite for coyness and indirection?

Bobbi doesn't understand. She's a poet, she can't help it. Oh, yes, I've tried to talk things out. Calmly, even tenderly, I've explained that the hole is merely a precaution and that my motives are anchored in the simple desire to fulfill my duties as a husband and father, to be vigilant, to protect. I've presented the raw facts. I've named names: Poseidon, Trident, Cruise, Stealth, Tomcat, Lance, Sprint, MIRV, Backfire, Pershing—the indisputable realities of our age. No fancy-ass metaphor, it's science.

Trouble is, Bobbi can't process hard data. The artistic temperament. Too romantic, too sublime. She's a gorgeous woman, of course, blond and long-legged, those shapely fingers, turquoise eyes, a way of gliding from spot to spot as if under the spell of a fairy tale, but she makes the deadly mistake of assuming that her beauty is armor against the facts of fission. Funny, isn't it? How

9

people hide. Behind art, behind Jesus, behind the sunny face of
the present tense. It's the head-in-the-sand principle. Bobbi finds
refuge in her corny poems; Melinda finds it in youth. For others
it's platitudes or blind optimism or the biological fantasies of
reproduction and continuity.

Me, I prefer a hole.

So dig.

Give it hell. Make it hurt. Melinda can giggle, Bobbi can taunt
me, but I won't be stopped.

I'll admit it, though. These past two weeks have been murder,
and at times the tension and frustration have turned into a redhot
sort of rage. This morning, for example. After a night of insomnia
and celibacy, I came to the breakfast table slightly funkish, a bit
under the weather, and it was difficult to see the humor in finding
another of Bobbi's snide ditties stapled to the Cheerios box. I
wanted to laugh it off, I just couldn't muster the resources.
Besides, the poem was cruel. It was a goddamned ultimatum.
Fission, she called it.

> Protons, neutrons
> Break the bonds
> Break the heart
> Fuse is lit
> Time to split.

A blatant threat, obviously. I'm not illiterate, I can read between
the lines: . . . Split, it's not even cute.

Who could blame me?

Sure, I lost my head for a minute. Nothing serious—some minor
yelling, some table thumping.

I apologized, didn't I?

"God," Melinda squealed. "Buggo!"

Bobbi remained silent, merely lifting her shoulders in a gesture
which meant: Yes, buggo, but let's not discuss it in front of your
father.

"Daffy Duck," said my daughter. "Hey, look at him! Look, he's
eating—"

I smiled. Yes, even that—a smile, a brave smile, a mark of
sanity, the cheerful face of a man in tiptop health—I smiled and
chewed and swallowed *Fission,* and then, patiently, with awesome

dignity, I asked if they'd be kind enough to put a lid on all the name-calling stuff, I was fed up with wisecracks and Mother Goose innuendo. I sipped some orange juice; my throat felt dry. "A little respect," I said. "Fair enough? A truce. Time for some understanding."

Melinda stared at her mother.

"You *see* that?" she said. "He ate your poem."

My wife shrugged.

"Holy crud, I think he's flipped," Melinda wailed. "He did, he *ate* it, I saw him."

"Now wait—"

"Daddy's flippo!"

"No," I said sternly, "Daddy's not flippo. Daddy's smart, Daddy's a goddamned genius."

"Buggo Bunny," said Melinda.

"Not me."

"Oh, sure. You and your stupid rabbit hole."

"It's isn't stupid," I told her. "Not at all. Damned brilliant, in fact. It's for *you*. Like a birthday present."

Melinda snorted and flicked her pale eyebrows. "Wow, thanks a lot. Just what I need. My whole life, that's all I ever wanted. My own personal hole." Folding her arms, she looked at me with an expression of fierce exasperation, something very close to disgust. "Selfish Sam," she muttered. "What about *my* feelings? What happens when everybody at school finds out? Ever think about that? They'll laugh at me . . . God, they'll think I've got the screwiest family in history."

"Let 'em laugh, princess."

"God."

I shrugged. "Eat your Cheerios," I told her. "And cut out the swearing."

"*You* swear."

"Hardly ever."

"I just heard it, you said—"

"Hustle up, you'll be late for school."

Authority, I thought. Don't bend. Don't crack. Win them over with firmness and tenacity. And somehow I did it. I ignored their coded mother-daughter glances; I made cheerful chitchat; I was a model of good-humored fatherhood, humming, stacking the dishes, buttoning Melinda's coat and then marching her out to

11

meet the school bus. A splendid morning, actually. Scrubbed mountains and sky, wildflowers everywhere, the wide-open spaces. Rural life, it has a lot going for it. The Sweetheart Mountains—beautiful, yes, but also functional, a buffer between now and forever. Shock absorbers. Heat deflectors. You can't buy that kind of peace of mind, you have to go out and find it.

Trouble was, my daughter had no great appreciation for matters of security. Standing there along the tar road, waiting for the bus, she wouldn't quite look at me, not straight on, and it was clear that the situation remained delicate.

"Well, Flub-a-dub," she finally grunted. "I hope you enjoyed your breakfast."

"Not too bad."

"Puke!"

I reached out toward her, but she yelped and spun away. Again, I offered extravagant apologies. Too much tension, I told her. Too little sleep. A lot on my mind.

"Holes," she said.

"Yes, holes."

Melinda glanced up for a moment, soberly, as if taking a measurement. "God, can't you just stop acting so freaky? Is that so hard?"

"I suppose it is sometimes."

"Eating *paper*."

"Right."

"You know what Mommy says? She says you're pretty sicko. Pretty screwy. Like a breakdown or something."

"No way."

"She said so."

"False, baby. Untrue."

"Yeah, but—" Melinda's voice trembled. She bit down on her lower lip, turning it white. "But you always act that way, real nervous, real flippy, like right now, and it makes me feel . . . You know what else Mommy says?"

"I can guess."

"She says if you don't stop digging that hole, she says we'll have to go away."

"Away where?"

"Away! I don't *know* where, just *away*. That's what she told me,

12

and she means it, too. That poem you ate—that's what it was *about*."

I nodded.

"Well, don't worry about it," I said. "Right now your mother and I, we're having this communication problem—can't quite get through to each other. Like when the telephone rings and nobody answers. Like a busy signal, sort of. You know? We'll work it out, though. That's a promise."

"Promise?"

"On my honor."

Later, when the school bus came grinding up the road, Melinda generously offered me her cheek, which I kissed, then I watched her ride away. A spectacular child. Very smart, too. And beautiful, like her mother—so blond it hurts the eyes. I love her. Both of them. Isn't that the purpose? To save those smooth, blond hides? To preserve the integrity of our nuclear family?

Split?

Doesn't make sense.

Dig.

Don't give up. All day long I've been at it, sweat and calluses, and my back hurts, and my arms feel like jelly, but there's also a nugget of sweet pleasure buried in the pain. It's duty-doing; taking charge. After all those years of pent-up terror, I'm finally showing the courage of a fighting man, and it feels terrific: tension translated into doggedness, anxiety into action, skittishness into firm soldierly resolve. I like the feel of a spade in my hands. I like its weight, the crunch it makes against this mountain soil, the blue sparks of metal striking rock.

Later I rig up the dynamite.

I know what I'm doing, believe me. Ollie Winkler taught me—I learned from a pro. Two sticks and the primer. Wire it up; crimp the blasting cap, take shelter behind the toolshed; think about Ollie and his Bombs for Peace; push the yellow button—"Fire in the hole!" I yell, and then the explosion, a muffled sound. The kitchen windows rattle. Bobbi comes to the back steps and stands there with a mystical smile on her lips. She doesn't speak. A wag of the head, that's all. In the backyard, like smoke, there's a light dusting of powdery debris, and my wife and I stare at each other as if from opposite sides of a battlefield, not enemies, but not allies

13

either. Bobbi bites her thumb. I smile and wave. Then it's over. She goes inside; I go back to digging.

The dynamite, that's what disturbs her. She thinks I'll miscalculate. Crazy, but she thinks I'll blow the damned house down, maybe hurt someone. Dangerous, she thinks. But what about plutonium? What about *bomb*, for Christ sake. Talk about windows rattling. Miscalculations? I'll show her. I'll show her two hundred million corpses. Leukemia and starvation and nobody around to read her goddamned literary masterpieces. I'll show her a daughter without hair. Where the hell's her imagination?

Screw it, just dig.

A crowbar, a pick, a spade. A pulley system to haul out the rock.

When Melinda returns from school, I'm still on the job. I straighten up and smile over the rim of the hole. "Hey there," I say, but she doesn't answer. She kicks a bit of dirt down on me and grunts "Nutto!" and then scampers for the house.

I don't let it rattle me. At dusk I plug in the outdoor Christmas lights. Who needs supper? I keep at it, singing *Jingle Bells*, working with the tough, high-spirited resolution of a man doing what must be done. It isn't obsession. It's commitment. It's fact-facing. It's me against the black-and-white realities.

Dig, no other answer.

Listen to the crickets. Watch the moon rise beyond the mountains. Pry out a boulder. Lift and growl and heave. Spit on your hands. Count the inches.

Obsession? Einstein was obsessed.

At ten o'clock I tell myself to ease off. It's hard to stop, though, and I take a few more licks at it, then a few more, then I unplug the lights and store my tools and reluctantly move toward the house. No signs of life. Rather eerie. In the living room, I find only the vague afterscent of lilac perfume; a spick-and-span silence; an empty closet; the indentation of Bobbi's lovely ass in the cushion of her reading chair. I stop and listen hard and call out to them— "Bobbi!" I shout, then "Melinda!" This strange quiet, it unnerves me. I can imagine the two of them packing suitcases and slipping away through the crevices of this dark night.

Melinda's bed is empty.

And when I move to Bobbi's bedroom—my bedroom—I'm stopped by a locked door.

I knock and wait and then knock again, gently.

14

"All right," I say, "I know you're in there."

No response. I jiggle the knob. A solid lock, I installed it myself. Now what? Pressing my ear to the door, I detect the sound of hushed voices, a giggle, bedsprings, bare feet padding across oak floors.

Another knock—not so gentle this time.

"Hey, you guys," I call. "Enough of this . . . Let's go, open up. Right now."

Nothing.

"Now," I say. "Hop to it."

Behind the door, Melinda releases a melodious little laugh, which gives me hope, but then the silence presses in again. My lungs ache. Studying the door, I have a sudden urge to smash the fucker down—a shoulder, a foot, like on television—break it down and storm in and pin them to the bed, both of them, grab those creamy white throats and bang their heads together and demand . . . demand *love*, demand some respect and understanding. Except they might take it the wrong way. They always do.

Instead I kiss the door and walk away.

Supper is cold chicken and carrot sticks. Afterward, I do the dishes. I take a shower, smoke a cigarette, mix up a batch of Kool-Aid, prowl from room to room. A lockout. Why? What possible reason? I'm a tender, loving man. A pacifist, for God's sake. The whole Vietnam business—I kept my nose clean, a resister, all those years on the run, a man of the most impeccable nonviolence.

So why?

At midnight I return to the locked door. At least they've had the decency to put my pajamas out for me. Freshly laundered, neatly folded. I find a sleeping bag and spread it out in the hallway. I undress in the dark. As I'm putting on the pajamas I hear a light scratching at the door, then a voice, muted and horse, and Melinda says, "Daddy?"

"Here," I say.

"Can't sleep."

"Well, gee," I tell her, "open up, we'll cuddle."

"Nice try."

"Thanks, sweetie."

She clears her throat. "I made this promise, see? To Mommy. She said it's a quarantine."

"Mommy's a fruitcake."

15

"What?"

"Nothing," I murmur. "We'll straighten things out in the morning. Close your eyes now."

"They *are* closed."

"Tight?"

"Pretty tight." A pause, then Melinda says: "You know something? I'm scared, I think."

"Yes."

"I mean—"

She makes a trilling sound, not quite a sob. In the dark, although the door separates us, her face begins to compose itself before me like a developing photograph, the cool eyes, the pouty curvature of the lips.

"Daddy?"

"Still here, pumpkin."

"Tell the honest truth," she says. "You won't . . . I mean, you won't ever try to kill me, will you?"

"Kill?"

"Like murder, I mean. Like with dynamite or an axe or something. I'm pretty young, you know. I'm barely a *kid*."

"Ah."

"Well?"

I examine my hands. "No killing," I tell her. "Impossible. I love you."

"Just checking."

"Of course."

"Mommy thinks . . . Oh, well. Night."

"Night," I say.

And for several minutes, ten, perhaps twenty, I'm frozen there at the door, just listening, pondering things, wondering where I've gone wrong. Kill? Where do kids get those ideas? Axes and dynamite? What happened to faith?

The world, the world.

I groan and lie down and zip myself into the sleeping bag, but then, as I'm squirming, I get jabbed in the heart. Another poem— it's pinned to the pajama pocket.

> *The Balance of Power*
> Imagine, first, the highwire man
> a step beyond his prime,

16

abandoned by skill and nerve,
caught like a cat
on the highest limb
seized by the spotlight
of his own blindness,
wounded, wobbling,
left to right,
locked in that treacherous
instant
between pride and fright.
Imagine, next, the brown-haired boy
alone on his teeter-totter
at the hour of dusk,
poised at the fulcrum,
one foot in fantasy
one foot in fear,
hands spread toward sun and moon,
shifting, shifting—
silly sight—
wrapped in that shadowed
moment
between youth and night.
Imagine, last, the Man in the Moon,
stranded in the space
of deepest space,
marooned
on his sterile sphere,
dust and rock and solar wind,
orphaned
widowed
divorced from Planet Earth
yet forever bound to her
by laws of church
and gravity.
Here, there is but the long thin wire
from sun to Bedlam,
as the drumbeat ends
and God is still
and clowns look up with tears
and families pray:

17

Be quick! Be agile!
The balance of power,
    our own,
    the world's,
    grows ever fragile.

Horseshit of the worst kind. Heavy on rhythm, light on reason. Bedlam—unbalanced, she means. Orphaned, widowed, divorced—a direct threat, nothing else. What can I say? At least it rhymes.

3.

My wife thinks she's leaving me. Already the suitcases are packed, and in the bedroom, behind a locked door, Bobbi spends the afternoon sorting through old letters and photographs. Her mood is truculent. Two months since she last spoke to me. When necessary—today, for instance—she communicates by way of the written word, using Melinda as a go-between, dispatching fierce warnings like this one:

> *Relativity*
> Relations are strained
> among kin
> of the nuclear family.
> It is upon us now—
> the hour of evacuation,
> each man for himself—
> the splitting of blood
> infinitives.
> Fission, fusion,
> critical mass.
> Panic comes to flight,
> and the ties dissolve,
> and Relativity claims itself
> as the final victim.

"Mommy's not too happy," Melinda tells me. "Pretty upset, I think. She *means* it."

"Mommy's not herself," I say. "Off the wall."

"Off what?"

"The wall. She's a brilliant poet, we have to expect it."

Melinda sniffs. She sits at the edge of the hole, legs dangling, peering down on me as I study *Relativity*. Her expression is grave and softly hostile. She tugs on her ponytail and says, "We're going away. Real soon, like tomorrow."

"It won't happen, angel."

"Tomorrow. In the morning."

"Won't happen."

"I *heard* her," Melinda says. "I'm not deaf, that's what she *said*— tomorrow morning! She already called the stupid goddamn *taxi*, I heard it."

"Don't say goddamn."

"Goddamn," she mutters.

No use lecturing. I pocket the poem, spit on my hands, grab the spade and go back to digging. Later I say, "This taxi business. What time?"

"Can't tell you."

"Early?"

"Real early. She says we have to sneak out while you're still asleep, because then you can't get crazy and try to stop us or something. It's a secret, though. I'm not suppose to talk about it."

"Better hadn't, then."

"I already *did*."

"You did, yes. Thanks, princess."

Shrugging, Melinda twists her ponytail and pulls it to her lips and quietly nibbles at it. Her position is precarious. I tell her to back away—it's a fifteen-foot drop—but she doesn't seem to hear. She watches my spade as if it were a loaded pistol. Those blue eyes, they're wired to my heart.

"Daddy?" she says. There's a pause while I lift a chunk of granite and wrestle it into my pulley-basket. Mid-June now, two months on the job, and I've got myself one hell of a hole. Fifteen feet and counting. Straight down into the mountain. "Hey, Daddy?" Dig, it's the project of a lifetime, a do-or-die undertaking. And the results are solid. No literary tricks—solid walls, solid rock. Amazing, what can be done with a spade and a jackhammer and a little dynamite. Gives me chills. Makes me feel . . . Strong. Yes, strong—in the belly and thighs, all over. Look at these hands.

19

Dangerous hands, like a boxer's big and rugged, muscled knuckles, mean-looking, hands you don't fuck with. I'm a tough customer. I don't take kindly to threats. Fission, fusion . . . Metaphor, for Christ sake, it's the opiate of our age. Poets should dig. Fire and ice—such sugar-coated bullshit. Bangs and whimpers—so refined, so elegant. So stunningly stupid. Nuclear war, nuclear war, no big deal, just a metaphor. Fission, fusion, critical mass . . . Blank verse for blank brains. "Daddy!" Melinda calls, and I look up and smile, then I put my spine to the spade and lean in and dig. No shit, it kills me. The end of the world: It's fucking *science*. It's machinery. You can *touch* it. And nobody's scared. Nobody's digging, just me. Idiots! They're drugged on metaphor. They dress up the realities in rhymes and sly similes, they paint on the cosmetics, they call it by fancy names, they pile on the adjectives and images and nifty little turns of phrase. Why aren't they out here digging? Nuclear war. It's not pretty-sounding. It's not subtle or coy. Nuclear war, nuclear war, nuclear war! Is it embarrassing? Too blunt? Too prosaic? Nuclear war: no metaphor. *Listen*—nuclear war, nuclear war. Those stiff, brash, trite, everyday syllables. I want to stand on my head and scream it: Nuclear war! Some say the world will end in fire, some say in ice, but from what I've tasted of reality, on the six o'clock news, in the cold-blooded jargon of Kahn and Schelling and Reagan and those crew-cut grad students in applied physics, from what I've tasted of fear and desire, I hold with those who favor the naming of names, the artless details, the out-of-key din of nuclear war, nuclear war. Where's the terror in this world? Where's the simple revulsion? Scream it: Nuclear war! The bombs are real. This spade is a spade, by God, and I'm digging.

"Daddy!" Melinda wails.

She drops a clod of hard clay from fifteen feet, a near miss. The real world. It gets your attention.

"Do something!" she shouts. "You have to . . . We're *leaving*, don't you know that? Do something! Get out of that goddamned hole and . . . Right now!"

"Baby," I say.

"Now!"

She smacks her hands together. She's crying, but it isn't sadness, it's fury. She pushes a wheelbarrow to the lip of the hole. "Do something!" she cries, then she growls and shoves and sends the wheelbarrow tumbling down. Frustration, that's all. She doesn't mean to kill me. "I don't want to leave," she chokes. "I want to stay *here*, I want you and Mommy to . . . " She's on her hands and knees, bawling, bombing me with rocks and chisels and fistfuls of dirt. I scramble up the ladder. Melinda rolls away and kicks at me and cries, "Daddy, please!" but I clamp on a bear hug and pin her down.

"Hurts," she says.

"I know it does."

"Let go."

"Not quite yet. In a minute."

So for a time we lie there at the edge of the hole, father and daughter. We're filthy, of course. I can smell sweat and moist clay. A warm afternoon—a Friday, I think, though I've lost track—and there are puffy white clouds above us, and mountains all around. Melinda's eyes are closed.

"Better now?" I ask.

She stiffens, still huffing. "You stink. You smell like that hole."

"Better?"

"Yeah, I guess. But you're breaking my back. God, you must weigh five billion pounds."

"At least," I say, and smile.

I sit up, taking her hand. Melinda sobs. She puts her head in my lap. A sweet, delicate child—these last two months have been tough on her. She doesn't understand. Twelve years old, how could she?

Nothing I can do but bend down and kiss her forehead.

"Tomorrow," she says.

"No."

"Mommy *said* so."

"Mommy's a poet," I murmur. "She's wrong. Nobody's leaving. It can't happen, I won't allow it."

Later, in the house, we take turns using the shower. She's at the age of modesty. There was a time, not long ago, when the three of us would do our showering as a team, a real family, Bobbi and Melinda and I. I love that little girl. I love my wife. Standing in the hallway, toweling off, I can hear Melinda singing *Billy Boy* behind the bathroom door, and I can hear Bobbi opening and closing drawers in the bedroom, and both doors are locked, and I realize that we've finally reached the point of decision.

I know what must be done.

"Won't happen," I say. "Nobody's leaving."

It's ugly, yes, but it's also a relief. In the kitchen, I'm whistling *Billy Boy* as I prepare a quick lunch of sausage and salad.

"I hate that song," Melinda says.

She eats standing up. She wears a pink robe and pink slippers, a white towel wrapped turban-style around her head. We chat around things. I ask if she'd like a pony someday, and she nods, then she thinks for a moment and says, "Except you'd probably dig a *hole* in it. You'd probably blow it up with dynamite."

"No, I wouldn't," I say.

"You probably *would*."

I grin and make a silly face. You can't argue. Kids and poets—they have trouble dealing with reality.

"Boomo," says Melinda. "Dead pony. No thanks."

Composure, I think.

Hard to be cheerful, but I wink and whistle *Billy Boy* and fix up Bobbi's lunch tray and carry it to the bedroom door. I knock twice and yell, "Room service!" There's no response. Not that I expect one. For a few seconds I listen with my ear to the door, just hoping, then I say, "Bobbi, Bobbi," then I put the tray down and knock again and head back to the kitchen.

"See what I mean?" Melinda says. "Tomorrow. It's all planned. She's really serious."

"Right."

"You better hurry up and *do* something."

"Done," I say.

"What?"

"Relax, sweetie. Consider it done."

A funny thing, but the afternoon goes by peacefully. I'm not worried; I don't talk to myself. It's the peace of decision, I suppose. Bobbi has her plans, I have mine. While she's busy packing and tidying up the loose ends of our marriage, I go about my daily business with confidence and good humor, almost happy, the kind of disconnected happiness that sometimes seems to nudge up against sadness. It makes your scalp tickle. You feel yourself straining to keep away the giggles, but then you giggle, and you slap yourself and shake your head and try not to cry.

Two things are clear.

I won't stop digging. I won't lose my family.

The trick now, of course, is to avoid arousing suspicion. Play it canny. Stick to the normal routines: Wash the dishes, sweep the floor, smoke a cigarette, lace up my boots and take a leak and then march back to the hole for the second shift.

Don't think about it. Squeeze that spade and dig. Progress, it's a lovely feeling. I was born to this sort of labor, a pickax and a spade, no metaphors, the jackhammer now and then, that ice-hot sensation of drilling point-blank into mountain rock. There's nothing like it. Here, in this hole, you can weigh progress by the pound, you can count the inches, and each inch takes you deeper into bedrock. It isn't psychological. I want to *feel* safe, yes, but I also want to *be* safe. You can't find peace of mind without first finding peace itself. These granite walls—they'll take anything but a direct hit. And when I'm finished, when I've installed a steel roof and a ventilation system and triple filters, that's when I'll look Bobbi in the eye and say, "It's yours, I've done what I can."

Until then, no quitting. I won't be blackmailed. This running away nonsense, I simply won't tolerate it.

Dig—it's my life.

Late in the afternoon I climb out of my hole and slip into the toolshed and make a few preparations. Some measuring, some easy arithmetic. I pile up a stack of two-by-fours and go to work with a saw. There's nothing humorous about it, but at times I start giggling, and my eyeballs sting, and I have to step back and take a breather.

Child's play, I tell myself. Follow the dotted lines: Fission, fusion, critical mass.

"Love," I whisper.

An hour later, when I leave the toolshed, the afternoon has gone dark, partly twilight, partly a soft rain.

I switch on the outdoor Christmas lights. The backyard glows in reds and greens, like a movie set, like Cape Canaveral before a night launch, and the rain is steady and warm and not quite real. I'm feeling fuzzy. I wish Sarah were here. "Be calm," she'd say, "let your body do the thinking." She had the nerve for this sort of thing; she made a career out of sabotage. But that's over now. I'm on my own . . . So I do it by the numbers. I cut the telephone line. I trudge over to the Chevy and open the hood and remove the battery and lug it across the yard and dump it into the hole. "Damn fine work," Sarah would say. "Terrorism isn't all that difficult—just takes some getting-used-to." For several minutes I'm not able to move. I waver at the edge of the hole, looking down, watching the rain make slop of a full day's labor, and I'm surprised to hear myself reciting aloud the names of my wife and daughter, then other names, Ollie and Tina and Ned and Sarah, that old gang of ours. What happened to them? And what became of the outrage and joy that kept us going all those years? "Enough speculation," Sarah would snort, "let's get on with business, William," but still I hesitate, wondering about the consequences of our disillusion, the loss of energy, the slow hardening of a generation's arteries. What *happened?* Rubin's on Wall Street, Fonda's doing diet books. Is it entropy? Is it genetic decay? Even the villains are gone. Where's Brezhnev when we truly need him? Where's Nixon and LeMay and Khrushchev and Johnson and Ho Chi Minh? There are no more heroes, there are no more public enemies. Villainy itself has disappeared, or so it seems, leaving a world without good or bad, without passion, and the moral climate has turned mild and banal. We've been homogenized, I fear. We wear alligators on our shirts. We play Space Invaders in darkened living rooms. Long hair is out, Adidas is in. We've become a generation of joggers and pasta-eaters and money makers. Our Moral Stance is supine. Who among us would become a martyr, and for what? Times change. As if to bow out before they were tarred and feathered, the fathers of our age have all passed away. Einstein's brains were pickled in formaldehyde; Teller made his final appearance on *Issues and Answers;* von Braun went quietly in his sleep; Rickover was buried at sea. Each of them beat the clock. And me—I'm digging a hole, just surviving.

"Oh, my," I say.

It's an era of disengagement. We're in retreat, all of us, and there's no use looking back.

I return to the toolshed.

I arm myself with hammer and nails. I sigh and bend down and pick up the two-by-fours and then make my way to the house under a heavy burden.

In the kitchen I try for stealth. One step at a time, cautiously. Past the stove, through the dining room, down a hallway to the bedroom door.

There I stop and listen. The sounds are domestic. Muffled but still comforting—Bobbi's hair dryer, Melinda's radio. "You guys," I say, "I love you."

First the wedge, which I tuck between the knob and the door's outer molding.

Next the two-by-fours.

I feel giggles coming on, but I maintain control. I blink and swallow hard and carefully check the measurements. When I begin hammering, the hair dryer clicks off and Melinda says, "God, what's going *on?*"

Speed is critical.

I nail a board flush to the door. "Daddy!" Melinda calls. Bobbi hushes her, and I hear bedsprings, but I keep my attention on the mechanics of carpentry. There's justice involved. And matters of love and preservation. So I nail down the second two-by-four, then the third, an overlapping system that anchors on the hallway wall.

"Stop that racket!" Melinda yells. Her voice is closer now, and a bit shaky. "Can you *hear* me? Stop it!"

Finally the braces. Six of them. Perfect right angles: door to molding. As an afterthought I remove the knob and use a screwdriver to jam the inner workings.

I kneel at the door.

The giggles have got me, I'm close to gagging, and for a moment or two it nearly spills over into sentiment.

Melinda jiggles the inside knob. "Well," she says, "I hope you're happy."

"Almost," I say.

"The *door* doesn't work."

"No, it doesn't."

She gives it a sharp tug. I hear the grunt, a metallic squeak, and then voices. There's a conference in progress. No doubt about the topic. Bobbi's a poet, Melinda's a child. It adds up to a paucity of imagination.

"Forget it," I say gently, "I'm years ahead of you."

My pace is brisk.

Not dawdling, not rushing either.

When I step outside, the night seems slick and treacherous—a much heavier rain now—and I take care to avoid silly accidents as I climb up the ladder. It's an eight-foot deadfall. At this point precautions are essential. I don't want broken legs, not mine, not theirs.

I press my nose to the bedroom window. It strikes me as a rather touching scene. In a way, in fact, I'm half-rooting for them, half-

25

proud, and I can't help smiling while Bobbi ties the bed sheets together. I'd like to lend a hand. A gorgeous woman, but she doesn't have the knack for knots, she never did. The physical principles of our universe are far beyond her. She sits on the bed, in profile, tying and retying, lips tighter than any knot. Her hair is bunned. She wears cords and sneakers and a yellow cotton sweater. Behind her, near the closet, Melinda struggles with the latch on a battered old suitcase. I feel a prickle along my backbone. It's a Peeping Tom tingle: I want to smash the glass and leap in and crush them with love.

If I could, I would.

Oh, yes—I *would.*

But I close the shutters and drive in the nails. If there were any other way . . . Then a couple of two-by-fours for good measure.

"We'll starve!" Melinda shouts.

They won't, though. I'll figure a technique.

I test the shutters, add an extra board, then call it a night. Guilt will come later. For now it's just heartache.

To share in their fast, I decide to skip supper, busying myself with little household chores. A thorough vacuuming and dusting. Defrost the refrigerator, scrub the kitchen floor. Ajax, I think, the foaming cleanser . . . In the basement, I toss in a load of laundry and sit on the steps and sing, "Clean clear through, and deodorized too, that's a Fab wash, a Fab wash for you!" My voice is strong. Many moons ago, when we were out to sanitize the world, I could carry a tune like nobody's business, I could do Baez and Dylan and Seeger, and it wasn't soupy, it was music to march to, it meant something. We cared, we really did. Ollie and Tina and Ned Rafferty—they knew the risks, they paid dearly, but they cared. It's nostalgia, I suppose, but where do you draw the line between mawkish sentiment and true *caring?* We were bleeding hearts in the old-fashioned sense—we indulged in idealism, we pursued our reckless dreams—and when we bled, which was often, we did so without moderation or embarrassment. There was evil at large. I blush to think it: Vietnam. The word itself has become a cliché: Vietnam. It's an eye-glazer, a party-pooper. But we *cared.* Chalk it up to naiveté, but we had the courage of our own indignation. We put up a damned fine fight. We stuck it out, some longer than others, Sarah longest, and it's not false sentiment to say that we had our hour of great honor. We were not the lunatic fringe. We

26

were the true-blue center. Middle-class, middle-of-the-road, middle-Americans—the last of the die-hard Conservatives, as patriotic as Nathan Hale, as conventional as Calvin Coolidge. It was not a revolution, it was a restoration. We believed in free speech and free assembly; we believed in the right to petition our government; we believed in a Constitution that requires formal declaration of war. In our hearts, bourgeois and bleeding, we were crusaders in a holy war to win back America from the infidels. And now it's over. Who among us remembers the convoluted arguments and counter arguments that kept us awake until five in the morning? Was Ho Chi Minh a nationalist or a spoon-fed Communist or both? Was he a tyrant, and if so, was his tyranny preferable to that of Diem and Ky and Thieu? Was it a case of naked aggression across state boundaries? Or was it a civil war? And who started it? And why? And when? What about the Geneva Accords? What about SEATO? What about containment and dominoes and self-determination? All those complexities and ambiguities, matters of history, matters of law and ideology—they've vanished, they've been reduced to a stack of tired old platitudes: The war could've been won; the war was ill-conceived; the war was an aberration; the war was hell. Vietnam, it was madness. We're all innocent by reason of temporary insanity. Yes, it's over. A sad chapter. And now we pat ourselves on the back. We did our bit. We marched a few miles, we signed a few manifestoes, we voted for McGovern. It's drop-out time; we earned our rest. We've become full-fledged members of the Pepsi Generation: "Be young, be fair, be debonair . . ." Someday, perhaps, we'll all get together for a bang-up reunion, like a VFW convention, thousands of us, veterans, thinning hair and proud little pot bellies, and we'll sit around in the lobby of the Chicago Hilton and swap war stories and show off our battle scars, the SDS bunch dressed to kill in their pea coats and Shriner's hats, Wallace in his wheelchair, McCarthy in his pinstripes, Westmoreland in fatigues, Kennedy in his coffin, Sarah in her letter sweater. And I'll be there, too. I'll show up in my hard hat, spade over my shoulder. I'll lead the song fest. I'll warm them up with some of the old standards, songs about overcoming and giving peace a chance, banning cannonballs, and we'll all get soppy with sentiment, hugging and embracing, even weeping, then we'll break out the booze and coke, we'll dance to Donna Summer, we'll parade through Lincoln Park singing our

27

lungs out: "Mister Clean will clean your whole house, and everything that's in it, Mister Clean, Mister Clean, Mister Clean!"

In times like these, what can a man do but dig?

I put my laundry in to dry. Upstairs, the house seems oddly empty, a kind of hollowed-out grandeur. There's a faucet dripping in the bathroom, which makes me smile—our domestic responsibilities never end—and I find pleasure in the task at hand, wrench and pliers, a new washer, the maintenance of an enduring peace.

If I could, I would . . . If only the world came with reliable components, a wife who would understand, a daughter who would trust. If at birth we were each presented with an ironclad certificate of warranty. If there were no Minutemen, if we were immortal, if we could somehow reverse the laws of thermodynamics . . . I would happily surrender my spade, I would kneel down in supplication to the great metaphor of our century—I surely would.

For now, though, I'm a handyman, a fixer of faucets, a digger of holes, humming jingles as I perform the odd jobs necessary to the survival of home and hearth.

Besides, I can't sleep. A frazzled feeling. I devote an hour to the oven, putting muscle to it, scraping away a year's worth of crud. If there were any other way . . . I scour the sinks, Drano the drains, carry out the garbage, gaze with quiet hope at the backyard Christmas lights.

It's nearly dawn when Melinda begins banging on the bedroom door.

"Daddy!" she screams, and I'm there in an instant. I tell her to calm down, but she won't, she keeps yelling and thumping the door, and there is now the inevitable weight of a guilty conscience. "Let me out!" she cries. "Hurry up, I have to *go!* Real bad—I can't *hold* it!"

"Angel, just try to—"

"Pee!" she yells.

It's a dilemma. One of those uncovered bases. Leaning against the door, I try to put the sound of patient fatherhood into my voice, as if we were in a car, as if the next stop were fifty miles down the road. I tell her to hang in there until morning, until I've had time to work out the plumbing arrangements.

"Wait?" she asks. "How long?"

"Not long. You're a big girl now, just count the telephone poles, go back to bed."

28

"Oh, right. *Wet* the bed."

"You won't."

"I will so," she says. "You better open that door. You better. One more minute and—"

"Use a bottle then."

"What bottle?"

"Look around, baby, you'll find one. Check Mommy's dresser."

For a moment she seems to be thinking it over. I can picture the droop in her eyelids, a tightening along the jaw.

"Gross," she snaps, and I can't blame her.

She hits the door.

"This is stupid. I'm a *girl!* I can't pee in any old bottle, I need . . . Stupid! God, I can't even believe it." Then she moans. It's a battle of nerves. She knows my tricks, I know hers. "Daddy," she says, "can't you act normal for a second? It's pretty cruel, don't you think? Sort of mean? First you blow up the backyard with dynamite and then you kidnap us and then you won't even let me go to the bathroom. Doesn't that seem like . . . Like maybe something's *wrong?* It's not too nice, is it? What if I did all that stuff to you— how would you *feel?*"

"Bad," I tell her. "I'd probably feel terrible."

"And what if I made you go potty in a bottle? In a perfume bottle. That wouldn't feel so wonderful, would it?"

"Awful."

"So there."

"There," I say, which is all I can manage.

She taps the door and speaks quietly, not scolding, not angry. It's a grown-up voice. "And listen," she says, "I bet you'd be pretty scared, too. I bet you'd cry. You'd get mad at me and then you'd start to cry, because you might think I was acting buggo, and because . . . because it's scary, that's why. And after a while you'd probably be so scared you couldn't even sleep at night, or else you'd have bad dreams and keep waking up all the time. And then—" She lets it hang. She knows I'm against the ropes. "Daddy?" she whispers.

"I'm here."

"You know what else?"

"What else?"

"You'd get sad. If you were me, you'd get so sad you couldn't stand it."

"I know, honey."

"Like right now. I'm sad, I guess."

"Yes."

"Let me out," she says.

It's a rocky moment, the most painful of my life, but I'm strong enough to tell her it can't be done, not yet. "The hot water bottle," I say. "Wake up your mother—she'll handle it."

Melinda is right, though. I can't stand it. When she says she hates me, I nod and back away, and later, when the tears come, when Bobbi finally takes command, I turn off the hallway light and move to the kitchen and try to patch myself together for the final bit of drama.

It's a splendid sunrise.

The mountains go violet, then bright pink, and just after six o'clock a taxi pulls up the long driveway. I have a word with the driver, make excuses, write out a handsome check. "Tip," he says. Just a kid, sandy beard and granny glasses, but he clearly knows what it's all about. He takes a twenty without blinking. "Could've called," he tells me. "Six fuckin' o'clock, no courtesy," then he shakes his head and sighs and leaves behind the smell of greed and rubber.

And that's it.

What happened, I wonder, to the rain? What more can I do? Roll out my sleeping bag before the bedroom door. Curl up like a watchdog.

What else?

If it were possible, I would join my wife and daughter, sharing their warmth, sleeping the dense narcotic sleep of the human race. I would gladly take my place in the devout procession from church to grave. I would vote Republican. I would subscribe to *Time*. At cocktail parties I would argue cheerfully in behalf of cautious optimism, the restrained pursuit of moderate causes. God knows, I'd prefer the tranquil hum of harmony everlasting, a Sunday in mid-summer. Melinda chasing thistledown, Bobbi in her hammock, speckled sunlight, butterflies, tomatoes ripening in weeded gardens, a temperature locked forever at eighty-one degrees. A yawning summer Sunday, a day when Christians barbecue. Not a cloud. Trimmed hedges and apple trees and a white bird bath. The Fourth of July, let us say, and I'd spend the afternoon grilling hamburgers and studying batting averages, a content man, middle-aged but truly happy. I would have hobbies. I would own life insurance. I would be secure in the certainty that the dollar will hold its value, that money will continue to matter, that matter will matter. I would stop smoking. I would plan trips to Yellowstone and Disneyland. If I had the power, if it were not for lunatics, I would sip martinis and root against the Yankees and firm up my golf game and invest heavily in the wide-open future. I would numb myself with Valium. I would join the taxpayers' revolt, denounce inflation, draw up a will, badger my broker, feed myself a diet of canned spaghetti and frozen vegetables. I'd *do* it, I really would. I'd dream the dreams that suppose awakening. If it were only believable, I would surely believe: Nuclear war, nuclear war—a fairy tale, a hoax, a great belly laugh in the Christian comedy. I'd slap my knee. A joke, for Christ sake! No bombs, no submarines, no ICBMs. I'd head out to the backyard and fill in the hole and plant grass and beg forgiveness. Yes, and I would live gracefully from day to day in the unspoken conviction that when it finally happens—when we hear that midnight howl, when we jerk up in bed, when the planet's zipper comes undone, when fail-safe fails, when deterrence no longer deters, when the jig is at last up— yes, even then I would cling to a steadfast orthodoxy, a man of abiding faith, confident to the end that E will somehow not quite equal mc^2, that it's a cunning metaphor, that the terminal equation will somehow not quite balance.

"Daddy, you're crazy," Melinda says. Then she shouts it: "Crazy, crazy!"

nominated by Edmund Keeley,
Sara Vogan and Ploughshares

HEMINGWAY'S WOUND—AND ITS CONSEQUENCES FOR AMERICAN LITERATURE

by Malcolm Cowley

from THE GEORGIA REVIEW

LONG AGO I was asked to edit the Viking *Portable Hemingway*, one of the early volumes in a new series. I accepted the commission eagerly, though it promised nothing in the way of financial recompense beyond a fee of $500. On the other hand, it might further some larger purposes, one of which was to correct a general misestimation of Hemingway's work. He was, as I felt, not merely an international celebrity but also an important figure in the history of American literature, which was my field of study. Though he was not among my friends at the time, he was a member of my age group and had expressed, more clearly than others, our special sense of life.

I worked hard on the *Portable*, and especially on the introduction, during the early months of 1944. Here I repeat my opening paragraph, for two good reasons. The first is that the end of it, which had a discernible effect on later assessments of Hemingway, is now under attack by the critical revisionists, a contentious sect.

The second is that what I wrote isn't widely available, the *Portable* having gone out of print in 1949.

> Going back to Hemingway's work after several years [I said] is like going back to a brook where you had often fished and finding that the woods are as deep and cool as they used to be. The trees are bigger, perhaps, but they are the same trees; the water comes down over the black stones as clear as always, with the same dull, steady roar where it plunges into the pool; and when the first trout takes hold of your line you can feel your heart beating against your fishing jacket. But something has changed, for this time there are shadows in the pool that you hadn't noticed before, and you have a sense that the woods are haunted. When Hemingway's stories first appeared, they seemed to be a transcription of the real world, new because they were accurate and because the world in those days was also new. With his insistence on "presenting things truly," he seemed to be a writer in the naturalistic tradition (for all his technical innovations) and the professors of American literature, when they got around to mentioning his books in their surveys, treated him as if he were a Dreiser of the lost generation, or perhaps the fruit of a misalliance between Dreiser and Jack London. Going back to his work in 1944, you perceive his kinship with a wholly different group of novelists, let us say with Poe and Hawthorne and Melville: the haunted and nocturnal writers, the men who dealt in images that were symbols of an inner world.

Was there an explanation for the "haunted" quality that distinguished Hemingway's work and placed it in a lasting tradition of American literature? I looked for clues in his fiction, where they abounded, and also in his life as it was then known to readers. The first clue I found was clearer than others: it was the wound he had suffered in Italy. On the moonless night of 8-9 July 1918, near the ruined town of Fossalta di Piave, he had stood in a frontline trench talking in pidgin Italian with three soldiers. A little after midnight an Austrian mortar bomb had exploded in the trench. "I died

33

then," Hemingway later told his friend Guy Hickok. "I felt my soul or something coming right out of my body, like you'd pull a silk handkerchief out of a pocket by one corner. It flew around and then came back and went in again and I wasn't dead any longer."

All three Italian soldiers had their legs blown off and two of them were dead. Hemingway's legs were full of steel fragments, 237 by the surgeons' later count; one fragment had penetrated his scrotum. Somehow he rose to his feet, heaved up the third soldier in a fireman's carry, and staggered up the road toward a forward command post. An Austrian searchlight caught him in its beam and he was wounded twice again by slugs from a heavy machine gun. He didn't know how he reached the command post, where he collapsed. By then the man on his shoulders was dead.

Such is an account of his first great wound, or of those many first wounds, as it can be reconstructed by comparing several reports. Hemingway was never to forget the mortar bomb that exploded in the darkness "as when a blast-furnace door is swung open." It was a memory that returned obsessively in his fiction. The heroes of his first two novels were both of them wounded men. Consequences of the wound reappear in several of his stories and help to explain their preoccupation with dying and corpses. Often the hero tries "never to think about it," and that effort is mentioned or hinted at in unexpected places—for example in "Big Two-Hearted River," which seems to be only the beautifully accurate record of a fishing trip. But one notes that the fisherman has to control his emotions and that there are memories he is glad not to be thinking about. After rereading the story in connection with others, one suspects that his most perilous memory is of being blown up at night and of feeling the soul or something go out of his body. Perhaps—or so I conjectured—that might help us to understand the emotional power of the story, which is otherwise hard to explain.

The conjecture was taken up and amplified by other critics, as notably by Philip Young in his *Ernest Hemingway* (1952). This is, on the whole, an illuminating work, but I suspected on reading it that Young had gone too far toward presenting a complicated personality chiefly in terms of the wounds, moral and physical, that Hemingway had suffered during his early life. The late Mark Schorer, a venturesome critic, went farther in the same direction; he said that a wound was to become the central symbol of almost everything Hemingway wrote. More specialized critics devoted themselves to the symbols, mostly of fear, that they had unearthed with pick and shovel after digging through the text of "Big Two-Hearted River." The search became popular in other countries, including Japan, where Keiji Nakajima wrote a compendious summary of the critical papers devoted to this one story.

After all this critical fabulation, some of it pretty hazardous, there was certain to be a reaction toward a more commonplace picture of Hemingway's work. The reaction was carried to an extreme by Kenneth S. Lynn in a very long review (*Commentary*, July 1981) of Hemingway's *Selected Letters*. It was reprinted in a collection of Lynn's writing (*The Air-Line to Seattle*, 1983), and I hear with trepidation that he has written a book on Hemingway, not yet published. In the review I play the villain's role. One of its principal points is that I had been perversely mistaken in my picture of Hemingway's character and writing. I had presented him as a victim of capitalist society at war and had thereby led other critics astray. In particular I had sinned by what I said about "Big Two-Hearted River." The story is, in reality, "a sun-drenched, Cézannesque picture of a predominantly happy fishing trip," and I had transformed it into something as "spooky," to use Lynn's word, as anything by Poe or Hawthorne. The truth according to Lynn is that the story is not about a returned soldier and has nothing to do with a wound suffered in Italy. For proof of this reinterpretation Lynn cites the *Selected Letters*. Those written home from Italy are cheerful about the wound, and after his return Hemingway had nothing whatever to say about it. By the time he made his fishing trip to the upper Michigan peninsula in the summer of 1919, he had fully recovered from the fear of being blown up at night. Perhaps there are shadows in the background of his fishing narrative, but if so they depend on something else in his immature psyche, that is, his obsessive grudge against his mother.

Lynn attacks my motives for writing about Hemingway, which he asserts were wholly personal and political. "When, in 1940," he says, "Malcolm Cowley finally ceased apologizing for Stalinism, he, too [that is, like Edmund Wilson], began to cast about for non-Marxist modes of continuing his assault on the moral credentials of capitalist society. America's entrance into the war against Hitler made this problem particularly difficult for him, but Wilson's overinterpretation of Hemingway seems to have showed him how to solve it. In addition to shoveling much more war-victim material into 'Big Two-Hearted River' than Wilson had done, Cowley's introduction to the Viking *Portable Hemingway* (1944) went on to insist that a haunted, hypnagogic quality characterizes all of Hemingway's work." I hadn't read Wilson's essay at the time, but that is a personal note. I wasn't deeply interested in what some other critic, even one I admired, had said about Hemingway's work. I was rereading the work itself and was trying to suggest an underlying quality that helped to give it literary stature.

Lynn almost never discusses literature in its own terms. What he endeavors to find in it are psycho-political motives to excoriate. Why was it that the introduction to the *Portable Hemingway* "slew the minds of so many critics"? That general disaster came about, he says, because my discussion of Hemingway's wound appealed to the anti-American prejudice of intellectuals who automatically identified themselves with powerlessness. After the triumph of American power in World War II, that prejudice "became more virulent than ever before, and anti-American interpretations of American literature sprang up like poisonous weeds."

That is a pretty broad, vehement indictment and I shall come back to it later. But first I should like to consider Lynn's notion that "Big Two-Hearted River" has nothing at all to do with Hemingway's wound in Italy. Much of his case against me, and against American critics in general, depends on this one story, and there is substantive evidence about Hemingway's frame of mind when writing it.

Lynn takes for granted that such evidence, if it exists, can be found in the big volume of *Selected Letters* edited by Carlos Baker. He doesn't pause to consider that the letters in the book, nearly 600 of them, are *selected* from thousands of others. Baker was conscientious in the task of selection, but there is always the possibility that some letters he had to omit for one reason or another might cast a different light on various questions, including the consequences of Hemingway's wound. That happens to be one of many topics discussed with candor in his 43 long letters to me, some of which go deeply into his state of mind. Only two of those letters, not crucial ones, are printed in Baker's book.

The correspondence with me had begun with two letters that mentioned the Viking *Portable Hemingway*. In the first he reported that some GI's in Buck Lanham's regiment, then fighting in

Hürtgen Forest, had read the book, which he still hadn't seen. They had teased him about being a haunted nocturnal writer and Hemingway had answered, "Well I'll be a haunted nocturnal son of a bitch." The second letter, this one included in Baker's selection, was written from Cuba in the fall of 1945. The first words are, "It was awfully good to hear from you [my letter has disappeared]. A few days after[ward] I got the book and liked the introduction very much. See what you mean about the nocturnal thing now."

In 1947 *Life* magazine asked me to write a full-scale profile of Hemingway. After some hestitation and an exchange of letters with the author, I undertook the project, which excited me; also it promised a visit to Cuba by myself and my little family. Hemingway had given his approval and letters became more frequent. I was finding that the profile was hard to put together, dealing as it did with a complicated person who had led many lives. I asked questions and Hemingway answered most of them, with candor; he liked to make confessions at night and was eager to have a confidant in the literary world. Our correspondence continued for some years after the profile—cut down by me from a much longer version—had appeared in the 10 January 1949 issue of *Life*. Arguments appeared in the letters, chiefly concerning the manuscripts of two books about Hemingway that had been sent to me by their prospective publishers; Ernest didn't like the suggestions I had made for improving them. I began to feel that the correspondence was taking too much out of me, since I had other pressing work. Late in 1952, I received a long, warm letter from Ernest and decided that it was a good point at which to stop. But we remained friends, if now distant ones, to the end of his life.

I treasured the correspondence in a thick folder, safe in my filing cabinet. The folder was shown to nobody, with a single exception. On one occasion I brought it out for Henry W. Wenning, a rare-book dealer in whom I had confidence, after telling him that I had no intention of selling it. Nevertheless, he described the folder to a wealthy collector in Hartford for whom he was acting as agent. The collector made me an offer of $15,000 for its contents, sight unseen. A condition of the sale was to be that I shouldn't copy the letters before letting them go.

The offer was tempting to a not-prosperous writer, even though accepting it would be against my standards of literary conduct. I consulted by mail with my friend Mary Hemingway, the author's widow and executor, and she consented to the sale. Wenning carried off the folder in April 1965, though first I had silently broken the agreement by copying one letter (25 August 1948) that seemed to me especially revealing. The story might have ended there, but it had a sequel. In 1977 the Hemingway-Cowley correspondence was put up for auction by Sotheby Parke Bernet (without my prior knowledge). A catalogue for that year devotes five double-columned pages to the collection. Two descriptive paragraphs read as follows:

> Throughout this complete file of his correspondence to Cowley (a friend whom Hemingway refers to in one letter as the "critic who best understands my work"), Hemingway talks of his own writing in detail, gives revealing biographical information about himself (on subjects ranging from his difficult relationship with his parents to his controversial activities in World War II), and discusses literature and other writers (with lengthy critical passages on Faulkner and Fitzgerald in particular). At the time Cowley was doing several pieces of writing on Hemingway [no, only one] and many of the letters are in answer to specific questions.
>
> This series of letters is so extensive (one 5-page letter running to 3000 words) and consistently of such high interest, that it is impossible to but suggest the remarkable quality of the contents.

The catalogue goes on to quote substantial passages from several letters. I didn't see it until long afterward, and of course I hadn't been present at the sale. What I heard was that there had been competitive bidding and that the collection had gone to Maurice F. Neville, a Santa Barbara collector. His bid was $32,500. For me at the time that was water over the dam.

I now wish that the entire collection could appear in a book that would include my twenty-five surviving letters to Hemingway, printed from their carbon copies. (I didn't make carbons of the earlier letters, most of which have disappeared.) Such a book, besides telling a story that is of interest in itself, would cast new light on aspects of Hemingway's character and episodes in his career. Carlos Baker's big life of Hemingway is an admirable work, as complete as he could make it, but there are questions it leaves only partly answered, including the new ones raised by Kenneth Lynn. On several of those questions my correspondence with Ernest would provide definite evidence.

I couldn't reproduce any of the letters here except after delicate negotiations. Their present owner might reasonably feel that printing them would lessen their market value. Also there is the lawyer for the Hemingway estate, whose consent would have to be obtained and who keeps diligent guard against infringements. But in one of my notebooks is the revealing letter I copied, and this can be summarized. In the Sotheby 1977 catalogue are those extracts, including one from the same letter, and these, by being printed, have lost their so-called "natural copyright."

As for the letter, it was written at five o'clock in the morning of 25 August 1948, when the first light was showing. Ernest had just been rereading my introduction to what he called "the Portable, or potable, Hemingstein"; for him this was part of a refresher course and was also a pleasure. Since I was having a bad time writing another piece about him, he thought he would tell me a few things that were really true, things he had learned in the Royal Air Force to call "the true gen." (He had explained in an earlier letter, one of the two printed by Baker, that "The gen is RAF slang for intelligence, the hand out at the briefing. The true gen is what they know but don't tell you.") Now he was giving me the true gen as he saw it at five in the morning, the hour when he made the decisions that he would fight on.

The next paragraph of the letter is one of the excerpts printed in the Sotheby catalogue. This gives the wrong date for it, 19 August instead of 25 August, but otherwise I copy it faithfully:

> In the first war, I now see, I was hurt very badly; in the body, mind and spirit and also morally. . . . The true gen is I was hurt bad all the way through and I was really spooked at the end. Big Two Hearted River is a story about a man who is home from the war. But the war is not mentioned. When I got off the train for the strip at Seney, which is a sort of whistle stop, I can remember the brakeman saying to the engineer. "Hold her up. There's a cripple and he needs time to get his stuff

down." I had never thought of myself as a cripple. But since I heard I was I stopped being one that day and from then on I got my stuff down fast and asking favors from nobody. But I was still hurt very badly in that story.

That one paragraph demolishes Lynn's misreading of "Big Two-Hearted River" and with it the factual basis of his attack on American critics. If he should wish for additional evidence, easily available, he might turn to A *Moveable Feast* and read the passage (page 76) in which Hemingway tells how he wrote the story. It was at a café table in the Closerie des Lilas. "When I stopped writing," he says, "I did not want to leave the river where I could see the trout in the pool, its surface pushing and swelling smooth against the resistance of the log-driven piles of the bridge. The story was about coming back from the war but there was no mention of the war in it." The war and the wound, too, were present notwithstanding. In an earlier book, *Death in the Afternoon*, Hemingway had said, "If a writer of prose knows enough about what he is writing about he may omit things that he knows and the reader, if the writer is writing truly enough, will have a feeling of those things as clearly as though the writer had stated them. The dignity of an ice-berg is due to only one-eighth of it being above water." After rereading "Big Two-Hearted River" in connection with his other stories, I had sound reasons for feeling that the wound in Italy was the submerged seven-eighths.

The experience of being blown up at night had been a trauma—though Hemingway never used the word—and for a long time it had kept him from sleeping at night. His fishing trip had marked a stage in his recovery, but not a final stage, since he continued to be engaged in a struggle against the fear of sudden death. A paradoxical result of the struggle was that he kept marching ahead into new dangers, as if proving to others—but chiefly, I think, to himself—that he was, after all, a brave man. Meanwhile, he kept telling the truth, or part of it, to his Corona Portable No.3, which he called his psychoanalyst. The rest of the truth is that he was actually braver than those others who hadn't his lively imagination and had never felt the soul or something go out of their bodies.

That letter of 25 August 1948 goes on to describe some further stages in the battle against fear, his private war. He hadn't been

40

afraid of big animals in Africa, it says, because they didn't carry guns. In Spain he had learned to fear only actual immediate danger: nothing in the future. The next step in his education was one that hasn't been recorded except in that single letter. It took place in China, 1941, during a thunderstorm, when his plane had to circle for a long time inside a range of steep hills; the ground was invisible. When the plane landed at last, and safely, Hemingway must have felt that a spell had been woven to protect him.

Later, when he was cruising in a heavily armed Q-boat off the north coast of Cuba, he and all his crew had believed that if they encountered a submarine they would all be killed, but first they would have destroyed the submarine. They were completely happy, the letter says, believing as they did that the adventure was worthwhile. In France with his guerrilla band, then later in Hürtgen Forest, he had been very little spooked—and he goes on to celebrate the joy of fighting for the first time in one's own language. He concludes by saying that everything in the letter is the True Gen.

He must have embroidered it at points, as always, but he was clearly trying to be honest about his long struggle with fear. This, as I said, had been reflected in much of his work and it had ended in victory, or so he felt in the summer of 1948. He would, however, return to the theme on one later occasion. Colonel Richard Cantwell, the last of his avatars (having been created later than Thomas Hudson of *Islands in the Stream*), finds the exact spot on the west bank of the River Piave where he had suffered his first wound. There he performs a private rite of defecation that closes out the experience. The rite is described in *Across the River* (1951), written more than thirty years after Hemingway himself was wounded.

So there is abundant evidence for the truth of what I wrote in the introduction to *The Portable Hemingway*. But had I any hidden political motives for writing it? Lynn makes that accusation, and at length, and it seems to me obstinately ill-informed.

I was writing early in 1944, before the Normandy landing, when the war against Hitler still hung in the balance. Two years before that time I had definitely withdrawn from political arguments, in which I felt out of place and out of character. If I was left with a

41

political purpose, it was one I shared with most Americans, namely, to strengthen our country and win the war as soon as possible. On the literary front, to which my work was confined, I could put forward the real achievements of American writers, dead and living. It was not a time to assault "the moral credentials of capitalist society."

In the unlikely case that I had wished to assault them, Hemingway's wound in the First World War was the weakest possible occasion. It was not the bitter fruit of American or European capitalism. Hemingway had chosen to expose himself beyond the call of duty, as I could judge from my volunteer service in an outfit that greatly resembled his. "Volunteer" is a key word in his case. During the early spring of 1918 he was a cub reporter on *The Kansas City Star,* one who felt ashamed of not being in uniform. He had learned that he would probably be rejected by the armed forces because of defective vision in one eye. He had also learned that the American Red Cross was enrolling young men to drive ambulances and that it was willing to overlook minor physical defects. He volunteered for that service eagerly and was sent to the Italian front. "He seemed always to want to be where the action was," said his assistant city editor. His sector of the front was quiet at the time, which was the first two weeks of June, and he decided that there wasn't much action or danger in driving an ambulance. So he volunteered again, this time to distribute chocolate, cigarettes, and postcards to soldiers just behind the front lines. He wasn't supposed to endanger himself. There was no military reason, none whatever, for his presence in a frontline trench on the night of 8–9 July. He had joyously sought out the wound and would later be proud of it (though deeply shaken). He was in fact the first American volunteer to be wounded in Italy, and there would not be many others.

The wound was in many ways a personal disaster for Hemingway, but my introduction to the *Portable* implied that it was a literary blessing. (Elsewhere I broadened the statement to include many Americans of his age group who had served in World War I. The future writers among them had profited by the experience, unlike the English, the French, and the Germans, who had served much longer.) It was the wound, I thought, that gave much of the depth to his fiction, besides the "haunted" quality that I admired. Unwounded, completely happy men and women are seldom the best writers. If American society, in spite of every appearance, was somehow culpable in his case, a critic of literature is tempted to exclaim, with the authors of the Missal, *O felix culpa!*

The critic might continue the quotation, but now with an embarrassed stammer, "O happy fault, which has deserved to have such and so mighty a Redeemer." Hemingway did a great deal for American literature, but he was not a redeemer, even uncapitalized. As a young writer he was, if possible, more self-centered than the others and more bitterly competitive. His ambition was not merely to outdo his coevals, all of them, but to win a place among the giants of fiction: Mr. Maupassant, Mr. Turgenev, Mr. Stendhal he called them, as they stepped one after the other into an imaginary boxing ring. If he achieved that ambition in his limited fashion (and with many qualifications), his success was in part (and again with many qualifications when speaking of that complicated man) a fortunate consequence of his wound. Such was my conjecture at the time, and after forty years of accumulated evidence I can see no reason for changing it.

Since my political reasons for writing about the wound are under attack, it is time for me to break a self-imposed political silence and state my position bluntly. I am a Little American. I am and have always been a patriotic native of some American neighborhood: at first it was Blacklick Township in Cambria County, Pennsylvania, then later—and for fifty years—it has been Sherman, Connecticut (present population about 2300, which I think is too many). There were intervening years in Pittsburgh, in Cambridge, Massachusetts, in Paris, and in Manhattan, but as a country boy I have never felt quite at home in cities. The United States as a whole is quite simply my own nation. It is also one nation among others, with very great comparative virtues and with faults, too, which I should be dishonest and disloyal if I tried to conceal. Many of them are my own faults. Some of the broader ones can be remedied; indeed, they must be remedied if we are to survive as a nation. Other faults are among the irreparable defects of human societies.

I have never dreamed of spending my life in any other country (except France long ago, and China in the days when it was being invaded). I like and love America, but not in any abstract fashion, having learned to distrust abstractions. I like the people, or most of them, I like the landscapes when they aren't defaced, and I feel at

43

home in almost any of the small communities in which Americans flock together. I like the sense of living securely on my seven acres of American soil (at least until the state decides to license a pipeline or build another superhighway). At the same time I like the feeling of being footloose that most of us enjoy: we are citizens free to try our luck elsewhere and let our tongues wag in abuse of the administration. I speak the American language. I like and love the American literature of this century, even while feeling that its past is still in process of creation, not to mention its future.

I don't like everything about us and, in particular, I detest superhighways, shopping malls, Standard Metropolitan Areas, chemical pollution, and international struggles for power. I wish I had a bumper sticker like one of those formerly seen in California: STAMP OUT PROGRESS. With the seeping away of earlier idealisms, I have become increasingly conservative (not neoconservative, a term that belongs with the jingo-jargon of the Cold War). Perhaps the America I love best is the country of my boyhood, with open fields to run barefoot in and never a chainlink fence in days of travel over dirt roads. I do not identify the America I love with any political or economic theory, whether it be the Free Market, Business Enterprise, or the Welfare State. Human beings have led tolerable lives under many systems, ranging from tribalism and primitive communism through absolute or limited monarchies and free republics to something approaching anarchism, provided only that people in the mass—and their leaders, too—were reasonably honest, aspired to justice, and felt a sense of loyalty to the earth and their fellow creatures. Let them go their separate ways.

And Soviet Russia (since it always comes into the argument)? It is not a country I ever visited, or strongly wished to visit even in the days when I regarded myself as a Marxist. Later the mere notion of living in Russia was one that filled me with horror. In historical terms the USSR now seems the greatest of failed experiments, since it had tried to effectuate the grandest of social theories. But was that social failure inevitable, given the nature of the theory, or was it partly the result of Stalin's character as a leader? The question is still being argued by historians, and meanwhile Russia has achieved a military strength that makes it one of the two great powers. It is still not a threat to Americans in their daily lives unless we choose to make it so. If we insist on living with the Russians in mortal rivalry, we run the risk of becoming like Russia in many respects, just as fascism and communism ended by copying each other. They were obeying an ancient law of social dynamics, namely, that polar opposites tend to assume the same structures. As a Little American I hate the notion of a world divided into spheres of influence by two superpowers. Sometimes I have a nightmare in which the US and the USSR loom up as giants locked in a deadly contest. The aim of the contest is to see which will be first and do most to destroy this pleasant earth—and Blacklick Township, and Sherman, Connecticut.

Kenneth S. Lynn is not a Little American. On the literary front he has been making himself a spokesman for the neoconservatives, the hard liners, the jingoes, as I would call them, who believe that the central reality of the contemporary world is a struggle for supremacy between American capitalism and Russian communism. They think in abstractions. For them America is not people, or landscapes and cityscapes, or human neighborhoods; it is a system based on business enterprise and the free market. That notion applied to literature gives them a simplified standard of judgment. Any piece of writing is "good," they seem to say, if it strengthens American self-confidence and American power. Everything else is malevolent or puerile.

From this standpoint Lynn has every right—so long as he bears the facts in mind—to attack my position as being moralistic, old-fashioned, lacking in realism, and—to use a word I detest—belletristic. He asserts that my misinterpretation, as he calls it, of "Big Two-Hearted River" helped to corrupt a whole generation of American critics, and he comes close to presenting it as a traitorous episode in a worldwide struggle for power. The critics, he says, were easy to corrupt since they "automatically identified themselves with powerlessness." The result—and I quote his words again—was that "anti-American interpretations of American literature sprang up like poisonous weeds." At this point, when he uses me as a club to beat down American critics in general, his picture of our critical history becomes not only mistaken but preposterous.

Let us look briefly at the facts in the case. Perhaps they will fit together into a picture that is exactly the opposite of his.

When I was in college, 1915-1920, American literature was at one of its low points in critical and scholarly estimation (after a brief

45

period of literary boasting during the 1890's). In academic circles here and abroad it was still a question whether the body of prose and verse produced by Americans truly constituted a national literature or whether it was no more than a provincial branch of English writing. I can't remember that so much as a single course in American literature was offered to Harvard undergraduates. The authors to be emulated by young Americans were Shaw, Wells, and perhaps Compton Mackenzie. But already a group of rebel critics inspired by Van Wyck Brooks had engaged in the search for a "usable past"—usable, that is, as an American tradition and a basis for future writing.

The situation changed after World War I, slowly at first, then more rapidly during the Depression. In 1930 Sinclair Lewis became the first American author to win the Nobel Prize, which had not been awarded to Mark Twain or Henry James; that was a political as well as a literary event. At home a considerable number of younger writers seized upon the dream of helping to create a new America ruled democratically by the working classes, but the dream faded step by step. Other writers, appalled by domestic and foreign dangers, had been delving into the American past as a hidden source of strength in perilous times. Historical novels and plays became widely popular, as witness *Abraham Lincoln in Illinois*. In the critical field Van Wyck Brooks projected his five-volume history of American literary life, which began grandly with *The Flowering of New England* (1936). At Harvard, F. O. Matthiessen was slaving over *The American Renaissance*, which, on its appearance in 1941, would be saluted as ". . . perhaps the most profound work of literary criticism on historical principles by any modern American."

I have been hurrying through a quarter-century of critical and academic history without even mentioning some of the crucial events. The earliest of these was the discovery about 1920 of a great American novel—of course it was *Moby-Dick*—that had gone almost unread for sixty years. Step by step this led to the establishment of Melville scholarship as a campus industry. Another event, one that followed after an interval, was the second coming of Henry James. Courses in American literature were by then being offered in all our colleges, even the smallest and most provincial; it had become the flourishing field of study. A big cooperative venture was the three-volume *Literary History of the United*

States (1948). Written and edited over a period of five years by a staff that included four editors, three associates, and forty-eight other contributors (all university men except Carl Sandburg and H. L. Mencken), it was not only a monumental work but also, in one neglected aspect, a mass demonstration of pride in American writing, as if the fifty-five scholarly contributors had marched down Fifth Avenue behind a brass band.

During those same years, 1943-1948, there was a vast change in the international standing of American writers. Partly it began with the discovery by respected French men of letters—Malraux, Sartre, and Gide, among others—that there was a vital new generation of American novelists. Sartre announced that his own novels were based on fictional methods invented by Dos Passos. In one of his *Imaginary Interviews* (1944), André Gide remembered what the German statesman Rathenau had told him in 1921. "America has no soul," Rathenau had said, "and will not have until it consents to plunge into the abyss of human sin and suffering." Gide praised our new novelists, especially Faulkner and Hemingway, for drawing their readers out of the soulless complacency that Rathenau abhorred. Gide was offering a literary, not a political, judgment, but his words had their effect in the international republic of letters.

His interview praising the new American novelists had been written from exile in Tunis, shortly after the city had been liberated by American forces. Here in the United States a series of victories in Africa and Europe and the Pacific was calling forth a surge of pride in American power, a feeling that affected every field of culture, criticism not excluded. Almost all the intellectuals, even those who had been rebels during the Depression years, were by now reconciled with American society; some had become imperialists in a bumptious fashion. We were witnessing the rebirth of American nationalism, if now on a grander scale. The whole world, so Henry Luce had proclaimed, was entering the American Century.

I too was drawn into the movement, if peripherally and with strong reluctances that tempered my enthusiasm. The reluctances had several causes, one of which was misgiving about the notion of an American Century: wasn't the century big enough to accommodate many countries? At the same time I deeply admired American writing and my enthusiasm, such as it was, for the new movement

47

was based on my conviction that many American authors—indeed, our literature as a whole—had long been misjudged and underappreciated. In my small way I might do something to raise its standing both at home and abroad. That purpose, I can see today, made me part of the movement in spite of my reluctances. I even helped to supply a component of the movement that had seemed to be missing.

At the end of the war students came flocking into our universities under the GI Bill of Rights. Many of them were eager to study American literature, and by now there were hundreds of scholars trained in the field and eager to teach them. The difficulty was that most of the scholars had specialized in some figure or group of figures from the American past. They knew less about the present, as I found to my dismay at meetings of contributors to *Literary History of the United States*. If our literature was to play its part in that American Century, it had to offer something more than imposing tombs; there had to be living authors worthy of standing beside the great Europeans.

That widely felt need gave an unexpected importance to *The Portable Hemingway* and later still more importance to *The Portable Faulkner* (1946). I had portrayed both authors as representing an American tradition, as weaving American legends, as writing a prose that was rich in symbols, and as plunging into the human depths. By speaking in literary terms, I had helped to make them *teachable* (of course with many collaborators in the task). Soon they were being taught: Faulkner more than Hemingway, as seemed proper, but Hemingway, too, as well as Fitzgerald, Hart Crane, and one or two of their coevals whom I also admired. It would not be long before the actual work of those authors was buried in a snowbank of doctoral dissertations.

During the 1950's and 1960's there was a high tide in American studies and in the world reputation of American literature. It often seems that our culture, instead of moving in one direction, has surged forward and backward in waves of fashion. During those postwar decades the wave of literary nationalism engulfed our universities and spread to those of Europe, where programs or professorships of American Studies were being established almost everywhere. In England by 1968, American subjects were being taught at all thirty-six of the universities and university schools, with thirty of these offering courses in American literature. The

United States hadn't fallen behind. At least two of our recent classics, *The Great Gatsby* and *A Farewell to Arms,* had reached a quarter-million copies each year in classroom adoptions. I couldn't help being heartened by this very wide academic attention to authors whose work I had cherished for a long time. But still I drew back a little and wasn't the only one to be disturbed by the neglect of other literary and historical fields. Edmund Wilson reported wryly in 1968 that Harvard had six professors occupied with American history, as compared with two in modern European history.

Wilson himself had won distinction as an Americanist, a word he never used. His monumental study of Civil War writers and statesmen, *Patriotic Gore,* had appeared in 1962, but he had then moved on to other branches of study, including Russian literature and Hebrew. In 1968 Kenneth Lynn was preparing to resign as chairman of the Harvard program in American Civilization. I don't think he reflected that the existence of his post, as well as of a later one to which he was named at Johns Hopkins, was due in large part to the efforts of critic-scholars whose opinions he was soon to deride as "poisonous weeds."

Now that the high tide of American Studies has somewhat receded—having been followed by other tides of academic fashion, Black Studies, Women's Studies, and now Computer Science—we can see that it left behind it many solid achievements; not everything was wreckage on the shore. As its greatest achievement, the body of writing produced by Americans has been raised to its proper position among world literatures (and even beyond that position, for a time). The federal government has created endowments for the arts and the humanities; together they come close to serving the function of something we had always lacked, a ministry of culture. Scholarly studies have been published in multitudes and not all of them have been trivial or pedantic; some have greatly added to our national self-knowledge. Among other achievements, a recent undertaking should be celebrated. Beginning in 1982 the American classics are at last being republished in a uniform edition, the Library of America, which consists of handsome and readable volumes not priced beyond our reach. This admirable series is the realization of a project first dreamed of and preached by Edmund Wilson, most prominent of the critics whom Lynn excoriates for being un-American.

All those achievements and others are lasting monuments to the national movement in literature. In my sceptical fashion I have long since drawn apart from the movement to play the part of a simple observer. Still I continue to ponder happily on the complete change in the standing of American literature and in our attitude toward the writing profession that it has helped to produce since the First World War. For me the change began a long time ago, perhaps when I read Scott Fitzgerald's first novel or sat on the hard benches of the Provincetown Playhouse during an early performance of *The Emperor Jones;* I was hearing new voices in our American world. But the change was intensified in my case by rereading Faulkner after 1940 and by reflecting at length on the literary consequences, often distant, of Hemingway's wound.

nominated by Frederick Busch
and Stanley Lindberg

THE FUNDAMENTAL PROJECT OF TECHNOLOGY

by GALWAY KINNELL

from AMERICAN POETRY REVIEW

> *"A flash! A white flash sparkled!"*
> *Tatsuichiro Akizuki*, Concentric Circles of Death

Under glass: glass dishes which changed
in color; pieces of transformed beer bottles;
a household iron; bundles of wire become solid
lumps of iron; a pair of pliers; a ring of skull-
bone fused to the inside of a helmet; a pair of eyeglasses
taken off the eyes of an eyewitness, without glass,
which vanished, when a white flash sparkled.

An old man, possibly a soldier back then,
now reduced down to one who soon will die,
sucks at the cigaret dangling from his lips, peers
at the uniform, scorched, of some tiniest schoolboy,
sighs out bluish mists of his own ashes over
a pressed tin lunch box well crushed back then when
the word *future* first learned, in a white flash, to jerk tears.

On the bridge outside, in navy black, a group
of schoolchildren line up, hold it, grin at a flash-pop,
scatter like pigeons across grass, see a stranger, cry,
hello! hello! hello! and soon *goodbye! goodbye!*
having pecked up the greetings that fell half unspoken

51

and the going-sayings that those who went the day
it happened a white flash sparkled did not get to say.

If all a city's faces were to shrink back all at once
from their skulls, would a new sound come into existence,
audible above moans eaves extract from wind that smoothes
the grass on graves or raspings heart's-blood greases still
or wails infants trill born already skillful at the grandpa's rattle
or infra-screams bitter-knowledge's speechlessness
memorized, at that white flash, inside closed-forever mouths?

To de-animalize human mentality, to purge it of obsolete
evolutionary characteristics, in particular of death,
which foreknowledge terrorizes the contents of skulls with,
is the fundamental project of technology; however,
pseudologica fantastica's mechanisms require:
to establish deathlessness you must first eliminate
those who die; a task attempted, when a white flash sparkled.

Unlike the trees of home, which continually evaporate
along the skyline, the trees here have been enticed down
toward world-eternity. No one knows which gods they enshrine.
Does it matter? Awareness of ignorance is as devout
as knowledge of knowledge. Or more so. Even though not
    knowing,
sometimes we weep, from surplus of gratitutde, even though
    knowing,
twice already on earth sparkled a flash, a white flash.

The children go away. By nature they do. And by memory,
in scorched uniforms, holding tiny crushed lunch tins.
All the ecstasy-groans of each night call them back, satori
their ghostliness back into the ashes, in the momentary shrines,
the thankfulness of arms, from which they will go
again and again, until the day flashes and no one lives
to look back and say, a flash, a white flash sparkled.

nominated by Philip Dacey, Sharon Olds,
and David Wojahn

52

HOT ICE

fiction by STUART DYBEK

from ANTAEUS

SAINTS

THE SAINT, A VIRGIN, was incorrupted. She had been frozen in a block of ice many years ago.

Her father had found her half-naked body floating face down among water lilies, her blonde hair fanning at the marshy edge of the overgrown duck pond people still referred to as the Douglas Park *Lagoon*.

That's how Eddie Kapusta had heard it.

Douglas Park was a black park now, the lagoon curdled in milky green scum as if it had soured, and Kapusta didn't doubt that were he to go there they'd find his body floating in the lily pads too. But sometimes in winter, riding by on the California Avenue bus, the park flocked white, deserted, and the lagoon frozen over, Eddie could almost picture what it had been like back then: swans gliding around the small, wooded island at the center, and rowboats plying into sunlight from the gaping stone tunnels of the haunted-looking boathouse.

The girl had gone rowing with a couple of guys—some said they were sailors, neighborhood kids going off to the war—nobody ever said who exactly or why she went with them, as if it didn't matter. They rowed her around to the blind side of the little island. Nobody knew what happened there either. It was necessary for each person to imagine it for himself.

They were only joking at first was how Kapusta imagined it, laughing at her broken English, telling her be friendly or swim

53

home. One of them stroked her hair, gently undid her bun, and as her hair fell cascading over her shoulders surprising them all, the other reached too suddenly for the buttons on her blouse; she tore away so hard the boat rocked violently, her slip and bra split, breasts sprung loose, she dove.

Even the suddenness was slow motion the way Kapusta imagined it. But once they were in the water the rest went through his mind in a flash—the boat capsizing, the sailors thrashing for the little island, and the girl struggling alone in that sepia water too warm from summer, just barely deep enough for bullheads, with a mud bottom kids said was quicksand exploding into darkness with each kick. He didn't want to wonder what she remembered. His mind raced over that to her father wading out into cattails, scooping her half-naked and still limp from the resisting water lilies, and running with her in his arms across the park crying in Polish or Slovak or Bohemian, whatever they were, and riding with her on the streetcar he wouldn't let stop until it reached the ice house he owned, where crazy with grief he sealed her in ice.

"I believe it up to the part about the streetcar," Manny Santora said that summer when they told each other such stories, talking often about things Manny called *weirdness*, while pitching quarters in front of Buddy's Bar. "I don't believe he hijacked no streetcar, man."

"What you think, man, he called a cab?" Pancho, Manny's older brother asked, winking at Eddie like he'd scored.

Every time they talked like this Manny and Pancho argued. Pancho believed in everything—ghosts, astrology, legends. His nickname was Padrecito which went back to his days as an altar boy when he would dress up as a priest and hold mass in the backyard with hosts punched with bottle caps from stale tortillas and real wine he'd collected from bottles the winos had left on doorstoops. Eddie's nickname was Edwardo, though the only person who called him that was Manny, who had made it up. Manny wasn't the kind of guy to have a nickname—he was Manny or Santora.

Pancho believed if you played certain rock songs backwards you'd hear secret messages from the devil. He believed in devils and angels. He still believed he had a guardian angel. It was something like being lucky, like making the sign of the cross before you stepped in the batter's box. "It's why I don't get caught even when I'm caught," he'd say when the cops would catch him dealing

and not take him in. Pancho believed in saints. For a while he had
even belonged to a gang called the Saints. They'd tried to recruit
Manny too, who, though younger, was tougher than Pancho, but
Manny had no use for gangs. "I already belong to the Loners," he
said.

Pancho believed in the girl in ice. In sixth grade, Sister Joachim,
the ancient nun in charge of the altar boys, had told him the girl
should be canonized and that she'd secretly written to the Pope
informing him that already there had been miracles and cures. "All
the martyrs didn't die in Rome," she'd told Pancho. "They're still
suffering today in China and Russia and Korea and even here in
your own neighborhood." Like all nuns she loved Pancho. Dressed
in his surplice and cassock he looked as if he should be beatified
himself, a young St. Sebastian or Juan de la Cruz, the only altar
boy in the history of the parish to spend his money on different-
colored gym shoes so they would match the priest's vestments—
red for martyrs, white for Feast Days, black for requiems. The
nuns knew he punished himself during Lent, offering up his pain
for the Poor Souls in Purgatory.

Their love for Pancho had made things impossible for Manny in
the Catholic school. He seemed Pancho's opposite in almost every
way and dropped out after they'd held him back in sixth grade. He
switched to public school, but mostly he hung out on the streets.

"I believe she worked miracles right in this neighborhood,
man," Pancho said.

"Bullshit, man. Like what miracles?" Manny wanted to know.

"Okay, man, you know Big Antek," Pancho said.

"Big Antek the wino?"

They all knew Big Antek. He bought them beer. He'd been a
butcher in every meat market in the neighborhood, but drunkenly
kept hacking off pieces of his hands, and finally quit completely to
become a full-time alky.

Big Antek had told Pancho about Kedzie Avenue when it was
still mostly people from the Old Country and he had gotten a job at
a Czech meat market with sawdust on the floor and skinned rabbits
in the window. He wasn't there a week when he got so drunk he
passed out in the freezer and when he woke the door was locked
and everyone was gone. It was Saturday and he knew they
wouldn't open again until Monday and by then he'd be stiff as a
two-by-four. He was already shivering so bad he couldn't stand still

55

or he'd fall over. He figured he'd be dead already except that his blood was half alcohol. Parts of him were going numb and he started staggering around, bumping past hanging sides of meat, singing, praying out loud, trying to let the fear out. He knew it was hopeless but he was looking anyway for some place to smash out, some plug to pull, something to stop the cold. At the back of the freezer, behind racks of meat, he found a cooler. It was an old one, the kind that used to stand packed wtih blocks of ice and bottles of beer in taverns during the war. And seeing it Big Antek suddenly remembered a moment from his first summer back from the Pacific, discharged from the hospital in Manila and back in Buddy's lounge on 24th Street kiddie-corner from a victory garden where a plaque erroneously listed his name among the parish war dead. It was an ordinary moment, nothing dramatic like his life flashing before his eyes, but the memory filled him with such clarity that the freezer became dreamlike beside it. The ballgame was on the radio over Buddy's bar, DiMaggio in center again, while Bing Crosby crooned from the jukebox which was playing at the same time. Antek was reaching into Buddy's cooler, up to his elbows in ice water feeling for a beer, while looking out through the open tavern door that framed 24th Street as if it were a movie full of girls blurred in brightness, slightly overexposed blondes, a movie he could step into any time he chose now that he was home; but right at this moment he was taking his time, stretching it out until it encompassed his entire life, the cold bottles bobbing away from his fingertips, clunking against ice, until finally he grabbed one, hauled it up dripping, wondering what he'd grabbed—a Monarch or Yusay Pilsner or Foxhead 400—then popped the cork in the opener on the side of the cooler, the foam rising as he tilted his head back and let it pour down his throat, privately celebrating being alive. That moment was what drinking had once been about. It was a good thing to be remembering now when he was dying with nothing else to do for it. He had the funny idea of climbing inside the cooler and going to sleep to continue the memory like a dream. The cooler was thick with frost, so white it seemed to glow. Its lid had been replaced with a slab of dry ice that smoked even within the cold of the freezer, reminding Antek that as kids they'd always called it hot ice. He nudged it aside. Beneath it was a block of ice as clear as if the icemen had just delivered it. There was something frozen inside. He glanced away, but knew already,

56

immediately, it was a body. He couldn't move away. He looked again. The longer he stared, the calmer he felt. It was a girl. He could make out her hair, not just blonde, but radiating gold like a candleflame behind a window in winter. Her breasts were bare. The ice seemed even clearer. She was beautiful and dreamy looking, not dreamy like sleeping, but the dreamy look DP's sometimes get when they first come to the city. As long as he stayed beside her he didn't shiver. He could feel the blood return; he was warm as if the smoldering dry ice really was hot. He spent the weekend huddled against her, and early Monday morning when the Czech opened the freezer he said to Antek, "Get out . . . you're fired." That's all either one of them said.

"You know what I think," Pancho said. "They moved her body from the ice house to the butcher shop because the cops checked, man."

"You know what I think," Manny said, "I think you're doing so much shit that even the winos can bullshit you."

They looked hard at one another, Manny especially looking bad because of a beard he was trying to grow that was mostly stubble except for a black knot of hair frizzing from the cleft under his lower lip—a little lip beard like a jazz musician's—and Pancho covered in crosses, a wooden one dangling from a leather thong over his open shirt, and a small gold cross on a fine gold chain tight about his throat, and a tiny platinum cross in his right earlobe, and a faded India-ink cross tattooed on his wrist where one would feel for a pulse.

"He got a cross-shaped dick," Manny said.

"Only when I got a hard-on, man," Pancho said, grinning, and they busted up.

"Hey, Eddie, man," Pancho said, "what you think of all this, man?"

Kapusta just shrugged like he always did. Not that he didn't have any ideas exactly, or that he didn't care. That shrug *was* what Kapusta believed.

"Yeah. Well, man," Pancho said, "I believe there's saints, and miracles happening everywhere only everybody's afraid to admit it. I mean like Ralph's little brother, the blue baby who died when he was eight. He knew he was dying all his life, man, and never complained. He was a saint. Or Big Antek who everybody says is a wino, man. But he treats everybody as human beings. Who you

57

think's more of a saint—him or the President, man? And Mrs. Corillo who everybody thought was crazy because she was praying loud all the time. Remember? She kneeled all day praying for Puerto Rico during that earthquake—the one Roberto Clemente crashed going to help. Remember that, man? Mrs. Corillo prayed all day and they thought she was still praying at night and she was kneeling there dead. She was a saint, man, and so's Roberto Clemente. There should be like a church, St. Roberto Clemente. Kids could pray to him at night. That would mean something to them."

"The earthquake wasn't in Puerto Rico, man," Manny told him, "and I don't believe no streetcar'd stop for somebody carrying a dead person."

AMNESIA

It was hard to believe there ever were streetcars. The city back then, the city of their fathers, which was as far back as family memory extended, even the city of their childhoods, seemed as remote to Eddie and Manny as the capital of some foreign country.

The past collapsed about them—decayed, bulldozed, obliterated. They walked past block-length gutted factories, past walls of peeling, multicolored doors hammered up around flooded excavation pits, hung out in half-boarded storefronts of groceries that had shut down when they were kids, dusty cans still stacked on the shelves. Broken glass collected everywhere mounding like sand in the little, sunken front yards and gutters. Even the church's stained-glass windows were patched with plywood.

They could vaguely remember something different before the cranes and wrecking balls gradually moved in, not order exactly, but rhythms: five-o'clock whistles, air-raid sirens on Tuesdays, Thursdays when the stockyards blew over like a brown wind of boiling hooves and bone, at least that's what people said, screwing up their faces, "Phew! they're making glue today!"

Streetcar tracks were long paved over; black webs of trolley wires vanished. So did the victory gardens that had become weed beds taking the corroded plaques with the names of the neighborhood dead with them.

Things were gone they couldn't remember, but missed; and

58

things were gone they weren't sure ever were there—the pickle factory by the railroad tracks where a DP with a net worked scooping rats out of the open vats, troughs for ragmen's horses, ragmen and their wooden wagons, knife-sharpeners pushing screeching whetstones up alleys hollering "Scissors! Knives!," hermits living in cardboard shacks behind billboards.

At times, walking past the gaps, they felt as if they were no longer quite there themselves, half-lost despite familiar street signs, shadows of themselves superimposed on the present, except there was no present—everything either rubbled past or promised future—and they were walking as if floating, getting nowhere as if they'd smoked too much grass.

That's how it felt those windy nights that fall when Manny and Eddie circled the county jail. They'd float down California past the courthouse, Bridewell Correctional, the auto pound, Communicable Disease Hospital, and then follow the long, curving concrete wall of the prison back towards 26th Street, sharing a joint, passing it with cupped hands, ready to flip it if a cop should cruise by, but one place you could count on not to see cops was outside the prison.

Nobody was there; just the wall, railroad tracks, the river and the factories that lined it—boundaries that remained intact while neighborhoods came and went.

Eddie had never noticed any trees, but swirls of leaves scuffed past their shoes. It was Kapusta's favorite weather, wild, blowing nights that made him feel free, flagpoles knocking in the wind, his clothes flapping like flags. He felt both tight and loose, and totally alive even walking down a street that always made him sad. It was the street that followed the curve of the prison wall, and it didn't have a name. It was hardly a street at all, more a shadow of the wall, potholed, puddled, half-paved, rutted wtih rusted railroad tracks.

"Trains used to go down this street," Manny said.

"I seen tanks going down this street."

"Tank cars?"

"No, Army tanks," Kapusta said.

"Battleships, too, Edwardo?" Manny asked seriously. Then the wind ripped a laugh from his mouth loud enough to carry over the prison wall.

Kapusta laughed loud too. But he could remember tanks, cam-

59

ouflaged with netting, rumbling on flatcars, their cannons outlined by the red lanterns of the dinging crossing gates which were down all along 26th Street. It was one of the first things he remembered. He must have been very small. The train seemed endless. He could see the guards in the turrets on the prison wall watching it, the only time he'd ever seen them facing the street. "Still sending them to Korea or someplace," his father had said, and for years after, Eddie believed you could get to Korea by train. For years after, he would wake in the middle of the night when it was quiet enough to hear the trains passing blocks away, and lie in bed listening, wondering if the tanks were rumbling past the prison, if not to Korea then to some other war that tanks went to at night; and he would think of the prisoners in their cells locked up for their violence with knives and clubs and cleavers and pistols, and wonder if they were lying awake, listening too as the netted cannons rolled by their barred windows. Even as a child Eddie knew the names of men inside there: Milo Hermanski, who had stabbed some guy in the eye in a fight at Andy's Tap; Billy Gomez, who set the housing project on fire every time his sister Nina got gang-banged; Ziggy's uncle, the war hero, who one day blew off the side of Ziggy's mother's face while she stood ironing in her slip during an argument over a will; and other names of people he didn't know, but had heard about—Benny Bedwell, with his "Elvis" sideburns, who may have killed the Grimes sisters, Mafia hitmen, bank robbers, junkies, perverts, murderers on death row—he could sense them lying awake listening, the tension of their sleeplessness, and Pancho lay among them now as he and Manny walked outside the wall.

They stopped again as they'd been stopping and yelled together: "Pancho, Panchooooooo," dragging out the last vowel the way they had as kids standing on the sidewalk calling up at one another's windows as if knocking at the door were not allowed.

"Pancho, we're out here, brother, me and Eddie," Manny shouted. "Hang tough, man, we ain't forgetting you."

Nobody answered. They kept walking, stopping to shout at intervals the way they had been doing most every night.

"If only we knew what building he was in," Eddie said.

They could see the upper stories of the brick buildings rising over the wall, their grated windows low lit, never dark, floodlights on the roof glaring down.

60

"Looks like a factory, man," Eddie said. "Looks like the same guy who planned the Harvester foundry on Western did the jail."

"You rather be in the Army or in there?" Manny asked.

"No way they're getting me in there," Kapusta said.

That was when Eddie knew Pancho was crazy, when the judge had given Pancho a choice at the end of his trial.

"You're a nice looking kid," the judge had said, "too nice for prison. What do you want to do with your life?"

"Pose for holy cards," Pancho said, "St. Joseph my specialty." Pancho was standing there wearing the tie they had brought him wound around his head like an Indian headband. He was wearing a black satin jacket with the signs of the zodiac on the back.

"I'm going to give you a chance to straighten out, to gain some self-respect. The court's attitude would be very sympathetic to any signs of self-direction and patriotism, joining the Army for instance."

"I'm a captain," Pancho told him.

"The Army or jail, which is it?"

"I'm a captain, man, *soy capitan, capitan*," Pancho insisted, humming, "La Bomba" under his breath.

"You're a misfit."

Manny was able to visit Pancho every three weeks. Each time it got worse. Sometimes Pancho seemed hardly to recognize him, looking away, refusing to meet Manny's eyes the whole visit. Sometimes he'd cry. For a while at first he wanted to know how things were in the neighborhood. Then he stopped asking, and when Manny tried to tell him the news Pancho would get jumpy, irritable, and lapse into total silence. "I don't wanna talk about out there, man," he told Manny. "I don't wanna remember that world until I'm ready to step into it again. You remember too much in here you go crazy, man. I wanna forget everything like I never existed."

"His fingernails are gone, man," Manny told Eddie, "he's gnawing on himself like a rat and when I ask him what's going down all he'll say is I'm locked in hell, my angel's gone, I've lost my luck— bullshit like that, you know? Last time I seen him he says I'm gonna kill myself, man, if they don't stop hitting on me."

"I can't fucking believe it. I can't fucking believe he's in there," Kapusta said. "He should be in a monastery somewhere; he should of been a priest. He had a vocation."

61

"He had a vocation to be an altar boy, man," Manny said, spitting it out like he was disgusted by what he was saying, talking down about his own brother. "It was that nuns and priests crap that messed up his head. He was happy being an altar boy, man, if they'd of let him be an altar boy all his life he'd still be happy."

By the time they were halfway down the nameless street it was drizzling a fine, misty spray, and Manny was yelling in Spanish, "*Estamos contigo, hermano! San Roberto Clemente te ayudará!*"

They broke into "La Bomba," Eddie singing in Spanish too, not sure exactly what he was singing, but it sounded good: "*Yo no soy marinero, soy capitan, capitan, ay, ay Bomba! ay, ay Bomba!*" He had lived beside Spanish in the neighborhood all his life and every so often a word got through, like *juilota* which was what Manny called pigeons when they used to hunt them with slingshots under the railroad bridges. It seemed a perfect word to Eddie, in which he could hear both their cooing and the whistling rush of their wings. He didn't remember any words like that in Polish, which his grandma had spoken to him when he was little, and which, Eddie had been told, he could once speak too.

By midnight they were at the end of their circuit, emerging from the unlighted, nameless street, stepping over tracks that continued to curve past blinded switches. Under the streetlights on 26th the prison wall appeared rust-stained, oozing at cracks. The wire spooled at the top of the wall looking rusty in the wet light as did the tracks as if the rain were rusting everything overnight.

They stopped on the corner of 26th where the old ice house stood across the nameless street from the prison. One could still buy ice from a vending machine in front. Without realizing it, Eddie guarded his breathing as if still able to detect the faintest stab of ammonia, although it had been a dozen years since the louvered fans on the ice house roof had clacked through clouds of vapor.

"Padrecitooooo!" they both hollered.

Their voices bounced back off the wall.

They stood on the corner by the ice house as if waiting around for someone. From there they could stare down 26th—five dark blocks, then an explosion of neon at Kedzie Avenue: taco places, bars, a street plugged in, winking festive as a pinball machine, traffic from it coming towards them in the rain.

The streetlights surged and flickered.

62

"You see that?" Eddie asked. "They used to say when the streetlights flickered it meant they just fried somebody in the electric chair."

"So much bullshit," Manny said. *"Compadre no te rajes!"* he yelled at the wall.

"Whatcha tell him?"

"It sounds different in English," Manny said. " '*Godfather, do not give up.*' It's words from an old song."

Kapusta stepped out into the middle of 26th and stood in the misting drizzle squinting at Kedzie through cupped hands as if he had a spyglass. He could make out the traffic light way down there changing to green. He could almost hear the music from the bars that would serve them without asking for ID's so long as Manny was there. "You thirsty by any chance, man?" he asked.

"You buyin'?" Manny grinned.

"Buenas noches, Pancho," they hollered, "catch you tomorrow, man."

"Goodnight guys," a falsetto voice echoed back from over the wall.

"That ain't Pancho," Manny said.

"Sounds like the singer on old Platters' records," Eddie said. "Ask him if he knows Pancho, man."

"Hey, you know a guy named Pancho Santora?" Manny called.

"Oh, Pancho?" the voice inquired.

"Yeah, Pancho."

"Oh, Cisco!" the voice shouted. They could hear him cackling. "Hey baby, I don't know no Pancho. Is that rain I smell?"

"It's raining," Eddie hollered.

"Hey baby, tell me something. What's it like out there tonight?"

Manny and Eddie looked at each other. "Beautiful!" they yelled together.

GRIEF

There was never a requiem, but by Lent everyone knew that one way or another Pancho was gone. No wreaths, but plenty of rumors; Pancho had hung himself in his cell; his throat had been slashed in the showers; he'd killed another inmate and was under heavy sedation in the psycho ward at Kankakee. And there was talk

63

he'd made a deal and was in the Army, shipped off to a war he had sworn he'd never fight; that he had turned snitch and had been secretly relocated with a new identity; or that he had become a trustee, and had simply walked away while mowing the grass in front of the courthouse, escaped maybe to Mexico, or maybe just across town to the North Side around Diversey where, if one made the rounds of the leather bars, they might see someone with Pancho's altar-boy eyes staring out from the makeup of a girl.

Some saw him late at night like a ghost haunting the neighborhood, collar up, in the back of the church lighting a vigil candle; or veiled in a black mantilla, speeding past, face floating by on a greasy El window.

Rumors were becoming legends, but there was never a wake, never an obituary, and no one knew how to mourn a person who had just disappeared.

For a while Manny disappeared too. He wasn't talking and Kapusta didn't ask. They had quit walking around the prison wall months before, around Christmas when Pancho refused to let anyone, even Manny, visit. But their night walks had been tapering off before that.

Eddie remembered the very last time they had gone. It was in December and he was frozen from standing around a burning garbage can on Kedzie, selling Christmas trees. About ten, when the lot closed, Manny came by and they stopped to thaw out at the Carta Blanca. A guy named Jose kept buying them whiskeys and they staggered out after midnight into a blizzard.

"Look at this white bullshit," Manny said.

Walking down 26th they stopped to fling snowballs over the wall. Then they decided to stand there singing Christmas carols. Snow was drifting against the wall, erasing the street that had hardly been there. Eddie could tell Manny was starting to go silent. He would get the first few words into a carol, singing at the top of his voice, then stop as if choked by the song. His eyes stayed angry when he laughed. Everything was bullshit to him and finally Eddie couldn't talk to him anymore. Stomping away from the prison through fresh snow, Eddie had said, "If this keeps up, man, I'll need boots."

"It don't *have* to *keep up*, man," Manny snapped. "Nobody's making you come, man. It ain't your brother."

"All I said is I'll need boots, man," Eddie said.

"You said it hopeless, man; things are always fucking hopeless to you."

"Hey, you're the big realist, man," Eddie told him.

"I never said I was no realist," Manny mumbled.

Kapusta hadn't had a lot of time since then. He had dropped out of school again and was loading trucks at night for UPS. One more semester didn't matter, he figured, and he needed some new clothes, cowboy boots, a green leather jacket. The weather had turned drizzly and mild, a late Easter, but an early spring. Eddie had heard Manny was hanging around by himself, still finding bullshit everywhere, only worse. Now he muttered as he walked like some crazy, bitter old man, or one of those black guys reciting the gospel to buildings, telling off posters and billboards, neon signs, stoplights, passing traffic—bullshit, all of it bullshit.

It was Tuesday in Holy Week, the statues inside the church shrouded in violet, when Eddie slipped on his green jacket and walked over to Manny's before going to work. He rang the doorbell, then stepped outside in the rain and stood on the sidewalk under Manny's windows, watching cars pass.

After a while Manny came down the stairs and slammed out the door.

"How you doin,' man?" Eddie said like they'd just run into each other by accident.

Manny stared at him. "How far'd you have to chase him for that jacket, man?" he said.

"I knew you'd dig it." Eddie smiled.

They went out for a few beers later that night, after midnight, when Eddie was through working, but instead of going to a bar they ended up just walking. Manny had rolled a couple bombers and they walked down the boulevard along California watching the headlights flash by like a procession of candles. Manny still wasn't saying much, but they were passing the reefer like having a conversation. At 31st, by the Communicable Disease Hospital, Eddie figured they would follow the curve of the boulevard towards the bridge on Western, but Manny turned as if out of habit towards the prison.

They were back walking along the wall. There was still old ice from winter at the base of it.

"The only street in Chicago where it's still winter," Kapusta mumbled.

"Remember yelling?" Manny said, almost in a whisper.

"Sure," Eddie nodded.

"Called, joked, prayed, sang Christmas songs, remember that night, how cold we were, man?"

"Yeah."

"What a bunch of stupid bullshit, huh?"

Eddie was afraid Manny was going to start the bullshit stuff again. Manny had stopped and stood looking at the wall.

Then he cupped his hands over his mouth and yelled, "Hey! you dumb fuckers in there! We're back! Can you hear me? Hey, wake up niggers, hey spics, hey honkies, you buncha fucken monkeys in cages, hey! we're out here *free!*"

"Hey, Manny, come on, man," Eddie said.

Manny uncupped his hands, shook his head and smiled. They took a few steps, then Manny whirled back again. "We're out here free, man! We're smokin' reefer, drinking cold beer while you're in there, you assholes! We're on our way to fuck your wives, man, your girlfriends are giving us blow jobs while you jack-offs flog it. Hey man, I'm pumping your old lady out here right now. She likes it in the ass like you!"

"What are you doing, man," Eddie was pleading. "Take it easy."

Manny was screaming his lungs out, almost incoherent, shouting every filfthy thing he could think of, and voices, the voices they'd never heard before, had begun shouting back from the other side of the wall.

"Shadup! Shadup! Shadup out there you crazy fuck!" came the voices.

"She's out here licking my balls while you're punking each other through the bars of your cage!"

"Shadup!" they were yelling and then a voice howling over the others, "I'll kill you motherfucker! When I get out you're dead!"

"Come on out," Manny was yelling. "Come and get me you piece of shit, you sleazeballs, you scumbag cocksuckers, you creeps are missing it all, your lives are wasted garbage!"

Now there were too many voices to distinguish, whole tiers, whole buildings yelling and cursing and threatening, *shadup, shadup, shadup,* almost a chant, and then the searchlight from the guardhouse slowly turned and swept the street.

"We gotta get outa here," Eddie said, pulling Manny away. He dragged him to the wall, right up against it where the light couldn't follow, and they started to run, stumbling along the banked strip of filthy ice, dodging stunted trees that grew out of odd angles, running towards 26th until Eddie heard the sirens.

"This way, man," he panted, yanking Manny back across the nameless street, jumping puddles and tracks, cutting down a narrow corridor between abandoned truck docks seconds before a squad car, blue dome light revolving, sped past.

They jogged behind the truck docks, not stopping until they came up behind the ice house. Manny's panting sounded almost like laughing, the way people laugh sometimes after they've hurt themselves.

"I hate those motherfuckers," Manny gasped, "all of them, the fucking cops and guards and fucking wall and the bastards behind it. All of them. That must be what makes me a realist, huh, Eddie? I fucking hate them all."

They went back the next night.

Sometimes a thing wasn't a sin—if there was such a thing as sin—Eddie thought, until it's done a second time. There were accidents, mistakes that could be forgiven once; it was repeating them that made them terribly wrong. That was how Eddie felt about going back the next night.

Manny said he was going whether Eddie came or not, so Eddie went, afraid to leave Manny on his own, even though he'd already had trouble trying to get some sleep before going to work. Eddie could still hear the voices yelling from behind the wall and dreamed they were all being electrocuted; electrocuted slowly, by degrees of their crimes, screaming with each surge of current and flicker of streetlights as if in a hell where electricity had replaced fire.

Standing on the dark street Wednesday night, outside the wall again, felt like an extension of his nightmare: Manny raging almost out of control, shouting curses and insults, baiting them over the wall the way a child tortures penned watchdogs, until he had what seemed like the entire west side of the prison howling back, the guards sweeping the street with searchlights, sirens wailing towards them from both 31st and 26th.

This time they raced down the tracks that curved towards the river, picking their way in the dark along the junkyard bank, flipping rusted cables of moored barges, running through the fire-truck graveyard, following the tracks across the blackened trestles where they'd once shot pigeons and from which they could gaze across the industrial prairie that stretched behind factories all the way to the skyline of downtown. The skyscrapers glowed like luminescent peaks in the misty spring night. Manny and Eddie stopped in the middle of the trestle and leaned over the railing catching their breaths.

"Downtown ain't as far away as I used to think when I was a kid," Manny panted.

"These tracks'll take you right there," Eddie said quietly, "to railroad yards under the street, right by the lake."

"How you know, man?"

"A bunch of us used to hitch rides on the boxcars in seventh grade." Eddie was talking very quietly, looking away.

"I usually take the bus, you know?" Manny tried joking.

"I ain't goin' back there with you tomorrow," Eddie said. "I ain't goin' back there with you ever."

Manny kept staring off towards the lights downtown as if he hadn't heard. "Okay," he finally said, more to himself as if surrendering. "Okay, how about tomorrow we do something else, man?"

NOSTALGIA

They didn't go back.

The next night, Thursday, Eddie overslept and called in sick for work. He tried to get back to sleep, but kept falling into half-dreams in which he could hear the voices shouting behind the prison wall. Finally he got up and opened a window. It was dark out. A day had passed almost unnoticed, and now the night felt as if it were a part of the night before, and the night before a part of the night before that, all connected by his restless dreams, fragments of the same continuous night.

Eddie had said that at some point: "It's like one long night," and later Manny had said the same thing as if it had suddenly occurred to him.

They were strung out almost from the start, drifting stoned under the El tracks before Eddie even realized they weren't still sitting on the stairs in front of Manny's house. That was where Eddie had found him, sitting on the stairs out in front, and for a while they had sat together watching traffic, taking sips out of a bottle of Gallo into which Manny had dropped several hits of speed.

Cars gunned by with their windows rolled down and radios playing loud. It sounded like a summer night.

"Ain't you hot wearin' that jacket, man?" Manny asked him.

"Now that you mention it," Eddie said. He was sweating.

Eddie took his leather jacket off and they knotted a handkerchief around one of the cuffs, then slipped the Gallo bottle down the sleeve. They walked along under the El tracks passing a joint. A train, only two cars long, rattled overhead.

"So what we doing, Edwardo?" Manny kept repeating.

"Walking," Eddie said.

"I feel like doing *something*, you know?"

"We are doing something," Eddie insisted.

Eddie led them over to the Coconut Club on 22nd. They couldn't get in, but Eddie wanted to look at the window with its neon green palm tree and winking blue coconuts.

"That's maybe my favorite window."

"You drag me all the way here to see your favorite window, man!" Manny said.

"It's those blue coconuts," Eddie tried explaining. His mouth was dry, but he couldn't stop talking. He started telling Manny how he had collected windows from the time he was a little kid, even though talking about it made it sound more important to him than it was. Half the time he didn't even know he was doing it. He would see a window from a bus like the Greek butcher shop on Halsted with its pyramid of lamb skulls and make a mental photograph of it. He had special windows all over the city. It was how he held the city together in his mind.

"I'd see all these windows from the El," Eddie said, "when I'd visit my *busha*, my grandma. Like I remember we'd pass this one building where the curtains were all slips hanging by their straps— black ones, white ones, red ones. At night you could see the lightbulbs shining through the lace tops. My *busha* said gypsies lived there." Eddie was walking down the middle of the street, jacket flung over his shoulder, staring up at the windows as if looking for gypsies as he talked.

"Someday they're gonna get you as a peeper, man," Manny laughed. "And when they do, don't try explaining to them about this thing of yours for windows, Edwardo."

69

They were walking down Spaulding back towards 26th. The streetlights beamed brighter and brighter and Manny put his sunglasses on. A breeze was blowing that felt warmer than the air and they took their shirts off. They saw rats darting along the curb into the sewer on the other side of the street and put their shirts back on.

"The rats get crazy where they start wrecking these old buildings," Manny said.

The cranes and wrecking balls and urban renewal signs were back with the early spring. They walked around a barricaded site. Water trickled along the gutters from an open hydrant, washing brick dust and debris towards the sewers.

"Can you smell that, man?" Manny asked him, suddenly excited. "I can smell the lake through the hydrant."

"Smells like rust to me," Eddie said.

"I can smell fish! Smelt—the smelt are in! I can smell them right through the hydrant!"

"Smelt?" Eddie said.

"You ain't ever had smelt?" Manny asked. "Little silver fish!"

They caught the 26th Street bus—the Polish Zephyr, people called it—going east, towards the lake. The back was empty. They sat in the swaying, long backseat, taking hits out of the bottle in Eddie's sleeve.

"It's usually too early for them yet, but they're out there, Edwardo," Manny kept reassuring him as if they were actually going fishing.

Eddie nodded. He didn't know anything about smelt. The only fish he ate was canned tuna, but it felt good to be riding somewhere with the windows open and Manny acting more like his old self—sure of himself, laughing easily. Eddie still felt like talking but his molars were grinding on speed.

The bus jolted down the dark blocks past Kedzie and was flying when it passed the narrow street between the ice house and the prison, but Eddie and Manny caught a glimpse out the back window of the railroad tracks that curved down the nameless street. The tracks were lined with fuming red flares that threw red reflections off the concrete walls. They were sure the flares had been set there for them.

Eddie closed his eyes and sank into the rocking of the bus. Even with his eyes closed he could see the reddish glare of the walls.

70

The glare was ineradicable, at the back of his sockets. The wall had looked the same way it had looked in his dreams. They rode in silence.

"It's like one long night," Eddie said somewhere along the way.

His jaws were really grinding and his legs had forgotten gravity by the time they got to the lake front. They didn't know the time, but it must have been around four and the smelt fishers were still out. The lights of their kerosene lanterns reflected along the breakwater over the glossy black lake. Eddie and Manny could hear the water lapping under the pier, and the fishermen talking in low voices in different languages.

"My Uncle Carlos would talk to the fish," Manny said. "No shit. He'd talk to them in Spanish. He didn't have no choice. Whole time here he couldn't speak English. Said it made his brain stuck. We used to come fishing here all the time—smelt, perch, every-thing. I'd come instead of going to school. If they weren't hitting he'd start talking to them, singing them songs."

"Like what?" Eddie said.

"He'd make them up. They were funny, man. It don't come across in English: 'Little silver ones fill up my shoes. My heart is lonesome for the fish of the sea.' It was like very formal how he'd say it. He'd always call this the sea. I'd tell him it's a lake but he couldn't be talked out of it. He was very stubborn—too stubborn to learn English. I ain't been fishing since he went back to Mexico."

They walked to the end of the pier, then back past the fisher-men. A lot of them were old men gently tugging lines between their fingers, lifting nets like flying underwater kites, plucking the wriggling silver fish from the netting, the yellow light of their lamps glinting off the bright scales.

"I told you they were out here," Manny said.

They killed the bottle sitting on a concrete ledge and dropped it into the lake. Then they rode the El back. It was getting lighter without a dawn. The El windows streaked with rain, the Douglas Avenue station smelled wet. It was a dark morning. They should have ended it then. Instead they sat at Manny's kitchen table drinking instant coffee with Pet milk. Eddie kept getting lost in the designs the milk would make, swirls and thunderclouds in his mug of coffee. He was numb and shaky. His jaw ached.

"I'm really crashin'," he told Manny.

71

"Here," Manny said. "Bring us down easier, man."

"I don't like doing downers, man," Eddie said.

"Ludes," Manny said, "from Pancho's stash."

They sat across the table from each other for a long time, talking, telling their memories and secrets, only Eddie was too numb to remember exactly what they said. Their voices—his own as well as Manny's—seemed *outside*, removed from the center of his mind.

At one point Manny looked out at the dark morning and said, "It still seems like last night."

"That's right," Eddie agreed. He wanted to say more, but couldn't express it. He didn't try. Eddie didn't believe it was what they said that was important. Manny could be talking Spanish; I could be talking Polish, Eddie thought. It didn't matter. What meant something was sitting at the table together, wrecked together, still awake watching the rainy light spatter the window, walking out again, to the Prague bakery for bismarks, past people under dripping umbrellas on their way to church.

"Looks like Sunday," Manny said.

"Today's Friday," Eddie said. "It's Good Friday."

"I seen ladies with ashes on their heads waiting for the bus a couple days ago," Manny told him.

They stood in the doorway of the Prague, out of the rain, eating their bismarks. Just down from the church, the bakery was a place people crowded into after mass. Its windows displayed colored eggs and little frosted Easter lambs.

"Onc time on Ash Wednesday I was eating a bismark and Pancho made a cross on my forehead with the powdered sugar like it was ashes. When I went to church the priest wouldn't give me real ashes," Manny said with a grin.

It was one of the few times Eddie had heard Manny mention Pancho. Now that they were outside, Eddie's head felt clearer than it had in the kitchen.

"I used to try and keep my ashes on until Good Friday," he told Manny, "but they'd make me wash."

The church bells were ringing, echoes bouncing off the sidewalks as if deflected by the ceiling of clouds. The neighborhood felt narrower, compressed from above.

"I wonder if it still looks the same in there," Manny said as they passed the church.

They stepped in and stood in the vestibule. The saints of their

72

childhood stood shrouded in purple. The altar was bare, stripped for Good Friday. Old ladies, ignoring the new liturgy, chanted a litany in Polish.

"Same as ever," Eddie whispered as they backed out.

The rain had almost let up. They could hear its accumulated weight in the wing-flaps of pigeons.

"Good Friday was Pancho's favorite holiday, man," Manny said. "Everybody else always picked Christmas or Thanksgiving or Fourth of July. He hada be different, man. I remember he used to drag me along visiting churches. You ever do that?"

"Hell yeah," Eddie said. "Every Good Friday we'd go on our bikes. You hada visit seven of them."

Without agreeing to it they walked from St. Roman's to St. Michael's, a little wooden Franciscan church in an Italian neighborhood; and from there to St. Casimir's, a towering, mournful church with twin copper-green towers. Then, as if following an invisible trail, they walked north up 22nd towards St. Anne's, St. Pius, St. Adalbert's. At first they merely entered and left immediately, as if touching base, but their familiarity with small rituals quickly returned: dipping their fingers in the holy-water fount by the door, making the automatic sign of the cross as they passed the life-sized crucified Christs that hung in the vestibules where old women and school kids clustered to kiss the spikes in the bronze or bloody plaster feet. By St. Anne's, Manny removed his sunglasses, out of respect the way one removes a hat. Eddie put them on. His eyes felt hard boiled. The surge of energy he had felt at the bakery had burned out fast. While Manny genuflected to the altar, Eddie slumped in the back pew pretending to pray, drowsing off behind the dark glasses. It never occurred to Eddie to simply go home. His head ached, he could feel his heart racing, and would suddenly jolt awake wondering where Manny was. Manny would be off—jumpy, frazzled, still popping speed on the sly—exploring the church as if searching for something, standing among lines of parishioners waiting to kiss the relics the priest wiped repeatedly clean with a rag of silk. Then Manny would be shaking Eddie awake. "How you holding up, man?"

"I'm cool," and they would be back on the streets heading for another parish under the overcast sky. Clouds, a shade between slate and lilac, smoked over the spires and roofs; lights flashed on in the bars and *taquerias*. On 18th Street a great blue neon fish

73

leapt in the storefront window of a tiny *ostenaria*. Eddie tried to remember exactly where it was. They headed to St. Procopius where, Manny said, he and Pancho had been baptized, along a wall of viaducts that schoolchildren had painted into a mural that seemed to go for miles.

"I don't think we're gonna make seven churches, man," Eddie said. He was walking without lifting his feet, his hair plastered with a sweatlike drizzle. It was around three p.m. It had been three p.m.—Christ's dark hour on the cross—inside the churches all day, but now it was turning three p.m. outside too. They could hear the ancient-sounding *Tantum Ergo* carrying from down the block.

Eddie sunk into the last pew, kneeling in the red glow of vigil lights that brought back the red flicker of the flares they had seen from the window of the bus as it sped by the prison. Manny had already faded into the procession making the Stations of the Cross—a shuffling crowd circling the church, kneeling before each station while altar boys censed incense and the priest recited Christ's agony. Old women answered with prayers like moans.

Old women were walking on their knees up the marble aisle to kiss the relics. A few were crying, and Eddie remembered how back in grade school he had heard old women cry sometimes after confession, crying as if their hearts would break, and even as a child he had wondered how such old women could possibly have committed sins terrible enough to demand such bitter weeping. Most everything from that world had changed or disappeared, but the old women had endured—Polish, Bohemian, Spanish, he knew it didn't matter; they were the same, dressed in black coats and babushkas the way holy statues wore violet, in constant mourning. A common pain of loss seemed to burn at the core of their lives, though Eddie had never understood exactly what it was they mourned. Nor how day after day they had sustained the intensity of their grief. He would have given up long ago. In a way he had, and the ache left behind couldn't be called grief. He had no name for it. He had felt it before Pancho or anyone was lost, almost from the start of memory. If it was grief, it was grief for the living. The hymns, with their ancient, keening melodies and mysterious words, had brought the feeling back, but when he tried to discover the source, to give the feeling a name, it eluded him as always, leaving in its place nostalgia and triggered nerves.

Oh God, he prayed, I'm really crashing.

He was too shaky to kneel, so he stretched out on the pew, lying on his back, eyes shut behind sunglasses, until the church began to whirl. To control it he tried concentrating on the stained-glass window overhead. None of the windows that had ever been special for him were from a church. This one was an angel, its colors like jewels and coals. Afternoon seemed to be dying behind it, becoming part of the night, part of the private history that he and Manny continued between them like a pact. He could see night shining through, its neon and wet streetlights illuminating the angel on the window.

LEGENDS

It started with ice.

That's how Big Antek sometimes began the story.

At dusk a gang of little Mexican kids appeared with a few lumps of dry ice covered in a shoe box as if they had caught a bird. *Hot ice,* they called it, though the way they said it sounded to Antek like *hot eyes*. Kids always have a way of finding stuff like that. One boy touched his tongue to a piece and screamed *"Aye!"* when it stuck. They watched it boil and fume in a rain puddle along the curb, and finally they filled a bottle part way with water, inserted the fragments of ice they had left, capped the bottle and set it in the mouth of an alley waiting for an explosion. When it popped they scattered.

Manny Santora and Eddie Kapusta came walking up the alley, wanting Antek to buy them a bottle of rum at Buddy's. Rum instead of beer. They were celebrating, Kapusta said, but he didn't say what. Maybe one of them had found a job or had just been fired, or graduated, or joined the Army instead of waiting around to get drafted. It could be anything. They were always celebrating. Behind their sunglasses Antek could see they were high as usual, even before Manny offered him a drag off a reefer the size of a cigar.

Probably nobody was hired or fired or had joined anything; probably it was just so hot they had a good excuse to act crazy. They each had a bottle of Coke they were fizzing up, squirting. Eddie had limes stuffed in his pockets and was pretending they

75

were his balls. Manny had a plastic bag of the little ice cubes they sell at gas stations. It was half-melted and they were scooping handfuls of cubes over each other's heads, stuffing them down their jeans and yowling, rubbing ice on their chests and under their arms as if taking cold showers. They looked like wild men—shirts hanging from their back pockets, handkerchiefs knotted around their heads, wearing their sunglasses, their bodies slick with melted ice water and sweat; two guys in the prime of life going nowhere, both lean, Kapusta almost as tan as Santora—Santora with that frizzy beard under his lip, and Kapusta trying to juggle limes.

They were drinking rum using a method Antek had never seen before and he had seen his share of drinking—not just in the neighborhood—all over the world when he was in the Navy, and not the Bohemian Navy either like somebody would always say when he would start telling Navy stories.

They claimed they were drinking Cuba Libres, only they didn't have glasses so they were mixing the drinks in their mouths, starting with some little cubes, then pouring in rum, Coke, a squeeze of lime, and swallowing. Swallowing if one or the other didn't suddenly bust up over some private joke, spraying the whole mouthful out, and both of them choking and coughing and laughing.

"Hey Antek, lemme build you a drink," Manny kept saying, but Antek shook his head no thanks, and he wasn't known for passing up too many.

This was all going on in front of Buddy's, everyone catching a blast of music and air-conditioning whenever the door opened. It was hot. The moths sizzled as soon as they hit Buddy's buzzing orange sign. A steady beat of moths dropped like cinders on the blinking orange sidewalk where the little kids were pitching pennies. Manny passed around what was left in the plastic bag of ice, and the kids stood sucking and crunching the cubes between their teeth.

It reminded Antek of summers when the ice trucks still delivered to Buddy's—flatbeds covered with canvas, the icemen, mainly DP's, wearing leather aprons, with Popeye forearms that even in August looked ruddy with cold. They would slide the huge, clear blocks off the tailgate so the whump reverberated through the hollow under the sidewalks, and deep in the ice the clarity shattered. Then with their ice hooks they'd lug the blocks across the sidewalk trailing a slick, and boot them skidding down the chute into Buddy's beery-smelling cellar. And after the truck pulled away, kids would pick the splinters from the curb and suck them as if they were ice-flavored popsicles.

Nobody seemed too interested when Antek tried to tell them about the ice trucks, or anything else about how the world had been, for that matter. Antek had been sick and had only recently returned from the VA hospital. He returned feeling old and as if the neighborhood had changed in the few weeks he had been gone. People had changed. He couldn't be sure, but they treated him differently, colder, as if he were becoming a stranger in the place he had grown up in, now, just when he needed the most to belong.

"Hey Antek," Manny said, "you know what you can tell me? That girl that saved your life in the meat freezer, did she have good tits?"

"I tell you about a miracle and you ask me about tits?" Antek said. "I don't talk about that anymore because now somebody always asks me did she have good tits. Go see."

Kids had been trying for years to sneak into the ice house to see her. It was what the neighborhood had instead of a haunted house. Each generation had grown up with the story of how her father had ridden with her half-naked body on the streetcar. Even the nuns had heard Antek's story about finding the girl still frozen in the meat freezer. The butcher shop on Kedzie had closed long ago and the legend was that after the cops had stopped checking, her body had been moved at night back into the ice house. But the ice house wasn't easy to break into. It had stood padlocked and heavily boarded for years.

"They're gonna wreck it," Eddie said. "I went by on the bus and they got the crane out in front."

"Oh-oh, last chance, Antek," Manny said. "If you're sure she's in there maybe we oughta save her."

"She's in there," Antek said. He noticed the little kids had stopped pitching pennies and were listening.

"Well, you owe her something after what she done for you—don't he, Edwardo?"

The kids who were listening chuckled, then started to go back to their pennies.

"You wanna go, I'll go!" Antek said loudly.

"All right, let's go."

Antek got up unsteadily. He stared at Eddie and Manny. "You guys couldn't loan me enough for a taste of wine until I get my disability check?"

The little kids tagged after them to the end of the block, then turned back bored. Manny and Eddie kept going, picking the pace up a step or two ahead of Antek, exchanging looks and grinning. But Antek knew that no matter how much they joked or what excuses they gave, they were going like him for one last look. They were just old enough to have seen the ice house before it shut down. It was a special building, the kind a child couldn't help but notice and remember—there, on the corner across the street from the prison, a factory that made ice, humming with fans, its louvered roof dripping and clacking, lost in acrid clouds of its own escaping vapor.

The automatic ice machine in front had already been carted away. The doors were still padlocked, but the way the crane was parked it was possible for Manny and Eddie to climb the boom onto the roof.

Antek waited below. He gazed up at the new plexiglass guard turrets on the prison wall. From his angle all he could see was the bluish fluorescence of their lighting. He watched Manny and Eddie jump from the boom to the roof, high enough to stare across at the turrets like snipers, to draw a level bead on the backs of the guards, high enough to gaze over the wall at the dim, barred windows of the buildings that resembled foundries more than ever in the sweltering heat.

Below, Antek stood swallowing wine, expecting more from the night than a condemned building. He didn't know exactly what else he expected. Perhaps only a scent, like the stab of remembered ammonia he might have detected if he were still young enough to climb the boom. Perhaps the secret isolation he imagined Manny and Eddie feeling now, alone on the roof, as if lost in clouds of vapor. At street level, passing traffic droned out the tick of the single cricket keeping time on the roof—a cricket so loud and insistent that Manny didn't stop to worry about the noise when he kicked in the louvers. And Antek, though he had once awakened in a freezer, couldn't imagine the shock of cold that Manny and Eddie felt as they dropped out of the summer night to the floor below.

Earlier, on their way down 26th, Manny had stopped to pick up an unused flare from along the tracks, and Antek pictured them inside now, Manny, his hand wrapped in a handkerchief, holding the flare away from him like a Roman candle, its red glare sputtering off the beams and walls.

There wasn't much to see—empty corners, insulated pipes. Their breaths steamed. They tugged on their shirts. Instinctively, they traced the cold down a metal staircase. Cold was rising from the ground floor through the stoles of their gym shoes.

The ground floor was stacked to the ceiling with junked ice machines. A wind like from an enormous air-conditioner was blowing down a narrow aisle between the machines. At the end of the aisle a concrete ramp slanted down to the basement.

That was where Antek suspected they would end up, the basement, a cavernous space extending under the nameless street, slowly collapsing as if the thick, melting pillars of ice along its walls had served as its foundation. The floor was spongy with water-logged sawdust. An echoing rain plipped from the ceiling. The air smelled thawed, and ached clammy in the lungs.

"It's fucken freezing," Eddie whispered.

Manny swung the flare in a slow arc, its reflections glancing as if they stood among cracked mirrors. Blocks of ice, framed in de-frosted freezer coils, glowed back faintly like aquarium windows from niches along the walls. They were melting unevenly and leaned at precarious angles. Several had already tottered to the sawdust where they lay like quarry stones from a wrecked cathe-dral. Manny and Eddie picked their way among them, pausing to wipe the slick of water from their surfaces and peer into the ice, but deep networks of cracks refracted the light. They could see only frozen shadows and had to guess at the forms: fish, birds, shanks of meat, a dog, a cat, a chair, what appeared to be a bicycle.

But Antek knew they would recognize her when they found her. There would be no mistaking the light. In the smoky, phosphorous glare her hair would reflect gold like a candle behind a frosted pane. He was waiting for them to bring her out. He had finished the wine and flung the pint bottle onto the street so that it shattered. The streets were empty. He was waiting patiently and though he had nowhere else to be it was still a long wait. He could hear the cricket now, composing time instead of music, working its way head first from the roof down the brick wall. Listening to it, Antek became acutely aware of the silence of the prison across the

79

street. He thought of all the men on the other side of the wall and wondered how many were still awake, listening to a cricket, waiting patiently as they sweated in the heavy night.

Manny and Eddie, shivering, their hands burning numb from grappling with ice, unbarred the rear door that opened onto the loading platform behind the ice house. They pushed out an old handcar and rolled it onto the tracks that came right up to the dock. They had already slid the block of ice onto the handcar and draped it with a canvas tarp. Even gently inching it on they had heard the ice cracking. The block had felt too light for its size, fragile, ready to break apart.

"It feels like we're kidnapping somebody," Eddie whispered.

"Just think of it as ice."

"I can't."

"We can't just leave her here, Edwardo."

"What'll we do with her?"

"We'll think of something."

"What about Antek?"

"Forget him."

They pushed off. Rust slowed them at first, but as the tracks inclined towards the river they gained momentum. It was like learning to row. By the trestle they hit their rhythm; speed became wind—hair blowing, shirts flapping open, the tarp billowing up off the ice. The skyline gleamed ahead, and though Manny couldn't see the lake, he could feel it stretching beyond the skyscrapers. The smelt would have disappeared to wherever they disappeared to, but the fishermen would still be sitting at the edge of the breakwater, their backs to the city, dreaming up fish. He knew now where they were taking her. They were rushing through waist-deep weeds across the vast tracts of prairie behind the factories, clattering over bridges and viaducts. Below, streetlights shimmered watery in the old industrial neighborhoods. Shiny with sweat, with the girl already melting free between them, they forced themselves faster, rowing like a couple of sailors.

nominated by DeWitt Henry and George Plimpton

SUNDAYS

fiction by ELLEN WILBUR

from WIND AND BIRDS AND HUMAN VOICES

(Stuart Wright, Publisher)

SHE COULDN'T REMEMBER when he'd started lying down on Sunday afternoons. He hadn't done it when they first were married. At least not regularly. Now he seemed to do it every week, each Sunday sometime after four. She'd notice the sudden quiet in the house when he lay down, but then she would forget it, lost in some task. She'd be wiping down the woodwork, washing windows, sweeping up the hall or cooking, humming to herself and peaceful in the way she only felt when she was busy. Of all the days she liked Sundays the best. The other days went by so fast, they jumbled all together. But Sunday was long. The hours passed slowly, with dignity, like time out of her childhood. She could catch up on things she'd missed or put off all the week while she was out at work. She liked to bake on Sundays. She made pies and home-made breads or muffins. All the things he liked. She'd prepare a roast of lamb or beef or chicken with potatoes. The kitchen windows steamed up in the winter and the cooking smells spread through the whole of the little house until it was so warm and homey that it seemed to cry out for the child they'd lost, the tiny girl who'd lived only one day, whose perfect little face was still so real to her that when she thought of it her hand would fly up to her mouth, and she would sometimes throw the kitchen door wide open to the chill and let the frigid air pour into the cheerful, steamy room.

It always took her by surprise to find him lying down. She'd be

81

carrying up the laundry or her sewing when she'd pass the open bedroom door and see him on their bed. Sometimes she'd hurry past the door without a word as if the sight of him embarrassed her. She couldn't imagine lying down during the day doing nothing. Just the thought of it made her jumpy. If he'd only sleep, it wouldn't bother her so much. But he never did. He lay there wide awake and he looked unlike himself. Sometimes not even gazing out the window, but staring up at the empty ceiling in a way that made her think of someone very old. Yet he was only thirty-five, a burly, lively man. He looked out of place, lying so still.

Why shouldn't the poor man rest, she told herself. He worked hard all week long. He was up before her every morning, wide awake the moment that he rose. She'd wake to the sound of him whistling in the shower and have to wrench herself up through a wall of sleep and hurry down to fix his breakfast. She'd have his orange juice fresh squeezed, his eggs done over light, his dark rye lightly buttered and his coffee steaming in his cup by the time he appeared with his briefcase in his hand.

"I don't know why you make yourself get up. I could just as easily eat out," he'd said hundreds of times. She didn't have to be at work till ten.

She stood at the window when he left the house. He liked to walk the mile down town to catch the train to work. Even in winter he went off through ice or heavy snow as if the weather couldn't touch him. He had a light, springy walk for someone so large. She'd never seen another man who walked exactly as he did.

He never watched t.v. or listened to the radio or read when he lay down on Sundays. His stillness and his silence fascinated her. When they went out to parties, people hurried up to greet him. They gathered all around him. He was such a talker and a story teller. She was shy in groups. She never laughed or joked or became close to people at her job the way he did. He was always calling her to see if he could bring somebody home to supper. Yet when they were alone together, he was quiet. She did most of the talking, as if there were no end to all the things she'd like to tell him.

"Tom?" she said some Sundays, stopping at the bedroom door. He'd turn and look at her with a little smile, never startled. He wasn't a nervous man, not at all like her. "What were you thinking about just then? You looked a million miles away." She stayed in the hall with her broom or dust cloth held tight, anxious to resume her work.

"Not anything really," he replied.

"You must have been thinking of *something*," she insisted. Her own mind was never still or empty. It was always focussed hard on something; something bothering her or pleasing, something coming up or in the past. It never stopped. Not even at night when she lay down to sleep. Her mind was always ticking.

"Come here," he'd say. He liked to stop her in the middle of her work.

"Lie down with me a minute," he would say while she stood perplexed with the broom gripped tightly in her hand.

"Come here," he'd urge her, smiling like a cat, lazy and happy, as if her irritation were amusing to him.

"Not now," she'd argue, but drawn to him and giving him her hand.

"Just for a minute," he would say, pulling her down on the tassled spread till she rested her cheek on his great chest and felt his chin on the top of her head.

"You fit against me perfectly," he'd whisper with his arm tight around her.

"I've got a million things to do," she'd say, all wiry with thoughts and wanting to jump up before the lethargy descended.

"Just lie a minute," he would say in a way that made her give in to the warmth of his shirt, his faint tobacco smell, and the silence building in the house till she could hear the birds outside so clearly and see their shapes streak by the window. The sky was violet or pink and she would feel the sweetness of the fading room begin to lull her.

"You're a devil," she would sigh, tipping back her head to gaze at him.

"I love you, May," he'd say, kissing her forehead or her hair. He never wanted to make love on Sunday afternoons. Only to hold her in the stillness for half an hour or more until it seemed to May that a spell came over them, a heavy sense of peace, as if the whole of life had swept away from them in a great wave and they'd become as motionless and changeless as the rocking chair beside the window, the tall white dresser and the row of pictures on the flowered wall that grew more dim and less distinct each minute in the dusky room. She would imagine the darkness growing in the house, filling up the unlit rooms downstairs, the empty kitchen growing desolate and grey and disappearing, until she'd suddenly jump up from the dark bed and with a beating heart she'd hurry like a child from room to room snapping the lights on, her face urgent and serious, as if she were preventing a great death.

nominated by Nona Balakian, Stephen Corey,
DeWitt Henry, and Joyce Carol Oates

EXODUS

by CAROLYN KIZER

from ANTAEUS

We are coming down the pike,
All of us, in no particular order,
Not grouped by age, Wanda and Val, her fourth husband,
Sallie Swift, the fellows who play bridge
Every Thursday, at Mason's Grill, in the back,
Two of them named George,
We are all coming down the pike.

Somebody whose face I can't make out
Is carrying old Mrs. Sandow, wrapped in a pink afghan;
Her little pink toes peep out from the hem
Of her cotton nightie like pink pea pods,
As pink as her little old scalp showing through.
Be careful, Mister, don't lose ahold of her.
She has to come down the pike.

Maybelle and Ruth walk together, holding hands;
Maybelle wears tennis shorts and a sweatband
As she strides along steadily in her golf shoes;
Ruth has on something flimsy,
Already ripped, and sling-backs, for God's sake.
Imagine her feet tomorrow, she'll have to drop out.
But right now they are both coming down the pike.

Richard had to leave his piano; he looks sort of unfinished;
His long pale fingers wave like anemone

Or is it amoeba I mean?
He's artistic, but would never have been
Of the first rank, though he's changed his name three times.
He doesn't like the mob he's with,
But you can't be picky
When you're coming down the pike.

One of the monitors wants us to move faster,
But you can't really organize this crowd;
The latch on the birdcage was loose so the budgie escaped
About two miles back, but Mrs. Rappaport still lugs his cage:
She's expecting the budgie to catch up any minute.
Its name was Sweetie. I can't stand pet names
And sentimentality at a time like this
When we should be concentrating all our efforts
On getting down the pike.

Who would have thought we would all be walking,
Except of course for Mrs. Sandow, and Dolly Bliss
In her motorized wheelchair and her upswept hairdo.
Someone has piled six hatboxes on her lap;
She can hardly see over, poor lady, it isn't fair,
And who needs picture hats at a time like this.
But they are probably full of other things,
The kind of useless stuff you grab up in a panic
When there's no time to think or plan,
And you've got ten minutes before they order you down the pike.

Bill Watkins is sore that he wasn't chosen monitor
Because he lacks leadership qualities.
But he rushes up and down the lines anyhow
Snapping like a sheepdog. The Ruddy family,
All eight of them red-heads, has dropped out for a picnic,
Using a burnt-out car
As a table. Not me, I'm saving my sandwiches.
The Ruddys were always feckless; they won't laugh tomorrow
When they run out of food on the pike.

Of course Al Fitch has nothing, not even a pocketknife
Let alone a gun.

He had to get Morrie Phelps to shoot his dog for him.
No pets! You can see the reason for that,
Although nobody fussed about the budgie.
I expect there's a few smuggled cats
Inside some of the children's jackets.
But old Al Fitch, he just strolls along
With his hands in his pockets, whistling "Goodnight Irene."

My husband says I shouldn't waste my breath
Describing us, but save it for the hike
Ahead. We're just like people anywhere
Though we may act crazier right now.
Maybelle drags Ruth along faster and faster
Though she's stumbling and sobbing, and has already fallen
    twice.
Richard, who's always been so careful of his hands,
Just hit Al, and told him to whistle something else
Like Bach: one of the hymns he wrote, that we could sing.
Will you be trying to sing, wherever you are,
As you come down the pike?

nominated by Sharon Doubiago, Edmund Keeley
Joyce Carol Oates and Sharon Olds

SORROW AND RAPTURE

by MAURA STANTON

from TELESCOPE

The April sun burned through the dirty glass.
My eyes burned. My wool skirt burned my knees.
Beyond the window of the city bus
As it turned up Forrest Hill, I couldn't see
Red brick, and frame, and budding maple trees,
But only the dark theater, where all alone
I'd watched *La Traviata* on the screen,
Surrounded by two hundred empty seats.
I'd bought the ticket from a nun at school
For two dollars, and a written promise
Not to go home, or shopping, or idling.
I'd sunk back in the tattered velvet seat,
Glad to be out of Civics and History,
Breathing the odor of popcorn and licorice.
I wondered if they'd show the film for me,
Just me. I sat in the exact middle.
I was sleepy and warm. I hoped for color.
And then the sound track blared and leveled off.
The black and white singers floated far above me,
Magnified. Their singing made me dizzy.
The voices drew me forward on my seat,
And my face prickled with heat, my chest hurt.
I was more Violetta than I was myself.
I wore her satin gown. I loved Alfredo.
I raised her handkerchief to my own mouth.
The subtitles that flickered underneath

A passionate embrace, or stricken look,
Seemed more foreign to me than the music.

Then the bus stopped on top of the hill.
I looked over the rooftops of Peoria
Shaken with rapture. What town was this?
I saw the brewery, my high school, a steeple,
Slate-colored shingles, the glimmer of river,
And beyond, smokestacks of Caterpillar
Where the wire mesh gates had just opened on thousands
Of laborers with their metal lunch pails.
Still dazzled, I got off at my stop.
At home our maple almost cast a shadow
With its early buds, and I threw myself down.
No ants were stirring in the pale, cold grass
But here and there, in thick, green clumps,
Violets had bloomed, not yet choked by weeds,
Purple petals the size of fingernails.
I stroked the violets' heart-shaped leaves.
I looked at my hands. I stretched them in the sun.
I could remember the face of Alfredo,
Violetta's room, the view of Paris,
But not a single tune. I was tone deaf.
Still, I rolled over and over in the grass
Unable to speak, burning and longing,
As cars from the factories arrived on our street
And the smell of supper drifted out of doors.

nominated by Ai and Jonathan Penner

89

THE ART OF SEEING
WITH ONE'S OWN EYES

fiction by SHARON DOUBIAGO

from NEW ENGLAND REVIEW *and* BREAD LOAF QUARTERLY

It is the need to enter what we loosely call the vision to be one with the Imago Mundi, that image of the world we each carry within us as possibility itself.

—*Robert Creeley*

Only off in the West is the glorious light of the setting sun telling us, perhaps, of light after darkness.

—*Edward Curtis*

I REMEMBER THE NIGHT as Halloween, the night of the Dead, Halloween as in "holy person, hence saint," the dictionary explains, but looking back in my journal I discover that it was the Autumn Equinox. At any rate, it was Vermont in Fall and harvest was greatly upon us. The first frost had come, we had brought in our garden: root-stringy, dirt-clodded green tomato plants hanging upside down on our apartment wells. *Allende dead*, my notes say, *Victor Jara's fingers cut off, Agnew may be impeached*. An I Ching quote: "*Superior man on the decline. Inferior man on the rise. A time of this.*" Someone coming up the stairs. A knock on the door. A young woman, a Jehovah's Witness, walking in with pamphlets: THE WORLD IS COMING TO AN END IN TEN DAYS. Me in my nightgown. "We are canvassing all of central Vermont. We are trying to give non-believers a chance."

All week at Goddard, the local college, the Stan Brakhage Film Festival had been occurring, the filmmaker himself hosting the event. Stan Brakhage's affinity with Charles Olson, the first poet to inspire me, made his presence in town exciting. "The sentence as an exchange of force rather than a completed thought," the journal notes exclaim. "FORM IS NEVER MORE THAN AN EXTENSION OF CONTENT!" My journals from those days are dominated by Olson.

At 7:30 p.m. we dropped windowpane acid. We had done some the week before, a trip that remains in my memory as one of the most wondrous of my life. That had been my first acid in a year and a half, our first in Vermont, a warm, emotional experience of great love between Maximilian and me. We spent that Sunday canoeing around a beautiful lake in the Northeast Kingdom, a lake named Eden. Of the many lakes of the Kingdom we picked Lake Eden because Eden is my maiden name. The photographs of that day are my favorite photographs of us. We are floating over an enormous mirror of giant flaming maple trees that line the shore, through a brilliant red, orange, maroon and gold paradise. If lysergic acid diethylamide can be photographed in the cells of the body it is in these pictures. We look at each other as if eternity cannot separate us. Max looks like Jesus with his full beard and long black curls, his image rippling back from the water. I am wearing lace and jewelry, a rarity for me. A red and green glass bead bracelet that had arrived that week from a friend traveling in Guatemala shimmers, catching the light above my oar. The smell of patchouli oil can't be photographed either but I smell it when I look at these photographs. On that day there was a big sun eruption estimated ten times the size of earth, equal to one hundred million atom bombs. "There was a 20 minute period after the flare reached its peak when long-distance short wave radio communications on earth experienced a complete fadeout," the Space Warning Center in Boulder, Colorado said. "Particles ejected by the flare are expected to reach the earth's vicinity tonight or early tomorrow causing magnetic disturbances and possibly auroral displays in the low latitudes." We walked in the dark woods, the sun filtering through the autumn leaves to the ferns on the floor. The whole world seemed benevolently aflame. And then we fucked, very gently, standing up, face to face, while a soft rain fell on us. We lay on the shore and stared into each other's eyes a long time. "What is

91

this?" he said, in a momentary flash of his normal embarrassment at intimacy. "A love trip?" That night we saw our first Brakhage film. I wrote "Infinite parts/The Body/The Self/floating in infinite directions./The myth outside/The stars inside./We are caught in the bodies of others." On our walk home from Goddard we stopped in at friends who were watching the movie, *Tora, Tora, Tora*. "Tora, Tora, Tora" was the Japanese code for the bombing of Pearl Harbor. I was struck for the first time by an understanding of the great difference between persons born before World War II and those born during or afterwards. The difference bombs make on the new psyche. We stayed up all night. The neighbor living below us said later he knew we had dropped acid when he woke at four in the morning and we were still giggling.

But tonight, as soon as we dropped, the phone rang. Max answered it. I heard him explain that we were on our way to a movie but that yes they were welcome to come over for about fifteen minutes. It was two friends of Passing Cloud, an old L.A. friend now living in Taos, New Mexico. Passing Cloud had given them our address when they left New Mexico for Montreal on an important business trip. We regarded Passing Cloud as one of our craziest, least-reliable friends—we had many in those days—so we prepared ourselves for the possibility of a screwy encounter. Or so we must have thought we prepared.

We were prepared for hippies from Taos. The two men who entered our apartment looked like Chicago gangsters, at least as they are portrayed in old movies. They were sturdy middle-aged men in dark suits, black silky dress shirts, white ties and identical Panama hats beneath which twitched pencil-thin moustaches. They seemed charged with a great conspiratorial air. When they removed their hats the glisten and smell of hair oil and the exposed skin around their ears and necks were shocking. This was 1973; this was not the current look. No one in their right minds, I thought, looks like these guys. Certainly no one I knew. Perhaps they walked in just as the acid started coming on.

We were as cordial and friendly as possible, engaging them in the usual questions of first encounters and explaining where we were going. We told them how to get to the theatre in case they were interested in seeing the film. I couldn't imagine that they would be. Such men as these could have little interest or patience in the art of Stan Brakhage. I was already a little hung-up on trying to figure out who they were. I was afraid of them and did not want to leave them in our home. In a while our children would return. They said they would walk around town and perhaps attend the film later. When we left the building we noticed their car: a highly waxed and polished black antique limousine with New Hampshire license plates. Again, I had the sense of gangsters, the shot of the car pulled up to do a job.

We walked the mile to the school. The film this night, culminating the festival, was to be Brakhage's current masterpiece, *The Act of Seeing With One's Own Eyes*. The hour and a half film takes place in the main Philadelphia city morgue. The subject is autopsy, the technique documentation. Our program explained that the etymology of "autopsy" is "seeing with one's own eyes." It was very cold and we, native Californians, were happily bundled in our new thriftstore coats and hats. Max said he read that LSD opens the lens of the eyes wider than normal, letting in more light so that you see more of what is actually here. "Hallucination is an incorrect word. It's just that the brain, used to the old programming, can't process what the eyes are newly seeing."

I was looking forward to an autopsy film. I was curious as to how a great artist would handle such a subject. One of the first stories I ever wrote was in reaction to the autopsy report in the Warren Commission's *The Assassination of President Kennedy*. The reading of that report was for me as bad as any bad acid trip I would ever take. I found little interest in the statistics proving how he died; that he was dead was the shock. The body of John Fitzgerald Kennedy is described in graphic detail: a muscular, well-developed, well nourished adult Caucasian male measuring 72½ inches and weighing 170 pounds. His hair is reddish brown and abundant, his eyes are blue. And skewed, divergent, deviated. We are told that he has an unremarkable bony cage. His teeth are in excellent repair. We are told of old wellhealed and recent incisions on the nipple line, the lumbar spine, and abdomen, the right thigh. His genitals are not described, but the cutting of the customary Y, beginning at the nipple line, deep into the rigor and algor mortis muscle to examine his body cavities, is. His lungs are well aerated with smooth glistening pleural surfaces and they are grey-pink in color. There is an area of purplish red discoloration. His right lung weighs 320 grams, his left 290 grams. A strawcolored fluid floats in his pericardial cavity. His heart is of normal external contour and weighs 350 grams. His coronary arteries are dissected and analyzed for us. His liver, spleen, kidneys, and intestines are described, as are the many hernias and lacerations and bloodclots. There is abnormal mobility of the underlying bone above the right eye caused by a sizeable metal fragment. He has a large skull defect with an actual absence of scalp and bone and exuding from it is lacerated brain tissue which on close inspection proves to represent the major portion of his right cerebral hemisphere. At this moment in the autopsy, federal agents bring the coroners three pieces of bone recovered from Elm Street and the Presidential automobile. When put together, these fragments account for approximately three-quarters of the missing portion of his skull. Then the scalp wounds in his coronal plane are extended to examine his cranial content. His brain is removed and preserved for further microscopic study. A Gross Description of his brain is given. Following formalin fixation it weighs 1500 grams. Photographs, colored and black and white, and roentgenograms are taken of his entire body, inside and out. He is sewed back up for burial preparation.

My story is of a young woman who never fully recovers from reading this report. Like so many, she had idolized John Kennedy. Knowing exactly how much his heart weighed, that he had an "unremarkable bony cage," were facts demonic to her psyche, facts she found herself wishing—though she was a Twentieth Century child and a full participant in its glories—could not be known by anyone. She thought of how the Indians from her home town said you lose your power if you tell everything. How much does the spirit weigh? In which cavity does the personality reside? What happens to these men in the minutes they are handling John Kennedy's brain? How do you weigh the shock the nation experienced at his murder? Which investigation will prove who killed him? Are there "lacerating," "herniating," "exuding," residues still? In the air, in our food?

Still, I anticipated identification with Stan Brakhage's effort. If I were a filmmaker it is conceivable that I would film an autopsy. I am making such a story now. The *art* of seeing with one's own eyes. Brakhage had made his career by seeing what our culture makes taboo. A 1957 film, *Flesh of Morning*, is "an intense, introspective and totally controlled work about masturbation." "It is so important to *see*," I said to Maximilian as we walked down

94

Highway 2, "to see our way out of the programming of our culture."

I told him of a car accident I was in when I was sixteen. "There were five of us. I was in the back seat. We were speeding down Clevenger Canyon when we met another car coming up on a blind curve. Both drivers made the same, instantaneous decision to crash head-on, rather than swerve off the five hundred foot drop into the granite canyon. Somehow we made it, everyone was O.K., though one of our wheels was off the edge, the fenders scraped and ripped. What I was most struck by afterwards was that while my friends buried their heads in their laps when they saw the car I sat up straighter, my eyes bulging, straining to see my own death coming at me. In that moment I felt fierce about this. I wanted to *see* myself die. It seemed everything was being taken from me and all I had left in this single split second of life was sight and so I would use it."

The theatre was nearly full when we arrived, students and hippies come down out of the mountains for a Friday night movie. The colors and costumes and abundant hair swirled and mixed wildly with the smells of woodstoves, patchouli, marijuana. The people were festive, inviting, orgiastic, the open invitation to sex exuding from many. Open marriage was the newest popular attempt to break through our puritanical programming and many couples this night, well-known among us all, seemed ecstatic with their new daring, their new discoveries.

But I couldn't talk. The acid was coming on strong, my throat was dry. I was afraid I might throw up. I held onto Max's arm and he found two empty seats in the front row. As we sat in them, I knew instantly they were a mistake. I felt on stage, exposed. At the same time I felt unable to get up, to move through the thronging people to the back. I waited for the lights to go out, for the veil of darkness. But then Stan Brakhage was introduced and an inhibiting silence fell through the room. He began a long talk about his films. I couldn't move.

It was an evening of strange men; perhaps this is why I remember it as Halloween. Brakhage seemed a sort of triplet to the two men who had come to our house. He too was large, big-boned, sturdy. He was wearing a black tuxedo. His thick black hair, with a streak of silver down the middle, was oiled and cut very short and he was clean shaven. All through his amazing lecture he would stop mid-sentence, turn his head to the right, simultaneously pulling from beneath his coattails a small silver spittoon. I could hardly believe my eyes. The arc of spit across the lights from this man dressed so severely, so strangely, so formally like the President, was bizarre. "Style," he said twice between spits, "is social manifestation of soul."

He described his films as "meditations of sexuality, meditations of light." "We are locked in creation at a certain level," he said, "and we can't get out. This is the fact of our existence. The trick is to find the key, the process is to get back to the garden, but the *purpose* of the riddle is to celebrate the mystery. My films celebrate the mystery.

"My themes are birth, sex, and death. I don't know about other artists, but when I work I sweat, snot comes out of my nose. Between me and film it can't be otherwise. I have a mold chamber. I grow mold on my films. I mean how do you keep on as a filmmaker in an area that struggles to be an art and not Hollywood-escapist, and I am left with the rags and tags of a Sam Peckinpah?"

I was feeling overwhelmed. Sam Peckinpah's daughter, a friend of ours, was in the room. "Max, can't we move?" I looked around. The theatre behind us was full now, people lining the three walls. "The way Hollywood separates the dream sequences from reality as if they aren't the same thing." Max whispered, "There's no place to go," and then added apprehensively, "Anything you want to tell me?" My paranoia was making him paranoid. Does he think Brakhage is turning me on? I put my hand on his thigh. I thought of the letter I had received that morning from my closest friend, Ramona, about her brother Verne being anesthetized and manacled to the hospital wall to receive twenty electric shocks. "Reich," Brakhage was saying, "was organically insane, I mean, not functioning at the end of his life." Maniacs, I was thinking, we are all maniacs, manacled to our bodies, speeding blindly down our lonely one-way canyons. "Vision," he was saying, "is a part of our separateness. Your vision is you, it makes you separate from others. Vision is just the inside of your head. These films are just what's inside my head. Fish, bodies, sand, wagon of my childhood. The word 'vision' is elevating and idealizing, but it's just simply one's take on the world."

Max whispered, "That smile of his is a trip."

"Remember Olson. *"There are no hierarchies, no infinite, no such many as mass. There are only eyes in all heads to be looked out of.'* I'm reading Pound again these days. The artist's business is to discover his *virtue*, the particularity that distingiushes him from all others. His signature.

"My goal is to photograph an angel." Suddenly he demanded from the audience, "Has anyone here ever seen an angel?" He waited for a response. To myself, I answered yes. A few in the crowd must have raised their hands. He challenged them. "I mean a *real* angel. With *wings*. Not some light around the body that looks like wings. Angels must be real or why would they be so prevalent in the paintings of European culture? Many have seen them. It is my goal to photograph an angel."

He began to prepare us for *The Act Of Seeing With One's Own Eyes*. The large, dark body took on a manner and tone that was apologetic, like a stern father who must do his duty toward his children. "It should be clear that this is not a window on an autopsy room. This film is made up of twenty-four still shots and an equal number of blank shots per second. It is made up of different kinds of films, for a greater range of color. Color is one of the themes of this film. One should make of this film a song. It is composed as a song. Still, my films do not have sound. Sound distracts the eyes from seeing. Any sound on a soundtrack is more distracting than the same sound in an audience of any situation. *Equality* of *seeing*: this is what I am after.

"There's humor in this film. Humor is everywhere. Humor of vision. Humor in sound. Humor in Beethoven. Humor of thought. Humor in nature. When you lie down in a field and notice one weed blowing faster than the others that's funny." He arced his wad into the silver cuspidor, a funny arc of light. "Art is gentle in that images are better than the light that people bounce off reality. Art is not escapist. It is not something different. This film is like the *Tibetan Book Of The Dead* in that it is a map of what the Dead experience." When he said it again, it was a command. "Art is gentle. One should make of this film a song. It is composed as a song."

The body is wheeled in on the guerney, the white sheet removed from a naked male of about sixty, the saw started up. The light is glaring, white fluorescent, without shadow. There can be no secrets here. Nothing can hide from us. The morticians, Brakhage has said, are artists. He also used the word *lover*. Noguchi, L.A.'s Coroner, for so long the bogeyman of my dreams, he who did Monroe, he who brags of having written the masterpiece of our times, the autopsy report of Robert Kennedy, leaps instantly into my mind.

In Stan Brakhage's full-length documentation we are shown the autopsies of a half a dozen bodies. It is true, one of the themes of the film is color. The shocking red of blood under the white light, the pink of lungs, and ash of flesh. I can't remember now the color of the brain, the liver.

There is a deft build-up in the drama of images. It is true, orchestration like a song. I begin to hear *no, no, no*. When the second body is wheeled in and the sheet removed, we, the audience, gasp. She is young and very beautiful, a small dark brunette. She is the star of this movie, a famous movie star without a name. The white lines of her bikini are in such sharp contrast to the deep tan of her beautiful skin, one thinks for an instant that she is wearing it. Perhaps she drowned today at the beach, so recently she bathed in the sun, walked her perfect body for us.

But this is a story of the Dead. This body is who she is. Two of them, one at her feet, one at her shoulders, lug her over to another table. She sags heavily between them. They are hard workers. I keep hearing *sorry, sorry, sorry*. The old man takes great pride in his work. He revs the saw, then grinds down her middle, counter the bikini lines. Her high pointed white breasts unzip, then slide under her shaved armpits. Black individual hairs of her pubis blow in the saw's wind. Her perfect hips, that arch high and erotically over the perfect line of her buttocks, are chainsawed in two. Everything oozes, is slush, the myths broken in a marshland. They scoop her out. Then, they burn open her skull. Her face, which in our culture would be described as cute, falls down around her neck, then is turned inside out. Later, when they put it back on, they stretch it over the remains of her skull which they have battered with hammers, just like a rubber halloween mask.

I've never had the experience of knowing or remembering a past life. But now I remembered being dead. I remembered being a corpse, of being handled this way. Flop me on the table, do your work. Drain my blood, weigh my brain, finger my heart, my cunt, remove everything, liver, intestines, kidneys, clitoris, muscles, my white fat, my bones. You are so desperate to find out. You believe that you can.

I felt great compassion and grief for myself. I remembered the pain in the dead body, the same, no less, for all the so-called anesthesia of death, as pain in life. I knew the full consciousness behind the fully paralyzed body. Now the monolith. Centered. Massive. They say of a common anesthesia used in childbirth that you feel the pain but later you have no memory of it. The cruelty of this statement is characteristic of our utter disdain and incomprehension of the present. We are anesthetized to the present, but our insides, our inner being gutted wide open to the world, for all time, for anyone, always knows, always remembers.

People were leaving the theatre, though not as many as one would have thought. We seemed riveted to our seats. There seemed to be some test involved, a test of courage, of intellectual courage. Or perhaps it was spiritual. I looked back once and saw the two New Mexico men and a pregnant friend leaving together by the same door.

You say this is not a window on an autopsy room, that this is a song. The coroner is talking. Behind him are six headless gutted torsos, six extremely remarkable bony cages. The image is truly grotesque, shocking. The poor, poor body, rifled, sacked, emptied, an utterly empty husk. I kept hearing *cask. cage. coffin. shell*. I kept hearing sobbing, an uncontrollable sobbing. Hang me in a locker, sell me as a side of beef. Throw me in a red baggie for further microscopic study. I saw Sioux children sleighing down snowy hills in the rib cage of bison. I was afraid I'd start sobbing. No. No. No. I remembered my lover Milton. He had worked as a mortician's assistant in L.A. and he would tell stories like the little old lady who fell out of her casket during the funeral, fell stiff, head over heels down a Forest Lawn hill. "Like a plank of plywood, like an upright tree," before the whole family. There is humor in everything. In the story of the mother who wanted the ring off her daughter's finger, so he broke the finger off, the quickest way to get the ring. When Milton and I made love he never came, not once did he ejaculate though we spent most of our time in bed. He just stayed hard. Ramona always excused her husband for being so cold and cruel because for the first three years of their marriage he had to work nights in the Pomona morgue to support his other family.

The walk back home was hard, like coming back from the dead. I don't know what Maximilian was feeling, he was very silent, but I felt crucified. Just keep moving, I told myself, try not to see the blood the blood everywhere. The organs hanging like fruit, like pine cones, like brightly-colored maple leaves, the liver, the heart, the brain, like fall colors, the beautiful lungs fallen to Earth. Art is gentle, but reality is violent, the real dead are everywhere.

When we got to the meadow we lay on our backs, mindless of the cold. Give up the body, let the world in. Down my right side it was hard to know where I left off, where he began. Beneath us the creation, above us the reception. "Can you feel the earth spinning?" How often in our years together Maximilian asked me this. "Do you remember? This is the Equinox. The day the sun crosses the equator, making day and night of equal lengths in all parts of the earth. Imagine," and he put his finger down my pubis, "all parts of the earth."

The word equinox made me think again of Olson. I had been trying to understand his essay *Equal, That Is, To The Real Itself*, with its address to Melville and its great discussion of language using the mathematical metaphor of congruence. The corpses in the movie seemed perfect illustrations of his thesis, of "what really matters, THE THING ITSELF, that anything impinges on us its self-existence, without reference to any other thing," the corpse itself, not the spirit or soul or history of the person as it leaves the corpse. "Matter," he writes of the whale, "offers perils wider than humanity if it doesn't do what still today seems the hardest for it to do, outside art and science: to believe that things, and present ones, are the absolute conditions. . . ."

The constellations passed above us. Max quoted bathroom graffitti he had just seen. "Know your own archetype.' "I'm blind Orion," I answered, "chasing the sun, seeking my eyes promised me if I can catch the light rising in the East."

"When I die," he answered, "I want to be cremated. Promise me you won't let them do an autopsy. Steal my body if you have to. Do you promise? They might accuse you of murder."

I promised. And then I made him promise the same thing. "But I don't want to be cremated. I want to be laid in the earth naked without a coffin. I don't want *anything* done to me. Oh, Max, don't let them put their hands on me then. I want to go back naturally, as it is meant, to the earth.

"The Sufis believe we are creating God as God is creating us," I said touching him, "so we and God can see ourselves. A continuous recurrence of creation. They believe we are the *place* of God. *I am creating you as you are creating me.* They say this twofold manifestation is the appeasement of God's sadness."

When we got up and continued our walk home, the world of the dead and the world of the living seemed a little more in balance. As we stood before our apartment building that held our sleeping children it seemed the archetypal house. The black archetypal gangster car was still parked in front of it. The stars and the planets whirled above the peaked roof that swayed on the curve of the earth into the deep blueblack night of infinity. But there is no infinity. He held me in front of him, his penis growing hard on my soft ass, my soft ass blooming erect to enclose him. The soul, someone said, is like a bucketful of water. It can be spilled.

At the top of the stairs the two men from New Mexico, or was it New Hampshire, were waiting in the hallway. Ophelia, our neighbor who was studying to be a witch, opened her door and invited us all into her apartment. "Let us enjoy Harvest together," she said authoritatively, sweeping her floor-length purple cape in a whirl around her, leading us in. This was a relief. We didn't want to be alone with these strange men. I didn't want them near my kids. From her stereo, as we entered, The Doors were singing *When You're Strange*.

She had brought in her garden too. The small apartment glowed with squash, pumpkins, the faces of giant sunflowers. Bundles of freshly cut herbs and tomato plants hung upside down from the walls, between the photographs that were one of her school projects, black-and-whites she had taken of herself in the bathroom mirror when she was crying for a lost lover. She showed me the rose hips we had collected the week before from the pond: they were now crawling with worms. The place smelled like a cave. She had made me a pumpkin pie. "For *you*," she said, staring deep into my eyes as she placed it in my hands. On the counter was the Jehovah's Witness pamphlet: Ten Days Till The End. "Great!" Max said. "To end with a bang rather than a whimper." We all sat down to eat pie. I guess it was the acid: I could distinguish the eggs from the pumpkin from the milk from the maple syrup from the spices—ginger, cinnamon, nutmeg. I felt I was eating each ingredient separately. Congruence? Is there such a thing? Synthesis. Another of Ophelia's projects to graduate from Goddard was photographing the local townspeople who fit the archetypes of the Tarot cards. I whispered in her ear, "Who do you think these men are?" She said, "They are the Capitalists. Beware. There is no card for them yet."

The men objected to the movie. "There are *some* things you don't have to see."

"But are you saying," I answered, "that there are things you *shouldn't* see?"

Ophelia said it made her think of Western Medicine. "Our approach is from the dead. Our knowledge comes from the study of corpses. But in China the approach is from the living, the healthy." We had more pumpkin pie. More raw eggs, syrup, milk, vegetable, nutmeg. The windows were frosted, the world turning into the dark fold of winter. "Is it snowing yet?" Max asked anyone in the room.

There began to be a little intimacy between us. The two men became warmer, more human. One of them rolled a joint, passed it around. They told us they met Passing Cloud at an art fair; that he makes leather belts now, paints sunsets and pinetrees on them, travels from fair to fair. When we first knew Cloud he was getting a Ph.D. in clinical psychology from USC. They told of their trip here from Boston. About the road and the weather. Neither had ever been to Montreal so they were looking forward to that. They seemed to be concerned about crossing the border and asked a number of questions concerning the procedure. They were such dark men against the colors and smells and glow of Ophelia's room. They hadn't removed their overcoats. I thought they must be Mafia, dope smugglers. A wave of happiness washed through me. I was happy the movie was over. Then the flashes: the face sliding off, the contents scooped out. The trunk of the girl, headless, limbless, gutted, washed ashore, ribs of what once was a canoe clutching mud at low tide.

The two men were consulting each other. They looked so much alike I asked if they were brothers. Just business partners. They decided they could trust us with the great secret they were harboring. That they were harboring a great secret was apparent in everything about them. They asked us if we would like to see something "incredible." They left the apartment. The three of us listened to them going down the stairs on the side of the building to their sinister car and then coming back up. "Do you think I should get rid of them?" Max asked. I shrugged my shoulders, even though I saw them coming back with submachine guns to kill us. "I don't think they are a danger to us," Ophelia said in her wise way. When they entered the room one of them was carrying a box of large envelopes, the other a heavy wooden crate.

They had us sit in a circle on the hardwood floor. They asked us if we knew who the photographer Edward Curtis was. None of us did.

Suddenly, Indians burst into the room like irradiated light, like pieces of shrapnel. They slammed against the walls, a thudding *boom-boom*. A wind off the ocean, the smell of iodine, blew through. Ophelia moaned. Max said nothing but sank deep into his body, crosslegged, in Indian fashion. God. They're looking at us. In a cold sweat, fighting nausea again, I eyed the path through the pumpkin-glowing, worm-crawling kitchen to the bathroom.

"These are old copperplate photogravures," the smaller man explained, as he passed large, antique pictures to us. "That's why they glow." All the drama of the evening was climaxing in photographs of Indians. Light exploded from Ophelia's tears on the wall. I heard a highpitched chant like women calling, like coyote yelps. Just one of the portraits would have been an aesthetic, spiritual shock, but these men seemed to have an endless supply. They were, truly, incredible. I was falling into a face, the texture and smell of the rough skin as powerful as a lover's, falling shattered through the large pores like windows when another face was handed to me. The heart pounded in each body, the thudding *boom-boom* that kept up all night. These photographs were a different kind of autopsy report. These people were as alive as the people in the film were dead.

"This Ed Curtis," the larger man was saying, "dedicated his whole life to photographing all the tribes of North America, except Mexico, before the old ways vanished. He had the endorsement of Teddy Roosevelt and financial support from J. P. Morgan. Morgan wanted to produce the finest book since the King James Bible."

I remembered then the Bible says you can't look on the Body of God and survive.

"Where did you get these?"

103

"Would you believe?" They both laughed crazily. "We found them! We found them in a basement in Boston, hundreds of them. Gold tones, copperplates, photogravures, unpublished negatives, it's Curtis's original collection. For some reason they were stored there years ago and forgotten. Can you imagine what it was like for us to *find* them?"

"We'd never heard of Curtis either," the smaller man said. "But we recognized their value instantly."

"Yeah," the larger man said. "Like being hit over the head with a brick."

"It took Curtis thirty years to complete the photographing," the smaller man said. "But only a few sets were ever produced."

"The original cost in 1906 for twenty volumes was $3500. It was too large a project. And Morgan died."

"I think they were too painful," the smaller man said. "It was too soon. Some of the people who bought them had made their money killing Indians."

"Yes," the larger man said. "But now enough time has passed. You and I . . ." he looked at his partner in the way Ophelia had looked at me when she handed me her pie, "will never have to work again."

Many of the photographs I saw that night I've never seen again. The popular reprint of Curtis's photographic epic, *North American Indians*, published a short time later, possibly from this collection, does not, even remotely, compare to the originals. *Hopi, Apache, Mojave, Navaho, Tiwa, Zuni, Southern Cheyenne, Sioux, Apsaroke, Mandan, Piegan, Northern Cheyenne, Cree, Sarsi, Assiniboine, Blackfoot, Walla Walla, Nez Percé, Flathead, Spokan, Yakima, Chinook, Hupa, Klamath, Pomo, Yokuts, Miwok, Mono. Cahuilla, Suquamish, Skokomish, Lummi, Quilcene, Quinault. Bridal groups in the totem poles, clam diggers on the beaches, wedding canoes, whaling boats, wickiups, sweathouses, tepee camps. The Sundance of the Piegans, the purification of the soul, the flame-riven mists of the Northern Seas, the cliff-hanging Alaskan villages, the Navaho's Canyon de Chelly. Hopi Snake Dancers, Mojave water carriers, prairie buffalo chases. The faces. The faces.* The vanishing race? I remembered the belief common to all traditional peoples, that the camera captures the soul. It was obvious that these photographs were of actual souls.

"Curtis's expeditions into the secret lands of the vanquished Indians were dangerous," the smaller man said, "and his camera supplies and equipment cumbersome. Sometimes it took months for the Indians to trust him, even though he sat in their tepees and beside their fires"—he said this with an air of reverence—"Not as a suppliant or a master, but as an equal being. Curtis saw the Buddha in everyone."

"And he didn't make any secret about his purpose," the larger man continued. Obviously, they had done research on these photographs, the new formality in their presentation sounding not unlike the opening of a sales pitch. "He told the Indians they were doomed to perish from the earth. All of them, their young and old men, women, and their children. But with his camera, he told them, he could record their stories in imperishable form so that they would live through the ages. Slowly they were won over. Having witnessed the death of so much they could believe that they were doomed."

"And so before the strange and inanimate focus of the camera," the smaller man continued, "they allowed their dances, games, array of battle, smoking of the pipes, so much that was intimate, occult or active in their lives, to be recorded on these plates so that other people in future times might know what a great people they were. They did magic things, sometimes unbeknownst to Curtis, to protect themselves, like performing dances backwards, but all in all, the attitude was if we are doomed then we will give ourselves."

Yes, I thought, they gave that which cannot be destroyed or stolen, the soul. *"My whole body is covered with eyes,"* an Eskimo sang. *"Behold it. I see all around."* I thought this is what a real American looks like, this is what thousands of years on this continent creates for a face. The wide cheekbone structure seemed like geography, faces like rain-beaten stones, a geo-historic diffusion forged by a time utterly lost to the world. *I am all the forces and objects with which I come in contact. I am the wind, the trees, the lakes, and the darkness. My eyes are two hawks perched on the peaks of the mountain range. The holy road to my mouth is to the other country. Our bodies are spiritual events. I take place out there. You take place in here.*

As the passing of the pictures continued they formed a wide

105

glowing circle in the center of the room and gradually as they were propped against the walls, they encircled us. The faces stared up at us and from behind us, into our backs, through the human glow of skin. Have you ever seen an angel? Brakhage asked. Ophelia dropped some of our windowpane, saying "We are the dead place between heartbeats." The two men said they didn't need any.

"You are correct in being so secretive about your mission." She prophesied, "It is a dangerous mission." She looked at them in her Russian Jewish way to suggest they probably had no idea of just how dangerous. "The powerplays, the intrigues, the behind-the-scenes maneuverings of dealers and collectors will reach monumental proportions."

The smaller man, sitting directly opposite me, winced. From behind him a Blackfoot woman said "I see through your eyes. I remember."

"Yes," the other man said. "There is a race on already among a small group of people to acquire as much as possible of Curtis's work. We've been a little concerned about reaching Montreal."

"Like a hold-up," the smaller man said.

I wondered if they had stolen the photographs themselves. They mentioned keeping them from Caspar Weinberger. I assumed they meant the government wanted to destroy the photographs for security purposes.

"Caspar is a ghost himself," Max mumbled, his first words since the showing of the pictures began.

"Caspar Weinberger wants them for their monetary value. He's the new Secretary of Health, Education and Welfare."

"You could make a killing on dead Indians," Max said, finding his old comic resiliency.

I held Geronimo in my hands. "He's unpublished," the smaller man said. "He's our good-luck piece. He's the one we'll never sell."

Geronimo is dressed in war regalia, war cap on his head and a feathered staff in his hand. It is the day of the famous 1905 inaugural parade for Teddy Roosevelt. The Chief's face is exceedingly grim but I swear twice the old coot winked at me.

Everyone was speaking at once on the wonders of photography, of film. "Souls stolen in this century by photographs surround all of us," Ophelia said, "anxious to possess our beings." As she said this I saw the Saigon police chief blowing the brains out of the peasant-soldier, the famous photograph of the time. I had always thought the puff coming from his head was the impact of the bullet, fragments of his brain beginning to fly. Now I saw that it was his soul.

"Some people are photogenic, like Jacqueline Kennedy Onassis, Marilyn Monroe," she said. "They always say of Jackie she is not as beautiful as her photographs. And Monroe they say was rather ordinary until a camera was pointed at her. Then she came alive."

"I'm afraid of cameras," I said, "I take awful pictures." I was surprised to find my voice. "Sometimes I think it's because I grew up in Hollywood. All the sun, the scouts everywhere looking for you. My soul hides, though so often I've wanted to give it."

"Curtis died in Hollywood," the larger man said. "He was the still photographer for the *Ten Commandments*."

"You have to have the kind of charisma the camera can capture," the smaller man said, who only now I saw had a severely pock-marked face, "to become famous in the Twentieth Century. It's the century of film." I remembered how I photographed everything when I was a teenager, driven by the need to capture the present, to save it. It was, along with baton twirling, my first art.

I felt the chemical surge in Ophelia and as it did it came on to all of us. The faces looked at us through the glow of skin. *My face is your mirror, my ancient face before mirrors, before self-conscious-ness.* A Cheyenne dressed all in white, tall as trees, in the moon dust that flew, waited for his lover. The paint on a child's face came off in my hands. Cottonwoods, clumped by a river, flickered their petals across Max's face, then shimmered in the thousand mirrors of the room, pale air and pale water. Ophelia's narcissistic tears for her lost lover splashed from the walls onto the people as they washed the wheat, as he snapped the camera, Antelope and Snakes at Oraibi, Zuni girls in the river. How we come through this cold song, we three Apaches, the rock, the sand, the cactus. I am trying to find my daughter, Angeline, across the Sound, but she is lost in dirty streets of her father's village, Seattle, who announces "*White men will never be alone. We will always surround you.*"

Stunned, we decided to stay there all night with the images, to wait for the sun to come over the New Hampshire mountains, the Winooski River that flowed behind and beneath our building. Occasionally, the movie reeled through the room. Then the two

107

men would be angry. The smaller, pockmarked man said, "Why this fanatical drive to *see* everything? The Indians say you lose your power if you expose all your secrets."

"There are ways to honor the dead," the older, more sinister man said. "Like Irish wakes."

"That's right!" the smaller man said, "Irish wakes are as much fun as Catholic weddings."

I thought of *Finnegans Wake*. I wondered if they were Black Irish.

"They put the corpse at the head of the table, pour it a drink, dance it around."

I asked who they were. As soon as I said it they hid again.

"I'm a saxophonist," the small man said. "It's good to believe in God for no other reason than as a safeguard against the possibility he's real. If you don't have a soul, then you're just a piece of dead meat."

"A piece of dead meat," I flared, "if you lay it on the ground disintegrates back to the earth. I *want* that experience. Who knows what it might be like. This country . . . , we're so anti-materialistic. We hate matter. I don't want to be burned. I don't want to be embalmed, preserved, trapped in plastic and steel. They dug up that six year old girl last week for the trial, the one in Philadelphia. It's been twenty years since her death and she's perfectly preserved. The rose in her hands was still fresh." I probably screeched it. "What the fuck for?"

"So the earth can't be renewed," Max answered.

"Autopsy," Ophelia said, "is like Manifest Destiny. It's God's will for the Indians to be swept aside. It's in the interest of science to weigh your heart. Our technology has destroyed the Goddess."

"Did you know?" the smaller man mused. "King Tut's pyramid was built for him before he was born." He added emphatically, "And don't forget, it's his tomb."

"Form is never more than an extension of concrete," Max said, winking at me.

The larger man dug into his files and pulled out a browntoned textured photograph of Sioux burial. A storm, this one from the Plains, blew through the room in all directions like a whirlwind, rain and snow in its heart. The body is placed on a platform on Cottonwood poles in the middle of the prairie, and left there. A small red bundle on a scaffold. To go back to both, sky and earth.

Bird and animal. Night and day. On the posts hang the playthings she loved: a rattle of antelope hooves strung on rawhide, a bouncing bladder with little stones inside, a painted willow hoop. On the scaffold, tied on top of the red blanket, is a deerskin doll, the beaded design that comes from far back in the family of her mother, Black Shawl. When you fall face down beside the body of your daughter you let the sorrow locked in your heart sweep over you, the rickety scaffold creaking a little under your weight. In the sky over you a few small clouds float white as swans on water. The wind dies in the sunset of that day and rises again with the sun's returning. An eagle with his buzzards following circles the far sky and over a low rise a bunch of antelope come grazing. Seeing the scaffold, they lift their heads and run down that way, circling a little, but coming closer in their curiosity, until they catch your man smell. Then they bound away, their rumps showing white. After a while a wolf comes along a little ridge, tail high, his nose in the air. He too gets the scent of you and with a leap is off over the prairie. And when it is night again a little mouse comes creeping up a post to sniff at the bundle of cloth, stopping, listening to a slow sound that comes and dies, and comes again. Suddenly the little animal leaps down and flees away into the grass, frightened that in the smell of death there was the thing of life, the breathing. The next daylight brings nothing of the sun, only grey clouds and a drizzling of fog closing in around the scaffold. When even the earth below the posts is lost, there is one pale flash of lightning and a fog-softened rumble of thunder. This you hear and you know, it is time to go.

I stared into the face of Crazy Horse, the lighthaired Oglala who was never photographed. *As the dead prey upon us,/they are the dead in ourselves.* I saw Ahab chasing the whale.

The smaller man said again, "See the Buddha in everyone."

How different, I thought, that is from Brakhage, who says it is the artist's business to discover the particularity that distinguishes you from all others. Your virtue. Your vision that makes you separate from others. I remembered that he quoted the poet Robert Duncan. "Soul is not universal. It is a created-creative event."

"We're a soulless people," Max said, staring into the black, small starred windows. "Misshapen, miscolored, the mixed blood of murderers without soul."

Ophelia agreed. "We are the broken hoop of the nation, the body gutted, without honor or land. This is why we hurt so badly. We killed the lover when we killed these people."

The eastern sky slowly streaked with blood, then a color like flesh, the second day of Fall. She read an Oglala prayer from one of her books, "So the God has stopped. Everything as it moves, now and then, here and there, makes stops. The bird as it flies in one place to make its nest, and in another to rest in its flight." She said we are at a stop now. "We are shaped by what we have seen. We have seen the dead. Now we are shaped like the dead."

In the instant the sun rose and hit the room like a flashbulb I saw us as a photograph of the dead family recently discovered in New Hampshire. From the coroner's report and from the neighbors the story was pieced together.

It appears that Cecelia, 84, died of natural causes two years ago. Her husband and the two others dressed her and laid her on the couch so that she could remain part of the family.

Her husband, George, 85, died a short time afterwards in the rocking chair facing his wife. A vase of white roses was arranged on the coffee table between them.

Grace and Roland, 76 and 72, continued living a normal life. But they were reclusive and shunned company. They did all shopping at night and even mowed the lawn after dark. Roland died around a month ago and was asleep in his bed at the time. Grace left him there and tried to continue her life, but found she could not. She lay in the same bed as Roland and died a few days or weeks later. A bag of groceries was found on the kitchen counter, unpacked.

The description of Crazy Horse at the burial scaffold of his daughter is adapted from *Crazy Horse. The Strange Man of the Oglala*, by Mari Sandoz.

nominated by Maxine Kumin, Alicia Ostriker and Pamela Stewart

TURNING OUT

fiction by GAYLE WHITTIER

from TRIQUARTERLY

"Plié!" The pink and black line at the *barre* drops down.

"Relevé!" The line lifts, more unevenly.

I am scrabbling for leverage, parts of my forgetful body tilting out of art back into nature. At last, late, I rise too on a brilliant point of pain. I am upheld mostly by the sinew of my mother's gaze. From across the hall she stares fixedly through me to the ideal daughter alive only in her dangerous maternal mind. Inside my staved toe shoe, a specific pressure reopens last Saturday's blister.

"Plié!" We begin again.

The hands of the schoolroom clock on the far wall have frozen at two of twelve. If I watch they will never move. But when I look away, "Time!" Sergei dismisses us. Although we dance in spell-bound, mispronounced French, we begin and end Group Ballet in a wide-awake and daily English.

"Time!" As the clock's hand darts across noon, the mothers discreetly check their watches to make sure of every paid-for minute. They smile, if at all, only at their daughters. They are as still, as grim as the face of a priestess casting bones.

My own mother wears even disappointment well. "Go *on*, Bonnie, take your toe shoes off. We haven't got all day." A towel, the admonitory smell of Lysol, come towards me. "Well, go *on*."

Turtle-shaped, my foot sticks, then springs suddenly free, the toes still invisible inside their protective "bunny pads." Worse is about to come. However gently I peel these cusps away, moist strands of rabbit fur clump where my flesh has oozed or, some-

111

times, yielded blood. Hair by hair I draw off the whistling pain. "Ow-w."

"Shh."

"Well, it hurts."

"I know it hurts. Here," she slips me the phial of iodine powder. "Be brave." But she is gazing elsewhere. "Just look at Gillian, will you. That girl never stops."

Away from the *barre*, Gillian, our class hope, poses in command of all the eight anatomical directions of the dance. Fatigue has not touched her. Her body arches and her torso tightens for a final budburst. She unfurls upward in a perfect *entrechat;* tries the circumference of space, a *cabriole*. Then the whole staff of her body blossoms, deft porcelain, ivory, not our common stuff. She turns and returns in the gyres of an almost endless *pirouette*. Faster she spins, the boundaries of the legs going; faster, her bright hair streaks into her scarf. Faster, she revolves, *spotting,* fixing an air-mark before her. Above the blur of arms and skirt and legs, her face seems still: she has been beheaded, reassembled by magicians.

"Well, Gillian shouldn't be in Group, it's not good for morale," my mother's judgment falls.

Now Sergei has paused to watch. Our elderly pianist revives too, scattering a few rosy bars of "Amaryllis" into the blank air of the studio. Even the other students watch, observing in her the reason why they practice every day, what they will turn into if they do.

"Your *plié* will *do*,'" my mother turns away, "but only because you're helped by gravity. But you'll have to work on *élevation*," a great discipline in her voice as Gillian leaps, *grand jeté, grand jeté, grand jeté*. Then Madame, massively caryatid, emerges from the office in her magenta satin class dress, flamethrower hair, thighs muscular with varicose grapes. Gillian, her raddled face says, has more than *placement, extension, line*, those brief commodities: Gillian has a future.

Applause, dropped beads, and "Bravo!" dries up quickly among the odors of talcum and sweat. Gillian resumes her place among us. Madame smiles and beckons to her mother.

"Marie Ravert may be my best friend," my mother tells the walls, "but sometimes I think she's just a *stage mother* after all!" For it is understood that Gillian dances to fulfill her mother's "ambition," while I, more penitentially, dance for Grace. "Shh!"

My mother strains to hear what Madame Orloff is saying. The word "exceptional" unrolls towards us; next, magic names, "New York . . . London," ascend to "Rome, perhaps," and consummate in "Paris, the Ballet Russe!" All the mothers start, look up as if they have heard their own names called.

But Mrs. Ravert's short arms crowd over her bosom. Her head bows no, no, no.

"You must get the money *somewhere*! *Borrow* it!" Now Madame booms whole sentences across the studio, but Mrs. Ravert's shoulders bend towards humiliation on a pulse of No, I'm afraid not, No.

"Why, the girl's a *natural!*" Madame informs everyone in earshot. "*Steal* if you have to, but get it somewhere! *Kill* for it!" she carries herself away, all Slavic extravagance. "*Kill!*"

"If there's one thing I can't stand, it's favoritism," my mother says. I sprinkle the iodine powder on my blister and wait for the reassurance of a local burn. "Bonnie, fluff your hair, it's stuck to your head."

"I can't help it."

"Group Class for *now*, then," Madame gives up on a hyperbolic gesture, you-can-see-what-I'm-up-against, to everyone who cares to watch. "But it's a *shame!*" On "shame," she turns towards us.

"Hold still while I tie it back with a ribbon, anyway," my mother says. "I wish you wouldn't twitch so."

Then it is certain. Madame is approaching us, a half-smile wired to her face. Is she going to ask *us* for Gillian's lesson money? I wonder.

"Mrs. Brent, could I see you a moment . . . ?"

"We're already paid up through next month. I've got the receipt right here. . . ."

"Oh, no. No, that's not what I wanted to talk about. In my office, please? You too, Bonnie. This concerns you."

We follow her at a distance. People are leaving now, and the studio resumes its great emptiness, to be filled by other classes today and, on Wednesday nights, the Bingo games they hold there.

"I bet she's giving you the 'Sugar Plum Fairy,' what do you want to bet?" my mother hisses. "Now act *surprised*, Bonnie."

In the smaller side room, over a table strewn with snippets of costume fabric, hundreds of younger Madames look down from glossies on a red velvet board: Madame as Pierrot, with rakish melancholy, hand under chin, and painted tear; Madame as a

113

large-featured Giselle in Black Forest bodice; and, of course, Madame as the Dying Swan.

"Mrs. Brent, I've made myself *sick* over this, just *sick*," her accent slips as she begins.

"What is it?"

"But I believe in being frank, I owe it to you, it's your investment, after all. There is"—her hand surrenders the room to fate—"no other way."

"But what's the matter?" My mother's Sugar Plum Fairy smile lingers, dead, on her face.

Madame, steadying herself, gazes into the wall of mirrors opposite us. Before them, a light oak *barre* runs prairie smooth. This is where I danced until my father "put his foot down," before I discovered, in the cheaper democracy of Group Class, the lie of my talent. This is the room for private lessons. Our glances meet in triplicate on the silver surface of the mirror.

"Where should I begin?" Madame wonders. Plunging, "It's my *sad* responsibility to tell you, Mrs. Brent . . . " the truth flows free, "that Bonnie's future in ballet is . . . well, *limited*. Believe me, I am sorry." Madame's hands ward off a protest my stunned mother cannot, as yet, make. "Truly sorry."

"What exactly do you mean by 'limited'?" she asks at last.

"You know," Madame sidesteps, "even *two* years ago she was nudging the height limit for a ballerina." She smiles hurriedly. "Bonnie's not exactly prima ballerina *size*, if you see what I mean."

In the mirror, my mother sees what she means, and I do too, my random, changing flesh flashed back at us.

"Oh, she's *shot up*." My mother cannot deny it. "But she won't keep on growing, will you, Bonnie. Anyway, I have no *illusions*. She may not become a first dancer, but I'm not a *stage mother* either. As far as I'm concerned, there's nothing wrong with the *corps de ballet*."

"My dear." Madame takes my mother's hand. She clears her throat of something worse. "I'm afraid Bonnie would unbalance the line even *there*. Exactly how old *are* you, Bonnie?"

My answer and my mother's intertwine.

"I'm sure she's reached her full height. I reached *mine* early."

"Fourteen last April," I confess.

A *faux pas*. In the Dance, your exact age is never calculated. "Teen," especially, evokes panic, for everyone holds her breath as you skid across the perilous mud of adolescence, Nature finger-painting you with hormones, blurring the artful line of years of lessons. For many Mothers of the Dance, a daughter's change of heart or bone may synchronize with their darker "changes of life." We dance in a time of endings.

"Only *fourteen!*" Madame seizes on it. "What, some girls keep on growing until they're *eighteen!*"

We all close our imaginations, not quite fast enough, against the spectacle of me, a dancing giantess of eighteen, demoted, year by year, from the Ballet Russe to the sideshow.

But my mother rallies. "You don't mean to tell me that it's only a matter of *size*, do you? Didn't you say it yourself, last year, Bonnie has *talent?* How can you have talent one year and not the next?"

"All my students have talent. I never accept a student who doesn't," Madame testifies. "But talent's not the whole picture. There's structure, too. With *Les petits rats*, the babies, who can tell? The older ones . . . well, one needs light bones, strict muscles, a long torso, *so*, and . . ." A complicated gesture cancels me out. "Time decides. What more can I say except that I am truly, truly sorry . . .!"

The fact upon her, my mother flattens into a chair. "You mean she should *stop dancing?*"

"Did I say that? Did you hear me say that, Bonnie? Of course not?" Madame laughs palely. "Haven't I always said that Bonnie's the most . . . most *industrious* dancer I've got. She *will dance!*" Color and confusion brighten my mother's face. "She should just shift to tap, that's all."

"Tap." The sentence is pronounced. All of us know that ballet is *the* Dance, an art, unlike the dazzling, double-jointed trickery of tap dancing, or, one more fall below, acrobatic "routines" and "baton lessons."

"Oh, she'll be *striking* in tap, just look at her! Why, a few weeks of private lessons and she'll catch up in time for the Christmas recital."

"Private lessons? Oh, I don't know. . . ."

"Wouldn't you like a solo, Bonnie?"

"Who, me?"

"A solo spot," Madame promises, right hand raised to the portrait of Pavlova. "I give you my word . . . *if* she applies herself."

"A solo in five months? Is that really possible?"

115

Madame looks offended. "Do I know my own business or not?"

"Of course, of course. I didn't mean to suggest . . ."

"I accept your apology," Madame declares, her accent now back in place. "Now, what would be a good time for this little one's new lessons? Thursday? Friday?"

"Either. Well, Thursday."

"I hope we can fit her in." Madame consults her big ledger. "Four-thirty? Five? . . . And you can apply the Group Lessons already paid for, *of course*. Bonnie, you are a very fortunate young lady. Practice every day now, don't disappoint us."

"Oh, don't worry. I'll see that she does."

"And thank you, Mrs. Brent, thank you for being so *reasonable*. You would not believe some of the people I have to deal with!" She rolls her eyes for heavenly help.

"Stage mothers." My mother understands.

Madame starts herding us out of her office. "One of these days," she consoles my mother, "you'll have a swan there. You'll wake up and see a *swan!*"

We emerge beside the sign INSTRUCTION MUST BE PAID FOR IN ADVANCE. The next hour's crowd of mothers and daughters swarms around us on their way to Group Tap. Theirs is a noisy, glossy craft, carried in round red or black patent-leather hat boxes. One tiny five-year-old wears, despite the heat, a leopard-skin coat. The Mothers of Tap have hard, bright faces, red nails, lips wide with Revlon's Fire and Ice.

Mine is a small, very elegant mother who has made a lifework of her good bone structure and her Good Taste. Good Taste directs that petticoats match skirts in one of three colors only: black, white and beige. Good Taste defines the brief season for white shoes (not before Memorial Day, not after Labor Day); it even measures and colors the rim of our company china, which may be white or cream with a "classic" gold border, but painted flowers only if they are "dainty." Daintiness, in fact, is one reason my mother has be-friended Mrs. Ravert, whose humility is rubbed smooth and small like a pebble, and whose Scots accent my mother thinks "refined." Also Mrs. Ravert wrestles skittishly with many small, but manageable, worries, a good sign in a good mother. "Oh dear, I hope Gillian doesn't become too *American*. Her manners put me to shame! What do *you* think, Ida?" and "Oh dear, Gillian uses so much slang I hardly understand her! Ida, what . . . ?"

116

The staircase clears. Marie and Gillian Ravert are waiting for us in the vacant entry below.

"Now just smile," my mother directs, sotto voce, "as if nothing's happened. There's no reason to be ashamed. Everybody knows only one or two girls ever make it."

"Only one or two will make it," Madame warns the mothers ritually. Each nods, though disbelieving that she has not earned, with her ambitious love, with the hard-saved dollar-fifty's for Group or the three dollars for a private lesson, a daughter's opportunity. Most of the mothers look plain and overworked, starved, like Mrs. Ravert, on American dreams. A startling number of them have, by some special curse, hatched peacocks, the challenge of uncommonly pretty daughters. Only my mother and I upend expectation. She walks, concluded, in a fading and ungiven legacy of beauty. I, it is charitably understood, am "still growing," not quite done.

"Only one or two" explains why silence so often covers the older students like a purifying snow. Yes, Barbara Cross actually tap-danced on the Ted Mack Amateur Hour, remember? And Judy Scolini *almost* got on the Ed Sullivan show with her Toy Shop ballet. But where are they now?

"I *heard* Barbara met somebody in New York, she got married."

"Is he rich?"

"I *heard* he's a millionaire!"

Of course. Because in every mother's mind fame flows to roses, red, red for the blood-pulse of the audience and for the passion of strangers. Millionaires all lined up outside the stage door just about to open. And if the scholarship dancer should come home quietly, failed, or pregnant, if she should be worn down to selling tickets, "Only one or two will ever make it. . . ." We have always known.

Outside Madame's studio, late summer thickens, bright and alkaline.

"I'm so embarrassed, Ida. I suppose everybody *heard*," Mrs. Ravert murmurs.

"*I* didn't. What did she have to say?"

"Well, she said Gillian ought to have private lessons, the way she used to." She adores Gillian with her eyes. "She says she's *talented*, a 'natural.' "

Gillian walks with us milkmaid-sweet, apple-breasted, arms a

117

graceful birthright, joints that must move on golden pins, not bone. Her feet turn out without being commanded. She steps over the sidewalk cracks without a downward glance.

"I just don't know. What do *you* think, Ida? Do *you* think she's got talent?"

"Anybody can see that."

"What did she say to *you*, Ida? Madame."

"Exactly the same thing. Madame told us Bonnie's talented."

"You don't say!" Mrs. Ravert's amazement checks itself diplomatically.

"I do say. She's been watching her and she's decided Bonnie's got a distinct talent for tap. Fix your barrette, dear, it's slipping."

"Tap?"

"That's where the *real* money is, you know, like Eleanor Powell, vaudeville . . ." she finds at last, "the Rockettes! Not in ballet."

"Bonnie *is* quite a strapping lassie."

"She's not big, she's statuesque. Bonnie's a long-stemmed American beauty."

"Hey, Bon." Gillian's elbow cuts into my side. "You really gonna do tap?"

"I guess so."

Gillian's jaws move up and down, *plié, relevé*, on her chewing gum while she considers this. "Well, Jeez Louise," she says.

"Of course I'm just thrilled!" my mother's voice is practicing behind us. "Tap's so much more natural. Did you know, Marie, that ballerinas never menstruate?"

"They don't? Oh, that can't be true, Ida, is that true?"

"It certainly is. I read it in the *Reader's Digest*. It's from starving themselves all the time, that's why."

"Imagine that!"

Gillian pushes me ahead of our mothers' lowered voices. By now Mrs. Ravert is or soon will be confiding how her husband came home drunk again and hit her—"right here"—her nylon glove touching her cheek as if to re-imprint it with the color of the bruise. "You ought to just *walk out*," my mother will advise, as usual. And Mrs. Ravert will agree that yes, she knows, she should leave that man, she *would* leave him if it weren't for the children, the children. . . .

Gillian walks faster. "Guess what! Guess who asked me out?"

"Who?"

118

"*Fred Vargulic!* He's a *senior!* It was right after Earth Science, he comes up to me, see, and he goes, 'You wanna go out next Saturday?' 'I dunno,' I says, real cool, 'why should I?' He says, 'I might take ya 'round the world, that's why!' "

"Where're you going?"

"The *drive-in*. Only my mother," she giggles, "she thinks it's a dance. They say Fred likes to French kiss." She is distracted, for a moment, by a passerby's stare. People often forget their manners in the face of such unexpected beauty.

"Bonnie! There's our bus!" my mother calls.

"So if anybody asks you, say it's a dance, O.K.?"

"O.K."

"We'll have to run for it!" my mother warns, running already. Lost girlhood strives inside her stiffening matron's body. She bunches up her skirt, against the wind. Her hair whips out weed tall, a graying ashblond paradox around her profile, fine and eroding. Still further down, pink laces of an invisible corset hold in the first dark place where once we blended into common flesh, a mother and a child. She runs awkwardly, wholly *en terre*. She runs to make me come true.

"You almost missed it, lady," the driver complains, impatient as she sorts out change. "I ain't got all day." My mother drops the exact fare for two into the slot and turns to find seats together for us.

From our window we watch Gillian, unhurried, unperturbed, ascend the steps to the bus. A veil of glances falls over her, and she smiles. The driver smiles back, turning her dollar into coins, lingering a little over her hand. The light changes to red, but no one cares. Time has paused for her.

"Beauty like that," my mother says, "it's a burden."

But I do not believe her. The faces of everyone, both genders, young and old, smile or stare in wonder at Gillian, the way sunflowers track the sun.

*   *   *

"I only hope Gillian's *grateful* for what her mother's trying to do for her. She's taking in *wash* to pay for those lessons."

"Other people's wash?"

"Yes. You've seen all those baskets of it, haven't you? Did you think it was *theirs*? Personally . . ." she settles a summer hat on her

119

curls—". . . I've always had a suspicion she was a *housemaid* back in Scotland. There was *some* scandal, that older husband and all . . . I bet Gillian's a *love child!*" She nods at her own thoughts. "That would explain it."

"Explain what?"

"Why she's so beautiful. I mean, otherwise it's really a *mystery*, isn't it?"

Gillian's loveliness, surely immoral, poises hummingbird static and swift in my mind. "She's going out with Fred Vargulic. He's got this awful reputation!"

"How's that?" She is asking herself whether her hat looks right.

"He puts his tongue in your mouth when he kisses. Yuk."

"There!" My mother stabs her hatpin through the straw. Below the lacy brim her face shadows with remembered beauty. "Let's get going, Bonnie, I just dread this, but we better get it over with."

That afternoon we—Gillian, her mother, me, mine—all sit on the scratchy, royal-blue, velvet seats of the Bijou Theatre while the matinee performance of *The Red Shoes* lurches, whirrs and skips from frame to frame. Before us Moira Shearer leaps up close, wafts away, at the commandment of the camera. Once, the projector jams, the picture clots to a stop, "Ohhhh!" Our disappointment brings it back in pink and purple burned spots to the exhaled relief of the mothers and Gillian's small solitary cheer. "Yeah!"

But Gillian is bored. Her flawless hand browses steadily from the popcorn box to her mouth, up and down, keeping its own time over the romantic crescendos of the movie score.

"Hey, Bon, you want some popcorn?"

"No thanks."

"Yeah, I shouldn't either. Gotta watch my figure. . . . Guess what! Didja hear about Marsha Norris?"

"No."

"She *went all the way.* Honest! I got it from Marge Donaldson and Marge, she got it from Marsh *herself*. So it's true all right."

"Who with?"

"Chuck Schultz. They're getting married, Marsha says, maybe this Christmas. A Christmas wedding."

"Shh!"

"But how old is Marsha?" I ask quietly.

"She's sixteen, a girl can get married at sixteen in this state without her parents' wanting her to, it's the law. . . ."

"We are here to watch this movie, not to listen to you," my mother announces as if to strangers.

It's the dénouement. Poor Moira Shearer drops suddenly, still in her demonic shoes, before the machinery of an oncoming train. The impact jars through the women, doubling on their shocked and indrawn breaths. Mrs. Ravert cups a cry back into her mouth. "Oh, look at that, Ida!"

Against a soiled pavement the dying dancer's fractured legs splay, still *en pointe*. Wind plays at the corolla of her skirt. The pale-pink gauze of her stockings darkens to the sound of Mrs. Ravert's weeping. She is sopping up tragedy in her fresh handkerchief, saved for this moment.

"Hey, Bon, where can you get stockings like that?" Gillian nudges me. "Do you know?"

"Quiet, girls!"

Out of the dancer's legs a darkness keeps flowing. It seeps through the pearly silk of her stockings. It stains the lighter satin of the Red Shoes. Blood, but moving more gently than blood really moves, and fading from black to purple to a thoughtful blue, the color at the heart of a poppy. *"Take off the Red Shoes!"*

We leave the theater, silent, for the glare of half-deserted Sunday streets.

"Wasn't it *sad*, Ida? I thought it was very *sad*."

"There are sadder things," my mother understands.

Mrs. Ravert tries to gather up all her feelings in something poetic—"She danced herself to death!" Her glance seeks out Gillian, tender, bewildered, watchful. "Oh, ballet is a cruel art, isn't it," she says, "but it's so beautiful. Isn't it beautiful, Ida?"

"This sun is giving me a headache," my mother answers.

"Did I tell you, Ida, I'm taking Gillian to Scotland next year? To my sister's in Aberdeen, to study?"

"You told me, Marie."

Gillian smooths the petals of her nine-gored skirt over crinolines. She sighs, mildly exasperated, then draws me back to confide, "Bon, guess what! I got into Secretarial. Next year I get to take typing, Typing I."

"I thought you were going to Scotland, to your aunt's."

"Maybe. Maybe not." But in the shimmer of her brilliant eyes, sky color bound by darker blue, slyness cannot take hold.

"Your mother says."

121

"Yeah, well. My mother works real hard and everything, you know? I mean, she's really sweet. But she's not too practical, know what I mean?" She blows a pink, fruit-scented bubble. "If you take Secretarial, you can always get a job. . . ." The bubble rounds out dangerously, but just before it bursts, she sucks it back in. "I'm gonna get a job and save up for my wedding. I already got the gown picked out, *you* know," she taps her skull, "in my head. White satin, or white velvet if it's winter. My cousin, she wore blush pink. You can wear ice-blue, too, only people don't, much. Anyway, I want real lace, not fake, down here on the neckline and on the train. A *six-foot* train. Sleeves cut like so. . . ." Her hand describes a fallen triangular wing, vaguely medieval. "What about *you*, Bon? What's yours like?"

"Maybe I won't even get married."

"Sure you will. Everybody does, almost. And I wanna have three kids . . ." She pauses, almost conscious of a golden pollen of male glances. ". . . no, four, real close together, *you* know, so's they can be friends. Two girls and two boys. Well, a boy, a girl, a boy, a girl," she conceives them on her fingers. "I'm gonna call the girls Dawn and Candy. Do you like 'Dawn' and 'Candy' for names? I don't know what to call the boys, though. I guess their father can name them."

The light changes to green just as we catch up to our mothers. Sinking into the softening asphalt, we four stride forward as if to merge with our images, closing in from the plate glass window of a furniture store across the street, in Darwinian enigmas. Somehow Gillian came from her small, speckled mother, a glorious mutation. But in me my mother's silver blondness has been thrown back to mouse-brown. A triumphant moment has declined. We both know this as she walks forward in her reconstructed dignity, and I walk in my body of original sin.

"Turn, dear." I turn. "A little more." I turn a little more. Mrs. Arcangelo talks around a slipped moustache of straight pins, held tight between pursed lips. She is fitting my costume, but her mind is on her masterpiece. "It's got hundreds of tiny little rhinestones, each one I got to sew by hand. 'Starlight effect,' that's what they call it. 'Starlight.' "

"I'm sure it's beautiful." My mother fingers the expensive slipper satin of a half-made sleeve.

"*Mrs*. Ravert, she's working extra just to help pay for it. Well," the seamstress lowers her voice, "she'd have to, it's costing over *two hundred dollars!*"

"Two hundred dollars!"

"And that's not counting *my* work. Well, it makes you wonder. . . . Turn, dear." I turn for her. ". . . what with all the starving people in the world! But Mrs. Ravert says it's an investment, the girl's dancing the Dying Swan and only the best dancer gets to do it. It's in a ballet . . . now, what did she call it? Blank? A ballet blank?"

"*Blanc,*" my mother corrects. "It means all in white."

"That's right. Well, Gillian! You could put your two hands right around her waist and touch your fingers, she's such a dainty little doll. They're taking her to Scotland, to study. . . ."

"Hold still, Bonnie, You're making it harder for Mrs. Arcangelo to do her work."

A straight pin just misses me, waist level. Mrs. Arcangelo turns, too, on her massive knees, and sets her yardstick up from the floor to my thighs. "Look at that, it's got to come down another quarter-inch! When is she going to stop growing?"

It is night; my mother is tired, but, "Bonnie's a long-stemmed American beauty," she defends me. "We expect *her* to audition for the Rockettes someday. When she's older, of course."

"What's that?"

"You never heard of the Rockettes? Why, they're famous for precision kicking. All over the world."

"Mmmm."

By now I know Mrs. Arcangelo's rhythm and turn without being told.

"You have to be over five-foot-seven just to try out for them!"

"My, my." Mrs. Arcangelo sits back on her haunches, finished.

"If you ask me, that waist's still not quite long enough," my mother reflects.

"There's nothing left to let down. Just step out of it, dear."

"Careful, Bonnie, don't step on the hem."

Almost negligently, Mrs. Arcangelo picks up my shed splendor, and I stand, unmasked before myself in her oval mirror, a startled, biscuit-colored shape in a cotton slip, slouched between girlhood and whatever else is coming.

"Beautiful material," she says, "a pleasure to work on."

"That's the best satin money can buy. Bonnie, put your clothes on, you'll get sick for the recital." A suffocating cape of Blackwatch pleats snaps shut on me until, with one sharp tug, my mother lets me breathe again.

"That Ravert girl, now . . ." I emerge to see Mrs. Arcangelo sketching in air, "she's got a cap of feathers, each feather's threaded on separately with a *seed pearl* at the base. . . ."

"Put your coat on, Bonnie, It's late. When's our next fitting?"

Outside, after the bitter wind, we settle onto the cold seats of the car. She starts rummaging in her purse: makeup, bankbooks, comb.

"Where's my pocket calendar?"

"The recital's the twenty-second, Mom." Who does not know his date of execution? "Eight o'clock. The Moose Hall."

"Oh, I know *that*. But when's your next period? The twenty-fourth? Later?" she hopes.

"I'm not sure. I don't know."

"What do you mean, *don't know?* Don't you keep track?"

"What for? It always happens."

"Bonnie, you're hopeless. Now where's my calendar? I didn't leave it home, did I? Did you see me leave it somewhere, on the kitchen counter maybe?"

"I *think* it's January second."

"That's next *year*, thank heaven. You wouldn't want to ruin your costume. . . ." We swing out into the November night. "Your *father*, of course, he doesn't understand anything. Wait'll I tell him what *Gillian's* cost."

My costume has already spoiled a dinner. "*Forty-five dollars!* What the hell, do you think I'm made out of money, Ida?"

"It'll last forever."

"Sure, in the attic. Half a week's pay packed up in a goddamned box!" Above my head the swords of failure poise: an overgrown metallic-gold tutu I wore two Christmases ago, as a Marigold in the Waltz of the Flowers, also last year's tulle skirt, dirty-white, to turn me into a Snowflake.

"I just don't have forty-five bucks."

"Use some of the vacation money."

"Oh, Ida."

"Please? It would make me happy."

"No, it wouldn't, but sure, go ahead, take the shirt off my back."

"I'm very surprised at you, John, denying your daughter like

124

that. Bonnie's talented. In just four months she's gotten a solo routine."

"Solo racket."

Now every afternoon between four and five, to the ratchety Voice of Music victrola, I practice without hope. It is like lying, to drag the cargo of a half-willing body through my Military Tap, cleats scratching the linoleum, eyes on the slow redemption of the clock. Where ballet required lightness, *ballon*, tap demands crispness, firecracker smiles, "bounce." To make me bouncier, my mother bobs my hair and ties it up in rags, but within moments it too falls limp.

"More life! Put more life in it!" She drives me, a dying horse, to the outpost of performance. "All right, all right, start over. Start from bar thirty." And when the phone rings, "Tell Gillian you can't talk long, you're working on *your* routine."

"Bon, listen." Gillian's voice comes to me conspiratorily soft. "I gotta see you. I've got something to *tell*. You won't *believe* it!"

My mother replaces the needle on the record. A few vacant grooves turn while Gillian urges, "After rehearsal tomorrow? O.K.?"

My mother gestures that time is up.

"Sure. I can't talk now."

My march starts. "Hey, is that yours?" Gillian asks, "Is that your music?" and starts singing,

> "'Oh be kind to your web-footed friends!
> 'For a duck! may be some! body's moth-er!' "

"Bonnie, hang up."

"I've got to go."

> " 'And if you! think that this! is the end . . .
> Well it is!"

Gillian hangs up first.

In bed that night the first black sweetness of my sleep breaks open. A dot of light is widening inside me. I lie still, as if listening, as it feathers, turns. A ribbon of cramp winds upwards through my belly. I swing out of the covers to start for the bathroom.

Outside it has been snowing, it still snows, wide steady flakes like petals falling off a peony. A seam of chill runs at the baseboard. Even the braided rugs feel cold to my bare feet. But from beyond my half-opened door quick air stirs in my parents' room. They are not asleep, but speaking softly, their voices distinct in the night darkness.

My mother's yields, "Oh, I'm not *blind*, you know. I can see it's over. Madame's right."

"Maybe she's wrong."

"She's right." The whole hall grows colder at the soft sound of weeping.

"Hey, it's not the end of the world."

At my window the georgette curtain lifts and falls in a current of thin heat. Below it, the radiator spits, then whistles. Perhaps I should make a noise, call out for somebody, stop them, my instinct for self-preservation tells me.

"You take things too hard, Ida honey. If you'd just stop wanting so many things, you'd be happy."

"Like you?"

"Well, yes, I guess I am, happy."

"No, ever since I knew you, you've been *contented* with what you have. Not like me. Sometimes it really makes me wonder."

Inside me fresh warm blood slips. Then out of a calm too good to last, her girl's voice, downy with wishes, speaks, "John," his name.

"What is it, honey? Let's get some sleep."

"John? What if we had another baby?"

"What?"

"I'd like that, wouldn't you? Wouldn't you?"

My father lengthens a silence around the house, its lonely shape in winter night. "Oh, Ida, we're too old for all that stuff."

"I am not, I'm not too old. John, we could start all over."

"Is that a threat or a promise?"

"Don't laugh at me."

"I'm not laughing, honey. Honest. Everybody likes to dream," he says. "It's nice to think about, anyway."

"I've always wanted another baby," my mother's voice rounds, rises in the darkness. "I always wanted to try again."

"Let's go to sleep now."

"John?"

"Let's go to sleep."

For a while I sit on the edge of the mattress. Brightness slips past the window shade. The dancer in the Degas poster on my walls blurs into a snowflower. At last water retreats banging down the radiator pipes, so that even the small heat vanishes. My bare feet have gone mineral-cold. I pull myself between the bedsheets, cold too now, draw my legs into a smaller self beneath the wide, indifferent quilt.

They must be sleeping now. Blindly, my heart tells itself over and over. If I don't get up, by morning the sheet will be stained. "I always wanted to try again." If I do get up, my mind will work on what I overheard. Still bleeding, knowing it, I fall asleep.

"Dress" rehearsal, everyone in old leotards anyway, "Hey, Bon," Gillian leads me to the back of the auditorium, glances around for eavesdroppers, and announces, "This is *serious*. First you gotta promise never to tell. Like *swear* . . ."

"Swear."

I gesture over my heart.

"Promise? O.K., then, *Well* . . ." She tries to delay dramatically, but her pride races forward. "*Well*, Fred and me, we went all the way the other night."

"You didn't!"

"I did." Off and on her starry eyes blink. "Well, we're really in love, *you* know, so it's all right and everything."

"It's *not* all right." Doesn't she know about V.D. and Pregnancy, my mother's big deterrents? "What *happened*? Did he get you drunk?"

"You shouldn't never drink," she admonishes, "it's bad for your skin." Her gum clicks and sloshes in excitement. "We just, uh, couldn't stop, *you* know." She chews faster, new juiciness.

On stage the baby swans, Beginners' Class, troop out in their soft bottoms and soft shoes, the random shoreline of our Swan Lake.

"But he won't *respect* you," the third reason Not To comes to me, "I mean, no boy really wants a girl somebody's . . ."

"Nobody's laid me, only Fred. Besides, your mother just says that so you won't. You know mothers."

Slowly I recognize that I am in the presence of an initiate, a living sourcebook. "Did you bleed much?"

"I didn't bleed at all. I bet they lie about that, too, huh? But I got worried, maybe Fred thought I'd been with somebody else, before, you know? I didn't say nothing. I just hoped he didn't notice."

From the stage Madame makes a scooping gesture toward Gillian.

"Hey, I gotta go."

"Wait. Does it hurt?"

"A little. Yeah." She half-turns her graceful back to me; it's her cue. "But, *you* know," her hand leads my glance downward to her feet, their perfect turnout, the slender pink cylinders of her toe shoes, "not as much as *this* . . ."

Recital night, someone has strung dressing rooms with flannel-blanket walls behind the Moose Hall stage. Decibels of laughter and trouble travel the central aisle. Unseen nerves snap to tears. The curtain's up. Excitement burns among us.

"Hold still." My mother strokes solemn pigments on my face. A towel tied around the neck protects my glossy soldier's costume. Above it, her compact mirror shows me in savage colors, desiccated peachskin base, woad-blue shadow, a lipstick orange enough to turn my teeth yellow. Not for me the wingswept ballerina's eye, the cold still red dot for a tear duct. In the small space between what my mother draws and the lines of my naked cheekbones, I feel a thin yet absolutely crucial margin, by how little I miss being beautiful. My mother's fingers move, electric with determination.

"Mom, I feel sick."

"That's just nerves. Hold still." She squints. Her sharp fingernail pares off a minute edge of paint. Up close her face terrifies my own, lipliner generous around her mouth, pores craterous with rouge. Resemblance hardens into me. "Don't look anywhere and don't blink, Bonnie, it'll smear." Then my eyes are on.

They have clamped me somehow into the white satin dress with its boy's bodice. My flesh pushes against Mrs. Arcangelo's French seams, a squash growing through rock.

"*Please* hold your stomach in." Her hands flatten her own to show me how. "If you don't, you'll look pregnant. And don't sit *down*, you might rip a seam."

"But I feel funny. Honest."

"Stage fright," she heads me off. "Everybody gets it. It's a good

128

sign," though she knocks on the nearest wood, a cigarette stand upholding blocks, jars and sticks of makeup, its own Chinese-red lacquer peeling off.

"I think I'm getting the curse."

"Oh, you're not due for a week yet, *more*." Briefly her face clears into candor. "Please just don't get sick now, Bonnie, this means so much to me. Just keep calm, will you, and do a good job? Just this once?"

Applause, a slow match striking, comes to us through the blankets. "O.K." The aisle makes way for three belly dancers in sparkles and finger-chimes.

"Who's on now?" she whips back the flannel wall to ask them. "Nina Martin? Nina's your cue, Bonnie! You go on after Nina! Now get out there," she rights one of the purple plumes on my helmet, "and break a leg!"

Behind the hot must of the velvet curtains, I stand breathing in all the other performances of that and other nights. Overhead the pulleys creak, the curtain lifts enormously on a socket of hall. I am poised on my chalk-mark, a white X center-stage, saluting hundreds of invisible onlookers, families and friends, while the moment crawls on and on and on. In the crescent of the footlights one dead spot interrupts the ring. "Never look right at the audience!" I remember. Because if you do, your own fear and commoness stare back.

In the stage wings my mother's presence keeps getting bigger and bigger with everything she has to lose. Her hands are fixed slightly apart, as if she holds some breakable commodity, and she starts counting—numbers whisper across the boards, "One, and, two, and . . ." my march rasps in its grooves, "three, and four AND. . . ." my foot takes over from her. In a noisy rush of turns, I come alive. There is the first naked awkwardness, the fear of tripping or forgetting, then my "routine" meshes with my body, takes me in.

Gradually I dance the rows of seats into shape out of the darkness. Out of the darkness wildflower faces come up, solitary, to the now-and-then blue dart of a camera pinning me to this place and this moment forever.

Hurtling out of every turn, I sight my mother. She mouths, "Smile! Smile!" Her hand tightens my salute. Her arms are waving "Arm movements!" and with the startling gesture of a woman

129

garrotted, "Head *up!*" By the finale she is flailing too, and as the curtains close on our farewell smile a loud, obligatory slap of applause says it is over.

"Oh, baby, I'm so proud of you!" she tells me, but she wilts into tears. I touch my own face to see if the makeup has come off. On one satin cuff an orange stain recalls my last salute.

"Now clean up and come down and sit with us . . . it's Row B, seats six and seven."

"O.K."

In my cubicle I rub my skin fiery to coldcream everything away except my simple, earlier face. Aftermath flattens out in me like the end of a birthday, like the daily texture and pallor of the street clothes I will be putting on for the rest of my life. Headed toward the audience, I walk past islands of ballerinas waiting for their cues.

"Bonnie!"

In the wings Gillian twinkles, two hundred dollars worth of light leaping and staying among the subtle rhinestones of her skirt. On her perfect, floral face worry hesitates, accepts the diminished form of puzzlement.

"Oh, Bon, am I ever scared!"

"You? *You've* got stage fright?"

"It's not that." Her eyes assess the cygnets on stage, pretending to swandom in uneven bourrées. "Denise's out of step again," she says, "as usual." While I am looking, "I'm *late,* that's what's the matter."

"No, you're not. It's not even your cue."

Her violet eyes roll upward. *"Late. Late,"* she repeats, " 'my aunt was coming for a visit' and she's *late.* You *know?"*

"I bet it's the recital. It's made you nervous or something."

"Oh, no, it's not. I'm real regular, Bon. And anyways, there's other . . . signs."

"Signs?"

"Oh, Bon." She lowers her eyes in perfectly practiced shame. "I'm *expecting.*"

It is the worst thing a girl could do, but even that, I sensed, you could do with talent, skill of some sort. "You're not?"

"Yeah. I'm sure. I got knocked up."

"Who?"

"Fred, who else?"

130

"Are you sure?"

Her glance shows damaged trust. Did I think she was one of those girls who "didn't even know the father"? Did I think she was an amateur?

"Does your mother know?"

"Bon, really. I mean, Fred and me, we'll tell her later. We're gonna get married right away, so it's O.K. Just don't say anything, promise?"

I start to cross my heart but the gesture feels foolish, childish. "But she'll find out. What about Scotland? What about the Dance?"

"Well, I'm certainly not gonna *dance* anymore!" Gillian puts on a matron's indignation.

"Oh, Gill."

"You gotta quit sometime, I mean, look at Madame." Her face pouts and she begins to cry, though carefully, a little wad of Kleenex damming up the tears to keep her mascara from flowing. "No. This is the last time."

From the stage a sharp crack of applause finishes the little swans.

"Oh, Gillian, that's awful."

"What?" The little cygnets, Beginners Class, giggle past us and she pulls back to preserve her fluid skirt.

"It's awful, you not dancing again."

"Oh. I mean, what I'm *really* worried about is maybe this could hurt the baby, mark it or something?" We hear the restless public murmur of the audience. "Well, me next," she says. "Cross your fingers, huh?"

"O.K."

Daintily Gillian pulls out a pink nubbin of gum and sticks it to the frame of the stage. A moment later she has assumed her place at center stage, legs effortlessly in the fifth position, arms *en couronne*.

In Row B I wedge past my mother's knees and sit between her and Mrs. Ravert, Seat 7, as the first bars of the Dying Swan draw a hush across the audience. On stage a wide confetti of pink and blue spotlights combine, settle on Gillian. The sweet soreness of her beauty, recognized, stirs in me, in everyone who watches. On our many drawn breaths she comes to motion.

Light plays on her rhinestones, bees on the living skin of

131

flowers. The drafts catch and turn the feathers in her swan cap, until she trembles into something more than human, like us but also winged.

Beside me my mother holds in her disillusioned lap, eyes bravely forward, like a schoolgirl undergoing punishment both rigorous and undeserved. I reach for her in the darkness and am surprised by the readiness of her answering grip. We sit hand in hand.

From the audience a ripple, half cooing, half regret, says that Gillian, in a *temps d'ange*, has taken a bowman's arrow and now is slowly folding back into mortality.

In a few moments now she will sink into the sharp shape of a swan's outstretched throat, trembling to her silent death. The space between perfection and applause will seal her off. Then, resurrecting on the beats of acclamation, higher, higher, she will rise and curtsey, will make her *révérence* to Madame, the throats will fill up with "Encore!" as Sergei offers her an armful of red roses. "Encore!" until the dream cuts some other onlooker to the heart, roots there, and it begins again.

Downbent, my gaze catches the gleam of patent leather, Mrs. Ravert's cushiony small feet crammed into the pony hooves of her new shoes. She wears opaque elastic stockings, new too. Between the lapels of her Sunday suit, a cheap lace quivers. Her gloved laundress's hands are moving in small, possessed gestures to the music of her daughter's body on the stage. But I am afraid to look higher, to witness her face in all its bright intensity, the stale hair netted in a dancer's knot. Motherhood is the cruel art. If I look I will have to see her spirit burning in her eyes, the rapt and unsuspecting love of the only innocent among us.

nominated by TriQuarterly

THE ELECT

by PETER COOLEY

from THE OHIO REVIEW

Many the shadowless under the rose leaves
untrembling mid morning
Many at early evening
the wings, ochre, henna, cinnabar,
which continue, unseen, singing
when night, never stirring, takes their air.

In this garden out of time
the stillborn until their moment linger.
Their souls climb the white down
of little tubers, footless; they suck
mouthless the orris root. Hoarfrost
their spoor foreshadows them, burned off by noon.

And from this place we called the child to us
that you might carry it
to give it up. And spare her breath
this life, the agony of body, the next, the next, the next.
Tonight on the long, clear wing of her voice
the soul of our daughter walks out
between the thorns, uplifted, no one

warbling her absence, everlasting.

nominated by Michael Waters

SHOOTING

by AUGUST KLEINZAHLER

from EPOCH

The sun is high
and the blacktop soft so   Hit
first from the corner
then from the key
because your hand is hot
and no one's watching   Hit
and the sun's an oscilloscope
among ghostly ruins   Hit
and out jumps memory—
Cerberus!   Hit
nothing happens   Hit
your brow's sore from salt
mixed with poisons escaping   Hit
for forget-me-nots
sprinkling the tall grass   Hit
for the poppies for birdsong
pale nubs   Hit
so your flanks start to glisten
like fish do   Hit
and young mothers pull their shades down
Hit   get hit back
till you're ripe for a juicing
Hit   on a hill in the Peloponnesus
your limbs oiled and kneaded
your focus burned clear   Hit
after dark and the stars shall

illumine
Put moves on the locals
They'll make you a god
Hit   for the sake of it
for the music of hitting   Hit
because will ordained it
and you can deliver
Hit   you the Hit Man
Hit   'cause Jim Dandy's
got nothing on you   Hit
because you've been hitting since when
at the playgrounds   Hit   underneath
then hook with both wings
Hit   twice for compassion
and 3 times for passion   Hit
one more time
and all sins are absolved
Hit   for the rhythm
that finds you and lifts you
The ball is a planet
and you make it go

nominated by Gary Soto

DINOSAURS OF THE HOLLYWOOD DELTA

by GERALD COSTANZO

from KANSAS QUARTERLY

Joe DiMaggio, who was married for three years to
Marilyn Monroe, has ended a 20-year standing order
for thrice-weekly delivery of roses to her crypt.
The florist said Mr. DiMaggio gave no explanation.
                                        —*The New York Times*
                                        September 30, 1982

In times of plenty
they arrived from everywhere
to forage among the palmettos
of Beverly and Vine, to roam
the soda fountains and dime stores
of paradise. For every Miss Tupelo

who got a break, whose blonde
tresses made it to the silver screen,
whose studio sent her on a whirlwind
tour to Chicago, and to the Roxy
in Manhattan where she'd chat
with an audience, do a little tap

dance, and answer questions
about the morality of the jitterbug,
thousands became extinct.
Their beauty, it was said, drove
men to wallow in dark
booths in the Florentine

Lounge dreaming of voluptuous
vanilla, though the rumor persists
that they were dumb.
They were called *Jean, Rita, Jayne,
Mae,* and *Betty.* The easy names.
No one remembers now

how the waning of their kind
began. Theories have pointed
to our own growing sophistication—
as if that were a part of natural
selection. At first we missed
them little, and only in that detached

manner one laments the passing
of any passing thing. Then posters
began to appear. Whole boutiques
adoring their fashion: heavy rouge,
thick lipstick. The sensuous puckering
of lips. Surreptitious giggling.

We began to congregate on street corners
at night, Santa Monica and La Brea,
to erect searchlights
and marquees announcing premieres
for which there were no shows.
We looked upward

as if what had been taken from us
were somehow etched in starlight above
their sacred city. We began
to chant, demanding their return—
to learn, for once, the meaning
of their desperate, flagrant love.

nominated by Ted Kooser

WHISKEY, WHISKEY GIN, GIN, GIN

fiction by GORDON WEAVER

from QUARTERLY WEST

> ". . . use a little wine for thy stomach's
> sake and thine often infirmities."
>
> *1 Timothy 5:23*

A constructive way to begin would be for you to make the simple admission, statement, if you like, that you're an alcoholic. Are you able to say that about yourself?

Not on your life! Not on my life. What we're really talking about is my life here. No way. Never. Far from it.

When he had something to celebrate, my father celebrated; he was a moody man, but he knew how to celebrate.

World War II for example. The war was very good to my father, at least for a time. He sold machine tools, a part of a machine necessary to make a machine that made something in some way vital to the war effort. Riding the crest of cost-plus contracts and military delivery priorities, he did extremely well until the war began to wind down toward victory over the Axis.

I like to think of him, remember him, celebrating.

I can see him, as clearly as though it were yesterday; my memory of things is like that, exact, alive, more real as memory than the fading facts ever were.

We are in a bar. I do not know which bar, what time of day or night it is. I am six. Seven? It is 1943? 1944? Memory can be like a dream, cause and effect non-existent, the reality all the more vivid for its isolation in a void of particular time and place.

It is World War II, we are in a barroom, my father and I. My mother is not there. She was not a woman who enjoyed barrooms.

My brothers are away at the war, Milton in Belguim, Leonard en route to the Philippines.

My father stands at the bar, celebrating. A winning contract bid? A commission paid? His return from another flying trip to Washington, where he confers with Dollar-A-Year men? He stands at the bar.

His suitcoat is open, thrown back, one hand cocked on his hip; one foot is up on the rail. His chest is thrust forward. Satisfaction? Pride? Bravado? Chin up, he talks, brags, throws back his head to laugh often, loud. The barroom, people, seem arranged for him, a stage setting. Everything, everyone is arrayed about him; he is the center, focus of attention.

With his free hand, elbow on the bar, he manipulates his Pall Malls, a Ronson lighter, a shotglass. Again and again. Memory is like that, incredible, yet more real than the possible.

Again and again, he lifts the glass to his lips, tosses off his drink. Something colorless. Gin? Schnapps? He tosses off his drink, raps the bartop with the empty shotglass, casually nudges money toward the bartender, flips a Pall Mall out of the pack lying in the tangle of bills and change, places it in the corner of his mouth, thumbs his Ronson, blows smoke, still talking, a cloud of smoke that shades into the layers that drift below the indistinct ceiling, obscures the faces of men and women who surround him, wait on his words.

Again and again. This is how I remember him. He tosses off his drink, calls for another round, lights a Pall Mall, blows redolent, luscious smoke. My father celebrates: the war, his success, himself.

Where am I in all this? Somewhere. There. I cannot remember when or how. I am there, observe. This is what I remember, how I remember it.

But my father was not a drinking man, what could be called a *drinking man*. Later, years later, I recall asking my mother if he drank a lot. Did he *drink?*

"No," she said, and, "Your father didn't have the courage for that."

"What?" I said. "What does that mean?"

"He was too afraid of hangovers to drink much. You father wasn't the sort of man to face the morning after the night before."

"I can't believe that," I said, "I remember being with him in a bar once, way back when, he was tossing off shots like he had a hollow leg."

"You're imagining things," my mother said, and, "Your father was a coward about physical pain. He'd never take the risk."

I was old enough to understand she meant more than she said. Another time, I might have asked another question, invited her to go on, speak about how she really felt about him. But all I was interested in at the moment was his drinking. I remember thinking that was funny, a man not drinking for fear of a hangover.

My father could be moody. I have another memory of him.

There was still the war, but it must have been almost over; it must have been the summer of 1945. The cost-plus contracts were evaporating, military delivery priorities revoked. The world war that was so good to him, for him, was ending, no longer a good war for my father.

We are at home, my father and I; my mother is there, but not in the room. It is the time when they are seeing lawyers, haggling over dwindling assets. Our home is dominated by long, tangible silences between them, broken only after I am put to bed for the night. I lie awake in the dark of my bedroom, listen to their strident voices, his hoarse shouting, her weeping. I lie awake, listen, try to assemble, make sense of references to a woman named Irene who lives somewhere he travels frequently on business. I have never understood the whole story.

My father and I are there, my mother somewhere else in the house, my brothers still gone to the war that is ending. Milton will return from Europe soon. Leonard is missing in the Philippines, will never be found. We do not know this yet.

My father and I listen to the radio. Mr. Anthony. People come to Mr. Anthony, tell him their problems. He asks them questions, deliberates, gives them, judge-like, solutions to the difficulties of their lives. My father listens. I listen, watch my father. He slumps in his easy chair, an expression of deepest, blackest depression set in his face like stone. It is night; the only light in the room comes from the large dial of the Philco console. A Pall Mall smoulders in the ashtray at his elbow; in his hand, he holds a highball, ice melting in the thick summer air.

Mr. Anthony, says a man with a problem, *my brother-in-law has lived with me and my wife for six months. Not once has he so much as lifted a finger to pay his share for groceries and the rent money.*

140

"Holy Jesus," my father says. He rattles the melting ice in his highball glass, lifts it to his mouth, no more than wets his lips.

Mr. Anthony, says the man's wife, *my brother has tried hard to find a suitable employment. He was 4-F for his bad back and also he got injured in a car crash shortly after.*

"Jesus H. Wept!" says my father. He twirls the chips of melting ice in his highball with his finger.

Mr. Anthony says, *I think we have a situation here where two people who should have failed to talk freely about what concerns them.*

"Sweet Jumping Jesus," says my father, looks into his drink, does not drink it. I do not understand; Mr. Anthony seems to be solving their problem. "Promise me one thing in your life," my father says to me.

"What? Sure," I say.

"Never do anything in your life the way I did. Okay? Promise me."

"I don't catch on," I say, and, "What?" again. Do I begin to cry? Do I try to listen for the sound of my mother in the house, hope, pray she will enter the room, turn on the light, tell me it is past my bedtime? I cannot remember.

"Promise!" my father says, drowning out Mr. Anthony.

"I promise," I say, and we sit there in silence together, listen to people's life problems being solved by Mr. Anthony's mellow voice. In the dark with the Philco's glowing dial, while the world war is ending outside, my father's fortunes crumbling, a woman named Irene waits for him, my mother waits for my bedtime, waits to begin her screaming accusations. My brother Milton waits for his rotation home from France. My brother Leonard is missing on the island of Luzon, though we do not yet know this.

My father was a moody man. Too depressed even to drink. Or afraid of a hangover. This is another of my memories. And I probably garble literal events, trying to tell it now.

I'm confused. What's the key here? You associate drinking with his exuberance, is that it? Drink is celebration? And this conflicts with your resentment of his philandering and his business failure? I'm thoroughly confused. The key's your image of your father?

Not at all. Of course you're confused. You can't see it with my eyes. You don't have my memories. My way of seeing it.

In 1947 there was a record blizzard; they always mention 1947 when we have a hard winter. I remember the two days and two nights of snow, the way the streets looked, drifted over, the bite of the wind on my cheeks when I played in the tunnels and forts I burrowed in the huge snowbanks, the crunching sound my boots made on the frozen crust, walking down the narrow lane plowed in the middle of a main street, my breath like smoke.

This is vague, a kind of collage, but the year was 1947, a matter of record.

I woke suddenly in the night. I was not dreaming, or if I was, I did not remember the dream when I woke. I was not frightened. I was sleeping, deeply asleep, and then, in an instant, I was wide awake, and all I knew was that I was awake in the darkness of my bedroom, only a pale moonlight at the window. I did not know what time it was, just that it was very late at night. My bedroom was cold; I wrapped myself in the quilt, went to the window, looked out at the cold stillness of the night, moonlight glittering on the snowdrifts, the high, plowed banks, the crusted streets. Then I heard them singing.

I do not remember what they sang. Songs from the war, dirty limericks, nonsense. Then I saw them, dancing, staggering in the street, and I recognized my brother Milton and his friend, Edmund Henry Clark. Milton wore his army fatigue jacket with the imprint of his chevrons still on the sleeves. Edmund Henry Clark wore his navy peacoat, black watch cap. They danced in circles on the snow-crusted street, slipped, fell into the frozen snowbanks, sparred with each other, sang, shouted, cupped their gloved hands to their mouths, called out obscenities to the sleeping neighborhood.

They stumbled out of sight. Then I heard them on our front steps, their booted feet stomping on the porch, the front door pushed open. I climbed back in my bed, sat up, huddling in the quilt, listening. I heard them creep through the house, heard Edmund Henry Clark curse when he bumped into something, Milton's loud whisper shushing him.

My brother opened my bedroom door, snapped on the light, and they stood there for an instant in the glare of the sudden bright light, grinning at me. Then my brother said, "Fancy finding you all up and alert at this wee hour," and Edmund Henry Clark laughed and Milton said, "Knock off the static, you want to wake up the

142

mater?" He pulled Edmund Henry Clark into the room and shut the door, and the two of them tip-toed in slow motion to my bed, sat down beside me, still grinning.

I said, "I heard you guys yelling and it woke me up."

Milton said, "That was my compeer here," and, "Swabbies can't hold their grog like GI's can." Edmund Henry Clark laughed so hard he fell over on his side of my bed. Milton said, "Brother of mine, brother-boo, I have a little proposition for you, now you're awake anyhow." Edmund Henry Clark fell asleep, a gentle snoring sound in his breathing.

My bedroom felt warmer with them there, as if they brought a source of heat through the subzero night into my room. They seemed to glow in the harsh light. Snowflakes dotted my brother's hair, melted to dewdrops. Powdery snow dusted his fatigue jacket, Edmund Henry Clark's peacoat and wool watch cap. Milton leaned close to me to speak; I smelled the tart, yeasty odor of beer.

He said, "Unbeknownst to you because of your tender age, the bars in this burg remain open for a good solid hour yet, but me buddy-boo and me finds ourselves temporarily tapped for funds. Now I happen to know you must have ample in yon Mr. Pig there . . . ," he turned to look at the large, pink plaster piggybank on my dresser—"which with your permissible permission I and this dumb swabbie here would like to borrow like a fin or maybe even a tenner at most, after which we'll tuck you in, say good *nacht* to all and to all good *nacht*, and be on our way in a trice if not a thrice or even quicker than that. What do you say?"

My memory is that he sat close to me on my bed, grinning, smelling of beer, warming my room, and we were silent for a long moment. My brother Milton grinned at me, wavering a little as he sat. Edmund Henry Clark snored lightly on the foot of my bed, and my memory tells me that I believed, in that very long moment of silence, that my brother, and his friend were very happy.

They had come home from a world war, and the government paid them twenty dollars a week for fifty-two weeks to buy cigarettes and beer while they pondered college educations on the GI Bill or pretended to look for jobs that would lead to satisfying and productive careers.

I believed, as I remember this moment, that the freezing black night outside, the city choked with snow this record winter of 1947, held joy and promise for them. They had come from a war, and they had no money, and our family had been broken by divorce and death, the future was so opaque as to be non-existent, but my brother Milton, nodding, drowsy with beer now that he was out of the terrible cold, was ecstatic as he waited for me to say he could raid my piggybank for beer money. And I believed Edmund Henry Clark, passed out on beer in his navy coat and hat, dreamed pleasant dreams at the foot of my bed.

"Can you help us out, bro?" my brother said. Before I could answer, my mother opened the bedroom door, tying her bathrobe closed, blinking against the light, furious.

"Do I have to have this!" she shouted. "Everything else, do I have to have this thrust on me on top of everything in this damnable life!" She jerked at her bathrobe tie, stood for an instant with her hands on her hips, hair mussed from sleep, blinking at the light, then came to us, stood over my brother and me to shout at him. "Is it enough his father deserted him for a slut, must you add to our misery!" she shouted at Milton.

Edmund Henry Clark woke up at once, sat up straight at the foot of my bed, stood up as straight as if he were on parade, walked, mumbling what may have been apologies, out of my bedroom, out of the house, into the night's bitter weather.

My brother did not answer her. "Leonard dead and gone in some Godforsaken end of the earth, rotting in the jungle for all we know, your father's a louse, is this the fine example you mean to be for your baby brother!" she shouted. Milton lowered his head, gloved hands in his lap, seemed to deflate, shrink under her words, the room chilly again.

I do not remember how it ended, how long before Milton and our mother left my room, turned off my light, the house dark and quiet again. I think I remember lying awake a while after it was over, snuggled under the quilt. And I suppose I thought of my father, my brother missing and presumed dead, my mother trembling with rage, weeping tears of hurt and anger, Milton with beer on his breath, melted snow in his hair, Edmund Henry Clark somewhere outside in the record cold and snow of the winter of 1947.

And then I suppose I must have gone back to sleep.

Traumatic. Or at least it would be, in context. Point?
The point is I am nothing like them. My father or Milton. My

point is it's a mistake to leap to easy conclusions. The point is that such memories are what you make of them.

Beer. Another winter. 1953? 1954? Somewhere along in there. No special winter, no record cold or snow. Just a winter night. I am sixteen or seventeen, and my two best friends and I are drinking quarts of Gettleman beer. We are parked in my rickety old Nash, lights out, motor running to keep the heater going, on a country road, having set out to drink as much beer as we can stand.

"It's warm enough you could take a bath in it," Nick says from the back seat as he takes the bottle from his lips, burps.

"Stand outside and drink it if you like it so much cold," I tell him.

"Next time," Larry says, popping the cap off a fresh bottle, "you be the one goes in to buy it, ask for refrigerated, show your spiffy fake I.D., they'll laugh you off the premises."

"Shut up," I say, "and drink your share before I get it," and, "Anybody gets sick cleans up after themselves."

"Anybody gets sick blames it on warm beer's a dork," Larry says.

"Big deal," Nick says, and, "Like it's real talented to be so overgrown you can pass for twenty-one."

"More than you can do, short Greek dork," Larry says, tips up his quart of Gettleman with both hands.

"Are we drinking beer or what?" I say.

"That's real neat," Nick says, and, "Maybe when you're twenty-one actually you can pass yourself off for thirty or so, huh?" He begins to laugh, says, "Imagine old Lar here the rest of his life, he can look real older than his age!" He laughs, gags when he tries to drink his beer.

"I never talk to short Greek dorks, it's a new rule I just made up," Larry says.

I tell them, "While you're yacking I'm drinking."

And then we do not speak for a long time, sitting in the dark of winter on a country road, drinking Gettleman quarts, my old Nash's motor running, the faulty heater clacking, the beer tepid. The only light is the dull winter moon, the points of stars in the black sky, the Nash's orange dash lights that make silhouettes of us as we lift our bottles to drink, wipe our mouths on our coat sleeves and the backs of our hands, the smack and gurgle of our drinking.

I do not know what made me think to speak as I did. I do not remember.

145

I said, "Each one say what he wants to be. Seriously. I mean in life, when you're an adult."

"When Nick grows up if he ever does he'll be this real short, real Greek old dork," Larry says.

"Seriously," I say.

"And you'll be this old man can pass for a hundred when you're say fifty," Nick says, laughs.

"I mean really," I say, and, "Just say, right this minute we're sitting here, getting sloshed, unless one of you two pukes first, each one say your best guess on what you want to be in your life. Seriously," I say.

And then we are quiet again in the winter dark, drinking our beer, and it would not have surprised me if nothing more had been said, or we began to tell jokes or talk about girls or school or the atomic bombs they were exploding in Nevada, half-drunk-on-warm-beer-talk.

But Larry said, "I'm getting serious as hell about b-ball. I'm knocking off smoking and drinking except for like parties, and working out on a schedule so I'm honed down in shape to get me a scholarship." I expected Nick to laugh, mock him, but he did not. Larry said, "I've got the size and the talent for college ball, and you make a lot of good contacts for your career in varsity sports. I'm joining the Masons for that too when I'm old enough."

When no one spoke, I said, "Nick?"

Nick said, "I want to grow up to be a short old Greek dork."

I said, "Seriously," and Larry said he was only joking, Nick should know that.

Nick said, "I'm going to college and majoring in business. I'm having my own business someday. Marketing or finances or something."

Larry said, "Sounds extremely boring," and, "Only joking, Nickie."

Nick said, "My old man's a goddamn waiter in a restaurant, man." When we were silent again, Nick said to me, "So what about you, Mr. District Attorney?"

I said, "You know, until I just now asked you guys, I never even once thought about it. I honestly have not got the foggiest." Nick laughed, and Larry said it was boring, and I was boring, and we opened more quarts of warm Gettleman beer to drink in my car, motor running, lights out, on a country road one winter night.

146

We spoke no more of it. I would guess we went on to tell jokes or talk about girls and high school, or the atomic bomb tests in Nevada, to get drunk and sick on beer. But I know I sat and thought about what they, what we had said about our lives, our futures. I imagined Larry playing college basketball, developing contacts that led to a career, joining the Masons. I imagined Nick, whose father spoke just enough English to wait tables in a hotel restaurant, majoring in business administration, founding a successful company, something in marketing or finance. And I thought of my future. And though there was nothing specific I could imagine, I believed in it; for all its vagueness, it was as real as the winter night or my Nash or Gettleman beer, and the whole of the future, for all of us, seemed natural, definite, tangible, a sure and certain path leading to the way things would and should be.

I'm lost.

So was I. Larry never finished high school. He joined the Air Force, but they gave him a mental discharge. The last thing I heard he was still in and out of veterans' hospitals for mental illness. Nick, the last I knew of him, was an accountant for some corporation. I'm sure his father must have been very proud of him. And I don't drink beer, haven't since I was in the army. I hate the taste and smell of it to this day.

I said, "Why do I love these quiet moments in life? Can you tell me that, Fat?"

Vos said, "Cut him off, Fat, he's starting to get all philosophical already."

Stu Pinzer shook the dice cup, rolled a full house hand of poker dice out on the bartop, said, "Read and weep, Fatty, you lose."

Fat poured all around, said, "If I win, I win. If I lose, I still win."

"How do you figure?" I said.

"Don't I get a drink too?" Fat said, and put away his rye.

"Really," I said, "I can't get over how good I always feel this time of day."

"It's called stinko," Vos said.

"That's just the buzz you're supposed to feel," Stu Pinzer said.

Fat said, "I don't feel a thing," and, "But don't mind me, maybe I'm numb on my way to bombed."

It was the quiet time in Fat's Bar, the slow hours between the

147

time the graveyard shift came off at the steel fabricating plant across the street to wash away the heat and metal dust at the bar, before the second shift came in for eye openers in the early afternoon.

Fat opened his doors at six in the morning for his regular winos on pensions and Social Security, stayed busy until nine-thirty or ten. The second shift started drifting in as early as one-thirty or two, and after that the bar was crowded, noisy until Fat locked up at two in the morning.

We did our drinking during the quiet, slow time, late morning to early afternoon, the summer after my discharge from the army. It was a hot summer, the sun heating the city into stillness and immobility. Everything seemed idle to me, waiting. I had my mustering out pay and some Soldiers Deposits savings, nothing I needed or wanted to do while I waited through the summer to start college in September.

I said, "These are the perfect hours." Fat lost another hand of poker dice, set up another around.

He said, "This is the perfect life, but then you kids are too young to appreciate my wisdom." Fat believed he had it made in life; he owned his bar, had plans to buy another in the same neighborhood.

He was only a few years older than we were, but he was married, to a fat woman we called Mrs. Fat, who spelled him as bartender, had two fat children as ruddy and red-haired as he was, was making some money, and liked to remind us, as we got drunk at his bar each day during the slow, quiet hours, that he drank more in a day than the three of us combined, yet never showed the effects. I think it was his size; he was six feet seven inches tall, weighed at least three hundred and fifty pounds. His face grew rosier and puffy as he drank, but I never saw him lurch or fall, never heard him slur a word.

Vos rolled the dice, said, "Be good to The Vos, he's flat busted!" It did not matter if he had to pay for a round. Fat carried his bartab, and Vos paid up every two weeks when his unemployment compensation came in. He lived and took his meals with his mother, who had a good job with county civil service. When I once asked him if he ever felt guilty for sponging off his mother, he said, "Why should I find work at twenty a day when I can steal ten a day from my old lady?" He said she only nagged him if he laid around

148

the house too much. "What the hell you think I hide out here every day for?" he said.

"If I thought like you I'd cut my throat," Stu Pinzer said. He attended extension night school, sold insurance, studied on his own for the Certified Life Underwriter's examination. He drove a company car, carried business cards, and always wore a necktie. He drank the least of us because he had to get out each afternoon and evening to run down prospects; he only killed the quiet time with us at Fat's because there was no sales percentage in chasing prospects in the middle of the day; nobody he tried talking to seemed to want to think about dying when the sun was high overhead. He said, "When I'm rich living off policy renewals, remind me to have my chauffeur cruise me by here and buy the house a round for old time's sakes."

Fat said, "Pinzer, I can buy you and sell you now, and I can buy and sell you the best day of your life."

Vos said, "Yeah, Fat, but he gets to wear a hat when he works," and, "Pour, Fat, put it on my tab."

I said, "You know, there's no place I can think of I'd rather be than right here and now. My brother writes me a letter, says come on out to California with him, go to school there, it's a paradise, my mother loves it already, but I can't see it."

"Fruits and nuts," Stu Pinzer said.

"That's because you're already half in the bag and we just got started," Fat said.

"Pour," Vos said, and, "Your dice, philosopher," sliding the cup on the bar to me.

But what I remember, what was most important, was the quiet. There might be a couple of winos at a table or nodding in a booth, and we could hear the hydraulic punch presses from the plant across the street, feel their vibration in the floor, and Fat's inefficient air conditioner chugged in the window, but we did not talk much, and I remember the quiet of those days, that long lost summer I killed time waiting to start my college education.

It was as if there were no time, no place except Fat's Bar. We heard cars pass on the street, and the blazing sunlight flared at the edges of Fat's dusty Venetian blinds. Fat had a Sylvania television on a corner shelf high above the bar, and a big Seeburg jukebox with colored lights, but we watched no soap operas or game shows, and nobody played the jukebox.

149

Sometimes I talked about what I might study in college come September, that I was considering pre-law. Stu Pinzer talked about a sale he had made or hoped to make, and Vos always tried to borrow a few dollars before we broke up for the day, and Fat laughed at us and told us how he had life made. We played liar's dice or poker dice or horse, and we drank away the quiet time of each day that summer. Whenever Vos or Stu Pinzer or I told army stories, Fat made fun of us because he had been in combat in Korea when we were still in high school.

But it was how slow and quiet and complete it was there, then, that I like to remember. And I remember how bad it felt to leave each day, walk outside, sun-blind for a minute, heat bouncing up from the concrete walks, softening the macadam street, the wet spot on the sidewalk just under the window where Fat's air conditioner dripped, how we stumbled to Stu Pinzer's company car, the suffocating, superheated air inside that rushed out when we opened the doors to get in.

There was each day, the mornings before we gathered at Fat's, and there was the bad, drunken, nauseated feeling when we stumbled out into the heat of the day, Stu Pinzer's company car, before the rush of second shift steelworkers crowded in for eye openers, and the stink and noise of the factory.

But I remember most the time between, different, special, because there seemed no time, no before or after. I remember saying to Vos and Pinzer once, as we lurched out of Fat's, "You know, these are probably the good old days we'll talk about when we're all a bunch of old men." I do not remember them saying anything.

And you mean to tell me you can't discern pattern here? Or is it won't?

Can't, won't, don't care to. It's just something I remember clearly.

And what became of these people?

How should I know? That was years, ages ago.

Mornings, starting each day, were horrible; I often think that if I had learned how to handle mornings I might still be married, have my family. The problem was I had the idea a man should tough out

150

his hangovers, since I had earned it the night before—if I had been willing to stash a bottle someplace, a closet, under the bathroom sink, I think it would have been fine. I might still be a man with a wife and children, but I never stashed a bottle at home, so I suffered hangovers, and lost my family, that phase of my life.

Mornings. Hangovers. Naturally I was hungover. Cheryl was already up and doing by the time I sat on the edge of our king-size bed in the master bedroom of our new split-level; we designed that house as our dream house, had it built. I sat there, looking at the bedside clock, trying to wake up through a monster hangover, listened to my wife move about our dream house, in the bathroom, waking our boys, washing and dressing them, in the kitchen, turning on the portable Sony on the breakfast bar to get the network wake-up shows.

It was morning, starting another day, and I listened to the sounds of my wife and sons in our dream house, and I looked at the bedside clock as if I thought it might speak the hour to me, encourage me, and suffered my well deserved monster hangover. My arms and legs trembled, and my hands shook; my stomach knotted and unknotted, my head throbbed, my eyes and lips were gummed shut from sleep, my mouth and throat so parched I could not swallow.

I sat there and suffered this, and listened to my wife and children talk, scrape chairs, the clack of spoons and knives and forks on their plates, the portable Sony television on the breakfast bar. I watched the second hand sweep around the lighted face of the clock, heard its faint electric hum, until I could force myself to stand, walk to the bathroom, shower and shave, dress, to go the kitchen to join Cheryl and my sons, Max, and his little brother Leonard, named for my brother who died in World War II.

"Do you feel like something substantial, or just toast or a roll?" Cheryl might say. Sunlight blared at me from the big picture window, reflected in my watering eyes off all the chrome and glossy formica in the kitchen of our dream house; when I could make myself look out the big window, I saw our patio slab, the natural stone barbecue, my lawn that was so even and green it looked artificial, the rear of my neighbors' dream houses, their patios and green carpet lawns.

"Just coffee," I would tell her.

I wish I could remember my sons from this time. I have

151

photographs, and I know what they looked like, blond like Cheryl, very fair complexions. I can say how tall they were, details, but when I try to think back to them it is as if I never saw them there in the kitchen at breakfast, as if I had only seen their pictures, been told details about them. I had to try to keep my stomach down and my hands still as I sipped my coffee; it is as if I never looked at them.

They were normal, noisy boys. They spilled their milk, giggled, fussed at each other, chattered at their mother. I cannot remember speaking to them, them speaking to me. All I seem to remember well is the terrible sunlight in the kitchen, the ache of my hangover, that it was morning, starting another day, the Sony's drone.

"You need to eat something for breakfast," Cheryl might say as I left for my office.

"What I *need* is the hair of the dog!" I remember telling her once. I remember how she looked at me, I looked at her, squinting because my eyes burned, and then, after a moment, she tried to smile, and then I left for my office.

The Hair of the Dog, then, when I was married, had sons, was the New Mecca Cafe, across the street from the County Courthouse and Commercial Building, where I had my law office. I saw a lot of the men I worked with—lawyers, police detectives, civil service people, a judge or two—in the New Mecca Cafe to get their Hair of the Dog. Some sat at the little round tables for coffee, doing business already, cutting deals, but most of us stood at the long bar, quiet, bleary-eyed, trying not to let our hands shake when we lit cigarettes, lifted glasses. We were silent, stared at ourselves in the backbar mirror as though we saw our faces for the first time, could not recognize ourselves.

My Hair of the Dog was two double whiskies, a house brand called Our Very Own, always at a special price, with half a glass of water to ease the rasp. The first one put my head and stomach and my tremor to rest; that was how I really woke up, ready to begin a new day. I stood a little straighter, looked at the men around me I worked so closely with each day, smiled, said hello, breathed deep. I looked at these men, and almost liked them, admired their affluence and success, the cut of their suits, the styling of their hair, the delicious smell of their talc and tonic and lotions.

After the first double Our Very Own I was sure who I was, there

152

with these men in the New Mecca Cafe, about to go to work across the street, a lawyer with an office in the Commercial Building, next door to the Courthouse, the center of the city, a family man, married to Cheryl, and I had two young boys, Max and Leonard.

The second double Our Very Own put me into motion. I was a *good* lawyer, doing better every day, married to a lovely woman, had two fine sons! Then I could step to the cash register stand, pay my tab, buy a packet of Sen-Sen for my breath, leave the New Mecca Cafe, start to work for another day, get on with my life. And I was glad to be who and what and where I was in my life.

I do not remember when I began taking a late morning nip to set me up for lunch. If I spent the morning in court, maybe I began to take a nip when I checked back in at my office for phone messages, felt I needed a jolt to clean out what went on in the Courthouse, set me up for the long lunches at the New Mecca, where lunch was always business at one of the small round tables, trying to cut a deal with a client or another lawyer, once in a while with one of the judges.

I drank the New Mecca's famous martinis at lunch; they kept their glasses in the freezer, served coated with a thick frost. I must have eaten something for lunch, but I do not remember anything I ever ordered, though their delicatessen sandwiches were also famous. "I guess," I would tell the waitress when she came to our small round table, "I'll open with one of your famous martinis. Make it a double. Rocks. It's been that kind of morning. No olive, no onion, no twist, okay? And just whisper *vermouth* at the gin on the way out of the bottle. Dry. Just the unadulterated juice of the juniper." I suppose I often sat at lunch with people, clients, who did not drink their lunches, but do not remember any of them.

The New Mecca was very crowded from noon until two o'clock, when court recesses ended, the air cloudy with cigarette and cigar smoke, noisy with the babble of conversations, deals being cut, waitresses carrying heavy trays, squeezing between tables. I ordered another famous martini, suppose I ordered something to eat. And I talked and listened, made notes sometimes in my pocket calender, cut my deals. With the second famous double martini I could talk and listen, make a note, did not see the crowded bar and jammed tables, did not hear the clammering voices. I could do what I had to do to be the good lawyer I was. I drank a third famous martini while I watched the clock over the bar, always careful to

153

get back to court at the end of a recess. I paid my bill at the cash register stand and bought more Sen-Sen for the afternoon.

The nip I took in my office before I drove home was to handle a lot of things. It washed away the day's work, the Courthouse, my clients, the deals I cut or failed to cut, all the men I had to work so closely with but did not like or admire or respect.

This nip was a kind of little bridge between my office and my home, and it set me up for the rush hour traffic. And it stopped any edge of daylight hangover that might start to creep in behind my eyes along about five o'clock. By *nip* I mean I kept a pint of bourbon in the deep-well drawer of my desk; I always closed my door so the secretaries could not see, then just took the bottle out of the drawer, unscrewed the cap, turned it up for a swig.

Then I could leave my office, say, "Goodnight ladies, and a good night to you," and go home to Cheryl, and to Max and Leonard.

I loved Happy Hour; when I think back on this time of my life, remembering the good times, I always remember Happy Hour as one of the best times of all.

We were all together in the den, with the big console Zenith on, the local news, and then the network news, but we really did not watch it closely. I mixed up a pitcher of manhattans, and Cheryl fixed snacks and soft drinks for the boys. I sprawled in my easy chair, sipped my manhattans, looked at the news a bit, watched my sons eat snacks and drink soda pop, glanced at the newspaper, listened to Cheryl talk about her day. I cannot remember anything specific she ever said—she talked about the boys, cute things they had said or done, about shopping, money she saved at a sale, a letter she got from her mother, an old girlfriend from college who called. Max and Leonard made a mess of their snacks, played at my feet.

What I loved was how it all made a kind of sense, the day, my life. I had finished another day. I had worked hard, done well, made some money, would make a lot more, faster, soon. And now I was home, and my wife told me about her day, and my children played at my feet, and the local, national, and world news ran in marvelous life-like color on the big remote control Zenith in the den of my dream house. I kept up with Vietnam, Watergate, whatever, but did not have to pay close attention, did not have to read my newspaper.

Cheryl told me things, and I responded, asked me questions I answered, and I spoke to Max and Leonard, touched them when they came close to my easy chair, and I kept up with what was happening in the world, but did not have to care about it. I sipped my manhattans, the tall pitcher on the coffee table close at hand. My family was close to me, and I was in our dream house, listening but not having to listen to all the voices, and it made a perfect, logical sense to me. I remember that feeling very clearly.

We ate a formal, family dinner. Cheryl was a wonderful cook; I remember how she planned our dinners so carefully, gourmet recipes and we ate together. The boys were not fussy eaters, so it was very pleasant. There was always wine, and I opened the wine at the table, poured. I had some interest in good wine, and Cheryl tried to share that with me, but she had to supervise the boys' eating. I always enjoyed our family dinners, but I suppose I could not really taste the wonderful food my wife prepared, did not do it, or her, justice.

I spent my evenings back in the den. I read briefs and depositions, did some light paperwork for the next day's court appearances. Cheryl was busy clearing the dinner dishes, getting the boys ready for bed. She brought them in to kiss me goodnight, and I hugged and kissed my sons. I remember how fresh and clean they were, how their blond hair smelled, their perfect skin. While she put them to bed, I got out the brandy, and after that I drank brandy until I went to bed.

Cheryl might join me once Max and Leonard were tucked in, and we often watched a nightowl movie on the television, but I did not pay attention to the movie. We sat in the den with the lights off, just the glow of the TV screen, did not talk. I drank the warm, warming brandy, and sometimes I dozed off there in my easy chair; Cheryl woke me when the movie ended, television signing off with a sermonette.

"Time to go to bed," she might say.

"What? Oh. Right," I would say, waking. I woke in my chair, head fuzzy with brandy, all the lights off, our dream house quiet. "Right," I would say, and, "Morning's going to come too soon to suit me," or, "I'm not sure I've got the will to get undressed when all you have to do is get up and dressed all over again in a few hours."

Cheryl might say, "You'll regret this in the morning," as she picked up my empty snifter, put the bottle away.

155

"How," I remember telling her once, "can you be so sure? You don't know how I feel."

And so you drank yourself out of a marriage. Lost your family.
Put simply, yes. Things are never so simple. And it worked out well enough.
Are you joking about this?
No. Cheryl remarried, very happily from all I understand, and my sons are fine young men. Max is in college now, and Leonard graduates from high school in another year. He attends a military academy, high class boarding school, really. They're both really excellent young men.
What you'd call a happy ending, is that what you're telling me?
There's more truth than not in that.
Now I know you're not serious.
But I am. Everything largely depends on how you look at it. How you see it, and where you're at at the time. That's what you can't understand. Nobody understands that.

My only drink now is vodka. Straight. Beer, whiskey, gin, cocktails, fancy mixed drinks—I never touch them. Vodka is pure. Cold. I drink it iced, with ice. *Purity*, I think is the quality of it that appeals to me. Cold, clear, like pure water.

Why do I drink? What do I mean when I say: I *drink?*

Not to celebrate, not to indulge my moods in any way. I am nothing like my father was. And my father is dead, and my mother, and of course my brother Leonard—somewhere in the Philippine Islands, almost forty years ago. My brother Milton is alive, but lives out in southern California, a grandfather several times over; it has been so long since I saw him, was in contact, he might as well be dead. This has something to do with my drinking.

Anyone, everyone, is born into a family. I have a father, mother, brothers, and my life with them remains with me, a part of me, forever. My family is broken by divorce, a world war, death, distance, time. It could make a man nostalgic. Sad.

I think of them, remember, and might be sad, but I drink. Not to forget. I drink. I fill my glass with ice, vodka that looks like purest water, drink. And I remember: father, mother, brothers, myself as I was then. And I am not sad. A man is born into a family, and they die, separate; that is the way it is. There is no reason for sadness, no point in nostalgia.

I fill my glass, drink. It is clear, cold, pure. It chills my mouth, warms my throat, my belly. I feel it soften me, relax my arms, legs, feet, hands. There is no aroma, no aftertaste. Things are the way they are.

A young man is ambitious and foolish. His ambitions are foolish. He has fools for friends. A young man believes whatever he wishes will come to be, is certain he will succeed. A man's friends, like his family, die. Surely Fat must be dead now. Or a friend can go mad, like Larry. Perhaps they succeed; Stu Pinzer is surely a success. Or they might as well be dead or mad, wherever they are. Where is Nick? Vos? I was young and ambitious, and I believed. And I succeeded.

So of course my success was foolish because I was too young to know what to want for my life. I dreamed the wrong dreams; what I realized of them is not what I should have wished for. But I do not regret my youth, that I was a fool. How could it have been otherwise?

I drink vodka, and it seems right to me that young men are fools. Such regret as I might feel for my life dissolves, dissipates. What else should a young man be but a fool? There is no regret, no nostalgia in this. I drink my vodka, and this is clearly the way things are, and should be.

And I fell in love, and married my love, fathered two beautiful sons all the while I was creating the fool's success I had imagined for myself when I was a young fool. And then my wife fell out of love with me, and took away my sons. I lost my love and my children, and this could hurt a man terribly for the rest of his life. But I am not hurt.

I do not hurt for this loss because I drink vodka, and can understand that this happens to many men, is what can happen for so many reasons. The woman I loved has a new love, and my sons are fine, excellent young men. I am sure they have ambitions, dream, and I suppose there is a chance they are not wholly foolish. But they were not hurt, I think, by me, and their mother is not hurt that I know. Why should I hurt? My vodka is clear and cold and pure; when I drink I see that things are the way they are, no reason for them to be any other way. I do not hurt.

157

When I drink vodka, I remember, whatever I remember, and understand, accept, feel no pathos, no self-pity, no anger. I remember whatever I remember, see myself, as I was, as I am, and there is only a great sense of the necessity of things, given time enough. I never wished to be tragic or pathetic, and I am not. I think I drink vodka only when I am confused. I am not confused when I drink.

Sometimes I am afraid of what will happen next, what may happen eventually. But then I drink, and I do not wonder about what is yet to come. I am not afraid when I drink.

I think anything, a man's life, my life, can only be known to me. No one else can know. When I am drinking, I am sure I know. No one knows a man except the man himself; I think drinking is how I know things, myself. I do not *drink*. It is simply a way that I am, who I am, have been. The way the world changes could confuse a man; when I drink vodka I am sure about what I know.

Is that all you have to say? You haven't anything else to say for yourself?

Nothing. Now, I think I'd like to leave. Talking about this is confusing. I am beginning to feel confused.

nominated by Quarterly West

THE SECRET LION

fiction by ALBERTO ALVARO RIOS

from THE IGUANA KILLER (Blue Moon and Confluence Press)

I WAS TWELVE and in junior high school and something happened that we didn't have a name for, but it was there nonetheless like a lion, and roaring, roaring that way the biggest things do. Everything changed. Just that. Like the rug, the one that gets pulled—or better, like the tablecloth those magicians pull where the stuff on the table stays the same but the gasp! from the audience makes the staying-the-same part not matter. Like that.

What happened was there were teachers now, not just one teacher, teach-erz, and we felt personally abandoned somehow. When a person had all these teachers now, he didn't get taken care of the same way, even though six was more than one. Arithmetic went out the door when we walked in. And we saw girls now, but they weren't the same girls we used to know because we couldn't talk to them anymore, not the same way we used to, certainly not to Sandy, even though she was my neighbor, too. Not even to her. She just played the piano all the time. And there were words, oh there were words in junior high school, and we wanted to know what they were, and how a person did them—that's what school was supposed to be for. Only, in junior high school, school wasn't school, everything was backward-like. If you went up to a teacher and said the word to try and find out what it meant you got in trouble for saying it. So we didn't. And we figured it must have been that way about other stuff, too, so we never said anything about anything—we weren't stupid.

But my friend Sergio and I, we solved junior high school. We would come home from school on the bus, put our books away, change shoes, and go across the highway to the arroyo. It was the one place we were not supposed to go. So we did. This was, after all, what junior high had at least shown us. It was our river, though, our personal Mississippi, our friend from long back, and it was full of stories and all the branch forts we had built in it when we were still the Vikings of America, with our own symbol, which we had carved everywhere, even in the sand, which let the water take it. That was good, we had decided; whoever was at the end of this river would know about us.

At the very very top of our growing lungs, what we would do down there was shout every dirty word we could think of, in every combination we could come up with, and we would yell about girls, and all the things we wanted to do with them, as loud as we could—we didn't know what we wanted to do with them, just things—and we would yell about teachers, and how we loved some of them, like Miss Crevelone, and how we wanted to dissect some of them, making signs of the cross, like priests, and we would yell this stuff over and over because it felt good, we couldn't explain why, it just felt good and for the first time in our lives there was nobody to tell us we couldn't. So we did.

One Thursday we were walking along shouting this way, and the railroad, the Southern Pacific, which ran above and along the far side of the arroyo, had dropped a grinding ball down there, which was, we found out later, a cannonball thing used in mining. A bunch of them were put in a big vat which turned around and crushed the ore. One had been dropped, or thrown—what do caboose men do when they get bored—but it got down there regardless and as we were walking along yelling about one girl or another, a particular Claudia, we found it, one of these things, looked at it, picked it up, and got very very excited, and held it and passed it back and forth, and we were saying "Guythisis, this is, geeGuythis . . .": we had this perception about nature then, that nature is imperfect and that round things are perfect: we said "GuyGodthis is perfect, thisisthis is perfect, it's round, round and heavy, it'sit's the best thing we'veeverseen. Whatisit?" We didn't know. We just knew it was great. We just, whatever, we played with it, held it some more.

And then we had to decide what to do with it. We knew, because of a lot of things, that if we were going to take this and show it to anybody, this discovery, this best thing, was going to be taken

160

away from us. That's the way it works with little kids, like all the polished quartz, the tons of it we had collected piece by piece over the years. Junior high kids too. If we took it home, my mother, we knew, was going to look at it and say "throw that dirty thing in the, get rid of it." Simple like, like that. "But ma it's the best thing I" "Getridofit." Simple.

So we didn't. Take it home. Instead, we came up with the answer. We dug a hole and we buried it. And we marked it secretly. Lots of secret signs. And came back the next week to dig it up and, we didn't know, pass it around some more or something, but we didn't find it. We dug up that whole bank, and we never found it again. We tried.

Sergio and I talked about that ball or whatever it was when we couldn't find it. All we used were small words, neat, good. Kid words. What we were really saying, but didn't know the words, was how much that ball was like that place, that whole arroyo: couldn't tell anybody about it, didn't understand what it was, didn't have a name for it. It just felt good. It was just perfect in the way it was that place, that whole going to that place, that whole junior high school lion. It was just iron-heavy, it had no name, it felt good or not, we couldn't take it home to show our mothers, and once we buried it, it was gone forever.

The ball was gone, like the first reasons we had come to that arroyo years earlier, like the first time we had seen the arroyo, it was gone like everything else that had been taken away. This was not our first lesson. We stopped going to the arroyo after not finding the thing, the same way we had stopped going there years earlier and headed for the mountains. Nature seemed to keep pushing us around one way or another, teaching us the same thing every place we ended up. Nature's gang was tough that way, teaching us stuff.

When we were young we moved away from town, me and my family. Sergio's was already out there. Out in the wilds. Or at least the new place seemed like the wilds since everything looks bigger the smaller a man is. I was five, I guess, and we had moved three miles north of Nogales where we had lived, three miles north of the Mexican border. We looked across the highway in one direction and there was the arroyo; hills stood up in the other direction. Mountains, for a small man.

When the first summer came the very first place we went to was

161

of course the one place we weren't supposed to go, the arroyo. We went down in there and found water running, summer rain water mostly, and we went swimming. But every third or fourth or fifth day, the sewage treatment plant that was, we found out, upstream, would release whatever it was that it released, and we would never know exactly what day that was, and a person really couldn't tell right off by looking at the water, not every time, not so a person could get out in time. So, we went swimming that summer and some days we had a lot of fun. Some days we didn't. We found a thousand ways to explain what happened on those other days, constructing elaborate stories about the neighborhood dogs, and hadn't she, my mother, miscalculated her step before, too? But she knew something was up because we'd come running into the house those days, wanting to take a shower, even—if this can be imagined—in the middle of the day.

That was the first time we stopped going to the arroyo. It taught us to look the other way. We decided, as the second side of summer came, we wanted to go into the mountains. They were still mountains then. We went running in one summer Thursday morning, my friend Sergio and I, into my mother's kitchen, and said, well, what'zin, what'zin those hills over there—we used her word so she'd understand us—and she said nothingdon'tworryaboutit. So we went out, and we weren't dumb, we thought with our eyes to each other, ohhoshe'stryingtokeepsomethingfromus. We knew adults.

We had read the books, after all; we knew about bridges and castles and wildtreacherousraging alligatormouth rivers. We wanted them. So we were going to go out and get them. We went back that morning into that kitchen and we said "We're going out there, we're going into the hills, we're going away for three days, don't worry." She said, "All right."

"You know," I said to Sergio, "if we're going to go away for three days, well, we ought to at least pack a lunch."

But we were two young boys with no patience for what we thought at the time was mom-stuff: making sa-and-wiches. My mother didn't offer. So we got out little kid knapsacks that my mother had sewn for us, and into them we put the jar of mustard. A loaf of bread. Knivesforksplates, bottles of Coke, a can opener. This was lunch for the two of us. And we were weighed down, humped over to be strong enough to carry this stuff. But we started walking anyway, into the hills. We were going to eat berries and stuff otherwise. "Goodbye." My mom said that.

After the first hill we were dead. But we walked. My mother could still see us. And we kept walking. We walked until we got to where the sun is straight overhead, noon. That place. Where that is doesn't matter; it's time to eat. The truth is we weren't anywhere close to that place. We just agreed that the sun was overhead and that it was time to eat, and by tilting our heads a little we could make that the truth.

"We really ought to start looking for a place to eat."

"Yeah. Let's look for a good place to eat." We went back and forth saying that for fifteen minutes, making it lunchtime because that's what we always said back and forth before lunchtimes at home. "Yeah, I'm hungry all right." I nodded my head. "Yeah, I'm hungry all right too. I'm hungry." He nodded his head. I nodded my head back. After a good deal more nodding, we were ready, just as we came over a little hill. We hadn't found the mountains yet. This was a little hill.

And on the other side of this hill we found heaven.

It was just what we thought it would be.

Perfect. Heaven was green, like nothing else in Arizona. And it wasn't a cemetery or like that because we had seen cemeteries and they had gravestones and stuff and this didn't. This was perfect, had trees, lots of trees, had birds, like we had never seen before. It was like "The Wizard of Oz," like when they got to Oz and everything was so green, so emerald, they had to wear those glasses, and we ran just like them, laughing, laughing that way we did that moment, and we went running down to this clearing in it all, hitting each other that good way we did.

We got down there, we kept laughing, we kept hitting each other, we unpacked our stuff, and we started acting "rich." We knew all about how to do that, like blowing on our nails, then rubbing them on our chests for the shine. We made our sandwiches, opened our Cokes, got out the rest of the stuff, the salt and pepper shakers. I found this particular hole and I put my coke right into it, a perfect fit, and I called it my Coke-holder. I got down next to it on my back, because everyone knows that rich people eat lying down, and I got my sandwich in one hand and put my other arm around the Coke in its holder. When I wanted a drink, I lifted my neck a little, put out my lips, and tipped my Coke a little with the crook of my elbow. Ah.

We were there, lying down, eating our sandwiches, laughing, throwing bread at each other and out for the birds. This was heaven. We were laughing and we couldn't believe it. My mother *was* keeping something from us, ah ha, but we had found her out. We even found water over at the side of the clearing to wash our plates with—we had brought plates. Sergio started washing his plates when he was done, and I was being rich with my Coke, and this day in summer was right.

When suddenly these two men came, from around a corner of trees and the tallest grass we had ever seen. They had bags on their backs, leather bags, bags and sticks.

We didn't know what clubs were, but I learned later, like I learned about the grinding balls. The two men yelled at us. Most specifically, one wanted me to take my Coke out of my Coke-holder so he could sink his golf ball into it.

Something got taken away from us that moment. Heaven. We grew up a little bit, and couldn't go backward. We learned. No one had ever told us about golf. They had told us about heaven. And it went away. We got golf in exchange.

We went back to the arroyo for the rest of that summer, and tried to have fun the best we could. We learned to be ready for finding the grinding ball. We loved it, and when we buried it we knew what would happen. The truth is, we didn't look so hard for it. We were two boys and twelve summers then, and not stupid. Things get taken away.

We buried it because it was perfect. We didn't tell my mother, but together it was all we talked about, till we forgot. It was the lion.

nominated by David Wilk

THE CIRCUMCISION RITES OF THE TORONTO STOCK EXCHANGE

by CRAD KILODNEY

from THE ORANGE BOOK (Charnel House)

AMONG THE MANY SECRET RITUALS that take place within the Toronto Stock Exchange, none is more complex or mysterious than the ritual of circumcision. Outside of the financial district, few persons are even aware that such a ritual exists. Only a very few learned men have been privileged to observe and document it.

It is not until the apprentice or novice on the floor of the T.S.E. becomes circumcised that he is entitled to call himself a trader in full standing *(moran)* and enjoy full freedom of action, a freedom which he uses especially for erotic purposes. Uncircumcised, he cannot marry; the same is true for young females of a brokerage house working within the Exchange. It is only through circumcision that the brokerage house acknowledges them to be sexually mature adults. Therefore, nothing is more desired by both sexes. The young male novice *(layoni)* becomes a man *(moran)*; the girl *(kyepta)* becomes a woman *(osotya)*.

Despite the universality of circumcision among all brokerage houses, the reason for it is obscure. If one asks a partner of the firm about it, he merely says, *"Zamani!"* which means "since ancient times." In answer to my question on the circumcision of females, a senior partner of Hector M. Chisholm said to me, "We don't want

165

anything hanging like that in the front of our women!" And he made a disdainful gesture with his little finger, signifying the clitoris.

But it seems to me that the fundamental reason for circumcision among young men is to make the act of intercourse easier. And of secondary significance is the period of convalescence following the operation, when the youth can be initiated into the mysteries of the stock market.

Among girls, the reason may be that of removing the erogenous zone, thereby ensuring that they will be perpetually unsatisfied and therefore more fit for the fast track of Exchange life.

The circumcision rites are conducted secretly approximately every four years and, in the case of both males and females, before their 26th birthday. The candidates then convene for that solemn act, which is undertaken as a group, but on different days for males and females.

There is much dancing the evening before the circumcision of the males. The *layoni* appear in colorful leisure suits. They have had their hair styled and their facial hair shaved. They dance, leap and hop until they are exhausted.

Very early the next morning the male candidates appear in pompous dress—grey three-piece suits and grey or black ties. They have just returned from the lake, where the circumcisor *(materyot)* sent them to bathe before sunrise. *"Lapat iun"* ("Go wash it"), he has said to them. Now they return to the Exchange, where circumcision always takes place. No uncircumcised male, no female, and no animal may be present. The *morans, boyot* (old men or senior partners), and those to be circumcised gather around the "burning pyre," represented by any small, smokeless flame, such as a can of Sterno. Now a senior partner approaches. He questions each novice as to whether he has ever had sexual intercourse with a circumcised woman (the uncircumcised do not count). Then the poor fellow must confess. He must look into the face of the electronic ticker tape, his god. Great suspense predominates. The excited *morans* listen to this confession because there is always the possibility that one of them will publicly learn that he has been cuckolded. The candidate for circumcision behaves quite ungallantly, without pangs of conscience over the woman he seduced. If he likes her, he says something like, "I took her to a drive-in and did it in the back seat." But if he is indifferent to her,

166

he says something like, "I went to a party, and she called me to her, although I did not want to at all." It is understandable why wives or girlfriends of the *morans*, or any other females in the Exchange, even those that prostitute themselves, have nothing to do with *layoni* in the face of such a scandal.

An iron staff, the *medyeuta*, resembling a chisel, has been glowing in the fire. On a bench a veteran trader or a partner of the firm mixes crushed chalk with milk, which is then rubbed onto the head of the candidate, who crouches on the floor. Now comes the *materyot* with his assistant, a junior partner. They seize the drawn-out foreskin; the one holds it fast, the other takes the glowing iron and passes it around the foreskin till it falls off, charred. The assistant throws it away while the master applies fat from the udder of a cow to the wound. During the whole operation the candidate must not cry out, or it would cost him his career. His salary would be permanently frozen at the entry level, and he would henceforth be the object of ridicule.

Now all the newly-circumcised (*tarusyot*) withdraw into the *mendjet*, a small, sparsely furnished room, to sing the Circumcision Song:

> *ya . . . ya . . . pa-ku-le-ro ma*
> *o le ree ya*
> *ya pa-ku-le-ro ma o le ree*
> *o ye a ye . . . ya*
> *ya guangue ya . . . ya guangua*

The *mendjet* becomes the abode of the circumcised for several weeks. A courier brings them their food: soft drinks, donuts, and fried chicken. In the meantime, their wounds heal.

The *materyot* remains with them. He initiates them into all the mysteries of Business and how to survive in a jungle of wolves and snakes.

After his convalescence, the *tarusyot* finally leaves the *mendjet*. Many questions must now be put to him. He is taken to the lake. One of the *morans* will ask, "What is a put?" "An option to sell," is the answer. "Indeed, how he knows," say his rejoicing friends. (Another possible question might be: "What resembles the sound of the vagina during coitus?" But this has not been asked in recent years.) Now he goes into the water, where the *morans* purify him with cow urine, examine his healed organ, and depart. He follows them back to the Exchange, where there is dancing and merriment. He is now wearing his "badge of manhood," which he will wear henceforth at all times. Women gather around and ask joyously, "Where is the trader of So-and-so?" naming his brokerage firm. He is pointed out to them.

At nightfall the ceremony may be continued in a private club or hotel suite at the discretion of each brokerage firm, although some celebrants may remain at the Exchange overnight, drinking and carousing.

The next morning the new *moran* is a free man and has the day off. He goes to the "old men's house," the private club of the senior partners, or a hotel suite hired to serve the same purpose. If he has no sweetheart, a girl is sent to him—usually a typist or file clerk. She utters the standard greeting, "I have come to give you my vagina."

The next day his best friend visits him at home, and he (the *tarusyot*) slaughters a goat for him. The day after that, the friend returns the favor by slaughtering a goat for him. They eat. The goats' stomachs are given to his mother.

The Toronto Stock Exchange is the only exchange in North America where circumcision is still accomplished by burning; everywhere else the knife is used for this purpose.

The circumcision of the girls *(kyeptas)* is an equally complex ritual. Those to be circumcised are obliged to have their hair styled, buy new clothes, and wear numerous plastic accessories. But the ornamentation is not yet complete. Each female candidate will be given the traditional thigh bells, or *kurkuriet*. These massive iron bells, six inches long, resemble half-open pods, within which several iron peas may be seen. The *kurkuriet* are attached to the thigh with a strap—preferably three on each leg. The more bells, the louder the noise made by the rhythmic shaking and stamping.

There is wild dancing on the floor of the Exchange the night before the circumcision of the girls. Both men and women appear in their most magnificent costumes. The men may appear in the traditional calf-skin *(goysit)* covering the buttocks, and the high baboon-skin cap. The women may wear huge earrings and a profusion of plastic bracelets; they anoint their faces with oil, so that the color of their make-up runs down their faces.

168

Late that night, each female candidate must be prepared for the circumcision to take place the next morning. An old woman, usually an executive secretary or sometimes the wife of the Chairman, brings the stinging nettles *(siwot)* of the species *Girardinia condensata*. The girl sits on a stool and spreads her legs; her genitalia are examined. If it is found that she is a virgin, she is kissed by the women. All are happy. Indeed, her immediate superior even has a cow slaughtered when he hears the good news! The nettles are now applied to the clitoris. It burns terribly, but the girl bears the pain with unbelievable patience. The clitoris swells and becomes large.

Early in the morning, an experienced woman, the female *materyot*, approaches the girl, who is crouching on the floor with her legs outspread. In a small grill over the fire is a glowing coal. The *materyot* places the coal on a spoonlike instrument and applies it to the swollen clitoris, which gradually chars. The girl endures this pain without a moan, for her thoughts are of the fast track and the sexual liberties she may take to advance her position. Her closest girlfriends now fetch garlands of dollar bills and hang them around her neck. Then the girl retires to begin a sick leave of four weeks. She is now called *tarusyot*, the newly-circumcised. But the guests dance on, all day long, singing their own circumcision song, *"Eyo leyo leyo la,"* and stamping their feet madly.

During her period of seclusion in the home of a girlfriend or older woman, the *tarusyot* will be attended by her girlfriends. She must wear a tight leather dress *(nyargit)* and a large three-cornered cowl *(soynet)*, which covers her entire head and which has two peep holes. No man may look at her at this time. As in the case of the young men, the girl receives instruction by her *materyot* in the secrets of Business and Sex.

When her wound is healed, a concluding feast is then given, which is celebrated very ceremoniously by the women employees of the brokerage firm and the Exchange. The highlight of this ceremony is the entrance of the lion, which has been brought into the Exchange by several older women. A jug of beer is offered to the lion. The old women stroke it to make it tame. All this time, the newly-circumcised girls have been kept in a dark room. The lion is brought into the room and begins to growl, causing the girls great fright. Now they must eat all the insects off the lion and sip his urine from the floor. Then the old women lead the lion out.

The circumcised girls believe in the authenticity of the lion with full seriousness. When I tried to hint politely that the "lion" was merely an Exchange official wearing a costume, the *tarusyots* almost wept because of the "dirty lie" I was telling about their grand experience. Consequently, I had to desist from further explanations.

The ritual is concluded by the giving of money and shares of stock to the *tarusyots* by the old men of the brokerage firms. Beer has been brought in, and now both men and women participate in the picturesque Beer Dance. Pressed close to each other, the married women from the various firms move in a circle, beating the leather parts of their clothing and thus giving a clapping accompaniment to their song. The dance is concluded by the *tarusyots*, who, in honor of the occasion, have painted themselves heavily with make-up.

Despite the pain that they have endured, both young men and women will always remember their day of circumcision as a sublime event and a joyous occasion.

From time to time, legal and medical authorities have attempted to put a stop to the circumcision rites of the Toronto Stock Exchange, but the combined power of the brokerage firms and the deep sense of tradition that pervades Exchange life make it unlikely that these attempts will ever succeed.

There can be no doubt that these rites, which may seem "barbaric" to the layman who is unconnected to the business world, serve an important social purpose and contribute to the stability and orderliness that one notices everywhere as one walks through the peaceful, shady valleys of the financial district.

nominated by Charnel House

BIG BROTHER IS YOU, WATCHING

by MARK CRISPIN MILLER

from THE GEORGIA REVIEW

> *The only comprehension left to thought is horror at the incomprehensible. Just as the reflective onlooker, meeting the laughing placard of a toothpaste beauty, discerns in her flashlight grin the grimace of torture, so from every joke, even from every pictorial representation, he is assailed by the death sentence on the subject, which is implicit in the universal triumph of subjective reason.*
>
> —*T. W. Adorno*, Minima Moralia

IN HIS COMMENCEMENT ADDRESS to the class of 1984 at Texas A&M University, Vice President George Bush, making a familiar point, invoked George Orwell's *Nineteen Eighty-Four*. Mr. Bush spoke of the novel as a prophecy that will not come true as long as America and her allies "stand together, firm and strong, in defense of our freedom." As he and/or his speechwriter(s) would have it, the novel is simply an attack on Soviet domination: "Big Brother may be all-powerful in Havana, but the United States will not stand idly by while Big Brother tries to extend his power and influence over our freedom-loving neighbors in Central America."[1]

This bellicose interpretation of *Nineteen Eighty-Four* is nearly as old as the novel itself. When it first appeared, some American rightists hailed *Nineteen Eighty-Four* as a vivid anticommunist

---

[1] "Bush Says U.S. Can Avert '1984' if Allies Are Firm," *The New York Times*, 7 May 1984, B8.

171

manifesto—a misreading that Orwell himself publicly repudiated. But even if Orwell had not thus tried to defend his text against its seizure by the right, he had already protested any such warlike appropriation, since *Nineteen Eighty-Four* is itself a satire of the same cold-war mentality that seeks to use it as a weapon. Vowing to oppose "Big Brother" by keeping the U.S. permanently mobilized, Vice President Bush spoke exactly like the fictitious managers of Big Brother's own regime, who also strive to keep their system "firm and strong" against the current enemy. Nor is the similarity merely general, but extends down to the vice president's striking misuse of specific terms. His proclamation that the governments of, say, El Salvador, Chile, Peru, and Guatemala, are "freedom-loving" recalls the perverse official language of Oceania, where the "Ministry of Peace" makes war, the "Ministry of Love" takes care of torture, and so on.

However, Orwell's novel does not simply expose the blindness of its own anticommunist boosters but illuminates the whole system that threatens to eternalize such blind aggressiveness, which comes automatically from both the "left" and "right," or East and West. *Nineteen Eighty-Four* describes a triune world of endless opposition and no difference: Oceania, allied with Eastasia or Eurasia, keeps itself "firm and strong" against Eurasia or Eastasia, which, allied with Oceania, does exactly the same thing. And, as the megastates within the text are made identical by their very opposition, so do the megastates outside the text resemble one another through the very belligerence that keeps them separated. This has been demonstrated, absurdly and yet fittingly, by the official function of *Nineteen Eighty-Four* itself in both the U.S. and the U.S.S.R., each power using it against the other. Just as, according to George Bush, Big Brother is "all-powerful in Havana," so, according to a major Soviet political journal, *Nineteen Eighty-Four* indicts not the Soviet system but "bourgeois society, bourgeois civilization, bourgeois democracy—in which, as [Orwell] feared, the poisonous roots of antihumanism, all-devouring militarism, and oppression have today thrust up truly monstrous shoots."[2] In the U.S., there is "complete uniformity of view on all subjects," and "a continuous frenzy of hatred for foreign enemies

[2] "Soviet Says Orwell's Vision Is Alive in the U.S.," *The New York Times*, 8 Jan. 1984, p. 8.

172

and internal traitors"—horrors represented and perpetuated by the very writing that thus decries them.

Thus Orwell's text, which captures the static agony of a world at once divided and unvaried, has been used to intensify the very face-off that it so memorably conveys. Perhaps this is inevitable. The enormous system that *Nineteen Eighty-Four* satirizes is surely too compelling to permit its managers to read with the care and detachment that might allow self-criticism. However, it is not only our vice president who has recently betrayed an inability to read *Nineteen Eighty-Four*. Throughout 1984, the novel has been at once celebrated and neglected in America, its significance for our society entirely denied in most of the TV newscasts, corporate advertisements, magazine articles, and other statements concocted especially for this Orwell memorial year. According to this barrage, *Nineteen Eighty-Four* is not satiric, not even literary, but an attempt at straightforward prophecy, like the works of Nostradamus, and therefore meant to be measured literally against the present. Because the present is obviously much preferable to the novel's world, *Nineteen Eighty-Four* has been used, predictably, as the basis for hearty affirmations of the status quo.

And those, of course, who have the most invested in the status quo have also been the novel's readiest detractors. Certain corporate "advertorials," for instance, placed in many magazines and newspapers, have anxiously refused the possibility that *Nineteen Eighty-Four* might somehow pertain to here and now. "The year is here at last, one is tempted to say," begins one ad for Mobil, "so let's get on with it and let the novel rest." "Whatever merits *Nineteen Eighty-Four* has as literature," claims an ad for United Technologies, "the book has failed as prophecy." Although there is no doubt what Orwell would have thought of these mammoth corporations if he had lived to appreciate their achievements, these ads disingenuously insist that *Nineteen Eighty-Four* is only "about the dangers of big, intrusive government," "government against people." And yet, as if to protest an indictment, both ads attempt to vindicate these corporations' products—and, therefore, their existence—by extolling the liberating effects of advanced technology: "Orwell was wrong about technology. Technology has not enslaved us. It has freed us." Because of the pervasiveness and accessibility of computers, each of us is freer than ever before: "Because the chip increases our choices, it ensures individuality."

But the refusal to admit that *Nineteen Eighty-Four* might in any way pertain to our own lives reflects and bolsters an ideology that extends well beyond the confines of big business. Arthur Schlesinger, Jr., writing in *The New York Times Book Review* (25 September 1983), reacted with a telling shrillness to the suggestion that Orwell's satire might illuminate its present readers' world. "Such arguments are shallow, if not frivolous," opined the historian, who went on thus to proscribe any such interpretation: "This is what '1984' is about—not some sort of continuous, incremental evolution from what we have today, but a shattering discontinuity, a qualitative transformation, an ultimate change of phase." In an effort to bolster this remarkable assertion, Schlesinger sought next to demonstrate that totalitarianism cannot succeed, a failure that presumably invalidates the novel as anything other than a chilling fantasy. Whereas the Oceanic system seems to prevail absolutely and for good, real human beings are too wayward to permit any such political finality: "There have been countless martyrs to the unconquerable faith in life, like Winston Smith himself. Today many, like Andrei Sakharov, intrepidly affirm this faith against cruel masters."

The judgment promoted by Vice President Bush and his Soviet counterparts, by Professor Schlesinger and the Mobil Corporation, depends not just on a refusal to read Orwell's satire carefully, but on the complementary refusal, or disinclination, to read the world with equal care. That satire and this world cannot possibly be severed from each other as Schlesinger insists they must be, for no expression can wholly transcend the moment that produced it, nor can contiguous moments be neatly disjoined: Orwell's history is in his novel, and that history connects with ours.

And what are the real points of convergence between *Nineteen Eighty-Four* and 1984? Those who have labored to deny the novel's importance may have helped us toward an answer. Despite their differences in emphasis, the liberal historian and the massive business enterprises share the assumption that Orwell's vision has been superannuated by the recent efforts of enlightened minds: "Thanks to the electronic microchip and the technology that brought it into being," exults the ad for United Technologies, "1984 has not become *1984*." The ad for Mobil alludes worshipfully to "the strides society has made since Orwell's day in electronics, communication, and computerization." Professor Schlesinger invokes the ideal of Enlightenment somewhat differently. His reference to Andrei Sakharov, affirming the Russian's faith in life against cruel masters, is a depiction that suggests the heroic conceptions of Voltaire and Jefferson.

And yet it is precisely the ideal of Enlightenment that is the implicit object of Orwell's painful satire. As we shall see, *Nineteen Eighty-Four* actually illuminates the assumptions of those who have tried to dismiss it—the same assumptions, paradoxically, that must also motivate any effort to correct those dismissive readings. Because *Nineteen Eighty-Four* is not a bald prophecy—not just a simple "warning," but a subtle and demanding work of art that tells us truths about modern politics—we must read it closely, both as a literary text and as an oblique reflection on our own world. In my attempt at such a reading, I will first analyze Orwell's novel as a critique of Enlightenment (after some discussion of that inescapable impulse), and then move on to a discussion of Enlightenment as it is manifest today, for us, in the forms of advertising and TV.

The opening sentence of *Nineteen Eighty-Four* recalls some of the oldest of English poetical traditions, but only to imply that they mean nothing in the novel's world: "It was a bright cold day in April, and the clocks were striking thirteen." With its two trimiter clauses and marked caesura, the sentence initially suggests the opening couplet of a folk ballad; but then this familiar rhythmic evocation is abruptly canceled out. The line's quasi-nostalgic appeal is undercut, first of all, by the futuristic revelation that Oceanic clocks strike more than twelve. And the effect of this surprising news is reinforced by the ending's metrical dislocation, as that spondee "thirteen" falls jarringly in place of the expected monosyllable. Moreover, as with the sentence's balladic rhythm, so with its peculiar "April" day, another reference that at first seems half-familiar, then wholly alien. Despite its vaguely comforting reverberations, this "April" day does not exemplify that balmy, revivifying April sung by the English poets since Chaucer, but is strangely "bright" and "cold," suggesting that, within the world we are about to enter, such antique associations have been eliminated.

The sentence seems at first to beckon us back home, but ends by leaving us bewildered, as on a sunny morning when you think you are awake until you sense that you are dreaming it. And yet the dreamlike eeriness of this new world is merely the final consequence of the most clear-sighted practicality. In the world liberated by the Inner Party, all vestiges of literary culture—both popular and learned—have long since been discarded as fantastic nonsense. Those obsolete texts by Chaucer, Shakespeare, Eliot, and others, with their impressionistic references to "April," have now been modernized for good, made equally accessible and clear in Newspeak versions; and the rustic traditions that once sustained the ballad have also been wiped out, even from among the unenlightened proles. Moreover, in its drive to junk all preexistent myth, the Party has excised not only poetry, but even those arbitrary terms and structures once used to mark the passage of time. Whereas, before the Revolution, the clocks had been attuned to go from one to twelve twice every day, that purely customary sequence need not persist in the Party's readjusted world, where the military scheme of hours makes better sense. Indeed, the bright, cold afternoon that starts the novel may not, in fact, represent an unseasonable "day in April," but a day in what we still call "March" or "January," since the months need not refer any longer to the quaint divisions of the Roman calendar; nor, for that matter, does the Oceanic "1984" necessarily denote a point along our temporal continuum, which still refers to the legendary birth of a deity outmoded by the Party.

"It was a bright cold day in April, and the clocks were striking thirteen." This disorienting line of anti-poetry does not just alienate us, then, but implicitly refers us to the intellectual origins of all contemporary alienation. Although in effect the sentence is surrealistic, with its sudden vision of a world that seems to have gone mad, this new world actually represents the final triumph of rationality itself, the distant source of the Oceanic madness that has so disastrously betrayed it. Thus the object of Orwell's horrific satire is not any one totalitarian regime, but a necessary modern urge that has indirectly brought about all modern tyrannies, whether of the left or right, whether centralized or pluralistic. What Orwell understood with such intolerable clarity was the appalling likelihood that the most destructive modern systems have emerged, paradoxically, out of the very impulse to transcend destruction: the impulse of Enlightenment.

Orwell had begun to intuit this paradox in the late Thirties, when he wrote the controversial second part of *The Road to Wigan Pier*; and as war broke out and then persisted, his intuition seemed to be continually reconfirmed by the massive barbarism that had somehow emerged out of civilization at its latest moment: "As I write," begins "The Lion and the Unicorn," composed in 1940, "highly civilized human beings are flying overhead, trying to kill me."[3] It was the war, a conflict at once atavistic and sophisticated, that led Orwell and certain others to contemplate the long self-contradiction of Western progress. In 1943, as Orwell was making notes toward his last novel, two other observers, although working out of intellectual traditions wholly different from Orwell's, were collaborating on a brilliant, dismal essay that illuminates precisely the same ruinous process that is the implicit subject of *Nineteen Eighty-Four*. Exiled in Los Angeles, Max Horkheimer and T. W. Adorno wrote the *Dialectic of Enlightenment* to elaborate their argument that mechanistic "Progress," as Orwell had once put it, "is just as much of a swindle as reaction."[4]

For Horkheimer and Adorno, "Enlightenment" refers not simply to the optimistic moment of the *philosophes*, but to the drive, as old as civilization, toward the rational mastery of nature; or, to put it more accurately, that drive toward mastery which is itself the source and purpose of civilization. The authors subvert complacent faith in progress by disproving the absolute distinction between primitive societies and the modern world that seems to have transcended them; for the aim of men, both then and now, has been to turn the natural world into the instrument of their own power. Just as archaic groups attempted to manage the inchoate forces of their universe through priestly ritual and human sacrifice, so too have modern men, from the time of Bacon's first intellectual prospectus, worked to make the material world both useful and

3 George Orwell, "The Lion and the Unicorn: Socialism and the English Genius," in *The Collected Essays, Journalism and Letters of George Orwell*, ed. Sonia Orwell and Ian Angus, 4 vols. (New York: Harcourt, Brace and World, 1968), II, 56. (This collection will hereafter be cited as *CEJL*.)

4 "The Rediscovery of Europe," *CEJL*, II, 205. Orwell makes this point in the course of comparing the optimistic works of the Edwardian writers with the darker mood of their postwar successors. The entire passage will reproduce the specific context of the observation: "Compare almost any of H. G. Wells's Utopia books, for instance, *A Modern Utopia*, or *The Dream*, or *Men Like Gods*, with Aldous Huxley's *Brave New World*. Again it's rather the same contrast, the contrast between the overconfident and the deflated, between the man who believes innocently in Progress and the man who happens to have been born later and has therefore lived to see that Progress, as it was conceived in the early days of the aeroplane, is just as much of a swindle as reaction."

predictable, through the application of technology and scientific method. What distinguishes the historical era which we call the Enlightenment, then, is not its objectifying tendency per se, but its total rationalization of that tendency, proclaimed "under the banner of radicalism."[5] Now nature will serve those who study it most coolly and relentlessly, having freed it from the obfuscations of folk wisdom, Church doctrine, and Aristotelian dogma: "The program of the Enlightment was the disenchantment of the world; the dissolution of myths and the substitution of knowledge for fancy."

This program was conceived by its earliest proponents as a means of universal renewal, "the Effecting of all Things possible," as Francis Bacon put it in *New Atlantis*. And yet the unrestrained demythifying impulse has led us not to rejuvenation, but toward apocalypse. In its efforts to appropriate the natural world by wiping out the myths that had made it legible, the Enlightenment began a process of erasure that soon moved beyond the defunct beliefs of tribe and church to subvert *all* metaphysical conceptions, particularly those which had justified the process in the first place: "God" and then "Nature" went the way of the countless spirits that had animated the global wilderness; and now such later abstractions as "History," "Man," "the people," "social justice," etc.—also impossible to defend as strictly rational—have likewise come to seem mere sentimental fabrications. Horkheimer and Adorno argue that "for the Enlightenment, whatever does not conform to the rule of computation and utility is suspect. So long as it can develop undisturbed by any outward repression, there is no holding it. In the process, it treats its own ideas of human rights exactly as it does the older universals."

Enlightenment, then, is finally bent on leaving nothing extant but its own implicit violence. As it proceeds to blast away each of its own prior pretexts, this explosive rationality comes ever closer, not to "truth"—which category it has long since shattered—but to the open realization of its own coercive animus, purified of *all* delusions—including, finally, rationality itself. Into the ideological vacuum which it has created so efficiently there rushes its own

[5] Max Horkheimer and T. W. Adorno, *Dialectic of Enlightenment*, trans, John Cumming (New York: Continuum, 1982), p. 92.

impulse to destroy and keep destroying: Orwell perceived the same suicidal process at work in Western thought, and explicitly expressed this perception several years before elaborating it in his last novel.

In a piece written for *Time and Tide* in 1940, Orwell considers that modern moment when Christianity had finally proven indefensible. At that moment, "it was absolutely essential that the soul should be cut away," for religious belief had "become in essence a lie, a semi-conscious device for keeping the rich rich and the poor poor." The major writers of the last two centuries, the heroic standard-bearers of Enlightenment—"Gibbon, Voltaire, Rousseau, Shelley, Byron, Dickens, Stendhal, Samuel Butler, Ibsen, Zola, Flaubert, Shaw, Joyce"—proceeded to demolish what was left of that old falsehood; but the outcome of that just campaign seemed to be a total, irreversible injustice:

> For two hundred years we had sawed and sawed and sawed at the branch we were sitting on. And in the end, much more suddenly than anyone had foreseen, our efforts were rewarded, and down we came. But unfortunately there had been a little mistake. The thing at the bottom was not a bed of roses after all. It was a cesspool filled with barbed wire. (*CEJL*, II, 15)

Like Horkheimer and Adorno, Orwell saw the unprecedented horrors of mid-century not as the aberrant results of any single system of beliefs, but as the inevitable consequence of the dumb, persistent, onward urge that had devastated one belief after another. It was the relentless impulse of Enlightenment that had enabled the conceptions of the death camp, the atomic bomb, the machinery of total propaganda—each one a highly rational construction devoted to a terminal irrationality. And that autonomous rationality, Orwell believed, would quickly supersede even those new myths devised to justify it in the present. Soon such notions as "the master race" and "socialism in one country" would seem as quaint as "Harry, England, and St. George," as Enlightenment approached that perfect disillusionment whereby the Inner Party keeps itself in power: "We are different," says O'Brien, "from all the oligarchies of the past in that we know what we are doing." For

Orwell and his German counterparts, the expert atrocities of the late Enlightenment foretold the emergence of a world wholly dominated by the self-promoting urge to dominate, an urge whose only manifesto might be expressed in these infamous tautologies: "The object of persecution is persecution. The object of torture is torture. The object of power is power."

And yet Enlightenment is necessary. "We are wholly convinced," write Horkheimer and Adorno, "that social freedom is inseparable from enlightened thought" (p. xiii)—a conviction to which Orwell, too, always held firmly. Neither he nor the two Germans ever crudely called for the repeal of the Enlightenment; for if progress "is as much of a swindle as reaction," the reflexive movement backward can only end up in that same abyss toward which the automatic movement forward always speeds. Rather, these critical advocates of Enlightenment recognized that progressive thought, while indispensable, at the same time "contains the seed of the reversal universally apparent today"; and so it was the two Germans' project to salvage the best original intentions of Enlightenment, by encouraging "reflection on [its] recidivist element": "The point is . . . that Enlightenment *must consider itself,* if men are not to be wholly betrayed" (p. xv). Our responsibility now, therefore, must be to read and reread *Nineteen Eighty-Four,* not as a piece of cold-war propaganda, but as a work that might enlighten us as to the fatal consequences of Enlightenment, including the current glare of publicity that has all but blacked out the text itself.

"It was a bright cold day in April, and the clocks were striking thirteen." Having thus adroitly engineered its total severance from the past, the Party represents the demythifying mechanism of Enlightenment at its most successful; but such success amounts to failure, since the Party's efforts to annihilate the past have only reimposed it. The Party's system, founded upon the total extirpation of cruel nature, has itself reverted to cruel nature. Life in the state of Oceania is nasty, brutish, and short, a furtive passage through an urban sprawl that is as primitive and dangerous as any jungle: London swarms with "gorilla-faced guards" and "small, beetle-like" men, and even its machines suggest the wilderness which they oppose: "In the far distance a helicopter skimmed down between the roofs, hovered for an instant like a bluebottle, and darted away again with a curving flight." And, as nature has been re-created at its most inimical, so has the patriarchal God, an overseer more wrathful and alert than ever:

> The little sandy-haired woman had flung herself forward over the back of the chair in front of her. With a tremulous murmur that sounded like "My Savior!" she extended her arms toward the screen. Then she buried her face in her hands. It was apparent that she was uttering a prayer.

And even the defunct conventions of poetry reemerge uncannily from the mechanism that was built to obliterate them. Although "composed without any human intervention whatever on an instrument known as a versificator," the lines sung continually by the washerwoman outside Charrington's shop repeat that strangely inexpungible allusion: "It was only an 'opeless fancy,/ It passed like an Ipril dye. . . ."

Thus Enlightenment hurries forward toward the very state from which it flees, a grand pattern that recurs in small and subtle ways throughout the novel, just as it defines the general structure of the narrative itself. As Winston Smith helplessly observes, "the end was contained in the beginning." Therefore the fateful number "101" not only designates the room wherein the hero relapses forever into primal incoherence but also symbolizes all such reversion—the terminal arrival at the point of origin. And this process is not only temporal, but spatial and psychological as well, informing every movement and every thought with an absoluteness that conveys, more poignantly than any dissertation, the full horror of whatever is "totalitarian." In Oceania there is no possible escape from Oceania, only continual rediscoveries of Oceania where one least expects it. "It was a bright cold day in April. . . ." Although this April seems at first to proffer a venerable pastoral solace, it is merely one more of the Party's inventions, a term irrelevant to that April known before the Revolution; and so this "day in April" is as "bright" and "cold" as "the place where there is no darkness," another promised refuge that turns out to have been devised by the very forces from which it seemed at first to offer sanctuary. And so it is with "the Brotherhood," with Charrington's retreat, with "Charrington" himself.

And, as there is no refuge for the novel's hero, neither is the hero himself a solid refuge for the novel's readers; for even Winston Smith embodies that cruel force which he ostensibly opposes. Like the "April" day that chills him, he represents an exception that turns out to be the rule:

> It was a bright cold day in April, and the clocks were striking thirteen. Winston Smith, his chin nuzzled into his breast in an effort to escape the vile wind, slipped quickly through the glass doors of Victory Mansions, though not quickly enough to prevent a swirl of gritty dust from entering along with him.

Although until his "reintegration" Winston Smith is clearly different from the rest of Oceania, it would be a sentimental overstatement to insist that, once the Party has hollowed him out, it has extinguished the world's last sturdy subject. Even at first, "the last man in Europe" is already losing his fragile selfhood, which is entirely contingent on his furtive, doomed refusal to accept the status quo. The figure who "slipped quickly through the glass doors of Victory Mansions" already seems as insubstantial as a breeze; whereas, conversely, that "swirl of gritty dust," by "entering along with him," seems to walk in on human legs. However, this first image of the hero implies not just that he is losing his tenuous uniqueness and coherence, but that he loses them precisely in attempting to retain them, since it is in making "an effort to escape the vile wind" that Winston Smith seems to turn into mere wind himself.

Until his final degradation, Winston Smith is repeatedly undone by this same paradox, as his very efforts to escape or to combat the Party become themselves the proof of his inviolable membership. In starting a diary, he deliberately commits what is probably a capital offense against the Party; and yet the first result of this dissident gesture is an effusion of perfect orthodoxy, enthusiastic praise for an atrocious war film seen the night before. Similarly, after his first sexual encounter with Julia, he realizes that the same belligerent coldness had entered into even this forbidden pleasure, thereby undoing it: "Their embrace had been a battle, the climax a victory. It was a blow struck against the Party. It was a political act." And his most explicit act of defiance—his promise to O'Brien that he will commit whatever subversive crimes "the

Brotherhood" requires of him—only demonstrates the futility of his ardent opposition, which makes him sound less like the Party's clear-sighted enemy than like one of its deluded founders: "You are prepared to give your lives?" "Yes." "You are prepared to commit murder?" "Yes." "To commit acts of sabotage which may cause the death of hundreds of innocent people?" "Yes." And so on, with the hero recalling those steeliest revolutionaries of the past, whose self-discipline prepared the way not for some hoped-for earthly paradise but for the enlightened Party that would vaporize them.

In opposing the Party, Winston Smith approximates it, because the Party has arisen from the same impulse that motivates his opposition: the impulse of Enlightenment. Having long since disabused itself of every metaphysical distraction, the Party not only sees all, but—more frighteningly—sees through all. What makes the Party's gaze so devastating, then, is not just its sweep, enabled by the telescreens, but its penetration. The Party sees through anyone who would see through the Party, because the Party has seen through itself already, demythifying itself—not to defeat itself, of course, but to make itself eternal. In struggling to see through the Party, therefore, Winston Smith inadequately emulates it. Each of his rebellious actions puts him in the ludicrous position of clumsily anticipating the system that he wants to terminate. Whether surreptitiously writing, defiantly rutting, or conspiring to subvert an odious regime, he merely reenacts old battles long since fought and won by the Enlightenment on its way to Ingsoc.

Nor does the Party thus superannuate only its opponents. In its relentless onward thrust, sooner or later it simultaneously by-passes and exterminates everyone above ground level, whether they hate the Party, zealously applaud it, or vacuously go about their business: Syme is vaporized, despite his exemplary commitment to Enlightenment linguistics, because, Winston thinks, "he sees too clearly and speaks too plainly"; but then Parsons too is vaporized—for "thoughtcrime," although he seems to have no thoughts.

To describe the Party only as a force that indiscriminately kills, however, is to mistake its sway for simple tyranny, like the reign of Caligula or of Henry VIII; the Party's sway is total, at once more subtle and extensive than the rule of any mere dictator, however bloodthirsty. For it is not the Oceanic bloodshed per se that proves

183

the Party's destructiveness, but the object of that bloodshed: the extinction of all resistant subjectivity. As Orwell put it in "Lear, Tolstoy and the Fool," it makes no difference whether one's would-be oppressors work cruelly or seductively, since in either case their intention toward the subject is to erase him in the name of their own power, to "get inside his brain and dictate his thoughts for him in the minutest particulars." In Oceania, the victim is extinguished long before his heart is stopped by force, or even if it never is, since, even while still breathing, that victim has already become a mere repetition of the state that may or may not have him shot, redundantly, one day. Thus Syme, "a tiny creature," is nothing more than the linguistic diminution that consumes him; and Parsons, wet and energetic, is only a particle of the general flood. Once vaporized, therefore, these nonentities are still no less extant than those model citizens who have survived them—Winston's wife, for instance, without "a thought in her head that was not a slogan," or the functionary whom Winston hears "quack-quack-quacking" at lunch, each official phrase "jerked out very rapidly, and, as it seemed, all in one piece, like a line of type cast solid."

If all of these blank members of the Outer Party have succumbed to the state's hollowing process, then perhaps the members of the Inner Party, the supervisors of that process, have not themselves been emptied by it: O'Brien, a representative of that invisible elite, does seem somehow to stand above the universal nullity—or so the hero thinks, yearning desperately for some communion with this ostensible exception, who "had the appearance of being a person that you could talk to, if somehow you could cheat the telescreens and get him alone." It is O'Brien's curiously aristocratic mien that excites this vague hope: his "peculiar grave courtesy," an "urbane manner" that contradicts his "prizefighter's physique." Winston Smith is heartened by O'Brien's strange detachment, his air of irony and secret knowledge, which suggests a sympathetic rebel hidden deep within the oligarch.

And yet O'Brien too is wholly a microcosm of the system that has both empowered and undone him. "So ugly yet so civilized," he embodies Oceania itself, or rather, that process of Enlightenment whereby Oceania has been forced forward to its origins. The hero has misread him absolutely. The discrepancy between O'Brien's coarse bulk and smooth deportment is not the sign of some dialectical potential, as Winston Smith had assumed, but, on the

184

contrary, just another instance of the same final contradiction that has arrested the whole world, its managers included. O'Brien's air of ironic detachment, in which the hero had discerned a promise of transcendence, is in fact the deadliest of all the Inner Party's secret weapons. "More even than of strength, [O'Brien] gave an impression of confidence and of an understanding tinged with irony." It is through relentless irony that the Party subverts anyone who, even inwardly, tries to resist its gaze.

Long before they have seized Winston Smith, the Party leaders have already neutralized his dissidence through derisive imitation, thereby transforming his struggle into an empty joke for their own unhappy entertainment. Since O'Brien himself helped to write the book attributed to Goldstein, that "heavy black volume"—Winston's Bible—turns out to be a satire; O'Brien's first encounter with the hero, in "the long corridor at the Ministry," is an implicit parody of the hero's first encounter with Julia in the same place. And the gentle "Mr. Charrington" is also an ironic spectacle, meant to draw the hero out—not to entrap him (an unnecessary step in lawless Oceania) but to make his desire laughable. But even if the Inner Party had never bothered to set the hero up for ridicule, it would still have played him for a laugh, simply by looking on, unseen and delighted, at the torment which he thought was private.

More fundamentally than by its instruments of torture, then, the Party is made mighty by its own mimetic subtlety and keen spectatorship—the weapons of pure irony, which is necessarily the attitudinal vehicle and expression of Enlightenment. Analogous to Enlightenment and fostered by it, pure irony denudes the world of every value, devastating—just with a little smile and deft repetition—whatever person, concept, feeling, belief, or tradition it encounters, until there is nothing left but the urge to ironize. And so the ironist, at last contemptuous even of the values that had previously bolstered his contempt, is forced to continue being ironic, because that attitude is all that can distinguish him from the nullity that underlies and enables it. Such an attitude depends, however, on the persistence of objects worthy of derision, even if all such objects have already been wiped out by enlightened thought and ridicule. The ironist must therefore revive anachronistic postures, reinvent the enemies long since put to rest, or else become depleted. Thus the ironist is forced to follow the ruinous

185

trajectory of Enlightenment, succumbing to his own process of erasure and in that process merely reevoking the objects which he had intended to destroy.

Posing as a conspirator, O'Brien "filled the glasses and raised his own glass by the stem. 'What shall it be this time?' he said, still with the same faint suggestion of irony. 'To the confusion of the Thought Police? To the death of Big Brother? To humanity? To the future?' " Only later do we realize that these apparent exhortations are nothing more than sardonic little jokes: O'Brien is sadistically equivocating, since—as he knows already—"the death of Big Brother" is impossible, "the confusion of the Thought Police" redundant, and "humanity" an essence that he means not to vindicate but to extinguish in "the future" (which, we learn eventually, O'Brien sees as "a boot stamping on a human face—forever"). Thus the hero's cherished, vague ideals are played for laughs by the resolute O'Brien; yet for all his resoluteness, O'Brien is, without the selfhood which he mimics, nothing. Similarly, once Winston's guardian agent doffs his excellent disguise as "Mr. Charrington," he at once regresses into "a member of the Thought Police": alert, hostile, and anonymous, like the Party that deploys him.

The obsessive thoroughness with which the Party re-creates what it purports to have transcended attests to a distorted longing for it. Although intended as ironic, the spectacle of Mr. Charrington and his shop is so fully and convincingly detailed, and the agent's performance so finely nuanced, that the actor and directors must unknowingly desire the past which they have parodied so expertly. And when O'Brien finally reveals his true identity (or nonidentity) to Winston Smith in the actual "place where there is no darkness," the ambiguity of his reply also suggests that his irony is itself an expression of the desire which it keeps cruelly mimicking:

> "They've got you too!" [Winston] cried.
> "They got me a long time ago," said O'Brien with a mild, almost regretful irony.

What the Party leaders laugh at in their victim is not a desire which they themselves have transcended but a desire which they themselves still feel and which they express pervertedly through their permanent campaign against it. Even in this perversion Winston Smith resembles and anticipates them. At the beginning of the novel, we recognize the hero's longing in his posture: "Winston Smith, his chin nuzzled into his breast in an effort to escape the vile wind," is a figure trying to evade Oceania by mothering himself, trying to escape the coldness of Enlightenment by reenacting that primal situation which Enlightenment attacks and yet restores in a warped form. Although still capable of acting on this desire, however, he is (like any other proper Oceanic citizen) both unconscious of it and, while driven by it, quick to side with every other Oceanic citizen against it—an indirect self-censure which he too carries out through ironic spectatorship.

Just after he has slipped into Victory Mansions in that revealing attitude, he writes, "only imperfectly aware of what he was setting down," an orthodox denunciation of the desire which he has just expressed out on the street, and which now continues to impel his jeering at it: "April 4th, 1984. Last night to the flicks. One very good one of a ship full of refugees being bombed somewhere in the Mediterranean." Both in the midst of this spectatorship and in recounting it, Winston Smith shares with the other members of the audience a cruel, sheltered pleasure in the methodical explosion of every figure on the screen: "a great huge fat man trying to swim away with a helicopter after him," then disappearing, torn by bullets, the "audience shouting with laughter as he sank." And yet this sadistic joy in the destruction of those fictitious "refugees" is also masochistic, as the hero unwittingly reveals in describing, still with evident approval of their fate, the next few victims, whose image expresses vividly his own desire as he has just betrayed it to us: "there was a middle-aged woman might have been a jewess sitting up in the bow with a little boy about three years old in her arms. little boy screaming with fright and hiding his head between her breasts as if he was trying to burrow right into her. . . ."

When, at the end, Winston Smith is rapt for good in credulous spectatorship, he is himself just like those refugees, a visible example of floundering and defeated opposition, shunned by all and waiting to be shot. The Inner Party is surely gratified by this atrocious spectacle—we can imagine them sitting and jeering his submersion into Oceanic nonconsciousness, just like that earlier "audience shouting with laughter as he sank." But there is no ultimate distinction between such viewers and the disintegration

187

that amuses them. In cheering the destruction of their own prototype, they cheer their own destruction. And so, in the end, all collapses into hateful liquid. Weeping "gin-soaked tears," his memory ebbing, the ex-hero is an old joke in the eyes of those who have been drenched along with him. He clings to the image of Big Brother's nonexistent face, as Enlightenment fulfills itself and humanity breaks down into a flood as vast and absolute as the flood in which all life originated.

As we leave the world of Orwell's novel dissolving into its own flux, we must turn back to our more tangible society, wherein the novel now receives so much perfunctory attention, and ask how Orwell's vision reflects on American life today. *Nineteen Eighty-Four* enables us to read with clarity not just itself but the whole current moment in which it is so widely celebrated and distorted. Orwell was, of course, not thinking of this moment in America when he conceived and wrote his novel, nor would it make sense to demonstrate a crude equation of America with Oceania. Orwell wrote not as a prophet but as an artist. Rather than simply itemize the world of *Nineteen Eighty-Four* into those details that have "come true" and those that haven't, we must discover within this satire of Enlightenment its oblique reflections on our own enlightened culture, whose continuities with Orwell's time and place demand our critical consideration. We can best begin this project of discovery by analyzing one explicit similarity between the novel's world and ours: in Oceania, as in America, the telescreens are always on, and everyone is always watching them.

The Oceanic telescreens are not actually televisual. Writing in the late Forties, Orwell could not come to know TV's peculiar quality; he conceived the telescreen, understandably, as a simple combination of radio and cinema.[6] Its sounds and images therefore suggest these parent media, which, beginning at mid-century, turned out to be alike in their capacity to drum up violent feeling.

---

[6] Horkheimer and Adorno also assumed that television would be such an amalgam, although their remarks on the emergent medium's potential suasiveness have proven more accurate than Orwell's conception, since they expected the televisual hegemony to arise out of the medium's tendency toward total homogenization, and not out of that inflammatory capacity envisioned in *Nineteen Eighty-Four*. See the *Dialectic of Enlightenment*, p. 124. For a wholly celebratory discussion of the same televisual tendency uneasily foretold by Horkheimer and Adorno, see Marshall McLuhan's remarks on TV and synesthesia in *Understanding Media* (New York: New American Library, 1964), pp. 274-75.

The telescreens' voices are abrasive and hysterical, like the mob whose regulated violence they catalyze; and the telescreens' images are also explicitly suasive, arousing primitive reactions, paradoxically, through sophisticated cinematic techniques. Ingenious tricks of Eisensteinian montage enable the telescreens to inspire extreme reactions, whether foaming hatred of this year's foe or cringing reverence for Big Brother (reactions that are fundamentally the same).

Television, on the other hand, inspires no such wildness, but is as cool and dry as the Oceanic telescreens are hot and bothered. Its flat, neutralizing vision automatically strains out those ineffable qualities wherein we recognize each other's power; nor can it, like film, reinvest its figures with such density, but must reduce all of its objects to the same mundane level. In order to overcome the muting effect of TV's essential grayness, the managers of all televisual spectacle try automatically to intensify each broadcast moment through the few sensational techniques available: extreme close-ups, marvelously heightened colors, dizzying graphics, high-pitched voices trilling choral harmonies, insistent bursts of domesticated rock 'n' roll, and the incessant, meaningless montage that includes all things, events, and persons. And yet these compensations for the medium's basic coolness merely reinforce its distancing effect. Repeatedly subjected to TV's small jolts, we become incapable of outright shock or intense arousal, lapsing into a constant, dull anxiety wherein we can hardly sense the difference between a famine and a case of body odor. The televisual montage bolsters our inability to differentiate, its spectacle of endless metamorphosis merely making all images seem as insignificant as any single image seen for hours.

Because of these formal properties, TV is casually inimical to all charisma and therefore seems an inappropriate device for any program like the Inner Party's. Televised, the "enormous face" of Big Brother would immediately lose its aura of "mysterious calm," and so those omnipresent features would appear about as menacing as Michael Jackson's. On TV, furthermore, the maniacal intensities of actual Party members would also lose their sinister allure—not by being canceled out but by coming off as overheated, alien, and silly. At those moments when his face takes on a "mad gleam of enthusiasm," even O'Brien would seem to have been bypassed, and therefore exterminated, by TV.

Thus TV would seem to be an essentially iconoclastic medium; and yet it is this inherent subversiveness toward any visible authority that has enabled TV to establish its own total rule—for it is *all* individuality that TV annihilates, either by not conveying it or by making it look ludicrous. Today's TV would therefore have suited the Party's ultimate objective perfectly. As TV would neutralize Big Brother's face and O'Brien's transports, so would it undercut the earnest idealism of Winston Smith, dismissing his indignant arguments about "the spirit of Man" by concentrating coolly on his "jailbird's face," just as O'Brien does. With its clinical or inquisitorial vision, TV appears to penetrate all masks, to expose all alibis, thereby seeming to turn the whole world into a comic spectacle of unsuccessful lying, pompous posturing, and neurotic defensiveness—behaviors that appear to be seen through the moment they are represented. It is from this apparent penetration that TV's documentary programs derive the ostensible incisiveness that makes them so engrossing: *60 Minutes, The People's Court, Real People,* and so on. And it is the need to withstand TV's derisive penetration that has dictated the peculiar self-protective mien of all seasoned televisual performers, whether they play love scenes, read the news, or seem to run the country. The muted affability and thoroughgoing smoothness that make these entertainers seem acceptable on TV also serve as a defense against its searching eye; yet by thus attempting to avoid subversion, these figures—finally interchangeable as well as evanescent—merely subvert themselves, giving up that individuality which TV would otherwise discredit.

Within the borders of its spectacle, TV continues automatically that process of Enlightenment which the Party hastens consciously—the erasure of all lingering subjectivity. Whereas the Oceanic telescreens are the mere means used by the ironists in power, our telescreens are themselves ironic, and therefore make those powerful ironists unnecessary. For it is not only *on* TV that TV thus proceeds to cancel selves; it also wields its nullifying influence out in the wide world of its impressionable viewers. Television's formal erasure of distinctness complements—or perhaps has actually fostered—a derisive personal style that inhibits all personality, a knowingness that now pervades all TV genres and the culture which those genres have homogenized. The corrosive irony emanating from the Oceanic elite has been universalized by

190

television, whose characters—both real and fictional—relentlessly inflict it on each other and themselves, defining a negative ideal of hip inertia which no living human being is able to approach too closely. For example, in situation comedies or "sitcoms"—TV's definitive creation—the "comedy" almost always consists of a weak, compulsive jeering that immediately wipes out any divergence from the indefinite collective standard. The characters vie at self-containment, reacting to every simulation of intensity, every bright idea, every mechanical enthusiasm with the same deflating look of jaded incredulity. In such an atmosphere, those already closest to the ground run the least risk of being felled by the general ridicule, and so those characters most adept at enforcing the proper emptiness are also the puniest and most passive: blasé menials, blasé wives and girlfriends, and—especially—blasé children, who, like Parsons' daughter, prove their own orthodoxy by subverting their subverted parents.

Nearly all of TV's characters—on sitcoms and in "dramas," on talk shows and children's programs—participate in this reflexive sneering, and such contemptuous passivity reflects directly on the viewer who watches it with precisely the same attitude. TV seems to flatter the inert skepticism of its own audience, assuring them that they can do no better than to stay right where they are, rolling their eyes in feeble disbelief. And yet such apparent flattery of our viewpoint is in fact a recurrent warning not to rise above this slack, derisive gaping. At first, it seems that it is only those eccentric others whom TV belittles. Each time some deadpan tot on a sitcom responds to his frantic mom with a disgusted sigh, or whenever the polished anchorman punctuates his footage of "extremists" with a look that speaks his well-groomed disapproval, or each time Johnny Carson comments on some "unusual" behavior with a wry sidelong glance into our living rooms, we are being flattered with a gesture of inclusion, the wink that tells us, "We are in the know." And yet we are the ones belittled by each subtle televisual gaze, which offers not a welcome but an ultimatum—that we had better see the joke or else turn into it.

If we see the joke, however, we are nothing, like those Oceanic viewers "shouting with laughter" at the sight of their own devastation. All televisual smirking is based on, and reinforces, the assumption that we who smirk together are enlightened past the point of nullity, having evolved far beyond whatever datedness we

191

might be jeering, whether the fanatic's ardor, the prude's inhibi-
tions, the hick's unfashionable pants, or the snob's obsession with
prestige. Thus TV's relentless comedy at first seems utterly pro-
gressive, if largely idiotic, since its butts are always the most
reactionary of its characters—militarists, bigots, sexists, martinets.
However, it is not to champion our freedom that TV makes fun of
these ostensible oppressors. On the contrary: through its derision,
TV promotes only *itself*, disvaluing not Injustice or Intolerance but
the impulse to resist TV.

Despite the butt's broad illiberality, what makes him appear
ridiculous in TV's eyes is not his antidemocratic bias but his
vestigial individuality, his persistence as a self sturdy and autono-
mous enough to sense that there is something missing from the
televisual world, and to hunger for it, although ostracized for this
desire by the sarcastic mob that watches and surrounds him. Like
Winston Smith, the butt yearns for and exemplifies the past that
brought about the present, and which the present now discredits
through obsessive mockery. Whether arrogantly giving orders,
compulsively tidying up, or longing for the good old days when
men were men, the butt reenacts the type of personality—marked
by rigidity and self-denial—that at first facilitated the extension of
high capitalism but that soon threatened to impede its further
growth. And it is just such endless growth that is the real point and
object of TV's comedy, which puts down those hard selves in order
to exalt the nothingness that laughs at them. Whereas the butt,
enabled by his discrete selfhood, pursues desires that TV cannot
gratify, we are induced, by the sight of his continual humiliation, to
become as porous, cool, and acquiescent as he is solid, tense, and
dissident, so that we might want nothing other than what TV sells
us. This is what it means to see the joke. The viewer's enlightened
laughter at those uptight others is finally the expression of his own
Oceanic dissolution, as, within his distracted consciousness, there
reverberates TV's sole imperative, which once obeyed makes the
self seem a mere comical encumbrance—the imperative of total
consumption.

Guided by its images even while he thinks that he sees through
them, the TV-viewer learns only to consume. That inert, ironic
watchfulness which TV reinforces in its audience is itself conducive
to consumption. As we watch, struggling inwardly to avoid resem-
bling anyone who might stand out as pre- or non- or anti-televisual,

we are already trying to live up, or down, to the same standard of acceptability that TV's ads and shows define collectively: the standard that requires the desperate use of all those goods and services that TV proffers, including breath mints, mouthwash, dandruff shampoos, hair conditioners, blow-dryers, hair removers, eye drops, deodorant soaps and sticks and sprays, hair dyes, skin creams, lip balms, diet colas, diet plans, lo-cal frozen dinners, bathroom bowl cleaners, floor wax, car wax, furniture polish, fabric softeners, room deodorizers, and more, and more. Out of this flood of commodities, it is promised, we will each arise as sleek, quick, compact, and efficient as a brand-new Toyota; and in our effort at such self-renewal, moreover, we are enjoined not just to sweeten every orifice and burnish every surface, but to evacuate our psyches. While selling its explicit products, TV also advertises incidentally an ideal of emotional self-management, which dictates that we purge ourselves of all "bad feelings" through continual confession and by affecting the same stilted geniality evinced by most of TV's characters (the butts excluded). The unconscious must never be allowed to interfere with productivity, and so the viewer is warned repeatedly to atone for his every psychic eruption, like Parsons after his arrest for talking treason in his sleep: " 'Thoughtcrime is a dreadful thing, old man,' he said sententiously. 'It's insidious . . . There I was, working away, trying to do my bit—never knew I had any bad stuff in my mind at all.' "

Thus, even as its programs push the jargon of "honesty" and "tolerance," forever counseling you to "be yourself," TV shames you ruthlessly for every symptom of residual mortality, urging you to turn yourself into a standard object wholly inoffensive, useful, and adulterated, a product of and for all other products. However, this transformation is impossible. There is no such purity available to human beings, whose bodies will sweat and whose instincts will rage—however expertly we work to shut them off. Even Winston Smith, as broken as he is at the conclusion, is still impelled by his desires, which the Party could not extinguish after all, since it depends on their distorted energy. For all its chilling finality, in other words, the novel's closing sentence is merely another of the Party's lies. What O'Brien cannot achieve through torture, we cannot attain through our campaigns of self-maintenance—no matter how many miles we jog, or how devotedly, if skeptically, we watch TV.

193

Like the Party, whose unstated rules no person can follow rigidly enough, TV demands that its extruded viewers struggle to embody an ideal too cool and imprecise for human emulation. And like Winston Smith, we are the victims of Enlightenment in its late phase, although it is the logic of consumption, not the deliberate machinations of some cabal, that has impoverished our world in the name of its enrichment. As the creatures of this logic, we have become our own overseers. While Winston Smith is forced to watch himself in literal self-defense, trying to keep his individuality a hard-won secret, we have been forced to watch ourselves lest we develop selves too hard and secretive for the open market. In America, there is no need for an objective apparatus of surveillance (which is not to say that none exists), because, guided by TV, we watch ourselves as if already televised, checking ourselves both inwardly and outwardly for any sign of untidiness or gloom, moment by moment as guarded and self-conscious as Winston Smith under the scrutiny of the Thought Police: "The smallest thing could give you away. A nervous tic, an unconscious look of anxiety, a habit of muttering to yourself—anything that carried with it the suggestion of abnormality, of having something to hide." Although this description refers to the objective peril of life in Oceania, it also captures the anxiety of life under the scrutiny of television. Of course, all televisual performers must abide by this same grim advice or end up canceled; but TV's nervous viewers also feel themselves thus watched, fearing the same absolute exclusion if they should ever show some sign of resisting the tremendous pressure.[7]

Television further intensifies our apprehension that we are being watched by continually assuring us that it already understands our innermost fears, our private problems, and that it even knows enough about our most intimate moments to reproduce them for us. The joy of birth is brought to us by Citicorp, the tender

[7] "Cameras and recording machines not only transcribe experience but alter its quality, giving to much of modern life the character of an enormous echo chamber, a hall of mirrors. Life presents itself as a succession of images or electronic signals, of impressions recorded and reproduced by means of photography, motion pictures, television, and sophisticated recording devices. Modern life is so thoroughly mediated by electronic images that we cannot help responding to others as if their actions—and our own—were being recorded and simultaneously transmitted to an unseen audience or stored up for close scrutiny at some later time." Christopher Lasch, *The Culture of Narcissism* (New York: Norton, 1978), p. 47.

concern of one friend for another is presented by AT&T, the pleasures of the hearth are depicted for us by McDonald's. And on any talk show or newscast, there might suddenly appear the competent psychologist, who will deftly translate any widespread discontent into his own antiseptic terms, thereby representing it as something well-known to him, and therefore harmless. As we watch TV, we come to imagine what Winston Smith eventually discovers: "There was no physical act, no word spoken aloud, that they had not noticed, no train of thought that they had not been able to infer."

Television is not the cause of our habitual self-scrutiny, however, but has only set the standard for it, a relationship with a complicated history. It is through our efforts to maintain ourselves as the objects of our anxious self-spectatorship that we consummate the process of American Enlightenment, whose project throughout this century has been the complete and permanent reduction of our populace into the collective instrument of absolute production. This project has arisen not through corporate conspiracy but as the logical fulfillment, openly and even optimistically pursued, of the imperative of unlimited economic growth. Thus compelled, the enlightened captains of production have employed the principles, and often the exponents, of modern social science, in order to create a perfect work force whose members, whether laboring on products or consuming them, would function inexhaustibly and on command, like well-tuned robots.

As the material for this ideal, Americans have been closely watched for decades: in the factory, then in the office, by efficiency experts and industrial psychologists; in the supermarkets, then throughout the shopping malls, by motivational researchers no less cunningly than by the store detectives; in the schools, and then at home, and then in bed, by an immense, diverse, yet ultimately unified bureaucracy of social workers, education specialists, and "mental health professionals" of every kind. The psychic and social mutations necessarily induced by this multiform intrusion have accomplished what its first engineers had hoped for, but in a form, and at a cost, which they could never have foreseen: Americans— restless, disconnected, and insatiable—are mere consumers, having by now internalized the diffuse apparatus of surveillance built all around them, while still depending heavily on its external forms—TV, psychologistic "counseling," "self-help" manuals, the "human potential" regimens, and other self-perpetuating therapies administered to keep us on the job.

And so the project of industrial Enlightenment has only forced us back toward the same helpless natural state that Enlightenment had once meant to abolish. Both in America and in Oceania, the telescreens infantilize their captive audience. In *Nineteen Eighty-Four* and in 1984, the world has been made too bright and cold by the same system that forever promises the protective warmth of mother love, leaving each viewer yearning to have his growing needs fulfilled by the very force that aggravates them. So it is, first of all, with Orwell's famished hero. The figure who had slipped quickly into Victory Mansions, "his chin nuzzled into his breast," had tried unknowingly to transcend the Oceanic violence by mothering himself, but then ends up so broken by that violence that he adopts its symbol as his mother: "Oh cruel, needless misunderstanding!" he exults inwardly before the image of Big Brother's face. "O stubborn, self-willed exile from the loving breast!" And, as it is with Winston Smith in his perverted ardor, so it is with every vaguely hungry TV viewer, who longs to be included by the medium that has excluded everyone, and who expects its products to fulfill him in a way that they have made impossible.

What is most disconcerting, then, about the ending of *Nineteen Eighty-Four* is not that Winston Smith has now been made entirely unlike us. In too many ways, the ex-hero of this brilliant, dismal book anticipates those TV viewers who are incapable of reading it: "In these days he could never fix his mind on any one subject for more than a few moments at a time." At this moment, Winston Smith is, for the first time in his life, not under surveillance. The motto, "Big Brother Is Watching You," is now untrue as a threat, as it has always been untrue as an assurance. And the reason why he is no longer watched is that the Oceanic gaze need no longer see through Winston Smith, because he is no longer "Winston Smith," but "a swirl of gritty dust," as primitive and transparent as the Party.

As this Smith slumps in the empty Chestnut Tree, credulously gaping, his ruined mind expertly jolted by the telescreen's managers, he signifies the terminal fulfillment of O'Brien's master plan, which expresses the intentions not only of Orwell's fictitious Party, but of the corporate entity that, through TV, contains our consciousness today: "We shall squeeze you empty, and then we shall fill you with ourselves." The Party has now done for Winston Smith what all our advertisers want to do for us, and with our general approval—answer all material needs, in exchange for the self that might try to gratify them independently, and that might have other, subtler needs as well. As a consumer, in other words, Orwell's ex-hero really has it made. "There was no need to give orders" to the waiters in the Chestnut Tree. "They knew his habits." Furthermore, he "always had plenty of money nowadays." In short, the Party has paid him for his erasure with the assurance, "We do it *all* for you." And so this grotesque before-and-after narrative ends satirically as all ads end in earnest, with the object's blithe endorsement of the very product that has helped to keep him miserable: "But it was all right, everything was all right, the struggle was finished. He had won the victory over himself. He loved Big Brother."

It is a horrifying moment; but if we do no more than wince and then forget about it, we ignore our own involvement in the horror and thus complacently betray the hope that once inspired this vision. Surely Orwell would have us face the facts. Like Winston Smith, and like O'Brien and the others, we have been estranged from our desire by Enlightenment, which finally reduces all of its proponents to the blind spectators of their own annihilation. Unlike that Oceanic audience, however, the TV viewer does not gaze up at the screen with angry scorn or piety, but—perfectly enlightened—looks down on its images with a nervous sneer which cannot threaten them and which only keeps the viewer himself from standing up. As you watch, there is no Big Brother out there watching you—not because there isn't a Big Brother, but because Big Brother is you, watching.

nominated by The Georgia Review

CHILD'S GRAVE, HALE COUNTY, ALABAMA

by JIM SIMMERMAN

from KANSAS QUARTERLY

Someone drove a two-by-four
through the heart of this hard land
that even in a good year
will notch a plow blade worthless,
snap the head off a shovel,
or bow a stubborn back.
He'd have had to steal
the wood from a local mill
or steal, by starlight, across
his landlord's farm, to worry
a fencepost out of its well
and lug it the three miles home.
He'd have had to leave his wife
asleep on a corn shuck mat,
leave his broken brogans
by the stove, to slip outside,
quiet as sin, with the child
bundled in a burlap sack.
What a thing to have to do
on a cold night in December,
1936, alone
but for a raspy wind
and the red, rock-ridden dirt

things come down to in the end.
Whoever it was pounded
this shabby half-cross
into the ground must have toiled
all night to root it so:
five feet buried with the child
for the foot of it that shows.
And as there are no words
carved here, it's likely that
the man was illiterate,
or addled with fatigue,
or wrenched simple-minded
by the one simple fact.
Or else the unscored lumber
driven deep into the land
and the hump of busted rock
spoke too plainly of his grief:
forty years layed by and still
there are no words for this.

nominated by The Kansas Quarterly

A LIBRARIAN OF ALEXANDRIA

by BARRY GOLDENSOHN

from SALMAGUNDI

She has the manuscripts of Sappho in her hand,
the personal body, not a scribe's work
but shining with her mark, Sappho's, actual.
She seals this papyrus in its own urn.

This is before Actium. She knows
the line of fire of the Roman mind,
learned in her body's long analysis.

Homer's two books, Moses' five,
their own hand, blotted and corrected,
Aeschylus and Sophocles, not one
play lost, and more Euripides
on the stupidity of Gods, and many voices
wholly lost to us whom the grammarians
did not quote, nor the invaders preserve
as mementoes of the Greek defeat.

She has buried them deep in her own earth:
the Psalms for preservation and Solomon's song.
She sways above them.

The books of the soul are dreaming underground
at their true depth, waiting to be found.

She has worked long at this, will defy
fire, time as fire, the fire in the mind,
using an Egyptian art. She has saved
all of Heraclitus, to mock him;
Aristophanes to make us sane;
of Archilochos the whole warm body.

In her white dress she is the one steady light
in the abandoned mine among the smoking lamps.
She preserves last
those that bear the real taste to the mouth
of love of tragedy—
                    kneels as she buries them—

with her face lowered in the golden tent of hair
that brushes the floor in a circle around her, she smells
her own spiced oils (that aromatic body
knows how the satyr plays)
                    —all the Satyr Plays.

nominated by Salmagundi

THE CONSOLATION OF TOUCH

by BIN RAMKE

from THE GEORGIA REVIEW

The sun in his blindness feels the way
up this wall, warming each brick by turns,
touching with lightness like my uncle's
fingers proofing his braille;

the sun in his blindness darkens
half a world at a time, turns
from the common fear oblivious, like
my uncle at home unafraid of the dark,

but afraid of a door ajar, of a chair
out of place. The sun in his blind-
ness warms the thin-skinned cheek
of my uncle asleep on the lawn, last

of his brothers alive, but first
to lose the light, to be brother
in blindness to the touching sun,
the creeping wash of senseless light.

nominated by Stanley Lindberg

THE HECTOR QUESADILLA STORY

fiction by T. CORAGHESSAN BOYLE

from THE PARIS REVIEW

HE WAS NO JOLTIN' JOE, no Sultan of Swat, no Iron Man. For one thing, his feet hurt. And God knows no legendary immortal ever suffered so prosaic a complaint. He had shinsplints too, and corns and ingrown toenails and hemorrhoids. Demons drove burning spikes into his tailbone each time he bent to loosen his shoelaces, his limbs were skewed so awkwardly his elbows and knees might have been transposed and the once-proud knot of his frijole-fed belly had fallen like an avalanche. Worse: he was old. Old, old, old, the graybeard hobbling down the rough-hewn steps of the Senate building, the Ancient Mariner chewing on his whiskers and stumbling in his socks. Though they listed his birthdate as 1942 in the program, there were those who knew better: it was way back in '54, during his rookie year for San Buitre, that he had taken Asunción to the altar, and even in those distant days, even in Mexico, twelve-year-olds didn't marry.

When he was younger—really young, nineteen, twenty, tearing up the Mexican League like a saint of the stick—his ears were so sensitive he could hear the soft rasping friction of the pitcher's fingers as he massaged the ball and dug in for a slider, fastball, or changeup. Now he could barely hear the umpire bawling the count in his ear. And his legs. How they ached, how they groaned and creaked and chattered, how they'd gone to fat! He ate too much, that was the problem. Ate prodigiously, ate mightily, ate as if there

203

were a hidden thing inside him, a creature all of jaws with an infinite trailing ribbon of gut. Huevos con chorizo with beans, tortillas, camarones in red sauce and a twelve-ounce steak for breakfast, the chicken in mole to steady him before afternoon games, a sea of beer to wash away the tension of the game and prepare his digestive machinery for the flaming machaca and pepper salad Asunción prepared for him in the blessed evenings of the home stand.

Five foot seven, one hundred eighty-nine and three-quarters pounds. Hector Hernán Jesus y María Quesadilla. Little Cheese, they called him. Cheese, Cheese, Cheesus, went up the cry as he stepped in to pinch-hit in some late inning crisis, Cheese, Cheese, Cheesus, building to a roar until Chavez Ravine resounded as if with the holy name of the Savior Himself when he stroked one of the clean line-drive singles that were his signature or laid down a bunt that stuck like a finger in jelly. When he fanned, when the bat went loose in the fat brown hands and he went down on one knee for support, they hissed and called him *Viejo*.

One more season, he tells himself, though he hasn't played regularly for nearly ten years and can barely trot to first after drawing a walk, One more. He tells Asunción too: One more, One more, as they sit in the gleaming kitchen of their house in Boyle Heights, he with his Carta Blanca, she with her mortar and pestle for grinding the golden petrified kernels of maize into flour for the tortillas he eats like peanuts. *Una más*, she mocks. What do you want, the Hall of Fame? Hang up your spikes, Hector.

He stares off into space, his mother's Indian features flattening his own as if the legend were true, as if she really had taken a spatula to him in the cradle, and then, dropping his thick lids as he takes a long slow swallow from the neck of the bottle, he says: Just the other day driving home from the park I saw a car on the freeway, a Mercedes with only two seats, a girl in it, her hair out back like a cloud, and you know what the license plate said? His eyes are open now, black as pitted olives. Do you? She doesn't. Cheese, he says. It said Cheese.

Then she reminds him that Hector Jr. will be twenty-nine next month and that Reina has four children of her own and another on the way. You're a grandfather, Hector—almost a great-grandfather if your son ever settled down. A moment slides by, filled with the light of the sad waning sun and the harsh Yucatano-dialect of the radio announcer. *Hombres* on first and third, one down. *Abuelo,* she hisses, grinding stone against stone until it makes his teeth ache. Hang up your spikes, *abuelo.*

But he doesn't. He can't. He won't. He's no grandpa with hair the color of cigarette stains and a blanket over his knees, he's no toothless old gasser sunning himself in the park—he's a big leaguer, proud wearer of the Dodger blue, wielder of stick and glove. How can he get old? The grass is always green, the lights always shining, no clocks or periods or halves or quarters, no punch-in and punch-out: This is the game that never ends. When the heavy hitters have fanned and the pitchers' arms gone sore, when there's no joy in Mudville, taxes are killing everybody and the Russians are raising hell in Guatemala, when the manager paces the dugout like an attack dog, mind racing, searching high and low for the canny veteran to go in and do single combat, there he'll be—always, always, eternal as a monument—Hector Quesadilla, utility infielder, with the .296 lifetime batting average and service with the Reds, Phils, Cubs, Royals, and L.A. Dodgers.

So he waits. Hangs on. Trots his aching legs round the outfield grass before the game, touches his toes ten agonizing times each morning, takes extra batting practice with the rookies and slumping millionaires. Sits. Watches. Massages his feet. Waits through the scourging road trips in the Midwest and along the East Coast, down to muggy Atlanta, across to stormy Wrigley and up to frigid Candlestick, his gut clenched round an indigestible cud of meatloaf and instant potatoes and wax beans, through the terrible night-games with the alien lights in his eyes, waits at the end of the bench for a word from the manager, for a pat on the ass, a roar, a hiss, a chorus of cheers and cat-calls, the marimba pulse of bat striking ball and the sweet looping arc of the clean base hit.

And then comes a day, late in the season, the homeboys battling for the pennant with the big-stick Braves and the sneaking Jints, when he wakes from honeyed dreams in his own bed that's like an old friend with the sheets that smell of starch and soap and flowers, and feels the pain stripped from his body as if at the touch of a healer's fingertips. Usually he dreams nothing, the night a blank, an erasure, and opens his eyes on the agonies of the martyr

205

strapped to a bed of nails. Then he limps to the toilet, makes a poor discolored water, rinses the dead taste from his mouth and staggers to the kitchen table where food, only food, can revive in him the interest in drawing another breath. He butters tortillas and folds them into his mouth, spoons up egg and melted jack cheese and frijoles refritos with the green salsa, lashes into his steak as if it were cut from the thigh of Kerensky, the Atlanta relief ace who'd twice that season caught him looking at a full-count fastball with men in scoring position. But not today. Today is different, a sainted day, a day on which sunshine sits in the windows like a gift of the Magi and the chatter of the starlings in the crapped-over palms across the street is a thing that approaches the divine music of the spheres. What can it be?

In the kitchen it hits him: pozole in a pot on the stove, carnitas in the saucepan, the table spread with sweetcakes, buñuelos and the little marzipan *dulces* he could kill for. *Feliz cumpleaños*, Asunción pipes as he steps through the doorway. Her face is lit with the smile of her mother, her mother's mother, the line of gift-givers descendant to the happy conquistadors and joyous Aztecs. A kiss, a *dulce* and then a knock at the door and Reina, fat with life, throwing her arms around him while her children gobble up the table, the room, their grandfather, with eyes that swallow their faces. Happy birthday, Daddy, Reina says, and Franklin, her youngest, is handing him the gift.

And Hector Jr.?

But he doesn't have to fret about Hector Jr., his firstborn, the boy with these same great sad eyes who'd sat in the dugout in his Reds uniform when they lived in Cincy and worshiped the pudgy icon of his father until the parish priest had to straighten him out on his hagiography, Hector Jr. who studies English at USC and day and night writes his thesis on a poet his father has never heard of, because here he is, walking in the front door with his mother's smile and a store-wrapped gift—a book, of course. Then Reina's children line up to kiss the *abuelo*—they'll be sitting in the box seats this afternoon—and suddenly he knows so much: He will play today, he will hit, oh yes, can there be a doubt? He sees it already. Kerensky, the son of a whore. Extra innings. Koerner of Manfredonia or Brooksie on third. The ball like an orange, a mango, a muskmelon, the clean swipe of the bat, the delirium of the crowd, and the gimpy *abuelo,* a big leaguer still, doffing his cap and taking a tour of the bases in a stately trot, Sultan for a day.

Could things ever be so simple?

In the bottom of the ninth, with the score tied at five and Reina's kids full of Coke, hotdogs, peanuts, and ice cream and getting restless, with Asunción clutching her rosary as if she were drowning and Hector Jr.'s nose stuck in some book, Dupuy taps him to hit for the pitcher with two down and Fast Freddie Phelan on second. The eighth man in the lineup, Spider Martinez from Muchas Vacas, D.R., has just whiffed on three straight pitches and Corcoran, the Braves' left-handed relief man, is all of a sudden pouring it on. Throughout the stadium a hush has fallen over the crowd, the torpor of suppertime, the game poised at apogee. Shadows are lengthening in the outfield, swallows flitting across the face of the scoreboard, here a fan drops into his beer, there a big mama gathers up her purse, her knitting, her shopping bags and parasol and thinks of dinner. Hector sees it all. This is the moment of catharsis, the moment to take it out.

As Martinez slumps toward the dugout, Dupuy, a laconic, embittered man who keeps his suffering inside and drinks Gelusil like water, takes hold of Hector's arm. His eyes are red-rimmed and paunchy, doleful as a basset hound's. Bring the runner in, Champ, he rasps. First pitch fake a bunt, then hit away. Watch Booger at third. Uh-huh, Hector mumbles, snapping his gum. Then he slides his bat from the rack—white ash, tape-wrapped grip, personally blessed by the Archbishop of Guadalajara and his twenty-seven acolytes—and starts for the dugout steps, knowing the course of the next three minutes as surely as his blood knows the course of his veins. The familiar cry will go up—Cheese, Cheese, Cheesus—and he'll amble up to the batter's box, knocking imaginary dirt from his spikes, adjusting the straps of his golf gloves, tugging at his underwear and fiddling with his batting helmet. His face will be impenetrable. Corcoran will work the ball in his glove, maybe tip back his cap for a little hair grease and then give him a look of psychopathic hatred. Hector has seen it before. Me against you. My record, my career, my house, my family, my life, my mutual funds and beer distributorship against yours. He's been hit in the elbow, the knee, the groin, the head. Nothing fazes him. Nothing. Murmuring a prayer to Santa Griselda, patroness of the sun-blasted Sonoran village where he was born like a heat blister on his mother's womb, Hector Hernán Jesus y María Quesadilla will step into the batter's box, ready for anything.

But it's a game of infinite surprises.

Before Hector can set foot on the playing field, Corcoran suddenly doubles up in pain, Phelan goes slack at second and the catcher and shortstop are hustling out to the mound, tailed an instant later by trainer and pitching coach. First thing Hector thinks is a groin pull, then appendicitis, and finally, as Corcoran goes down on one knee, poison. He'd once seen a man shot in the gut at Obregon City, but the report had been loud as a thunderclap and he hears nothing now but the enveloping hum of the crowd. Corcoran is rising shakily, the trainer and pitching coach supporting him while the catcher kicks meditatively in the dirt, and now Mueller, the Atlanta *cabeza*, is striding big-bellied out of the dugout, head down as if to be sure his feet are following orders. Halfway to the mound, Mueller flicks his right hand across his ear quick as a horse flicking its tail, and it's all she wrote for Corcoran.

Poised on the dugout steps like a bird dog, Hector waits, his eyes riveted on the bullpen. Please, he whispers, praying for the intercession of the Niño and pledging a hundred votary candles— at least, at least. Can it be? Yes, milk of my Mother, yes— Kerensky himself strutting out onto the field like a fighting cock. Kerensky!

Come to the birthday boy, Kerensky, he murmurs, so certain he's going to put it in the stands he could point like the immeasurable Bambino. His tired old legs shuffle with impatience as Kerensky stalks across the field, and then he's turning to pick Asunción out of the crowd. She's on her feet now, Reina too, the kids come alive beside her. And Hector Jr., the book forgotten, his face transfigured with the look of rapture he used to get when he was a boy sitting on the steps of the dugout. Hector can't help himself: He grins and give them the thumbs-up sign.

Then, as Kerensky fires his warm-up smoke, the loudspeaker crackles and Hector emerges from the shadow of the dugout into the tapering golden shafts of the late-afternoon sun. That pitch, I want that one, he mutters, carrying his bat like a javelin and shooting a glare at Kerensky, but something's wrong here, the announcer's got it screwed up: BATTING FOR RARITAN, NUM-

BER THIRTY-NINE, DAVE TOOL. What the—? And now some-body's tugging at his sleeve and he's turning to gape with incom-prehension at the freckle-faced batboy, Dave Tool striding out of the dugout with his big forty-two ounce stick, Dupuy's face locked up like a vault and the crowd, on its feet, chanting Tool, Tool, Tool! For a moment he just stands there, frozen with disbelief. Then Tool is brushing by him and the idiot of a batboy is leading him toward the dugout as he were an old blind fisherman poised on the edge of the dock.

He feels as if his legs have been cut from under him. Tool! Dupuy is yanking him for Tool? For what? So he can play the lefty-righty percentages like some chess head or something? Tool, of all people. Tool, with his thirty-five home runs a season and lifetime B.A. of .234, Tool who's worn so many uniforms they had to expand the league to make room for him, what's he going to do? Raging, Hector flings down his bat and comes at Dupuy like a cat tossed in a bag. You crazy, you jerk, he sputters. I woulda hit him, I woulda won the game. I dreamed it. And then, his voice breaking: It's my birthday for Christ's sake!

But Dupuy can't answer him, because on the first pitch Tool slams a real worm burner to short and the game is going into extra innings.

By seven o'clock, half the fans have given up and gone home. In the top of the fourteenth, when the visitors came up with a pair of runs on a two-out pinch-hit home run, there was a real exodus, but then the Dodgers struck back for two to knot it up again. Then it was three up and three down, regular as clockwork. Now, at the end of the nineteenth, with the score deadlocked at seven all and the players dragging themselves around the field like gutshot horses, Hector is beginning to think he may get a second chance after all. Especially the way Dupuy's been using up players like some crazy general on the western front, yanking pitchers, jug-gling his defense, throwing in pinch runners and pinch hitters until he's just about gone through the entire roster. Asunción is still there among the faithful, the foolish, and the self-deluded, fum-bling with her rosary and mouthing prayers for Jesus Christ Our Lord, the Madonna, Hector, the hometeam, and her departed mother, in that order. Reina too, looking like the survivor of some disaster, Franklin and Alfredo asleep in their seats, the niñitas gone off somewhere—for Coke and dogs, maybe. And Hector Jr. looks like he's going to stick it out too, though he should be back in his closet writing about the mystical so-and-so and the way he illustrates his poems with gods and men and serpents. Watching him, Hector can feel his heart turn over.

In the bottom of the twentieth, with one down and Gilley on first—he's a starting pitcher but Dupuy sent him in to run for Manfredonia after Manfredonia jammed his ankle like a turkey and had to be helped off the field—Hector pushes himself up from the bench and ambles down to where Dupuy sits in the corner, contemplatively spitting a gout of tobacco juice and saliva into the drain at his feet. Let me hit, Bernard, come on, Hector says, easing down beside him.

Can't, comes the reply, and Dupuy never even raises his head. Can't risk it, Champ. Look around you—and here the manager's voice quavers with uncertainty, with fear and despair and the dull edge of hopelessness—I got nobody left. I hit you, I got to play you.

No, No, you don't understand—I'm going to win it, I swear.

And then the two of them, like old bankrupts on a bench in Miami Beach, look up to watch Phelan hit into a double play.

A buzz runs through the crowd when the Dodgers take the field for the top of the twenty-second. Though Phelan is limping, Thorkelsson's asleep on his feet and Dorfman, fresh on the mound, is the only pitcher left on the roster, the moment is electric. One more inning and they tie the record set by the Mets and Giants back in '64, and then they're making history. Drunk, sober, and then drunk again, saturated with fats and nitrates and sugar, the crowd begins to come to life. Go Dodgers! Eat shit! Yo Mama! Phelan's a bum!

Hector can feel it too. The rage and frustration that had consumed him back in the ninth are gone, replaced by a dawning sense of wonder—he could have won it then, yes, and against his nemesis Kerensky too—but the Niño and Santa Griselda have been saving him for something greater. He sees it now, knows it in his bones: He's going to be the hero of the longest game in history.

As if to bear him out, Dorfman, the kid from Albuquerque, puts in a good inning, cutting the bushed Braves down in order. In the dugout, Doc Pusser, the team physician, is handing out the little

210

green pills that keep your eyes open and Dupuy is blowing into a cup of coffee and staring morosely out at the playing field. Hector watches as Tool, who'd stayed in the game at first base, fans on three straight pitches, then he shoves in beside Dorfman and tells the kids he's looking good out there. With his big cornhusker's ears and nose like a tweezer, Dorfman could be a caricature of the green rookie. He says nothing. Hey, don't let it get to you, kid— I'm going to win this one for you. Next inning or maybe the inning after. Then he tells him how he saw it in a vision and how it's his birthday and the kid's going to get the victory, one of the biggest of all time. Twenty-four, twenty-five innings maybe.

Hector had heard of a game once in the Mexican League that took three days to play and went seventy-three innings, did Dorfman know that? It was down in Culiacán. Chito Martí, the converted bullfighter, had finally ended it by dropping down dead of exhaustion in centerfield, allowing Sexto Silvestro, who'd broken his leg rounding third, to crawl home with the winning run. But Hector doesn't think this game will go that long. Dorfman sighs and extracts a bit of wax from his ear as Pantaleo, the third string catcher, hits back to the pitcher to end the inning. I hope not, he says, uncoiling himself from the bench, my arm'd fall off.

Ten o'clock comes and goes. Dorfman's still in there, throwing breaking stuff and a little smoke at the Braves, who look as if they just stepped out of *Night of the Living Dead*. The hometeam isn't doing much better. Dupuy's run through the whole team but for Hector, and three or four of the guys have been in there since two in the afternoon; the rest are a bunch of ginks and gimps who can barely stand up. Out in the stands, the fans look grim. The vendors ran out of beer an hour back, and they haven't had dogs or kraut or Coke or anything since eight-thirty.

In the bottom of the twenty-seventh Phelan goes berserk in the dugout and Dupuy has to pin him to the floor while Doc Pusser shoves something up his nose to calm him. Next inning the balls-and-strikes ump passes out cold and Dorfman, who's beginning to look a little fagged, walks the first two batters but manages to weasel his way out of the inning without giving up the go-ahead run. Meanwhile, Thorkelsson has been dropping ice cubes down his trousers to keep awake, Martinez is smoking something suspicious in the can and Ferenc Fortnoi, the third baseman, has begun talking to himself in a tortured Slovene dialect. For his part,

211

Hector feels stronger and more alert as the game goes on. Though he hasn't had a bite since breakfast he feels impervious to the pangs of hunger, as if he were preparing himself, mortifying his flesh like a saint in the desert.

And then, in the top of the thirty-first, with half the fans asleep and the other half staring into nothingness like the inmates of the asylum of Our Lady of Guadeloupe where Hector had once visited his halfwit uncle when he was a boy, Pluto Morales cracks one down the first base line and Tool flubs it. Right away it looks like trouble, because Chester Bubo is running around right field looking up at the sky like a birdwatcher while the ball snakes through the grass, caroms off his left foot and coasts like silk to the edge of the warning track. Morales meanwhile is rounding second and coming on for third, running in slow motion, flat-footed and hump-backed, his face drained of color, arms flapping like the undersized wings of some big flightless bird. It's not even close. By the time Bubo can locate the ball, Morales is ten feet from the plate, pitching into a face-first slide that's at least three parts collapse and that's it, the Braves are up by one. It looks black for the hometeam. But Dorfman, though his arm has begun to swell like a sausage, shows some grit, bears down and retires the side to end the historic top of the unprecedented thirty-first inning.

Now, at long last, the hour has come. It'll be Bubo, Dorfman, and Tool for the Dodgers in their half of the inning, which means that Hector will hit for Dorfman. I been saving you, Champ, Dupuy rasps, the empty Gelusil bottle clenched in his fist like a hand grenade. Go on in there, he murmurs and his voice fades away to nothing as Bubo pops the first pitch up in back of the plate. Go on in there and do your stuff.

Sucking in his gut, Hector strides out onto the brightly-lit field like a nineteen-year-old, the familiar cry in his ears, the haggard fans on their feet, a sickle moon sketched in overhead as if in some cartoon strip featuring drunken husbands and the milkman. Asunción looks as if she's been nailed to the cross, Reina wakes with a start and shakes the little ones into consciousness and Hector Jr. staggers to his feet like a battered middleweight coming out for the fifteenth round. They're all watching him. The fans whose lives are like empty sacks, the wife who wants him home in front of the TV, his divorced daughter with the four kids and another on the way, his son, pride of his life, who reads for the doctor of philosophy

212

while his crazy *padrecito* puts on a pair of long stockings and chases around after a little white ball like a case of arrested development. He'll show them. He'll show them some *cojones*, some true grit and desire: The game's not over yet.

On the mound for the Braves is Bo Brannerman, a big mustachioed machine of a man, normally a starter but pressed into desperate relief service tonight. A fine pitcher—Hector would be the first to admit it—but he just pitched two nights ago and he's worn thin as wire. Hector steps up to the plate, feeling legendary. He glances over at Tool in the on-deck circle, and then down at Booger, the third base coach. All systems go. He cuts at the air twice and then watches Brannerman rear back and release the ball: Strike one. Hector smiles. Why rush things? Give them a thrill. He watches a low outside slider that just about bounces to even the count, and then stands there like a statue as Brannerman slices the corner of the plate for strike two. From the stands, a chant of *Viejo*, *Viejo*, and Asunción's piercing soprano, Hit him, Hector!

Hector has no worries, the moment eternal, replayed through games uncountable, with pitchers who were over the hill when he was a rookie with San Buitre, with pups like Brannerman, with big leaguers and Hall of Famers. Here it comes, Hector, ninety-two m.p.h., the big *gringo* trying to throw it by you, the matchless wrists, the flawless swing, one terrific moment of suspended animation—and all of a sudden you're starring in your own movie.

How does it go? The ball cutting through the night sky like a comet, arching high over the centerfielder's hapless scrambling form to slam off the wall while your legs churn up the base paths, rounding first in a gallop, taking second and heading for third . . . but wait, you spill hot coffee on your hand and you can't feel it, the demons apply the live wire to your tailbone, the legs give out and they cut you down at third while the stadium erupts in howls of execration and abuse and the *niñitos* break down, faces flooded with tears of humiliation, Hector Jr. turning his back in disgust, and Asunción raging like harpie, *Abuelo! Abuelo! Abuelo!*

Stunned, shrunken, humiliated, you stagger back to the dugout in a maelstrom of abuse, paper cups, flying spittle, your life a waste, the game a cheat, and then, crowning irony, that bum Tool, worthless all the way back to the washerwoman grandmother and the drunken muttering whey-faced tribe that gave him suck, stands tall like a giant and sends the first pitch out of the park to tie

213

it. Oh, the pain. Flat feet, fire in your legs, your poor tired old heart skipping a beat in mortification. And now Dupuy, red in the face, shouting: The game could be over but for you, you crazy gimpy old beaner washout! You want to hide in your locker, bury yourself under the shower room floor, but you have to watch as the next two men reach base and you pray with fervor that they'll score and put an end to your debasement. But no, Thorkelsson whiffs and the new inning dawns as inevitably as the new minute, the new hour, the new day, endless, implacable, world without end.

But wait, wait: Who's going to pitch? Dorfman's out, there's nobody left, the astonishing thirty-second inning is marching across the scoreboard like an invading army and suddenly Dupuy is standing over you—no, no, he's down on one knee, begging. Hector, he's saying, didn't you use to pitch down in Mexico when you were a kid, didn't I hear that someplace? Yes, you're saying yes, but that was—

And then you're out on the mound, in command once again, elevated like some half-mad old king in a play, and throwing smoke. The first two batters go down on strikes and the fans are rabid with excitement, Asunción will raise a shrine, Hector Jr. worships you more than all the poets that ever lived, but can it be? You walk the next three and then give up the grand slam to little Tommy Oshimisi! Mother of God, will it never cease? But wait, wait, wait: Here comes the bottom of the thirty-second and Brannerman's wild. He walks a couple, gets a couple out, somebody reaches on an infield single and the bases are loaded for you, Hector Quesadilla, stepping up to the plate now like the Iron Man himself. The wind-up, the delivery, the ball hanging there like a *piñata*, like a birthday gift, and then the stick flashes in your hands like an archangel's sword, and the game goes on forever.

nominated by Sara Vogan

AGRICULTURE

fiction by WILLIAM KITTREDGE

from CONFLUENCE PRESS

IN THIS OLD BEGINNING of the end Streeter thinks about starting out in agriculture, and remembers coming home drunk from Winnemucca in the morning hours before daylight, and finding a man named Andre Leeman sitting on the front steps and smoking a cigarette, his long chin and concave cheeks briefly illuminated when he touched the cigarette to his lips.

It was June and the barley crop was in the ground, and the alfalfa haying wouldn't start for another couple of weeks, a time of brief freedom which had led Streeter to a spate of drinking and running the back roads. This night had brought him miles from the tavern in Paradise Valley without much memory of more than sagebrush desert flowing at the edges of his headlights, and he was surprised by the year-old Ford pickup with a caved-in tailgate which was parked by his front gate, and then by the glow of cigarette over there on the concrete steps to the house.

"Takes you long enough," the man said, and then he told Streeter about being a flyer, and wanting the brush spraying contract. "Been sitting here six hours," he said, "which must mean something."

"Means you got more time than sense," Streeter said, almost at once hating the sourness of drink in himself, which led to such talk. So he offered this Andre Leeman a hit from the pint of Old Crow he was packing, and asked him to wait until the next day for any serious talk, and stumbled into the house, and into his bedroom where his wife was sleeping with the two children in the bed, one on each side of her, and no room left for him.

Streeter went back to the living room and slept about an hour and a half on the couch, then slipped out so his wife wouldn't hear him, and drove slowly to a circle of willows near the upper limits of his property, where the headgates were flowing with water out of the creek. The flyer, Andre Leeman, found him there just after noon, asleep and sweating in the sun with his feet hanging out the windows on the driver's side of the pickup. He shook Streeter's foot.

"Been hunting all over for you," he said, when Streeter had got himself awake and washed his face in the cold water come off the snow in the Warner Mountains.

"Sorry," Streeter said, but this Andre Leeman had already gone limping off to his pickup. He came back with his own half-empty pint of Old Crow, and they sat together on the wooden frame of the headgate, resting in the sun and sipping whiskey and talking about the deal on the brush spraying.

Like most of those old time spray pilots, Leeman flew an ancient Steerman bi-plane, one of those rough-looking remnants of the 20's and 30's with a massive stub-nosed radial engine and a maze of struts and wires between the wings, heavy looking aircraft with an open cockpit where the pilots with their leather helmets and goggles looked like World War I flying aces, dropping their aircraft close to the earth in the stillness of an early morning and churning along over the cool dewy croplands, leaving an undulating path of misty chemical spray while their wheels sometimes skimmed the leaves. Leeman claimed to have inherited his Steerman from his father, who caught a Baptist church steeple while spraying cotton in Arkansas. The old man had been crippled for life, and the Steerman mostly wrecked, but now it was rebuilt and ready for work. Leeman didn't say why he had brought it so far from Arkansas to Idaho.

"I been around this all my life," he said. "I can do you good work, close down as anybody. I was in Korea, flying a little Piper, and they kicked me out." He shook his head over this bit of old history, as if the motives of some men and organizations were impossible to imagine. "I been doing this ever since," he said.

They finished the whiskey and Streeter gave him the job. Leeman was new in the country, and had nobody to vouch for him, but Streeter liked that hour or so in the sun, talking about foreign

216

lands beyond the Pacific between little sips of whiskey, and that was reason enough.

A week later Leeman showed up with the old silver-painted Steerman and two boys to flag for him in the brush, one of them driving his Ford pickup with the crushed tailgate and the other bringing his '59 flatbed International truck with a 500 gallon mix tank chained down on the back. It was all shipshape, three yellow 55 gallon drums of chemical in the back of the pickup and the chain binder tied secure with heavy telephone company wire.

It was early daybreak when Leeman buzzed the main house twice, and Streeter came floundering out of sleep and got himself down to the highway, wearing only house slippers on his feet, and no socks. Leeman brought the Steerman soft onto the narrow pitted asphalt, and taxied up to where Streeter stood and revved the radial engine to a crackling roar, and shut it down and grinned. Dust from the prop-wash settled out into the pretty morning, and the birds took up again and the day was perfect, with smoke rising in an unwavering string from the crooked pipe over one of the tin-sided houses where two of Streeter's ranch-hand pensioners batched together.

Leeman stood down off the wing of the Steerman, and stretched like his back was aching, and rubbed his hands over his whisker stubble, then twanged one of the strut wires like he was tinkering with a stringed instrument. "She never lets me down," he said. "Not hard, anyways." He grinned at Streeter.

And things went fine. Leeman was good at his work. Streeter sent a man with him, to help out on the mix truck, pumping chemicals from the yellow concentrate drums to dilute with creek water in the big tank, and then over to the spray tanks on the Steerman. The contract was for spraying almost four thousand acres of brush, on land where the native grasses had been killed out by overgrazing. Given time, with the sage knocked down, the feed would come back. That was the theory. The work involved endless trips with the Steerman, and had to be done in the absolute stillness of early morning, so the spray would not drift.

By the time a gusty little breeze came up just before noon of that first day Leeman had already covered a little more than 400 acres, and he was staying down close, as a spray pilot should, and it was fine to watch in the clear light, the mist swirling out behind in the draft from the propeller and turning through bright rainbows over the smokey green of the sage. With any sort of luck the job wouldn't take more than ten days, or two weeks at the most.

Streeter asked Leeman to dinner that night, and Leeman showed up carrying another pint of whiskey, cleaned up and new shaven, with his hair slicked down. "Gift," Leeman said, and he shoved the flat bottle into Streeter's hands.

"This here is my wife," Streeter said. "Her name is Patty."

Leeman nodded his head, and looked like she was a surprise, and Streeter wondered how long since Leeman had eaten a meal in somebody's house, cooked by a wife.

After they had finished the steaks and mashed potatoes and spinach and cauliflower under some yellow sauce, Streeter and Leeman sat around the living room while Patty stacked the dishes in the dishwasher, and Streeter began to wonder if he had made a mistake with this invitation. Leeman wouldn't talk. Streeter would say something about the work, and Leeman would nod his head, and then they would sit in silence another couple of minutes, until Patty came in with a tray and three whiskey glasses of Creme de Menthe.

"What's it like?" she asked, looking at Leeman once they were all settled and through the first sip. Patty was sitting across from them on a footstool, and all at once Streeter wished she would pull down her skirt. Her reddish hair was curled tight around her head that summer, and she was wearing a plain white blouse that was tight around her breasts, and Leeman was looking at her in a curious way as he turned the glass of Creme de Menthe in his hands. Finally he shook his head like he didn't understand.

"Flying so close to the ground," Patty said. "I'd like to see what it was like." She scooted forward on the stool. "I mean there must be a moment," she went on, "when you settle down to the field and it looks like it would come right up around you, and you've got to stop yourself from sinking. I've been trying to imagine it."

"I guess you don't think much about it," Leeman said.

"Seems like a swing," Patty said. "You go down, but you know you can never go so low, you can never really touch even when it seems like you will."

"Never thought about it that way."

Patty went on like she was excited, twisting on the stool and leaning forward with that glass held in both her hands, and pretty soon trying to talk Leeman into giving her a ride in the Steerman. Her skirt had worked higher, and Streeter was thinking he ought to break this up when Leeman said, "Tomorrow, when the breeze comes up."

"You get out there," Leeman said, "and I'll give you a ride." Then he looked to Streeter to see if it was all right, and swallowed the last of his drink and stood up.

"Sun comes early," he said, and then he was out the door and heading toward his pickup. Patty was in the kitchen washing the drink glasses when Streeter looked around from the doorway. After that they argued a little, and she made it up to him in bed like they hadn't done in months. She surprised Streeter that night, like she would do every so often, and he lay awake when she was sleeping and knew it was a good thing she wanted to get out and do something.

The breeze came early the next day, and by eleven o'clock Streeter had Patty up on the gravel roadway through the brush Leeman had been using as a landing strip. Leeman was pumping fuel into his aircraft from the barrels in the back of his pickup with an old hand-crank pump, and Patty was biting at her lower lip as she watched. Remembering that morning, Streeter would think he had never felt so good with Patty since they were married children as he boosted her onto the wing and held her hand to steady her as she climbed over into the cockpit.

"Don't dump her out," Streeter shouted, and Leeman smiled. Patty was wearing a Levis jacket of Streeter's with the sleeves turned up a couple of rolls, and her hair was tied down with a silk bandana. As she waved over the sides of the open cockpit Streeter thought she looked like some girl he might have dreamed about years before and could have known if they hadn't got married at eighteen.

Dust blew and the engine roared, and Streeter stood back as the Steerman bounced along and then lifted from the gravel roadway, Streeter watching until they turned low over the rolling sand hills and dropped from sight against the sun, and he thought about Patty frightened, and felt sorry for her because she would be angry with herself when this was over, and say she should have known better, and he couldn't blame her for wanting to try something.

219

Streeter ducked his head in the wind, which was coming in gusts from the southwest, like it did sometimes in early summer, and sat in the pickup and nipped on another little pint of Old Crow.

The Steerman was gone longer than he had guessed, and he wondered if the wind meant rain. Late spring storms would most often come riding a blow like this, the country dry and already blowing dust one minute and then moist the next morning, the tilled soil dark and the sage softened and green under the soft rain.

Streeter had sipped at the whiskey four or five times when the Steerman returned, skimming low over the brush and then rising slightly and wheeling in the sky and dropping to the gravel roadway, touching down and bouncing slightly and then braking abruptly before taxiing toward Streeter, where he stood beside his pickup.

The prop-wash was still blowing dust behind them when Patty leaned forward from behind the pilot's seat, and shouted something in Leeman's ear, gesturing at Streeter and then repeating whatever it was until Leeman shook his head and waved Streeter toward them. Leeman pulled his goggles up over his old leather helmet, and grinned.

"Piggy-back," he shouted over the dull noise of the idling engine, gesturing toward the cockpit where Patty was crouching behind the surprisingly small and cramped pilot's seat, her knees on a grease-stained sofa cushion. There were no safety straps for the rider, nothing to keep you in but gravity and your grasp on the tubing around the cockpit. Streeter thought what the hell, and crawled awkwardly in behind her, and wedged himself, hunched forward with his arms around her and hands clamped to the cockpit edge.

Leeman revved the engine, dust and wind stinging around them, and the Steerman bumped and hurtled forward, rising as the sound diminished and they were skimming out over the sage flatlands before dropping over the rim along the north side of the valley swamps and down over the hayland meadows, lifting and falling over the sloughs and running sometimes only eight or ten feet off the ground, rising away from their shadow to flow over the banks of willow and wild rose along the fencelines and then falling so slightly again, until they were at the highway and lifting and nosing toward the sun and turning as they ascended over the roadside string of Lombardy poplar, and falling into the turn as Streeter knew he was going to be sick.

The familiar fields and patterns were foreign and swept to a lost featureless blurring, like the sea under a green summer evening as the tipping horizon fell sideways in a long jerking sweep, and the warm bourbon came into Streeter's mouth as he managed to turn and twist himself, straining against the solid bulk of his wife as the horizon went on revolving, and then the vomit was gone, just that quick, in a long spew lost in the wind, and he was hunched there half out of the cockpit with Patty looking back to him and grinning as he wiped at his mouth. The Steerman began to lift and throttle into another steeply banking turn as Patty ducked to huddle her head against the back of Leeman's seat, her expression in the quick glance Streeter caught not so much sickened as haggard, as if watching him had turned her old while he fought to keep from falling.

A week later it did rain, and the work was stopped with maybe four or five hours to go. After breakfasting with his crew in the bunkhouse, Streeter turned them loose for the day and went home to crawl into bed with Patty, the bedroom door locked against the children, who were playing in the living room. It was almost noon when Streeter left the house again, and he took the children with him, a little boy and little girl, maybe four or five at the time, standing in the pickup seat beside him and keeping quiet and being good, as if awed by this special favor as Streeter drove the muddy meadow roads for an hour or so, checking his irrigation water, the wipers sweeping at the windshield and Streeter drawn to sadness with himself which left him surprised when he came home to find Leeman's pickup with the crushed tailgate parked in front of the house.

Patty opened the door as the children came running through the rain, and Leeman was sitting in the living room with a half-empty beer in his hand. Patty seated herself on the hassock stool again, sitting there hunched forward and nobody saying anything, studying her hands. After a slight hesitation, Leeman lifted his beer to Streeter as though in salute. "I ain't going to finish," he said.

Which was putting Streeter in a bind, and Streeter told him so. "Who the hell am I going to get?" Streeter asked. "You got any ideas."

"Not a one," Leeman said. "I'm sorry about that, but I'm pulling out." He looked away from Streeter, and shifted his feet a little, and finished the beer.

"You know what I wish?" Patty said. "I wish I could just go off like that. I really do, for the rest of my life."

"She says she does," Leeman said. "But she don't."

There was a little quiet, and then Leeman got to his feet. "I'll be seeing you," he said. "Maybe you could write my check."

"My privilege," Streeter said, and he took out his personal checkbook, and looked to Patty for a pen. She sat looking back to him like he was gone crazy if he expected her to fetch him anything. "Need something to write with," Streeter said, and there was no sense to the anger in her eyes as she sat unmoving, the three of them locked there in place until Leeman fished in his shirt pocket and came out with an old give-away ball point. "Try this," he said.

"Just round it off," Leeman said, "at five thousand."

"Since I'm leaving you early," Leeman said, and he folded the yellow check into his shirt pocket, and clipped the ball point there, and was out the door.

"I could have gone, I wish I could," Patty said. "With him. I would have made him get me an Airflow trailer, and I would have gone, easy."

Streeter was running his fingers back and forth on the smooth hardwood of the mantel above his fireplace, just feeling the slight texture of the wood he had sanded and varnished so many years before. "How come?" he said.

"I could have asked him," she said. "He might have done it."

"Sounds to me like you did." This wasn't anything Streeter could imagine with any ease, and after one last swipe along the mantel where Patty polished away the dust every day, he slipped his hands flat into his back pockets and asked what this was getting at. "I don't think this is making any sense," he said.

Patty just sat there and shook her head like she was about to cry while the rain streaked the windows, and Streeter walked to the kitchen and back, and then they heard the crackling roar of the Steerman from where it was parked over by the highway, and listened as it was climbing through the rain and turning and leaving until the dull throb of it was gone.

"It's nothing to do with flying," Patty said, looking up to Streeter and no longer fighting back her tears. "He just understood what things were worth."

There was no sensible answer. "Sounds to me like he turned you down," Streeter said, and the bottom of what he knew of himself was falling away, because it was true, for sure, and he walked out and spent the next eleven days sleeping down at the bunkhouse under the old blankets and heavy tarp from his hunting camp bedroll, until one night he was drunk and went up to the house, and Patty shrieked at him for a fool, which seemed correct when he thought about it, and they ended up in bed.

The next morning was silent and they began a wary series of days in which nothing more was ever explained while the motions of their lives began to reassert themselves, and they slowly came together again as if nothing had ever happened, and maybe it hadn't, Streeter could never bring himself to really ask. In the end it wasn't so bad and Streeter could lie in their bedroom before sleep and in the eye of his imagination see someone who might be her with another man, just the man's white and muscular naked back, and feel them trembling, and try again to understand that transgressions and betrayals and violations of trust and guilt had nothing to do with anything which was his life while the children grew and the grass grew back where the brush had been killed by chemicals, and Patty learned to laugh and study him like only another problem in her life which would never be solved on the ground.

nominated by Raymond Carver,
DeWitt Henry and Theodore Wilentz

CRANES

by ANNEKE CAMPBELL

from TELESCOPE

Your five-month belly leads. You follow
the nurse whose black braid bounces
against white. She milks a vial of blood
from your arm, a drop from your finger,
to fan red molecules on glass for tests.
You fear a harm that can't be measured.
The doctor enters. O-isha-san is young,
you think, born since then. We'll take
special care of you, he nods, he smiles.
Thirty-nine is late to start a child.

You cut the picture from the paper one week
before your wedding, decided on the pill.
Amchitka Island: A Crack in the Globe.
Two scientists with their white faces,
in hikingboots and dark down jackets, inspect
effects of underground explosion, their stances
jaunty like explorers over Everest, pointing
at the earth's peeling skin.

You waited and you read.
Do not expose yourself to X-rays,
to paints and fumes, to children with
contagious diseases, to litterboxes and lead.
Avoid coffee, tea, salt, sushi, and undercooked
red meat. Attach a waterfilter to the faucet.

224

Don't drink, don't smoke, don't take drugs,
not even aspirin. And don't forget,
the placental barrier's a myth.

The doctor lays a warm hand
on the curved shelf of your belly.
He asks why you didn't come here sooner.
There were too many reasons to hold back.
You studied photographs of a fetus
growing, traced its steps of evolution
in the womb, praying to harbor these
exact same stages. Then it happened.
You felt movement, a being touched
inside by fingers of air and light.
You wanted to shout: It moves, it lives.
But awe took your voice, and joy
like a flight of cranes taking off
in your blood.

You felt awe at seven years of age,
standing on Inasa mountain,
staring down at where the day before
a city lived under these same stars,
now only a pillar of fire climbed
the sky to burn the wan new moon.
You felt awe at the twisted trees
midsummer bareness, at the quiet herd
crossing Kōjin bridge slow as in sleep,
they were men or women shedding skin,
they were red mud moving, whispering
with their thousand voices, water.

The doctor reads your birthplace
in the chart. He's read studies
of the hibakusha. His voice grows
gentle, but his questions pry and probe,
more intimate than his gloved hand
inside you. The words that leave
your lips are thin as paper.

That bright blue morning Mother left
to buy pickled plums at market,
left the sleeping baby in your care.
You played in shade of latticed bamboo,
when suddenly the light, the sound
roared down to your knees.
You were pinned to ground by air.
You couldn't still your brother's cries,
pull rooftiles from the cradle.
You saw across the field coming running
that slight, familiar figure.
You felt so reassured. Nearer,
Mother looked funny. She freed
the baby, held him close to suck.
You watched the nipple come away
and from the torn breast squirted
red milk. Mother lay down.
Big black drops of rain began to
fall on the white mud wall.

The doctor brushes water from his eyes.
He places the doptone on your belly
to magnify the fetal heart.
You feel a moment's fear pulsate
at your throat, one moment of no right
to this fragile flutter of life,
before the rapturous rhythm
beats like a wild horse into the room.
You want to hug this man in white.
You want to tell him what might heal
the crack in the globe.

nominated by Maura Stanton

CLOUD PAINTER

by JANE FLANDERS

from POETRY

Suggested by the life and art of John Constable

At first, as you know, the sky is incidental—
a drape, a backdrop for trees and steeples.
Here an oak clutches a rock (already he works outdoors),
a wall buckles but does not break,
water pearls through a lock, a haywain trembles.

The pleasures of landscape are endless. What we see
around us should be enough.
Horizons are typically high and far away.

Still, clouds let us drift and remember. He is, after all,
a miller's son, used to trying
to read the future in the sky, seeing instead
ships, horses, instruments of flight.
Is that his mother's wash flapping on the line?
His schoolbook, smudged, illegible?

In this period the sky becomes significant.
Cloud forms are technically correct—mares' tails,
sheep-in-the-meadow, thunderheads.
You can almost tell which scenes have been interrupted
by summer showers.

Now his young wife dies.
His landscapes achieve belated success.
He is invited to join the Academy. I forget
whether he accepts or not.

In any case, the literal forms give way
to something spectral, nameless. His palette shrinks
to grey, blue, white—the colors of charity.
Horizons sink and fade,
trees draw back till they are little more than frames,
then they too disappear.

Finally the canvas itself begins to vibrate
with waning light,
as if the wind could paint.
And we too, at last, stare into a space
which tells us nothing,
except that the world can vanish along with our need for it.

nominated by Philip Dacey and Maura Stanton

BIRTHDAY STAR ATLAS

by CHARLES SIMIC

from THE MISSOURI REVIEW

Wildest dream, Miss Emily,
Then the coldly dawning suspicion—
Always at the loss—come day
Large black birds overtaking men who sleep in ditches.

A whiff of winter in the air. Sovereign blue,
Blue that stands for intellectual clarity
Over a street deserted except for a far off dog,
A police car, a light at the vanishing point

For the children to solve on the blackboard today—
Blind children at the school you and I know about.
Their gray nightgowns creased by the north wind;
Their fingernails bitten from time immemorial.

We're in a long line outside a dead letter office.
We're dustmice under a conjugal bed carved with exotic fishes
    and monkeys.
We're in a slow drifting coalbarge huddled around the television
    set
Which has a wire coat-hanger for an antenna.

A quick view (by satellite) of the polar regions
Maternally tucked in for the long night.
Then some sort of interference—parallel lines

Like the ivory-boned needles of your grandmother knitting our
    fates together.

All things ambiguous and lovely in their ambiguity,
Like the nebulae in my new star atlas—
Pale ovals where the ancestral portraits have been taken down.
The gods with their goatees and their faint smiles

In company of their bombshell spouses,
Naked and statuesque as if entering a death camp.
They smile, too, stroke the Triton wrapped around the mantle
    clock
When they are not showing the whites of their eyes in theatrical
    ecstasy.

Nostalgias for the theological vaudeville.
A false springtime cleverly painted on cardboard
For the couple in the last row to sigh over
While holding hands which unknown to them

Flutter like bird-shaped scissors . . .
Emily, the birthday atlas!
I kept turning its pages awed
And delighted by the size of the unimaginable;

The great nowhere, the everlasting nothing—
Pure and serene doggedness
For the hell of it—and love,
Our nightly stroll the color of silence and time.

*nominated by David Bromige, Rodney Jones,
Edmund Keeley, Sherod Santos and Mary Peterson*

HEAVEN AND EARTH

fiction by ANTONIO BENÍTEZ-ROJO

from NEW ENGLAND REVIEW AND BREAD LOAF QUARTERLY

PEDRO LIMÓN said good-bye to Pascasio and told him in creole—
so that he would know that he still remembered and that in spite of
all the time between them he was still one of them—that it was
good to see him working in the sugar refinery, taking apart the
machines and reading engineering manuals. Then he put on his
pack, and looking back every now and then, left, taking the path of
red earth and sun that connected the *bateyes* where the cane
cutters of the Camagüey region lived.

Initially Pascasio had not recognized him, behind the face that
had been pasted together bit by bit in the hospital, the sad face
that burned through to the bone on muggy nights and that,
according to the doctor, had turned out all right but really should
be touched up for the last time in a couple of years (it was always
the last time); but straight off he asked Pascasio about Ti-bois and
Pascasio let go of the ropes and smiled, extending his arm and
shaking his hand, and Ti-bois was fine, grumbling when he wasn't
communicating with the greatest voodoo spirits, complaining that
the young men from Guanamaca left to hang on the fine black
women from Florida and Esmeralda, preaching to the old hags that
Fidel was crazy and had shaken up the world, taking for himself
the land that the *bon Dieu* had given to the Cubans. He then had
no choice but to tell Pascasio about his life in the army, in the
Sierra, in Havana, of the shrapnel that struck him in the face
during the Bay of Pigs thing, and later his discharge, the hospital
alternating with the teaching school; the things that he had
learned, the things that he had done thinking about the people

231

from Guanamaca—he was about to say "thinking about your brother Ariston," but didn't get it out—thinking of you and Ti-bois and Aspirin and Julio Maní and of the rest, and of Léonie. And now Pascasio had moved to the main factory and was an assistant mechanic and was studying; he pointed to the book with boiler diagrams on the cover, and since we only received that one letter of yours, we thought they had killed you in the Sierra. No, we never knew about your parents. Léonie. Léonie lives with me now, and we have a son. A six year old.

Yes, Pedro Limón: Léonie lives with Pascasio and just yesterday they moved to the factory neighborhood; Julio Maní became a mason and he builds shelters for cane cutters in the south of the province; Aspirin married, quite legally, a widow from Florida, and went there to drive a cab, you know that he was always a good talker, anyway, and Pascasio laughed and then you understood that those who you loved most will never return to Guanamaca, and only Ti-bois remained, the *houngan* scaring the women and the kids, filling the afternoons of the old folks, the solitary, shriveled old men from the cabins, with his stories, the sorcerer Ti-bois, as the whites called him, Pascasio and Ariston's grandfather, also your grandfather in some ways.

Pedro Limón stopped following the curve of the railroad tracks and walked down by the narrow road that ran by the cranes of the *bateyes*, and he picked up a yellow sugar cane that had slid off some crate; he took off his boots and socks and the grass by the edge of the railway was warm; he pulled his knife from the sheath and cut a section of cane; he peeled it and bit into the sweet, light nectar, and suddenly he was a child again, a naive Haitian youngster, who killed the hunger of the flour spirit with a shot of cane juice fought for tooth and nail, and he'd better get going because Mama and Papa, carrying baby Georgette, would already be at Adelaide Macombe's, Ti-bois's oldest daughter, with all of their bundles, and surely they must have already sent Pascasio and Ariston to find him around the tracks, for the harvest was over and they were going to Oriente in the rented car of one of Adelaide's mulatto friends; they were going to the mountains near Guantánamo, to fill coffee cans on the land of Monsieur Bissy Porchette, honorary consul of the Haitian Republic.

We walked to the highway with all our bundles under the strong sun. The driver was already at the roadside stand having a beer.

Papa took a nickel from his pocket and asked for a soda with plenty of ice. He didn't give me a single piece; the driver didn't care if we arrived late; he had another beer and started joking around with us until he finally offered a glass to Adelaide, who sweated a lot. He knew some creole. Maybe that's why Papa unbuttoned his jacket, removed the straw hat which he had worn when he got off the boat before he met Mama—and started to fan himself with it and later used it to wave away the flies that surrounded Georgette, and he no longer looked as stiff as before, and he accepted a drink from the man and that time let me suck on some ice.

The driver put Adelaide's wooden suitcase in the trunk of the car, and helped Papa to arrange our things on the roof and he tied them with rope and he left the doors open to cool off the car a bit and then we left, with me between Pascasio and Ariston, in the front seat. Every now and then you could see water at the end of the highway, but when we got closer it disappeared. We counted many imaginary puddles. Many.

Ariston slapped me awake and it is almost night and we have to push. It could be that the battery is dead, surely with one little push it will start and Papa takes off his white linen jacket and folds it carefully over the back of the seat, then everyone gets out and gives it everything they've got, until the car picks up speed, and I push next to Adelaide and I hear her puff and puff; Adelaide is too fat. The motor starts at the bottom of the hill and the car doesn't stop. We don't either. We run, we shout, Adelaide falls down. The car doesn't stop so we have to let it go. We shout again. Nothing. It's leaving. It has left with all our baggage and with Papa's money, sewn into the lining of his jacket. Adelaide gets up and casts a spell on the driver that can't miss; she says Ti-bois taught it to her. My father is in the middle of the road. With his arms outstretched. I have never seen him so long and so thin. He doesn't move. He looks like the Jew that we burned last year during Easter week. Mama has stayed behind with Georgette, but I hear her cry. We slept in the sewer that night.

We are half-way there and Adelaide wants to keep going. Papa doesn't know. He looks at Mama and Georgette, shakes his head and looks at them again. He says that he has twelve cents, that we would have to walk for two days, that we are too many for any truck to take us. Mama gets on her feet and begins to walk with Georgette. Papa follows her, thinking that it is insane, he doesn't

233

think that it's worth it because two days from now he is not going to find work, nor I, nor Adelaide, nor the kids, no one. Mama starts to sing. Adelaide starts to sing too and she forces Pascasio and Ariston to sing along. Then I begin and later so does Papa.

We were still singing when the winds arrived and with the wind, the dust, and Papa said that it's been a while since it rained and if we got jobs the work was going to be tough, and Adelaide removed the colored scarves from around her waist and we covered our faces as if we were bandits and we continued to sing beneath the dust and the scarves and we arrived.

Monsieur Bissy Porchette didn't need more people although Adelaide screamed right into his face that he must have been lying to say he was a Haitian; we returned to Guanamaca on foot.

That summer we went hungry and my sister Georgette died.

Although I talked about the war, Pascasio didn't mention Ariston, he only said "and since we only received the one letter of yours, we thought that they had killed you in the Sierra." And he said it almost smiling, without resentment in his eyes, and who knows, maybe they don't hate me in Guanamaca after all; maybe they understood the letter, they understood that I did my duty. It's also possible that Pascasio doesn't know, that no one knows, that Maurice had kept it from them, Maurice, such a good person, the most educated man in Guanamaca, my father's best friend.

Papa looked again at the twenty cents and put them in Ti-bois's hand, and by the afternoon the four pesos had been collected so that Maurice could run across the Biram mountains and get to Santiago de Cuba to see the new consul. Because we did not agree with the forced deportation, the law that the Cubans had created to throw us out of their country, so that we could no longer work for less pay and not take jobs away from anyone. But no. We did not agree. No sir. We are ashamed to get off the boat and have the family over there see us without clothes and without money after so many years. And we were still against it although Maurice had returned within the week without having seen the consul and we already knew that it was useless.

"The ships have arrived. They are waiting in the docks," said the spirit of President Dessalines through Ti-bois's mouth.

And the next day the rural police gallop two by two past the border patrol with their machetes in hand. Inside their hats they carry a list of the families that must leave. Without dismounting, they go from *batey* to *batey* shouting the names that the Cubans have given us, the names that appear on the plantation's payroll because the French surnames are too difficult, those names that they coined at the social welfare centers, that complicated any transaction, José Codfish, Antonio Pepsicola, Juan First, Juan Second, Andrés Silent, Alberto Hardhead, Ambrosio Limón, Ambrosio Limón!, and my father comes to the doorway laden with bundles and later my mother, dropping their eyes to the garden of sweet potatoes and squash so that the officials wouldn't see them cry; we are a proud race, we have a history, we are a race of warriors that defeated Napoleon's armies. But now something is wrong. They are crowding us into the center of the *batey*. They do a head count. They whip and herd us to the refinery train. The boats are waiting. The train leaves. I do not see it. I do not leave with Papa and Mama. I fled three days ago and am far from the refinery. I am staying here because I was born in Cuba and I love Léonie, since I lay with her in the cane fields, and she's not on the list and I don't want to look for more hunger in Haiti and I may end up there like a zombie without a name.

I live in Adelaide's shack, next to Ti-bois's. My parents' shack was burned down by the rural police believing that I was inside. I sleep with Pascasio and Ariston. They fall asleep right away. I don't. Through the cracks in the boards I hear Ti-bois talking with the gods and the dead. Ti-bois is a powerful *houngan* who even knows Cuban black magic. He also turns into a snake and eats the plantations owner's chickens. I respect him very much. Ti-bois loves Ariston more than any of his grandchildren. He says that he will make Ariston a *houngan,* that he will teach him how to shed his skin and turn into an owl or a snake. That would frighten me. What I want to do is work enough to be able to live with Léonie. Some day I will dare to ask Ti-bois for this.

That summer I go and make money from the coffee growers of Oriente and I buy two shirts, a pair of pants and a hat. I bring Léonie a dark red dress, almost new. Julio Maní, a distant grandson of Ti-bois, appears with a box of shoes. He calls everyone around to see them, he wants to amaze them, they are two-tone shoes, an American brand; Julio Maní is happy, now he breaks the string and opens the box, but there are no shoes, they have cheated him and inside there is only a brick. Ti-bois starts to hit him with his cane.

235

The rural police must have already forgotten about me, besides, you have grown and are almost as tall as a man. But nonetheless I am afraid to ask for a job in the cane fields. Adelaide pushes me because you owe me lots of room and board and you must make money.

And I go.

And nothing happens. Nothing bad.

They are going to pay me for lifting the cane that Ariston cuts.

I am pleased because I know that no one will cut more cane than he. And that's what happens: Ti-bois has been preparing his arms with magical herbs and snake lard and now the blade is like lightning in his hand, and people look at him, and he has many friends, and women. Once he argued with Splinter, a Jamaican who has killed two people. We agree to the duel. We went out into the plain, we followed the narrow path that leads to the locust trees. We scared away the cows and sat in the shade of the green sky. Ti-bois starts making signs with his cane and calls the spirits of the air and the earth. Splinter laughs, he is a black man who believes in the whites' religion. He takes a gulp of rum and then spits it out noisily, splashing Ti-bois, and he takes out his machete and confronts Ariston. Splinter knows a lot, he continues to laugh and dodges Ariston's wild sweeps with the machete. He jumps around making faces and mocking him, and so the time passes. He has tried to tire out Ariston, but it is he who is tired, and he no longer laughs; he doesn't look confident or serene anymore. Ariston shouts and jumps him with rapid-fire punches that sound like a swarm of wasps. Splinter jumps back, he arches away too late: Ariston has cut into his belly and now he can only look into his guts.

That night Ti-bois assured us that Oggun Ferraille had entered Ariston, that he had spoken with the god, and he was very pleased to have been able to move and fight inside the muscles of his grandson. We all thought this very fine. During those days Adelaide received many visitors, many gifts of rum, tobacco, codfish, lard, flour and beef. She gathered her friends around her, and it was funny to see her tell of the fight, playing the part of Splinter and of her son, jumping around, sweating and choking and shouting curses, but no one laughed. Finally, when she had to stop, she struck her chest and waved her arms speaking just like Ariston.

"I will be a greater *houngan* than Ti-bois. Oggun Ferraille

236

protects me, Oggun the Marshal, Oggun the Captain, Oggun of Iron, Oggun of War. I am Oggun!"

Ariston was gone for a week, precisely the week when Adelaide Macombe was dying from a burst vein. He didn't see her alive. He didn't see her dead. He returned to the *batey* a day after the burial, a Sunday afternoon, with palm fronds on his shoulder. He walked like a god, very straight and tall, and stepped firmly on the red earth. The children ran after him, touching his thighs and the case of his machete. He sighed when Pascasio told him about Adelaide, then he turned solemn, he put the palm fronds under the bed, ate half a bunch of bananas and went to sleep. At dawn, before we left for work, he called me and Pascasio over and he pulled from the palm fronds a Paraguayan machete, a rifle, an ammunition belt, and a hat from the rural police. Right there I dug a hole and buried the stuff wrapped in one of Adelaide's dresses. He didn't answer a single question, but in the cane fields we learned that a sergeant had been found mutilated on the outskirts of Esmeralda. In the *batey* we all guessed who the killer was. And we were proud.

Before Easter week I spoke with Léonie's parents. It turns out that I was too young, was in the country illegally, didn't have money for a steady job and you must understand that we aren't going to give away Léonie just like that. I didn't insist, and that disturbed Léonie, but they really were right, anyway they can't keep me from seeing you; I will speak with Ti-bois and he will find me a good job, you will see.

Ariston, Pascasio and I joined the *bande rara* that Maurice organized. Maurice organized everything in Guanamaca, the whites called him Mayor; he could also read the newspaper and write letters in Spanish. Nicole, his wife, was the *reina* and we practiced at night in the back of his house, lighting the place with oil lamps. Léonie played *princesa* and marched with Nicole. The "lead machete" was played by Ariston; it was thrilling to see him do tricks with it. Pascasio was chosen as "lead baton" but I was not skilled enough and only got the part of flag-bearer. We left on Ash Wednesday after dinner, dressed in costumes that the women had made, singing and dancing with the entire *batey* following behind us. We returned on Saturday, tired from visiting the villages and all the *bateyes* of the plain, tired already of so much rum, so much *merengue*, so much *fiesta*. We followed the ancient custom and burned the Jew, and drank the ashes of the rags mixed in water and sugar. Of all my weeks, this was the happiest.

The happiest?

Yes. Because in some way (like they say in Havana) Guanamaca was, in spite of all the misery, my little piece of heaven, and I was never happier than during those nights with Léonie, next to Ti-bois's bonfire, beneath the trees of the plain, listening to him tell stories of the old country, listening to him speak of the maimed Makendal, of how he had put three handkerchiefs in his glass, and then removed them one by one, first the yellow one, then the white one and finally the black one, the race that would reign in Saint Domingue, and that is how it had been, and that is how it will be one day all over the world, and then I would kiss Léonie and Maurice would start to play the harmonica and Pedro Maní would play the conch, and the dancing and singing would begin again until the new day would find us in another *batey* and we would meet up with another *fiesta*.

"The happiest," I say, and now I sit on the train tracks and I put on my socks and my boots: I am not going to go into Guanamaca barefoot: two kilometers and someone may see me.

I put down my backpack: it weighs more than usual: I am carrying lots of things: presents for Ti-bois and for the old men from the cabins, who are so influential. I also stop to have a cigarette and suddenly I realize that I have bought these things because I am afraid. Me, afraid. It infuriates me. I am tough. A man of blood and fire. A young Marxist-Leninist Haitian. Lies. I am afraid of Guanamaca, afraid to inaugurate the school and have no one show up, afraid of failure, that they will not want to see me because of the Ariston thing and that they will throw the presents in my face. At this face of mine. Now I am nothing more than a poor school teacher with the face of a zombie, and I am afraid. And it is not only Guanamaca that I fear: I am afraid of everything: afraid of the gun shots, of the officials, of books, of doctors, hospitals; I am afraid of women, of children who stare at me, I am just like my father, a poor bastard of a Haitian not worth shit.

"If you don't come fight with me, I'll kill you," Ariston said to me one night, and I had also felt afraid. Oggun says that I have to fight, to set the earth on fire, that I have to fight at your side, that you are my protection and that the bullets will not harm me if you are

238

there. They will not touch you either. Oggun told me, and he said the same to Ti-bois. Fight or I kill you. Choose.

And because I was afraid I left Léonie and I followed Ariston to the mountains of Oriente. This time we weren't going to pick coffee beans: we were going to war because Oggun had demanded it; to fight against the tanks and cannons of Batista that rolled down the highway; we were going to fight against the airplanes, against the ships and against the army, we, who had not meddled in the white men's things for a long time, were fighting.

Aspirin, Maurice's son, knew the way. The peoples from the *batey* called him that because he was always buying aspirin at the boss's drug store, his headache never went away; as a kid a horse had trampled him during the uproar over the deportation. In spite of this, he was a very bright guy, and Maurice had taught him to speak like the whites in the office of the refinery. He liked to get out of Guanamaca and roam around for days, and a man once told him "Look, in those hills over there the rebels are holed up," and in order to fulfill Oggun's wishes, we had to join them. I spent the entire afternoon with Léonie. We went to the fields but I could do nothing, nothing more than listen to her assure me that she would wait for me all her life, and I was silent. We left at night. Ti-bois said that Toussaint Louverture's soul was with us and he gave us sweets to offer to Papa Lebba, the Owner of the Roads. We said good-bye: "Good-bye, Léonie. Good-bye, Pascasio. Good-bye, *houngan* Ti-bois."

The sun rose when we had already crossed the plains, and Ariston sang to the sun. Ariston would sing to the trees, to the rain, to everything; he knew lots of songs that Adelaide had made up, and he had learned them unconsciously and would always sing them.

We soon entered the hill plantations, at the foot of the Sierras where the coffee was grown, and there were the soldiers. Ariston was dressed in the uniform of the rural police. I was afraid that they would stop us. I told him to at least take off the hat, but he insisted that as long as I was at his side, misfortune could not touch us; in addition, he had Adelaide's magic scarves hanging from his waist. "No, Pedro Limón, nothing can happen to us." And it was true: when the airplane saw us and Ariston pulled out his machete and shouted to it to come down if it dared, that he was going to cut off its wings, when it turned around and flew down low firing many shots and I threw myself in the stream listening to Ariston's insults, when the plane flew by again and dropped a bomb and there were no sounds as they had said there would be, and I saw him crouching, trying to dig it up, then I realized that it was true, that Ariston and Ti-bois were right and then I was less afraid because certainly Oggun would also protect me.

Aspirin didn't show up, so it was difficult for us to find the rebels. At first they didn't want to accept us. But Ariston's arrival with the bomb counted for something.

Pedro Limón gets himself together and secures his pack. He looks at the smoke coming from the chimney of the refinery. He continues looking at it for some time. Now he turns his back to it, throws away his cigarette, touches his face and begins to walk towards the island of palms in the middle of the cane fields. Behind those palms is Guanamaca, he thinks.

Pascasio wanted him to stop (if only for a moment) to see Léonie (it would make her so happy) as they passed by the offices of the refinery and had given him the address of the house (new and painted indigo blue).

But he had chosen the long way around, the path that skirted the *batey;* fear, and again, his face before Léonie's, so suddenly: his face repaired with blade and buttock skin; the look compassionate at best, the mistrust of the child, barely six years old; a six year old son, what do you think, Pedro Limón, oh, how we are growing old; how quickly life flies away, yes.

"There is no one who could kill me," Ariston would say, charged by the spirit of Oggun. It was curious watching him fight: before the first gun shot, as we watched the passage of the tanks and the trucks full of soldiers. Oggun would take possession of him, he would come into him silently like a snake. Ariston wouldn't notice; he let himself be swallowed up without moving, and his skin became scaly and cold and ashen; his eyes became like those of dead oxen killed in the floods, the god coming through his eyes and his skin, Oggun Ferraille.

Much later, when we stayed close to camp and I learned to read, the man from Havana closed the book, lit his cigar and began to speak of the gods, of Ariston, of Ti-bois, of Haiti, of Guanamaca. He spoke of them as if he had been there in the middle of the *batey* or in the mountains of the old country. That night we didn't sleep, we stayed practically out in the open beneath the branches of a tree, and he, talking and talking while the stars moved across the skies, explaining everything in great detail and with much patience, like when he taught me to read, and I had never heard anyone explain things as well as he, no, no one put things together in quite that way to get them into one's head, and he told me that he was happy to know that I had made my plans, and that after the war, they would need people like me, and it was then that he spoke of studying to become a teacher and I understood why he had refused to write down all that had happened to Ariston.

But now we were only beginning the war and I did not dream of reading and the discipline was too severe and the leaders kept saying that morale must remain high. I didn't have any problems; I remembered every single one of the Habanero's words about the regulations. Ariston; yes; they had promoted him three times and each time he was left without stripes. "It's a shame that he has no brain, a man so strong, a man who has balls," said the Habanero. Although Ariston could really care less. All he cared about was fighting and killing.

That dawn the Habanero got me out of my hammock and later woke Ariston. It was still a while before daylight. We had coffee with some of the other men and we received our orders: there was word that they were preparing a siege and it was necessary to make sure; if it was true we would have to move the camp, go further up, to the summit of the Sierra. The Habanero divided us up into squads. Ariston and I and the Blond, a student from Manzanillo, would take care of the northern quadrant. I was leading; Ariston had a poor sense of direction and the Blond was pretty new to this. Soon it was daybreak and Ariston decided to sing and there was no way to shut him up. The Blond got nervous, he wanted to cover Ariston's mouth. I took a green mango from my pocket and gave it to Ariston, that shut him up. But he didn't finish eating it. He stood still, smelling the fibers stuck to the seed, and when he looked up it was no longer Ariston who looked at us, and I knew that Oggun had caught the scent not of the mango but of war, and suddenly a flash of light exploded over the boulders and struck the Blond and infuriated Ariston.

The shots didn't last long, although we killed three men. Ariston killed the last one with his machete because we ran out of ammunition. I crouched next to the Blond and he was dead, and suddenly shells began to fly and explode like ripe *guanábanas* and we had to leave the Blond and run into the hills.

We weren't fleeing. Rather, I was fleeing and he wasn't.

Because Ariston didn't know what fleeing was: Oggun must have warned him that the fighting was far away, that he could no longer kill and that that type of war didn't interest him.

I *was* afraid, and I was fleeing. I flee.

And now we return, sweating, through the weeds. To the camp.

And I look back and I don't see Ariston pushing back the branches that I've just parted: I only see the edge of the line of plants, dazzling in the afternoon, next to the broken cane, the cane that sweetens the air of Guanamaca. And in the distance, there is an old man making signs with a twisted reed, and some women and children and they wait for me, and it is going to be something like another war, but I am no longer afraid.

The news of the siege was true and we had to leave there, retreat into the clouds. Ariston still walked with the god inside him, maybe because he still wanted to fight, and his feet came down hard, like children when they play soldier, very tall and dignified, carrying his machete on his shoulder and his rifle slung across his chest. I looked for the Habanero to tell him the news; he was with some other man from the plains who came and went with messages for the camps.

"I don't know what happened. I think we met up with an entire patrol of them," I said, and I told him about the shooting, the shower of shells and what happened to the Blond.

There are people who shouldn't speak, who shouldn't open their mouths because all they do is offend. And the man from the plains was one of them.

"What happened is that you are a pair of ass-hole niggers, a pair of faggots who shit as soon as you hear a gun shot. If I had anything to say about it I'd execute you right this minute . . ."

He couldn't continue talking: Ariston raised his machete and split his head in two with a single blow, right through the middle, from top to bottom, as if it had been a papaya.

That is what the man from the plains died from. Immediately.

The trial was also quick.

That night we had to leave the campsite.

Ariston was there, standing, surrounded by the troops, silence.

242

The leaders were over there, sitting on the crates of rifles that had arrived just the other week, all very stern and speaking softly.

He didn't defend himself: he began to move his head, just like a horse and began to say that he didn't remember anything, that he was very sorry and that he wouldn't do it again, and no one could make him say more. And since the Habanero was the judge, it was me who had to tell them what happened and tell them about Tibois and Oggun.

When the captain pronounced the sentence, he stalled a bit. Later he explained carefully, as they always did, why things had to happen that way. But no one wanted to be on the firing squad, no one.

Then Ariston raised his head, smiled and asked permission to choose the men, and I was the first, "Pedro Limón," he said, and then he named the others.

"Don't worry," he said to me as they tied his hands. "If you are with me nothing can happen."

We walked along the sewer towards the *ceiba* tree. Every three or four steps he turned his head and spoke to me of the scare they were going to have when Oggun performed the miracle. Finally we reached the tree. He let himself be blindfolded and turned his back to the tree. The firing squad formed a line about twelve paces away from him.

"Ready!" yelled the Habanero and I cocked my Springfield. Ariston was, as usual, cheerful, with his rural police hat, the rim pinned up with the religious medals of the Virgin that he had taken from the dead, placed sideways on his kinky hair, dirty with earth; I looked at him to imprint him on my memory, in case Oggun turned him into an owl or something; and I saw that he wore two beaded necklaces and I had always thought that there had been more, and the colors of Adelaide's scarves were white, black and yellow, and I had to look really hard as they were ripped and faded; and I looked at his face again and it had already turned grey, and certainly the noise of the firearms had brought Oggun down and now the fun would begin.

"Aim!"

"I am Oggun Ferraille! No one can kill me with Pedro Limón here!"

"Fire!"

243

He bounced against the tree. He made a sound like a cough and let out a mouthful of blood. He slipped slowly down the trunk; he sighed and sunk into the thicket. The Habanero walked to the *ceiba* tree with his pistol in his hand. He bent down. I don't know what kind of snake it was, but when the smoke from the shooting settled, a wisp of ashes ran through his legs and lost itself up in the mountains. It was not my imagination, we all remained looking up at the slope of the hill.

The next day, after settling down at a new campsite, I asked the Habanero to write a letter for me: to write to Maurice so that they could know what happened to Ariston; I asked him to explain it clearly, as he knew how to say things. But the Habanero did not want to say anything about the snake. He refused, he who explained everything in such detail. He looked at me directly, for a long time, and then began to write, and without looking up he told me to leave, to leave and to decide, because in life men have always had to decide between heaven and earth, and it was about time that I did so.

TRANSLATED BY MARTA SIBERIO

nominated by Sharon Doubiago

THE EASTER WE LIVED IN DETROIT

fiction by JANET KAUFFMAN

from THE PARIS REVIEW

THE BEST DAY REMEMBER was the Easter we lived in Detroit, locked in the apartment all day. The furniture, the rugs, began to breathe. Geraniums hummed. I thought, so this is a lively place. It's what happens when somebody's got a chance to think.

Early, about seven o'clock, I said to my husband, Loren, it's bright out, which was at first a complaint. But Loren can sleep with the sun in his eyes; he didn't wake. I believe it's more natural, though, with the eyes closed, to be in the dark, and that is why, very deliberately, when the sunlight compressed itself from a general glow to a four-cornered field next to the bed, I got up and pulled down the green shades in both rooms. The floorboards were cool or warm, depending where I stepped, and checking around, I found a warmed-up spot near the living-room window where I stood for a while with my feet pressed flat, so the heat moved upwards through my ankles. My feet are spongy and pale, the white kind of feet that sculptors put at the ends of women's legs. I know what luxury-living means, soaking them in the sun.

In the kitchen, I took a blue-painted egg from the refrigerator, poured some milk, and let my eyes travel the walls in the indoor light. It was greenish, undersea light, very mild. I peeled the egg and sliced it with a steak knife onto a big plate, where the two halves slid together. They arranged themselves, it certainly

245

seemed to me then, as down-hearted, pitying eyes. I just whispered, don't you worry. Not today.

The air was unusually pretty, iridescent. The watercolor light of the room washed into the milk and swirled some pastels; the white of the egg shone aquamarine. Through the plumbing, or through the floors, I heard the rush of water falling, and I washed the knife, to add to it, and even after I'd set the knife off to one side to dry, I let the water run, full force, from the faucet into the drain, for somebody's pleasure down below. Noises coming from far away, I decided then, the ones that have nothing to do with your life, can be more important than anything anyone says in your own ear. It may be for that kind of reason, too, I turned on the radio, for the noise of the Easter broadcasts, a Sunday sound which seemed to come from a great distance and out of some other scenery. I've advised Loren, many Sundays, listen, they're dreamy. You shouldn't mind it, I tell him. Let them pursue happiness, that's what I say about that. But he won't listen.

For Easter, "92 Rock" was given over to a man with a damaged, smoker's voice who read haltingly, like a beginning reader, the story about the women at the tomb, where the rock had rolled away, making a space as wide as a door. I kept the sound low and listened off and on; and since I knew the story anyway, I could picture very clearly the roundness of the rock and the dark hole in the hill. It was desert there, with no trees, and the soil thin and shallow, with bedrock practically under your feet, so that caves were used as tombs. Or was it for criminals only that caves were tombs? I don't recall ever hearing the full explanation.

I sat in the kitchen eating the egg. With the radio on and the light in the rooms going green to gold, the morning just lulled—it held itself steady, unattached to things in the room, and I tell you I sat with my back against the back of the chair, content as a queen who, when the palace was ransacked, carried off her own throne and set it somewhere in the woods. She was worn out; she didn't have a thing; but there she was.

I chewed and swallowed and let the cells of my brain go to work. I thought, this is an opportunity. You can't think in bed. You can't think on the radio. But I sat still and the less I moved, the more I noticed how, one after another, the thoughts lined up, linked themselves, and ran together like frames of a moving picture. I sat there and let it happen.

Of course, in the past, I had given thought to a number of things. I'd thought about Loren, who'd lost, or surrendered, the use of his hands. I'd thought about that, from all of the angles. And with the *Free Press* delivered every day, I paid attention to events, foreign or domestic, violent or nonviolent, since it all counts in the end. And, lately, I'd also tried to decide how it happened that during the winter our daughter Patty had made me a grandmother at thirty-four, for God's sake, but that was a simple matter of arithmetic, and not so surprising considering she'd run off from school the day before Thanksgiving vacation with the evangelical Mr. Stutz, the book burner with the megaphone, the one the *Free Press* called the Noisemaker. The paper said in one article that Patricia Dove, 224 N. Grand River, described this Mr. Stutz as "a person you trust through and through." What is harder to understand, when you think about it, is the fact that I didn't know, as of Easter, if the grandchild was boy or girl—I'd never seen it, and never would see it—because Patty was keeping the child for God. *Harboring* was her word on the phone. I am harboring the child for God. I'd thought after that about harboring, about crimes perpetrated, one way and another.

All of this thinking led nowhere. It knotted up. My mind kept a list of concerns, a mix, like a canned soup label with a long paragraph of ingredients, so that you wonder as you taste it if all those things are really necessary.

But the Easter we lived in Detroit, it was a clear, surging day from the start, with fair-weather clouds crossing the window-square above the sink, an outside activity that recalled to any human who looked these clear-minded conclusions: one, the blue patch was, in fact, sky—blue by its own rules; and, two, the prevailing winds still held.

It was easy to look around. To the right of the living-room door, on the metal radiator cover, was the spider plant; and to the left, on a shelf, was Patty's junior picture, in a cardboard frame—she had her father's straight brown hair, parted in the middle. From where I was, with a slow, continuous turning, I could take in the sofa, which was red plaid, a decent-looking thing where Loren usually sat to watch T.V., and on through the bedroom door I could see Loren's feet at the end of the bed, his toes pointing up, slightly outward. I could look at his feet. Separate objects in the rooms, even though I kept them separate and shadowed with thick lines

247

like the crayon lines of a child's drawing, were nonetheless part of a train of thought. Even a small thing, a book, or a scrap of dust in the corner, took up a quantity of space, and the room seemed full of things to be seen and space to be seen between. When I looked at something, I saw it. I noticed on the wall space next to the front door the old photograph of my grandmother standing beside a newly-planted pine tree, holding me, her youngest grandchild, a baby over her shoulder. The frame was oval, gold metal. In the picture, my head was blurred, turned away, and smudged into the sky of the background. I decided: this is a picture of the pine tree, that's what. I was glad to know it. Count the years, you can figure the tree has grown into something huge, very dark, in somebody's back yard. It is probably so dark, day or night, it looks like empty space.

I decided if I saw Patty again, I'd give her the picture.

On the radio, the man's voice stumbled, mispronouncing *sepulchre*—you'd have thought it was a brand-new story for him. He coughed, trying to cover up, and went on.

Years ago, when Patty was a child small enough to hold on one arm, I remember holding her on Christmas morning and telling her it was the day Jesus was born, and she said, very sweet and mournful in my ear—yes, she'd heard about Him, she'd heard they put Him in a tube. A tube! Well, you can understand that when she was swept up last fall with the Noisemaker, I thought I'd lighten things up and remind her of her first Christian knowledge. But she couldn't laugh. She said, Mother, shame. What's shame, I said. You think your Jesus couldn't take a joke, I said. Knowing what *He* knows, I said. But Patty's a serious girl; she always was.

A choir sang. I stretched my legs and shoulders, crackling vertebrae in my back, and I remembered I hadn't got the paper yet from the hall. With the mid-morning noises from outside—cars braking for the light and gunning off, a whistling kettle across the alley—I could move around easily without waking Loren. I unlocked the front door, picked up the paper, and locked the door again. Even while it was folded, I could see the *Free Press* had a very predictable three-color picture on the front page, of a mountainside near Jerusalem, where a touring dramatic club had staged an Easter pageant. Except for the winged angel who sat on one side, the scene came close to the one of the tomb I had pictured myself.

After the headlines, I slid myself back into bed, where the sheets on my side had cooled, and I pushed against Loren, curling myself to his back like a shadow, which he had occasion to notice, and he said, here, Mummy, here you go. He rolled over to me with what I would call real intent. I don't deny that I had been thinking, too, a kind of a thought: dear God, a double bed and two bodies in it—Easter—and no place to go.

Loren was forty-two. He claimed his hands were dead hands, although they were very beautiful, and patterned with veins and with criss-crossed lines in the shape of stars on his knuckles. Sometimes he let his hands hang from his wrists as if they'd been chopped off and reattached with a hidden stitching. Every day he would set the hands flat on the table top and look at them. With a snap of his elbows, he'd flip the hands over and examine the palms. They looked fine to me. But he'd study them as if any time he expected them to move against his will. I think he'd prepared himself to recalculate, at the moment that happened, everything he knew. He didn't use the word *miracle*, but I think he believed one had already hit him, and that possibly it would happen again and undo itself. If he'd been a scientist with the habit of tracking an idea down, instead of a welder, he might have been able to figure out what was what. But being the man he was, he veered. He wasn't a bitter man, but he couldn't put two and two together. He learned to stare. When he saw something going on, when he saw Patty pack up the red suitcase and leave, for example, he stood in the doorway and flicked his head as if he were snapping his welder's helmet in place, and having trouble with it. But he didn't blink; and he didn't say anything more than goodbye. By Easter, I'd allowed myself to admit that I lived with a vacated Loren, a shadowy man who'd discovered silence and who made love much more carefully now.

Loren liked to read the paper and he read every column, including the ones in the Business section. After I gave him breakfast, he sat with the paper in his lap, the back pages propped against the table. While he read and while the radio man talked on, I washed dishes. From the kitchen, I didn't mind watching him. The past can cut itself off very smoothly. It's possible that Loren's life from birth had been surrounded with a silence nobody noticed, and I certainly never noticed, until he wasn't working. But then the quiet accumulated; it polished him, waxy and definite. That Easter morning, at a distance of twenty feet, I could see the capsules, like layers of color, around him. I took some time, looking at him. I watched him the way you watch, unpitying, an insect going its own way in the alley, working its legs over chunks of gravel. You feel lucky just to see it.

"It's the Noisemaker," Loren said. "Here's where she is." He nodded and pointed with his forehead to an article in the paper.

"So. So," I said. I read the article over Loren's shoulder. It was a brief note: Richard Stutz, 28, arraigned for trespassing, breaking and entering, and malicious destruction of property, after an incident at the Allegan High School. Rock and roll records, brand name articles of clothing, books—some of them stolen out of the library—had been heaped on a bonfire in the schoolyard. Apparently, Mr. Stutz had broken a window in the library, climbed in, and thrown out selected titles. The article didn't mention his megaphone, but I knew it was there, calling from inside the building, describing each step, naming each book as he pulled it off the shelf. There was no mention of Patty; I didn't expect any. She'd have been somewhere out of sight. And nothing about the Noisemaker's baby.

"She's in Allegan," Loren said.

"I'll look it up."

On the Rand-McNally map, Allegan was marked in the western fruit-growing area, a greenish strip with grey hatching. The whole section was stamped with small, rounded trees, the symbol for orchards and vineyards.

"Drop her a line," Loren said. "Maybe in care of the Court House?" He pushed at the paper and flipped the page.

The letter was simple to write. I wasn't very hopeful about it, one sheet of paper, but I knew it wouldn't hurt. After a certain point, nothing hurts. In the living room, bright streaks from the sun came in around the shades, and I snapped them up and let the daylight in, a liquidy milk sort of light that flowed across the room, straight for the table. But it was cool, and I moved the Olivetti from the sewing table into the lighted space opposite Loren. Without planning ahead what to say, I started in, typing at my top speed, which is above average, and which Loren sometimes smiles at, as if the tapping noise and the running of fingers from key to key means something different to him.

I can tell you exactly what I wrote, because I have the letter here. It came back after a month. Someone had opened it up and taped it shut. I don't know who.

I told Patty it was Easter and did she remember that. I told her just because she was in the orchards and not in a desert region not to feel left out of it all, that I didn't. Loren, at this point, said to say hello, and I typed in: Patty, your father says hello. When I saw those words, I knew that Patty, because of the Noisemaker, would think about God the Father, that's how she thinks, and that is why I went on with this talk about her father. I told her, your father is right here, across the table from me. You know who I'm talking about. You know who your father is, I told her. And I know who your baby's father is, Richard Stutz. Think about this, Patty. I am your mother, and you are your baby's mother. My guess is, I told her, the baby is a boy. I asked her point-blank. I am your mother, and I ask you, Patricia, would you harbor a girl for God. Oh no, I told her. You were *my* little girl, I told her, and I harbored you for *nobody*. Look at yourself. You're grown up. I told her to sit down in the sunlight somewhere to read the letter and remember, as she well knew, that she was a daughter of mine and of her father's, that's whose. God doesn't want your baby any more than God wanted you. I tried to say it plain. Sometimes when you think the worse, you have to say it. I told her I didn't know where she was but I thought she should walk the baby boy on the beach and tell it who its father and mother were, and who its grandmother and grandfather were. Tell him his grandmother has new white capped teeth, better than anything you'd believe, and that his grandfather says hello from Detroit. Sit in the sand all afternoon, I told her, and think. I told her, do you really believe God has the chance to think the way we do? None of this will surprise you, I said. We are thinking of you. Your father, who is no better, is also no worse, and he says, fare thee well, which he did say. He also said, be gentle now, but I didn't check back. I said, be well, my dearest one. With love, your mother.

Loren and I finished reading the paper. At noon, he took a nap, which went on all afternoon. I opened the living-room window and sat on the sill, listening to the radio. The window had no screen; I could open it wide and sit there, watching the space over the roofs, where the light of the morning held on. It was a pale light that slowed people down and hushed them up. Kids on bicycles riding no-hands swerved smoothly and turned up the alley as if their bikes were on automatic. Nobody shouted to anybody.

For supper, I cooked a steak, and we watched the news on T.V. A reporter outside a crumbled building in Jerusalem said that no incidents of violence disrupted the Christian holiday.

"No violence here either," I said to Loren.

He shook his head.

After the news, I turned on the radio again and we had our ice cream. Loren went to the window. On the radio a preacher was saying, it fills us with amazement, *amazement,* he said, that Jesus rose up from the arms of death. He was dead, he was in the tomb, but he rose up and walked again. The preacher sounded so surprised.

Loren sat down on the sill with his arms in his lap and watched the street. Listen, Mummy, he said. Turn off the radio. Look.

I turned it off and walked over beside him. There were sirens. A haze had wound itself over the city, gauzy and pinkish-orange.

Loren leaned back against the window frame and I sat opposite. I told him I'd had a whole day to study what was on my mind, and see, I came through it. It didn't surprise me that a person who knew what God knew, given the time to think, would throw over the idea of staying dead, and come back, and keep on going.

Loren said, hold my hand. I took his hand and I held it up to my mouth. All of his fingers pointed to the ground. The skin on his arm was soft, untanned, with fine brown hair, and I drew my tongue across the hairs.

The sirens moved in and then came blue flashing lights, headed downtown. Patty's letter lay somewhere behind me, in the middle of the table, sealed and stamped. Loren and I sat on the windowsill while the dark took over the living room and took over the ground outside, too. The dark, which is like a shelter around each person, is a lovely thing to see, once you see it.

nominated by M. D. Elevitch

LEDGE

by SANDRA McPHERSON

from GRAND STREET

Butterfly-lily
and roan puff-pea
raise a sparse meadow
in gravel.
So does a patch
of snow downslope,
solitary and dirty
like a goat.
From timberline
Jeffrey pinecones
roll into the lake.
Clothes lie on a rock.
I too
float into Lake Shirley.

The bottom atomizes
at a toe-touch,
disperses upward,
rapturizes
its green, hairy,
restless insolidity.
The lake floor
is suspense.
Human presence
shoos like a draft
its elderly

incohesion—
each fathom sneezes
to my step.

"Follow the outlet
down and never,
never go uphill."
But a hawk's back
reddens and veers off—
below. A short
shore where
I drink from my hands
bridles into a cliff,
an inchworm
rears its waist
to read "omega."
And the dropping
low voice of the stream

teases me
to suspect I climb.
Until across an aeon-cut
between summits
sulfur as a Zen wardrobe,
not snow
but something freshly
fallen there—
a white crash,
a private patch
of plane
which the rescue helicopter
at frost-dawn yesterday
frowned upon

and today newsprinted
as waffled wings,
an engine's deep
metal eyes
in a burrow,

a meteor, a marmot.
Here on this ledge
the strange
stream I must follow
splits two ways.
A water ouzel
turns its tail,
uncurious, calm, and gray—
oh but even he

must see this;
how a guide of water,
slipping and falling,
does better than a person
trying to descend
alone, keening
to belong
in the grassy,
red-ant valley
a day beneath
this ledge
from which Shirley Creek
hangs in two sashes
such as my lost

grandmother used to tie
behind me.
I crouch at the knot
in a print of odors
of Jeffrey lemon
bark, twigs
snapped cold as vanilla,
violets, pineapples,
apples: illusion,
a high
to cover the hard panic
centered
above two waterfalls
growing apart.

I like granite.
It can act like a tin basin.
But I wish I were not
alone, unsure,
and strange to the ouzel.
I feel the quartz rapids,
shallow-grained, deep-striped,
trying to twist the water
round my little finger.
Springy, it all
loosens of itself.
Goes where?
Past, past where
I lift off my shirt
              and wash.

nominated by Pamela Stewart

KODIAK WIDOW

by SHEILA NICKERSON

from *Into The Storm: The Fifth Orca Anthology* (Orca Press)

The curtains speak to me.
Even the spoons
slipping in and out of my mouth
don't know as much—
the man who seeded me,
the sons who swam away
like fingerlings.
The curtains tell me how it was—
how I unfurled like sails before wind,
how I shook with light,
danced with storm.
Now when gales blow
south from the Barren Islands,
the curtains sing to me—
sometimes a lullaby in Russian,
sometimes a song
that only I can understand.
I need no instrument, no telephone.
The curtains hold the news,
the gossip of flying geese and tears.

nominated by Richard Eberhart

DOG FIGHT

by CHARLES BUKOWSKI

from THE WORMWOOD REVIEW

he draws up against my rear bumper in the fast lane,
I can see his head in the rear view mirror, his eyes
are blue and he sucks upon a dead cigar.
I pull over. he passes, then slows. I don't like
this.
I pull back into the fast lane, engage myself upon
his rear bumper. we are as a team passing through
Compton.
I turn the radio on and light a cigarette.
he ups it 5 mph, I do likewise. we are as a team
entering Inglewood.
he pulls out of the fast lane and I drive past.
then I slow. when I check the rear view he is
upon my bumper again.
he has almost made me miss my turnoff at Century.
I hit the blinker and fire across 3 lanes of
traffic, just make the off-ramp . . .
blazing past the front of an inflammable tanker.
blue eyes comes down from behind the tanker and
we veer down the ramp in separate lanes to the signal
and we sit there side by side, not looking at each
other.
I am caught behind an empty school bus as he idles
behind a Mercedes.
the signal switches and he is gone. I cut to the
inner lane behind him, then I see that the parking

lane is open and I flash by inside of him and the
Mercedes, turn up the radio, make the green as the
Mercedes and blue eyes run the yellow into the red.
they make it as I power it and switch back ahead of
them in their lane in order to miss a parked vegetable
truck.
now we are running 1-2-3, not a cop in sight, we are
moving through a 1980 California July
we are driving with skillful nonchalance
we are moving in perfect anger
we are as a team
approaching LAX:
1-2-3
2-3-1
3-2-1.

nominated by Gerry Locklin and Tony Quagliano

from THE GREAT PRETENDER

by JAMES ATLAS

from TRIQUARTERLY

IT WAS 1968, and I was twenty. I had gotten a summer job as a manuscript reader for *Poetry* magazine, and toward the end of June I moved down to the North Side, where one of my Evanston friends, Herbert Lowenstein, had an apartment. A composer who was studying at Roosevelt University downtown, Herbert lived in a ground-floor apartment on Sheffield, west of the elevated tracks, a neighborhood of wooden houses layered over with aluminum siding or brick-patterned tarpaper, the scruffy yards enclosed by waist-high cyclone fences. From the kitchen window I could see backyards cluttered with tricycles and junked refrigerators beneath a fretwork of laundry lines and creosote-stained telephone poles.

Herbert's apartment was willfully minimal: the walls were hospital-green, the linoleum floors high-school brown, the windows spotted with grime. The only furniture was a card table littered with Herbert's scores and monographs, an upright piano, two mattresses, a few folding chairs, and bookshelves constructed from raw planks propped up on cinderblocks. The kitchen was never used; the paint-specked sink had a bone-dry look about it and the faucet was flecked with rust. Swollen clots of ice bulged from the freezer compartment of the refrigerator. Just visible beneath the crust was a package of Green Giant peas. There was nothing on the shelves but a box of Domino sugar and a jar of freeze-dried coffee.

Herbert took all his meals at the Victoria Restaurant, a coffee shop beneath the Belmont elevated tracks. "It gives me an excuse to go out," he explained.

The son of a dentist in Evanston, Herbert reminded me of the urban poor described in Michael Harrington's *The Other America:* he never got any mail and didn't even have a phone until I arrived on the scene. Dr. Lowenstein lived in one of those stolid old buildings on Sheridan Road with a marble foyer and a sun porch overlooking Lake Michigan, but Herbert was a Marxist, and money was "shit." (When I recommended Michel Foucault's *The Order of Things,* he scoffed, "You mean *The Ordure of Things.*") In his cheap brown slacks and ivory short-sleeved shirts from a discount men's-wear outlet on Belmont, Herbert looked more like a storefront insurance salesman than a composer. He was an "internal émigré," as he put it, an heir to Isaac Babel, Walter Benjamin, E. M. Cioran—victims in one way or another of our terrible century. Cesare Pavese, a suicide; Osip Mandelstam, dead in a Soviet labor camp; Guillaume Apollinaire, fatally wounded in the trenches during World War I: these were Herbert's representative men. Hunched over the card table in the front parlor, fists clenched, a cigarette burning in a tin ashtray by his side, he read "in order to survive." North Sheffield was exile. "Chicago is meteorologically and topographically identical with certain regions of Central Siberia," he had written me at school the previous winter, offering me what he called my "poet's daily dose of transfiguration." "Chicago really becomes itself in winter. Only then does the inner torture of its inhabitants find confirmation in the outer aspects of the city." Shivering in his overcoat beside a porcelain-glazed gas stove, Herbert was as far from his father's cheerful office in the Old Orchard Shopping Plaza, with its piped-in Muzak and tinsel-decorated waiting room, as a dissident hauling wood in a Siberian penal colony.

Herbert was always trying to draw me into discussions of "the means and the mode of production," the "early" and the "late" Marx. "Read this, so we can discuss it," he would say, handing me Trotsky's *Literature and Revolution* or some essay by T. W. Adorno in *New Left Review*. I shut my ears to the tinny Latin music blaring from the juke box in the El Lago Club next door, the landlady's television rumbling overhead, the kids yelling in the street—"Louie! Hey, Louie! Where the fuck's my bike?" "On the back porch where it always is, asshole!"—and applied myself to dialectics as if I were cramming for an exam.

By the time I'd gotten through one of these assignments, Herbert invariably had some new enthusiasm. "I'm beginning to see how wrong Lukács was about so many things," he announced after I'd struggled through four hundred pages of *History and Class-Consciousness*. "You really have to read Gadamer to know what's up." The year before he'd written me at school recommending "The Real Bahamas in Music & Song," and for months the vibrations of steel drums and exuberant voices singing "Yellow Bird" filled my room in Dunster House. But when I arrived home babbling about how great Calypso was, he gave me a peculiar look and put on his latest find: Bulgarian folk music.

Why did I subject myself to this rigorous course of study? To root out my reactionary impulses. "Saw your poem in *Poetry*," Herbert had acknowledged in a letter devoted to the problems of composing twelve-tone music in "our late-capitalist moment." "If you are a poet, I hope you can use language not just as it is, an oily lubricant for the frictionless working of the system." He had no patience for my nostalgic family poems ("My heart simmered with angry love/ Like chicken soup on grandma's stove"). "Why don't you write about North Vietnamese peasantry?" he suggested. "How they live, work the fields, the satisfaction they must experience in such a unified and just effort. Or the joy of a group of villagers who've just shot down an American plane?"

Herbert was right. My poems didn't have a whole lot to do with the class struggle shaping up right outside my window, where sirens shrieked and warbled in the steamy night and the blue flashers of squad cars accelerating up Sheffield flitted past our open door. This was Amerika, 1968.

"Listen to this," Herbert said one sweltering night when the Puerto Ricans were drag-racing up and down the street, their tuned-up engines splintering the air like a chain saw. Seated across from him at the wobbly table, I was working on a new poem, "The song of a lover who loves his death/And sees the few years as the long." *Señor Ministre de Salud*," he recited in a stern dictatorial voice. "*Qué hacer? Ah, muchisimo qué hacer.*"

"What's it mean?"

He squinted at me through the smoke of his cigarette. "They don't teach you things like that at Harvard? 'Too much. There's too

262

much to do.' It's a poem by Vallejo that I set to music: 'Manifesto for Woodwinds and Voices.' " He went over to the piano and played a few notes that sounded as if someone were dusting the keys. "That's the oboe," Herbert explained, "and then a bassoon comes in"—he pounded out a thunderous chord—"defiant, bitter, furious. Followed by a chorus of a hundred mournful women." He sang in a piping voice, " 'Too much to do.' They're supposed to sound imploring, desperate: 'What can we do for the revolution?' "

"You really think you could get a hundred mournful women?"

"Sure. Mahler scored his Tenth Symphony for a thousand voices. A hundred's nothing."

Maureen, the waitress on the day shift at the Victoria Restaurant, was a real city girl. Hefty and double-chinned, she leaned against the counter smoking, her white uniform spotted, her skin pearly and coarse-pored. She had grown up on the South Side in one of those Italian neighborhoods of bungalows with concrete stoops and scalloped curtains, the yards marked off with necklaces of chain. Her father worked in a Gary steel mill. Maureen had dropped out of college after a semester at Chicago Circle because she was pregnant by a masseur at the Standard Club, but she had no intention of getting married. "My kid's gonna have a masseur for a father?" she said indignantly. "Forget it. If I can't do better than that, I'll bring it up myself."

Arriving with our morning coffee, she would perch on the edge of the booth—"jus' for a second; I can't sit around all morning like you guys"—and tap a cigarette out of her pack. Her stomach was beginning to fill out beneath her soiled apron. A pregnant girl: I found the whole thing deeply mysterious. In the bright fluorescent light, I studied her grubby nail-bitten hands, her straw-dry hair, her gray cat's eyes: couldn't I stop thinking about girls for *ten seconds?* Not that it ever turned out like it did in *Sexus*. " 'Jesus, Henry, I never thought it could be like this. Can you fuck like this every night?' " I should have been reading *The Sun Also Rises*.

The truth is I was happiest on those nights when I didn't have a date. I would come home from the office, get a beer out of the fridge, and go sit on the front steps in the cottony heat, watching the sky become a deep lavender as the sodium-vapor streetlamps flicked on and the windows were kindled by the sunlight. Popping open my can of Budweiser, I savored its metallic, chilly taste and

263

talked to the landlady's five-year-old daughter, Melody, who came down after supper to dig in the yard with a plastic shovel, filling her pail with dirt, then emptying it out again. Squatting on the scrubby grass, her smudged yellow shorts tight against her thighs, she worked with purposeful absorption, distractedly pushing aside a wisp of damp blond hair that had come loose from her barrette. My heart quickened when she came up and put her little arms around my neck, grabbing for my can of beer. Her skin smelled of camomile lotion. "Want a Pez?" she said, whipping out her Goofy dispenser.

"No thanks, Melody. Beer and Pez don't mix."

"Can I have a sip of your beer?"

"That's probably not a very good idea. Your mother would get mad." When I held the can away, she climbed up on my lap to reach it.

"Well, pull me in my wagon then."

She got in and sat down, hugging her knees, an expectant look on her face. I grabbed the handle and headed off down the sidewalk, pulling her back and forth in front of the house until Mrs. Underwood leaned out the window and called "Mel-o-dy"—a melancholy three-noted song in the dusk. I lifted her out and she tromped poutily upstairs, dragging her pail behind her. Another girl betrayed.

Across the street the glad, syncopated beat of Latin music came through the open door of the El Lago Club. A phone rang two doors down. Go in and work, I ordered myself. Go write a poem about the sunset. But after Melody had gone upstairs I was overcome by a familiar desolation, that ache of solitude I used to feel wandering through our empty house in my underpants when I was seventeen, *Satisfaction* blasting out on the stereo while I stared at myself in a full-length mirror and wondered if I would ever grow up. "I can't get no-o sa-tis-fac-shun. . . ." You're not the only one, Mick. I strolled over to World Drug in the twilight and leafed through magazines, breathing in the medicinal air. The white, octagonal tiles, the propeller-like fan suspended from the stamped-tin ceiling, the combs in a cardboard easel beside the cash register and the grimy beach balls in a bin reminded me of my grandparents' drugstore on Peterson Avenue.

Maureen. She was working nights now. Maybe I'd walk by the

Victoria. . . . I peered through the dusty plate-glass window and saw her wiping the counter. "Hi," she said when I came in. "We're just closing up." She undid her apron, and I could see the faint swell of her stomach where the baby was waiting in the wings.

"You want to go for a walk or something?" I said.

"Sure."

Loose change clinked in her pocket as we walked down Belmont toward the lake. The storefronts were dark, and we glimpsed ourselves in the window of a surgical supply store, two shadowy faces superimposed on a display of walkers and prosthetic limbs. "Are you scared about having a baby?" I said.

"Nah. I need the company. It'll be fun to go with it to the zoo and stuff, pushing around a pram. I'll be a good mother."

"But, like, don't you think it will make you feel old?"

"If you're old enough to get knocked up, you're old enough to be a mother," Maureen said. "I mean, it wasn't anything I planned on, but what the hell? Things don't always work out the way you thought they would."

Lying beside her on the grass, I felt like a boy with his mother. A sudden sadness crept over me as I remembered how my mother used to drive me to local tennis tournaments in the summer. There was a secret between us, some furtive understanding; I couldn't look her in the eye. Out on the court, I watched her through the chain-link fence, reading or knitting, as patient as a chauffeur. Once, when I was fifteen, she had driven me and Noreen Fleisher to an open-air performance of "As You Like It" in the Grant Park bandshell, and I'd made her go sit by herself. All through the first act I kept glancing over at her, alone beneath a tree. But when I went to keep her company between acts, she made me go back to Noreen: "She's your date. I'm fine." But Mama, I want to sit with you.

In the harbor, yachts knocked against the pier. Children pounded up and down the esplanade in the dark while their parents sat on the grass in canvas lawn chairs and talked. The smelt were running now; on the beach below, men armed with nets and lanterns waded in the shallows. Maureen guided my hand over her stomach. "Feel the baby?" I leaned down and laid my ear against her blouse, pretending I could hear it. "Are you in there?" I said. Her uniform gave off a clean, laundered scent.

"What are you going to call it?"

"Deirdre if it's a girl, Raymond if it's a boy," she said promptly. "Aren't those pretty names?"

"They are. They're really pretty. You'll have a beautiful child, Maureen."

She would. In the glow of the old-fashioned cast-iron lamps on the esplanade, her pale skin had a porcelain tint. It had lost the fishy sheen that made her look so washed-out in the Victoria. I brushed my lips against her neck. "You want to go back?"

Within a block, the odor of rotting fish gave way to the city's heat, a stifling blend of tar and asphalt. The stars over the lake were swallowed up in the milky light that suffused the sky.

Maureen lived down the street from me, in a storefront that had been converted into an apartment; curtains hung in the plate-glass windows. There was a wooden staircase at the back, and we climbed up to the roof, where it was cool. The tarred gravel still gave off heat from the day. Just across the alley was the trestle of the elevated tracks, and every few minutes a train hurtled by. Electric sparks crackled between the rails as the metal wheels shrieked around the turn and the earth-brown tenement walls lit up like a cave illuminated by torchlight. Faces flashed past in the yellow windows and vanished in the dark.

Beside me, Maureen's skin gave off the fragrance of girls in summer, a bouquet of dried sweat and perfume. I stroked her bare white arm. Miles to the south, the towers of downtown office buildings rose in glittering pillars of light.

"Are you staying over?" Maureen said.

"If you want me to."

"I do." If it feels good, do it: the credo of our time. She pulled the curtains shut, lit a scented candle in a saucer on the floor, and stood before the mirror caressing her stomach. Reaching behind her, she started to pull her uniform up over her head.

"No, leave it on," I said. Its starchy whiteness excited me. Maureen as a nurse. She stepped out of her cotton underpants and hiked up her dress in the flickering light, then turned away and dipped her legs, hands on knees like a referee. I stared at the orbs of her ass and the dark furrow that divided it. There was something unnerving about that furry cleft; it drove all thoughts from my mind, and left a clear, vacant concentration on what we were about to do. I undid my pants and stood behind her, watching her face in

266

the mirror; eyes closed, lips pursed, she looked as if she were thinking hard. I crouched like a quarterback waiting for the hike, and slipped in.

Studying our bodies in the mirror, I was in the same deep trance that came over me when I leafed through porn magazines in the sex shops on South Wabash, gazing with stunned eyes at the cum-smeared faces and outsized cocks, the toiling threesomes giving it to each other every which way: did people really do such things? Dimly I heard a car swish past, its headlights flashing through the gauzy curtain. Maureen looked at me in the mirror and began to move up and down while I spread my trembling knees. Suddenly she shuddered, her shoulders quaking as if she had a chill. I clasped my hands around her swelling stomach and came in a spasm so fierce that I cried out with a bereaved sob more like a mourner's lament than a moan of pleasure.

"Jesus, Maureen," I murmured as we collapsed on the bed. "What was that all about?"

"There's something about sex when you're pregnant," she admitted. "I never used to come like that. It's like my body's all keyed up for the big event."

"I just had my big event," I said, reaching for a cigarette. My hand shook so much I could hardly get it lit. Maureen got up to go to the bathroom, and I had an impulse to grab my clothes and get out. There was always that moment when it was over and I just wanted to be alone. Fleeing the scene of the crime. Emission accomplished. One advantage to living at home was that you couldn't stay out all night. Driving back from a date after midnight in high school, I would turn on the radio, downshifting through the empty streets in my father's MG as I hastened home to the glass of milk and the plate of brownies that nullified my corruption. I didn't have any excuses now.

But what about Maureen? What did *she* want? She padded back to bed, her doggy face illuminated by the guttering candle on its saucer. Could it be that she was as lonely as I was and just wanted company? There's no need for remorse, I reassured myself. You're not depraved; you did no wrong. She likes you. "Why, to get laid is actually socially constructive and useful, an act of citizenship"— thus Herzog. I was striking a blow against the repressive sexuality that deformed human relationships under capitalism. No one ever said the revolution would be fun.

267

When I woke up, the transom was filled with gray light, floating above the door like a Rothko. Beside me Maureen's body gave off a warm sleep odor. There was a chalky taste in my mouth from cigarettes and beer. I slipped out of bed, pulled on my clothes, and walked back to Sheffield. It was early, but a haze rose off the empty street and the trees had the parched dusty look they got in midsummer, wilting in littered patches of dirt. The rows of wooden, two-family houses with sagging porches and scrubby yards gave this part of Chicago a strangely rural look; except for the elevated tracks, it might have been some dying Georgia town. Hardly the kind of neighborhood to nourish fantasies of literary fame, but its shabbiness didn't trouble me. Byron and Teresa Guicchioli floated in a gondola through the canals of Venice; Maureen Duffy and I hung around the Victoria Restaurant. Did that make the nervous exaltation I felt in her presence any less momentous? Hours later, lighting a cigarette at work, I could still detect the musky odor of cunt on my hands. I glanced over at Eloise, the spinster secretary whose office I shared, held my fingers under my nose, and inhaled.

My friend Bob Wolin and I had lunch on the North Side once a week. He was working at *Playboy* for the summer, editing their Party Jokes page. (As usual, he towered over me; I could see his office, on the twenty-ninth floor of the Palmolive Building, from my ground-floor window at *Poetry*.) "Got some great jokes for you," he would announce, striding through the midday gloom of Eli's Stage Delicatessen on Oak. "Dear Joke Editors," began a typical submission, scrawled in pencil on a torn sheet of yellow legal paper:

>What do a ball, a bat, a snake and a circle all have in common?
>Answer: There all sex sembles.
>   Please send my $25 to BOB BRUSKI, 3477 Champlain Street, Terre Haute, Indiana.
>   (P.S. Don't use my name. My wife would have a cow.)

"How can you read this junk?" I said.
"I'd like to see some of the stuff you have to plow through."
It was true: the sack of manuscripts the mailman dragged into the office every morning contained some pretty dismal efforts.

How did these people keep their spirits up? I wondered, glancing through the day's submissions, fifty or sixty fat envelopes crammed with a dolorous assortment of villanelles, sonnets, ballads, haiku, and "free verse" effusions from all over the world. Most required only a glance at the first few lines ("Eagle and lambs, together, share/Of the sweets of the wilderness"); and there were "repeaters" whose manuscripts I didn't have to read at all after awhile: a nun from St. Paul, Minnesota, who specialized in "Jesus" poems ("Christ came to me in bed one night/His head with a crown of thorns bedight"); Louis Ginsberg, a retired New Jersey school-teacher, who was Allen Ginsberg's father; the inmate of a mental institution in Upstate New York, who covered yellow legal sheets with an illegible scrawl; and Bejan J. Daruwalla, a poet from Bombay, who submitted many versions of his "Apostrophe to a Nihilist" in the hope of "getting it right":

> If always you are looking
> For items to pick at,
> Or objects and people to hurtle a brick at,
> You are sure to find NOTHING
> For which to thank heaven
> No matter what fabulous
> Fortune is given.
> And would you persist
> In this line if you knew
> That it would wreck everything,
> Including YOU?

If these people had only known that their submissions were doomed to languish in a file cabinet for six weeks before they were sent back—a policy designed to discourage eager poets from inundating us with manuscripts.

I usually came across two or three poems in each mail that required further attention, either because they were by contributors to the magazine or had possibilities; the rest got a rejection slip. Stuffing the manuscripts back in their stamped, self-addressed envelopes, I felt sorry for the authors and couldn't resist scrawling a few words of encouragement on their slips: "Try us again" or "You have a feel for words." But these consoling messages only provoked more thick envelopes. "I don't know who you are," wrote a court stenographer from Flint, Michigan, "but yours are the first personal words I've received from an editor in twenty-seven years. I wonder if you would mind reading my novel, *O Bloody Land*." Enclosed was a 300-page manuscript, the pages faded to parchment yellow. I read the first two sentences: "Abe Lincoln leaned forward in his chair and buried his face in his hands. 'By God, Mary,' he cried, 'I'll see the slaves freed if it's the last thing I ever do.'"

One day Bob came in to Eli's and handed me a new poem: "One of the few sonnets ever written in the bleachers at Comiskey Park." I pushed aside a plate of borscht and laid it on the table.

NIGHT GAME

I sit in the bleachers among a chanting crowd,
My eyes stunned by the emerald lawn.
High above the upper deck, night lights
Blaze down through the steamy dark. A cloud
Scuds past the pearly moon.
The players trot out in their dazzling whites.
The stadium is a luminous bowl
As Lollar chops one through the hole.

Loitering among the hopped-up fans,
I watch a pop-up arc through the tropical night
And think of those exotic ancient clans
—Egyptian, Sumerian, Coptic, Hittite—
Who scanned the skies for omens and prayed to strange gods.
On the mound, the pitcher looks in for the sign and nods.

"I don't like 'hopped-up' and 'pop-up,' " I said.
"Hey, thanks a lot. I can always count on you for a generous response."
"Sorry." What was it Yeats said at a crowded meeting of the Rhymers' Club? *"The only thing certain about us is that we are too many."* As far as I was concerned, two was too many. "It has some good things," I conceded, scanning the poem. "I like 'pearly moon,' and the line about 'exotic clans.' But the meter's off, and I don't get the last couplet. Are you trying to say that the pitcher is as primitive as these old clans?"

270

"No, I'm saying that Sherm Lollar is the reincarnation of King Tut."

Five minutes into the meal and we were ready to step outside. What was it about Bob? His seersucker jacket had a crisp, summery look, and his close-cropped hair gave him a boyish air. Just right for *Playboy*, where the editors lounged around in big offices with television sets in the corner and Abstract Expressionist prints in steel-edged frames on the wall. The secretaries were former Playmates of the Month who looked as if they'd just gotten off a bearskin rug and slipped into those tight-fitting jumpsuits with necklines down to their *pupiks* that were the standard uniform over there. I shared an office with Eloise, who buttoned her long-sleeved blouses up to the chin. "But what's this poem really saying?" I pursued. "I mean, what's it about? Baseball is one of our rituals?"

"You just don't think a poem can be written about baseball," Bob said hotly. "Nuclear war isn't the only subject there is, you know."

"I'm not saying it is. It's just this is somehow so . . . obvious."

"Fuck it," Bob said, grabbing the poem. "There's no point in showing you my work." His blue eyes were furious. But goading him had mollified me—a tidy transfer of resentment.

"Come on, Bob," I said, spearing a knish. "Lemme see it." I studied the poem again with a professorial eye. "It's really good. The rhyme scheme's very taut." Magnanimity was a pleasant emotion. It was satisfying to dole out praise once you'd made your real feelings known.

"You think it's good enough for *Poetry?*"

In the dim booth, I weighed my response. It wasn't easy having all this power. You wanted to be encouraging, but not create false hope. Besides, did Bob really need to get published in *Poetry?* I mean, he was six feet tall, with a face right out of a back-to-school ad; he had won the Illinois High School Poetry Contest two years in a row; enough was enough.

Still, it wasn't a bad poem. "It might get in," I said, having hesitated long enough to convey my doubts. "I'll send it on." And be credited with a good deed.

"Thanks, Bobo." Bob signaled for the check. "This one's on me." On the sidewalk in front of Eli's, he lit a Tiparillo. It was time for our ritual summing up. "So here we are," he said. "The two North Shore boys in the big city."

271

"It's amazing," I agreed. With us everything was amazing. We marveled over ourselves the way we had once marveled over the gigantic walk-in heart at the Museum of Science and Industry, awed that such a rudimentary organism could support life. I had been moved by the rustle of blood in the huge plastic auricles and ventricles, the rhythmic thump of the pumping muscle as Mrs. Rady led our fifth-grade class through the heart. I could still remember sitting with Bob on the long bus-ride home. We had nearly come to blows over what the aorta did. And now we were standing on a hot sidewalk in the city with ties around our necks. Life! Was it possible that everyone grew up, left home, got jobs, ended up "in the city" having lunch and heading back to the office with their jackets hung over their shoulders on a thumb? It couldn't be; it was too momentous. We would have read about it by now.

"Well, Bob," I declared, "I wish you luck in your endeavor to find jokes that will leap off the page, stun readers with their savage wit, and earn you a permanent niche in the pantheon of *Playboy* Party Jokes editors."

"And you, Kippy," Bob solemnly replied. "May you go forth and discover a poem beside which *The Waste Land* will seem the mere puling babble of a madman, a poem that will illuminate what you call 'our predicament' and transform the landscape of contemporary literature."

Back at the office, I settled down with the afternoon's batch of manuscripts. The air-conditioner rattled and hummed in the window, and bars of sunlight filtered through the dusty venetian blinds. Eloise's ancient black Underwood clacked in the drowsy silence. My first real job. (I had been a ball boy at Birchwood one summer, chasing down housewives' forehands in the backcourt while the pro yelled, "Put a little hustle in it, Mrs. Sugerman.") A hundred and twenty-five dollars a week. Sitting with my feet up on the desk, the phone by my side, a cigarette in the ashtray, a styrofoam cup of coffee on the desk and a stack of bad poems within easy reach, I was happy. I had a good life.

Toward the end of the afternoon, Derek Holmes, the editor of *Poetry,* phoned from down the hall, summoning me for our daily conference. A bachelor near retirement, he came to work in sandals and bermuda shorts, smoked Gitanes and kept a bottle of

Cinzano in his office; he had once done a year of graduate work at the Sorbonne. "What is it now, dear boy?" he would say in his coquettish voice whenever I came in, the phone tucked under his chin like a cello—then, to one of the friends he gossiped with all day: "Could you hold on for *one* minute, Richard? The boy has just walked in."

Derek had published a couple of my poems, but he was capricious about it. One day he would deliver a crushing remark— "These are rather silly, I'm afraid," or "These are third-rate Lowell"—then turn around and accept some long-winded monologue I had put in the mouth of a dead Bulgarian poet. One afternoon he shuffled down the hall with a fat new biography of Hart Crane in hand and asked if I was "at all interested" in reviewing it. "Shall we say a thousand words?" That whole afternoon I was too excited to read. Leafing through the glossy new book, I glanced at the illustrations, the author's photograph, the promotional letter, the printed slip listing the price and publication date. They gave it authority: whoever owned this book hadn't just gone out and bought it, but had a special purpose, a mandate to "review" it. For weeks afterward I left the fat biography on the card table with the reviewer's slip sticking out so Herbert could see it.

"Any new *finds* today?" Derek said when I came in for our daily conference. He put his bony feet up on the desk. "I'm afraid we'll have to pass on these." He handed me a sheaf of poems—among them my dramatic monologue "Kafka's Prayer."

How could he not like it? I brooded on my way back down the hall. Spoken by Kafka as he lay dying in a Swiss sanatorium, it engaged the big themes: the collapse of Europe, the holocaust, the pathos of the writer's life. The last stanza, where Kafka atones for the vitriolic "Letter to His Father," was especially good:

> What I needed, father, you could never give.
> You made me the invalid I became.
> But now we both need to forgive,
> Or endure the memory of our shame.

What was the matter with Derek, anyway? Slumping down in my wooden swivel chair, I noticed Bob's poem on the desk. "Night Game." I looked out the window for awhile, listening to the bleat of traffic on Rush Street. Then I slipped the poem in an envelope, tucked in a rejection slip, and dropped it in Eloise's OUT box. Why make him wait six weeks?

During the last weeks of August, the *Sun-Times* was full of accounts of the Democratic Convention that was to be held in Chicago and the Yippies who were converging to disrupt it. While Herbert sat at the card table making his way through Kropotkin and Althusser, I lounged on the front steps reading about Jerry Rubin's plot to release a bunch of pigs on the streets of Chicago. Mayor Daley had refused the demonstrators a permit to sleep in Lincoln Park, and it looked like there might be trouble. One steamy night I decided to walk over and see what was happening. "You're wasting your time," Herbert said, looking up from his book. "They're just a bunch of suburban kids playing at revolution."

"Come on, Herbert," I protested. "Things are really heating up out there. I'm sick of *Capital*. I want some action." I laced up my Keds and stuffed a paperback copy of *The Liberal Imagination* in my hip pocket. "It'll be an experience."

"You know what Kafka says about experience?"

It's on the tip of my tongue. "No, what does he say?"

"It's like a seasickness on dry land." But he was putting on his windbreaker. In his white short-sleeved shirt, brown polyester slacks, and scuffed priest's shoes he looked like a 1930s Communist, one of those gaunt union organizers who stood shivering at the gates of factories in the dawn, handing out leaflets.

It was dusk when we got to the park. The sky over the lake was deep lavender, and the air had a warm, grassy fragrance. Beneath the leafy elms thousands of demonstrators were camped out on blankets or wandering around in second-hand Army jackets, T-shirts, Civil War caps, headbands, cowboy hats, bandannas, work shirts, dungarees, blue jeans, sandals, boots, shawls, capes—more ragged than the troops routed at Antietam. Fires smoldered in trash cans and columns of sparks rose through the trees. The faces of the demonstrators shone in the flaring light with a Goya-like intensity. The damp air was perfumed with dope.

It was nearly ten, the curfew stipulated by the police, and the crowd in Lincoln Park had begun to mill about uncertainly. A group of black-clad priests near the platform raised up a giant cross and other people were busy making a barricade of garbage cans and picnic benches. I spotted Allen Ginsberg, Jean Genet, and William Burroughs under a tree. Ginsberg's patriarchal beard flowed down his face and he was nearly bald, but he had the brainy look of a high-school math wizard. Genet wore khaki slacks and huaraches. His forehead was wrinkled like a rotting fruit. Burroughs had a gaunt, papery face, and his gray suit needed pressing.

A girl who had been talking to the trio of writers walked away. Now was my chance. "Mr. Ginsberg?"

The burly poet glanced my way. "Yeah?"

"Um, I just wanted to tell you how much I admired *Howl*. It's really a great poem."

"I suppose you're a poet?" His voice was angry, bored, a basso rasp.

"Well, I don't know about that. But I do write poetry."

"*Qu'est-ce qu'il dit?*" It was Genet, gazing at me with moist eyes full of tenderness.

"*Un poète*," Ginsberg said shortly.

"*Il est beau*," Genet murmured. He gave me an adoring look and reached up to stroke my hair.

Just then a boy raced up and yelled, "They're coming, man, the pigs are coming!" A herd of demonstrators pounded by. "I don't feel like getting my ass whipped," Ginsberg said. "Let's get out of here." The writers trotted off beneath the trees, and I trotted beside them for a few yards, but they didn't notice me—except Genet, who waved at me with a tiny hand as they hurried away in the dark.

Spotlights swept through the fog of tear gas and cast a marshy glare over the scene. I could hear glass shattering on Lincoln Avenue and, close by, the pop of tear-gas canisters. My heart skipped with fear. "How do we get out of here?" I yelled to Herbert.

"I guess we don't," he said.

Just then a squad car's beacon flashed through the trees and a wedge of cops charged over the knoll. "Don't run! Don't run!" people chanted as they sprinted by. Suddenly the tear gas hit me. My eyes winced shut, my throat burned, my face stung as if it had been swabbed with ammonia. I stumbled forward, lost sight of Herbert, and slipped on the wet grass. There were cries and groans in the darkness, and the hollow thud of nightsticks. My lungs were on fire as I raced the last few hundred yards to the edge of the park.

Herbert was leaning against the hood of my mother's Oldsmobile, holding a handkerchief over his face. "I thought I'd never find you!" I shouted over the whoop of sirens and the crunch of tires kicking up gravel as cars skidded out of the parking lot. I fumbled for the key, flung open the passenger door, and we lurched forward through the swarm of cars heading away from the park. Wooden barricades had been set up at the intersections. The street was strewn with broken glass. Wisps of tear gas hung in the air.

"This isn't a good neighborhood to be in," Herbert said. "You want to stop at Miyako's?"

"Excellent. I could use an order of tempura."

I drove past the taverns on Division, their neon Pabst and Schlitz signs pulsing over the doors, and parked in front of a restaurant with a beaded curtain in the window. It had the look of an ordinary luncheonette, with a counter and three booths; only a paper lantern overhead and the old Oriental men who hung around reading tissue-thin newspapers dense with columns of spidery characters distinguished it from a neighborhood coffee shop.

The restaurant was nearly empty. A Japanese family sat at one table, and there was a man in a threadbare business suit at the counter. "What an incredible scene!" I exulted. My heart was storming in my chest. History!

"This is child's play, hippie pranks," Herbert said. "It has nothing to do with politics."

"I don't know," I said doubtfully. "I thought we made a point."

Herbert squinted through smeared glasses. "What point?" There was impatience in his voice; he would explain it to me again. "Without the proletariat there is no such thing as revolution. Until the proletariat is enlisted in the struggle it's just a game."

"But how do you do that? I mean, how are you supposed to go about enlisting them?"

"Study." He pulled out a cigarette and tapped it on the table. "First you have to grasp dialectics, which I think you don't," he pursued. "The difference between the means and the mode of production, the labor theory of surplus value, dialectical materialism. Forget Yeats. Forget about running around in the street dodging cops. What's important is to master the objective truth."

The waitress arrived with our dinner, a clear soup in a red enameled bowl and shrimp in a lacy glaze of batter. I unwrapped my chopsticks from their paper sheath and raised the bowl of soup to my lips; the steam was like a warm washcloth. My eyes still ached from the tear gas, and adrenalin was pouring through me. But the bright restaurant, the bowl of black sauce, the cooks' urgent cries in the kitchen had calmed me down. I popped a shrimp in my mouth, hoping Herbert would notice how adept I was with my chopsticks, but he was eating with a knife and fork. "Look, why not see yourself as the petty bourgeois producer you are?" he said. "Your product—poetry—is determined just like the shopkeeper's product. The idea that he can decide what to stock on his shelves is an illusion. He supplies demand. You identify your own feelings with those of society because you must; the petty bourgeois grocer identifies his interests with those of society for the same reason."

"But what about you?" I protested. "What are you doing for the revolution? I mean, you just sit around by yourself like I do."

"Not so," Herbert said in that definite voice of his. "My music is an allegory of revolutionary development. The order and arrangement of the notes is necessary, like the revolution. And I mean a revolution of the working class, not this anarchist bullshit." He drained his tea while I paid the check. Whoever had money paid: to each according to his needs, property is theft, and so on. Only somehow it was always my allowance that got appropriated.

Out on Division, a squad car sped past, its dispatcher crackling. The air was dense with ozone, gasoline, tear gas. Down by Lincoln Park, sirens yelped and fluttered in the night. I was tempted to go back and see what was happening, but couldn't bring myself to propose it. Herbert was eager to go home and finish *The Eighteenth Brumaire*.

The phone was ringing as we came up the steps. "Kippy!" Bob cried when I picked it up. "I've just been down to Lincoln Park. Incredible scene! Tear gas, cops: the revolution is definitely happening."

"I was there, I was there," I said wearily. "It was just a lot of anarchist bullshit."

nominated by Richard Burgin

HEART LEAVES

fiction by BO BALL

from THE CRESCENT REVIEW

W HEN SHE WAS NINE SHE BLED. She daubed the flow with leaves and didn't wonder till later when the better grainy wetness caught her by surprise. She was following the bells of the cows who had roamed into the woods and stubborned. She stopped to fondle rhododendron. The wetness came.

A bird's nest full of eggs could bring it on—the smell of heart leaves. But mostly rain. When thunder bassfiddled heaven, her fingers traveled to her thighs to play.

Pearl Duty said it was dying. For two years Bethel kept hands from thighs. Unless it rained.

Then after Christmas recess, she glanced up from her speller to the back of the room and saw the eyelashes of the new boy dance. She crossed her legs and tried to think of i before e. But she died.

Pearl said Doll Newberry's daddy killed a man in West Virginia and that his mama kept hounds in their house on Cherry Mountain. But he rode a spotted horse and Pearl petted its mane.

Her mama and her daddy said the Newberrys were no count—that his daddy shot a branch walker and was serving time. But Doll smelled of all her nose had taught her of perfume.

She gave her dinner bucket to Nez Wampler for the last desk in the seventh grade. It was right across from his, in the sixth.

He couldn't read. He couldn't spell. His talk was from tongues that hadn't learned from paper, but he could count in tens and he liked to hear the teacher tell of Abe Lincoln's eyes in lamplight.

While the grades—primer through seventh—followed their les-

278

sons, each different, his ears and eyes followed Mr. Armentrout and history.

The teacher plagued him only once. The first day he was asked to stand and read. He sat and stared red-faced into the book.

At dinner recess, those who brought food brushed snow from the well box to spread biscuits and sugar cake, to open lard cans filled with cornbread and milk.

Doll unhitched his spotted horse from the woodshed and rode off.

Bethel slipped a gingerbread baby in his desk. From the corner of an eye she saw his fingers pick crumbs to his mouth.

The next day her desk had walnuts, hickory, hazel. She kept some for a love box she was building.

She gave up the games of children. A farmer in the dell ground his heels in a circle to follow her eyes aimed upward at Doll Newberry on the big rock above the schoolyard. At "Hi-ye-o, my dearie-o," she broke circle and ran to the schoolhouse porch. She glanced upward. His nose and fingers were inspecting the winter sap of spruce. But he turned his face downward for her.

From then on, all games were just children in a ring.

At little recess, at dinner, and at big, her eyes stalked happy when they could catch a patch of him.

If a storm came up at free time, the scholars could play seat games or stand on the porch and flirt with fever.

Bethel flirted with Doll who made eyes at the sky. She let her whole face feast on half of his, and when his eyes shifted slightly to contain her, he would sigh and shift his weight, but she could see his britches grow as her thighs tightened to hold the wetness in.

At books, she learned how his page-turning finger caught spit. How, when he thought no one was looking, another finger joined to tug at a thin moustache. How at spelling his britches would sag, his legs bow to catch the belly of a horse that wasn't there.

But at history his legs would tighten when the teacher told of frozen Delawares.

It was in a morning drizzle she first touched him. She lingered on the porch till she heard hooves splash. She went to the little cloakroom and waited.

Mr. Armentrout cracked the Bible for devotion just as Doll's shoulders filled the cloakroom door.

Bethel's hand, fluffing dryness to her hair, caught the damp wool of his mackinaw. His fingers, fumbling for buttons, brushed hers.

"They's courtin' in a cloakroom," she heard Pearl Duty say above the teacher's "it shall come to pass."

Doll's hands darted to his pockets.

She took her seat for morning singing. She felt her cheeks fry.

She dared peep at him over a grade of history. The rose of a blush spotted his neck.

In February, she found an early violet blooming under a little rock that jutted out. She covered it from freeze at night, opened it to the thaw at day, and on the fourteenth, she picked it and put in it a red valentine of her own making—a boy and girl on a spotted horse in the middle of a heart. The horse was pretty. She traced that. The boy and girl she put on it looked squatty.

Her valentine came a day late—a bouquet of heart leaves tied with the bark of birch. All day long she breathed the sweetness of the gather. In geography, she forgot all her capitals.

Mr. Armentrout kept her after school to talk low. She was supposed to go away free to Normal next year. Bethel lowered her eyes and watched her right foot tap out no.

On her way home she put a heart leaf in her bosom. She hugged the bark of birches.

Doll started nodding to people and during big recess on a March day that played at being spring, he rode the primer on his horse. From the porch, she watched him gallop easy in the sun.

The next day, though a flurry made vague the horse's haunches, he rode the first grade in a circle around the schoolyard. When the last of five slid from the horse, Pearl Duty said, "When ye gone ride me an' Bethel?"

He nodded to Bethel. He pranced his horse to the well box. Her galoshes mounted. A hand swooped down to pull her for a side ride without a saddle.

She had made up how even her hair would flow. It would part in equal manes and tickle his neck as they rode off into the wilds.

But her hips kept the rest of her busy holding on. His left arm crooked for the same purpose. It gave her too much of a circle for bouncing.

When he let her down on the well box, she thought she felt her hair brush his face.

The long thaw came. He was absent more than present. The

government couldn't force him. He was over sixteen and they had his daddy. He had to stay home to plow.

Bethel smelled despair in the chalk. In the nests of mud daubers. In the over-ripe sweat of feet.

At home she paled and mumbled. Her mama boiled her spring tonics. Rolled rosin pills.

At school she kept her head on her desk. But she wouldn't miss a day in case he came.

He came for three rainy days in a row.

She left letters in his desk. He left in hers an Indian baby doll whittled from the sweet scented root of pine.

The last week in April he didn't come a single day.

She languished so that Mr. Armentrout sent her home with a note. She tore it up and stayed in the woods listening to the cow bells and talking to redbuds.

Though the last day of school was sunny, he came for his report card. She knew it would be fail. He could come back for two more years, if he wanted to.

Hers said pass, with no note for Normal. She could not come back.

Into his hands she placed pressed flowers and, for old time's sake, a fresh heart leaf.

In her desk was a bird's egg necklace—all blue and rounded to perfection. He rode off on his spotted horse before she could show him the neck it prided.

The first week away from school seemed longer than Moses' trip her mama made her read her every day. When Bethel came across a word she didn't know, she'd whisper Doll and lift her eyes toward Cherry Mountain and wonder what his hands and eyes were doing five miles away in wildness.

As a child she had fought sleep to catch fireflies or try to peep the dusky eyes of whippoorwills. Now she complained of aches and went to bed early. Katydids sawed their itch, night birds swelled their throats, but they blended with her dreams—wide-eyed and closed—of Doll and their twelve children who would escape snakebite and fever to grow up to take his image. When a storm came at night, she flailed love for him into the featherbed.

She asked to go herbing, but her mama and her daddy wouldn't let her. Galavanting they called it. They pointed out how Canady Crabtree lollagagged and ended up with a woods' colt at fourteen.

In late May she got to wear her necklace to a graveyard meeting to decorate her mama's dead. In early June to decorate her daddy's. She didn't catch a glimpse of Doll. His dead, she reckoned, were down in West Virginia.

When she could escape her mama's one good ear, she whispered to a schoolmate, "Seen Doll?"

Sardis Hess had seen him at the Jockey Grounds swapping the spotted horse for a mule.

Nez Wampler saw him digging May Apple root.

Pearl Duty said she saw him almost every day, but Bethel knew different.

At home she helped her mama in the garden. Found the cows and drove them home. Milked and churned. Read the kin of Moses past the Promised Land.

In early July, the oldest cow Piedy butted rails from the fence and roamed up the mountain. Clover and Cloudy followed. Her daddy walked the pasture fence to mend it, and though a red sky warned of rain, Bethel was sent to hunt the cows.

Two miles up the mountain she heard Piedy's old-timey bell clank tin. Another mile, the happy ring of Clover, like a handshook dinner bell. Cloudy wore a little brass one made for goats—a tinkle that hinted Christmas. Cloudy could not be told, but with the tin of Piedy in front and the iron of Clover in the middle, Bethel imagined the tiny bell baby out of the sound.

A half-mile away she could say what they were up to—the regular ring of walk. The unpatterned pause and ring of grass eating. The twisting side rings as their necks fought for buds. The more frantic clapper when they nudged away flies.

She knew a storm was brewing, for their bells became flaps of fear, hanging quiet for thunder.

She let them hide so she could follow another sound—the high whine of gee, the fall of haw, the bass of whoa, that came from a spur on the ridge above her.

She came to a clearing. She parted rhododendron to see Doll, naked to the waist, follow a black mule through corn rows. She caught the slight nod of his head right with the gees, left with the haws. The lift of chin upward for the whoas. She counted the knobs of muscles on his arms and back. The brave tremble of his chest.

She held her sides and rocked. She watched for two more rows, and when her knees stretched they could hold her, she answered her lips' say of go.

He stopped the mule in mid-field. He looked to the black clouds in the West, where the best storms came. A sudden breeze gathered leaves and turned them white.

She walked up beside him and said, "Ye ain't heard no bells?"

The belly of God rumbled. Dull lightning streaked the western sky.

"Best get 'fore hit pores," he said. He unhooked the mule and led it into the woods. She followed, around the spur on a small path that came to cliffs that jutted out to make a cave.

He tied the mule to a limb that elbowed inward for the shelter.

On rocks were whittled objects, dried and drying herbs, nuts from last year's swell. Her valentine in a high dry place.

He pointed to a bed of pine boughs. "To dream time 'way," he said.

She lay down on the bed and breathed the sweetness.

Thunder rolled. Lightning quickened.

He lay down beside her. He nibbled a heart leaf from her bosom. His lips played juice-harp on her breast. Minnowed her belly.

She smelled summer in him. She kissed the sweet lay of hair on his belly—up through naval to the little knob that said three ribs were passed, and then to the dark thickets that grew on both hills the nipples made, up to the ponds of collarbones where she lipped his salt. Then the ears that caught and held the seed of hay.

She kissed the lower lip in its tremble, the upper in its spread of joy, the whole mouth for the jerk his belly gave to her thighs that knew to open, knew to close.

"You killin' me," he said.

She sucked growth into his moustaches.

He rolled over on his back to let his muscles jerk. She waited for the apples on his shoulders to say fall. Then her chin caught the cup of a shoulder blade and her left hand babied navel.

The rain came down in heavy sheets.

He turned over to greet her snuggle.

"Let's die again," she said.

He straddled her to help them.

She ground her hips sideways and squeezed until the sweet hurt came.

"You killin' me," he said.

Her hips rose to meet the ride.

He slept. Through thunder. Through gulley washes.

She watched the two butt dimples rise and fall with his breathing. The storm darkened them from her eyes. Her fingers traced them through down.

He woke to breathe the sweet sourness sleep had fed him.

When a rainbow told them to, they rose to put on clothes. Doll reached out a hand to try to rake the color in. He settled for the new green that rain had given wildflowers.

She heard the clink of Piedy's tin, the clear ring of Clover, the tink of Cloudy.

"Day after tomar?" she asked.

He nodded.

"Noon?"

He nodded.

She gathered the cows and switched them into chimes. She laid her plan. She would cow hunt every other day on Cherry Mountain. She would stifle with rags the clappers of the cow bells. She would tie Piedy to a tree. Clover and Cloudy would linger beside her. She would slip all three forbidden winter hay at their milking to make up for lost graze.

She lied to her daddy that she had found the cows on Abner's Gap.

Her eyes were closed before the washed sky could blacken. Her thighs gathered feathers to pillow the burn past bruise into memory.

She woke to disappointment. Her daddy took one look at Piedy's tail and said, "Cuttin' up." He took her to a known bull in the valley. The silly daughters stuck their heads over the yard gate and mooed till milking time.

Bethel was fitful. Day after tomorrow would be delayed, for that night her daddy did the milking.

She sat on the front porch and read her mama the psalms of David and tried to catch the harps in her mind.

She couldn't hide the cows till Thursday evening's milking.

When they didn't come home by morning, her daddy said she would have to go find them. Once she was out of his sight, she followed a straight path up Cherry Mountain.

At the cave, the pine boughs were gone. In their place was a full bed of moss with blue-eyed grass and heart leaves duly spread. She let her face take their tickle.

She walked to the field. It was finished. She heard no gees, no haws.

She returned to the cave and prayed for him to come.

She rose to measure her shadow for noon.

She heard the nose of the black mule splutter, the click of Doll onward.

She quickly spread the heart leaves into pattern.

Her hand trembled when it helped him knot the strap of the bridle round the limb.

She told him how her daddy and Ole Pied had kept her from him.

They lay down together. Soreness made them gentle. His hands played pity-pat on her thighs. Her fingers forgot fumbles as they loosened his belt to trace down. She smelled the drip of work in him.

New blood drove away the blue from bruises.

They let the moss lip them, let the heart leaves slow impressions. Their thighs obeyed without a crop of thunder.

The day after tomorrow was Sunday. Her daddy would not violate the Sabbath for field work, but he would claim an ox in the ditch to hunt cows. She would have to hide them Sunday, see him Monday.

She led home the bewildered Piedy. Her bell, obedient to the fasting, told tin. Clover iron. Cloudy brass.

She milked them. Not much.

Stole them hay. A lot.

Her daddy deemed the bull's topping hadn't taken. On Sunday he led Piedy placid to the valley where the bull turned up his nose.

Yet Bethel's plan worked Monday, and for three weeks till her daddy sold Piedy. Said she taught them all to roam and stubborn. They were going dry.

Bethel tied Clover to a tree, but Cloudy traipsed home without her and lolled her head over the yard gate.

After three days away from Doll's eyes, she risked death.

She waited till snores told her she could gather dress from bed post. She held her breath for the count of fifty footfalls.

Bushes hugged for her hair. Sawbriars tried to tangle feet.

She slapped and kicked at thickets.

By midnight she crossed the field she knew. Then a tobacco patch. A stream. A garden. She saw his cabin stilled in moonlight.

She inched her way to the one window. She saw the face it gave her back—eyes rounded past recognition, lips pouted with fear. She heard the house hounds throat their warning. She jerked reflection away and waited behind the dahlias for what the dogs' teeth or Doll could give her.

She got Doll, his long fingers pushing at the noses of the dogs.

He took her elbow and they walked beyond the voice of his mother asking who.

The dogs, wagging now, smelled her out. She gave them her hands. They purposed tails and noses for night roam.

She told of the thwart. His arms answered she could count on him.

When the dew divided them, she said, "Come to me."

He came every other night through August. She held him under the crabapple tree, or when thunder squeezed the mountains into awe, in last year's corn shucks in the crib.

Once her mama rose to feel the bed and wonder where she was. Bethel claimed sleepwalking had taken her by surprise.

Her thighs caught wonder three months without daubing. She told Doll she was big. He replanted to be sure.

Her daddy found them and prized them apart before frost could. He threatened death and prison.

Bethel clutched her dress to her and said, "You kill three."

Her daddy lifted his right hand to the heavens and declared her dead.

"Go," he said. "With 'at woods' colt in yore belly."

She had only the one dress on her back. Her mama later slipped her others with love notes in the pockets.

They didn't marry. Doll and his mama didn't like the State. She asked his mama's blessing. She smiled through snuff and gave it in wide wink.

They stayed with her till the State gave back his daddy. Then they moved to a higher mountain where she taught wildflowers to grow in her yard, where he tilled fields and caught the bees in trees and told them to make honey.

The pregnancy was false. And every one thereafter. She would swell, but the egg would not ripen on her.

She made up the names and lives of twelve who escaped snakebite and fever to grow up to take his face. Doll would lie quiet in bed to listen to her tell what the children of her mind had done that day.

She grew too fat. He grew too thin. And they learned to snore many nights away. But when a storm would come, she'd rustle the bed clothes and turn to him.

And he'd say, "You gone kill me."

She did, in the flood of '52. At a clap of thunder, as he spent, he gave a gurgle she hadn't heard before. Then he lay heavy upon her.

She turned him over and, through lightning, she courted the skin time had blotched. Her lips traced the gray hairs to the knob that said three ribs were passed. Her arms cradled him till dawn.

She rose to see a rainbow. Her hands reached out to try to rake it in, but they settled on the new green rain had given.

She told them all—the flowers, the children, the bees—and, on her weak way down the mountain, the Queen's Lace, the Penny-royal, heart leaves.

nominated by Josephine Jacobsen

DICKINSON

by MARTHA COLLINS

from THE VIRGINIA QUARTERLY REVIEW

Deep in the hills, in the noon sun,
through the white gate, through the white front door,
up the stairs to the room, and the white dress—

up the stairs, to the cupola,
where the turning world—the trees, the hills,
the hills beyond circumference—returned.

>Is this what body comes to, then,
>after the dinners, the talk, the wine,
>hello, goodbye, is this the way,
>most I, most who I am?

He was perfect muse, the god who was
and was not there. She had no mother,
she said, her mother was awe.

But awe was also muse, was house,
was hills, beyond the hills—

Mother, wife, the earth at last.
For us it goes the other way:

>the deep green cave, the flesh
>of love, the wings
>   of the white election—

nominated by Kelly Cherry

A SETTING

by DONALD REVELL

from THE ANTIOCH REVIEW

(in memory of John Cheever)

There is nothing Orphic, nothing foreign.
The deep greens of a suburban June,
the lawns, the orientalia,
are enough, for now, to make you sing.

The deep greens of a suburban June
drift from oriel to oriel and
are enough, for now, to make you sing
into the dark you've watched

drift from oriel to oriel. And
now the air around the porchlights curves
into the dark you've watched,
changing into the colored air of romance.

Now the air around the porchlights curves
like hours in summer, like desire,
changing into the colored air of romance
your first home breathed into you.

Like hours in summer, like desire,
what you cried out each June
your first home breathed into you,
became the best of you.

What you cried out each June—
"There is nothing Orphic, nothing foreign!"—
became the best of you,
the lawns, the orientalia.

nominated by David St. John and Michael Waters

GRASMERE

by AMY CLAMPITT

from THE PARIS REVIEW

Rainstorms that blacken like a headache
where mosses thicken, and the mornings
smell of jonquils, the stillness
of hung fells thronged with the primaveral
noise of waterfalls—contentment
pours in spate from every slope; the lake fills,
the kingcups drown, and still it rains,
the sheep graze, their black lambs bounce
and skitter in the wet: such weather
one cannot say, here, why
one is still so happy.

Cannot say, except it's both so wild
and so tea-cozy cozy, so snugly
lush, so English.

A run-into-the-ground complacency nonetheless
is given pause here. At Dove Cottage
dark rooms bloom with coal fires; the backstairs
escape hatch into a precipitous small orchard
still opens; bedded cowslips, primroses,
fritillaries' checkered, upside-down
brown tulips still flourish where
the great man fled the neighbors:
a crank ("Ye torrents, with
your strong and constant voice, protest

the wrong," he cried—i.e., against the Kendal-
to-Windermere railway). By middle age a Tory,
a somewhat tedious egotist even (his wild
oats sown abroad) when young: "He cannot," his sister
had conceded, "be so pleasing as my
fondness makes him"—a coda
to the epistolary cry, "Oh Jane
the last time we were together he
won my affection . . ." What gives one
pause, here—otherwise one might not
care, as one finds one does,
for William Wordsworth—
is Dorothy.

"Wednesday. . . . He read me his poem. After dinner
he made a pillow of my shoulder—I read to him
and my Beloved slept."

The upstairs bedroom where the roof leaked
and the chimney smoked, the cool buttery
where water runs, still voluble, under the flagstones;
the room she settled into after his marriage
to Mary Hutchinson, and shared with, as
the family grew, first one, then
two of the children; the newsprint
she papered it with for warmth (the circle
of domestic tranquillity cannot
guard her who sleeps single
from the Cumbrian cold) still legible:
such was the dreamed-of place, so long
too much to hope for. "It was in winter
(at Christmas) when he was last at Forncett,
and every day as soon as we rose from dinner
we used to pace the gravel in the Garden
till six o'clock." And this,
transcribed for Jane alone from
one of his letters: "Oh my dear, dear Sister
with what transport shall I again
meet you, with what rapture . . ." The orphan
dream they'd entertained, that she had named

The Day of My Felicity: to live
together under the same roof,
in the same house. Here,
at Dove Cottage.

"A quiet night. The fire flutters, and
the watch ticks. I hear nothing else
save the breathing of my Beloved . . ."

Spring, when it arrived again, would bring
birch foliage filmy as the bridal veil
she'd never wear; birds singing; the sacred stain
of bluebells on the hillsides; fiddleheads
uncoiling in the brakes, inside each coil
a spine of bronze, pristinely hoary;
male, clean-limbed ash trees whiskered
with a foam of pollen; bridelike
above White Moss Common, a lone wild cherry
candle-mirrored in the pewter of the lake.
On March 22nd—a rainy day, with William
very poorly—resolves were made
to settle matters with Annette, in France,
and that he should go to Mary. On
the 26th, a black day, followed by a morning
of divine excitement: At breakfast
William wrote part of an ode. It was
the *Intimations*.

The day after, they took the excitement to Coleridge
at Keswick, arriving soaked to the skin. There, after dinner,
she had one of her headaches.

A bad one's ghastly worst, the packed ganglion's
black blood clot: The Day of My Felicity
curled up inside a single sac with its
perfidious twin, the neurasthenic
nineteenth-century housemate
and counterpart of William's incorrigibly
nervous stomach: "I do not know from what
cause it is," he wrote, "but during

293

the last three years I have never
had a pen in my hand five minutes
before my whole frame becomes a bundle
of uneasiness." To ail, here in this vale,
this hollow formed as though to be the vessel
of contentment—of sweet mornings
smelling of jonquils, of tranquillity
at nightfall, of habitual strolls
along the lakeshore, among the bracken
the old, coiled-up agitation
glistening: birds singing, the greening
birches in their wedding veils,
the purple stain of bluebells:

attachment's uncut knot—so rich, so dark,
so dense a node the ache still bleeds,
still binds, but cannot speak.

*nominated by George Plimpton, Sherod Santos
and Richard Wilbur*

GREENBAUM, O'REILLY & STEPHENS

fiction by KENNETH GANGEMI

from CONJUNCTIONS

SAM GREENBAUM, KATHY O'REILLY, AND BOB STEPHENS are in their mid-twenties and recent graduates of Yale Law School. For about a year they have been in business as the law firm of Greenbaum, O'Reilly & Stephens, operating out of a storefront office located on East Ninth Street in New York City.

The time is the present, and the job market is very tight for law school graduates. Major firms receive dozens of resumes every day. Sam, Kathy, and Bob went to a prestige law school and would certainly fare well in the competition for jobs. But the prospect of working in a corporate law firm, and the lifestyle associated with it, is unappealing. In a sense they have dropped out from the typical young lawyer's route to a "good" job.

They each raised $7500 capital to start their own firm. It wasn't enough, and they are undercapitalized, but it was all they could put together. They figured they would learn more about law, and much more rapidly, with their own firm than any other way. And as instant partners they would be independent. There would be no senior lawyers telling them what to do.

It is an unusual kind of law firm. They type many of their letters themselves. A secretary comes in during the afternoon to answer the telephone and do other typing, mostly contracts and other legal papers. Except when they appear in court, the three don't look much like lawyers. They look like most of the other young people in the neighborhood, wearing clothing that includes jeans, flannel shirts, sweaters, down parkas, hooded sweatshirts, running shoes, and so on.

Their fees are low. They have their clients do as much of their own legwork as possible. The low-cost no-frills law firm is a struggle, often touch-and-go. None of them has an outside income. They must pay the rent on the storefront, the secretary's salary, office expenses, and their own rents and expenses. But they have managed to survive in spite of some embarrassing mistakes. Every month they are getting better and more effective. In just one year they have learned a great deal about practicing law in New York City. They have also learned much about the vast problems of the American judicial system.

Sam, Kathy, and Bob are very different in their interests, backgrounds, and personalities. Like most successful partnerships their strengths and weaknesses are balanced and complimented. One important reason they have stayed in business is that they work together very well. In addition all three are willing to compromise.

Before opening the office they knew that the legal world was unfair, archaic, and overcrowded. They wanted to be one of the new kinds of law firms. At first they were going to call their venture the Ninth Street Legal Clinic, but decided against it. Other lawyers advised them that such an operation would invite too much unsavory off-the-street business, people with problems but no money. The storefront location and the neighborhood gives them enough of that kind of business anyway. Sam had idealistic plans for them to be "people's lawyers," but this concept was quickly forgotten during the first few months.

In another time Sam, Kathy, and Bob might have chosen other fields. They were caught up in what was almost a national movement to go to law school. By their third year they shared a common disaffection with their profession. But they were in too deep and had invested too much to pull out. The firm is partly an attempt to regain control of their lives.

They also share much disenchantment with the life of a typical young lawyer. Some of their fellow graduates are unhappy with their jobs, where they often do repetitive, laborious work for the senior partners. The three have all had summer jobs in corporate law firms and sometimes tell stories of what they observed. But dropping out of the system means financial sacrifice, which can be painful. Occasionally they have to suffer the tales of classmates who are making high salaries at prestigious law firms.

Greenbaum, O'Reilly & Stephens is in general practice. The partners have provided a wide variety of legal services, many of them relevant to the lives of the television audience. They have defended various types of petty criminals. A few times, due to inexperience, they have taken on hopeless cases no other lawyer would touch. So far there have been a couple of assault charges and one manslaughter case, but no murders.

East Ninth Street between First and Second Avenues is one of the most attractive blocks in the East Village, with trees and many small shops and storefronts. It is in the center of an ethnically rich and economically diverse neighborhood. The process of gentrification is taking place, which provides many contrasts. Bleak, crime-ridden Avenue C is only a few blocks from the bohemian elegance of Stuyvesant and East Tenth Streets. But the neighborhood is still mostly populated with poor and low-income residents of every description.

The people are Polish, Italian, Jewish, Puerto Rican, Ukrainian, black, Irish, Czech, Korean, and Chinese, to name just a few. There are many illegal aliens, most of them from Latin America. Much of the population is white middle-class of no particular ethnic background. Some are students at Cooper Union, New York University, and other institutions. Aspiring poets and writers, young actors and actresses, and dancers and musicians from all over the United States have traditionally lived in the tenements of the East Village.

The neighborhood is undergoing change. Landlords are no longer abandoning buildings as they did a few years ago, and speculators are moving in. Young people with good incomes who want to live in neighborhoods like the Upper East Side are now settling for the East Village, because there is simply no other place to go. Some of the low-income residents regard it as a battle for turf.

Most of the original capital went into fixing up the storefront as an office. The basics of the space are completed, the floor, walls, plumbing, and wiring, but the money began to run out before it could be finished and furnished properly. With their ingenuity and some used office equipment, however, it is remarkably attractive. There are plants hanging, and it could be a loft in Soho. GREEN-BAUM, O'REILLY & STEPHENS is painted on the window.

The floor is the original wood, which has been sanded and prepared with care. The walls are painted white, except for one which has been taken down to the bare brick. All the desks are together in one big room, as there was not enough money to build partitions for separate offices. Beside each desk is a chair for the client. A bookcase holds a variety of law books and legal guides.

Some of the furnishings were provided by clients in lieu of payment. Several prints and paintings hang on the walls, payment from artists they have represented. A coffeemaker and cups are on a table. A water cooler is from a junk shop on First Avenue. An answering machine by the telephone takes messages after the office closes. One of the first things they do in the morning is to play back the messages, some of which are very funny.

Sam Greenbaum grew up in modest circumstances in the Mid-wood section of Brooklyn. He attended Columbia University while living at home and working part time. He graduated with honors, won a scholarship to Yale Law School, and finished near the top of his class. Sam is of medium height and build, has dark hair and a bushy moustache, and always seems to be in motion. He is single but lives with his girlfriend, who is an actress, in a loft on Mercer Street.

Sam did some acting in high school and at Columbia and Yale, and is still very interested in the theater. He occasionally drops a line or two from Shakespeare and other playwrights. For many years he planned to be an actor, but in the end chose law school. One way he compensates is by frequently seeing plays. Through Sam and his girlfriend, the series has access to the theater world of New York City.

Sam is lively, very funny, the natural comedian of the three. He has a remarkable ability to imitate foreign accents, somewhat like Sid Caesar. When talking with clients he gradually slips into their accents and patterns of speech.

The three partners are equals in the firm, and their names are in alphabetical order, but more often than the other two Sam takes the lead. For one thing the storefront law office was his idea. He was living there with his girlfriend when they decided to move to the loft on Mercer Street.

In addition Sam has built up a network of acquaintances who are in different areas of law practice. He also has an uncle nearby who is a lawyer doing much the same kind of work. Because of frequent conversations with him and the other lawyers, Sam usually knows more than Kathy or Bob.

Sam Greenbaum is a total New Yorker as opposed to his partners, one of whom grew up in the suburbs and the other in Connecticut. He spends a lot of time on the telephone, although his conversations are usually short. He is superb in the courtroom, witty, forceful, and articulate. Because of his background he relates well to the judges and members of the juries, most of whom are also New Yorkers.

Sam has made several trips to Mexico. He speaks a little Spanish, enough to talk with Hispanic clients. He is liberal in his politics and active in an independent Democratic club. He has worked on campaigns and may run for office himself someday, possibly from his native Brooklyn.

Sam drinks very little, an occasional beer or glass of wine. He loves Chinese restaurants and goes to Chinatown once or twice a week. He keeps in shape by running, which he sometimes does with his girlfriend. Sam is filled with energy and inner drive. He wastes no time at anything he does, and turns out the most work of the three.

Sam's parents moved to Los Angeles a few years ago. He has a younger sister who lives with them and attends U.C.L.A. His parents have adjusted to California and like it, but they also miss New York, where they were born and spent most of their lives. Sam often hears their grievances on the telephone, and reads about them in letters from his sister.

Kathy O'Reilly is from an affluent family and grew up in Rye in suburban Westchester County. She attended a parochial school as a child and then Rye High School before going on to Vassar College. Kathy has two younger brothers. She is an attractive young woman, taller than average, with shoulder-length brown hair and blue eyes.

Kathy is single and lives on the top floor of a brownstone on West 69th Street between Columbus Avenue and Central Park

West. She shares the apartment with a woman journalist who is about the same age. Kathy was going with a man during her last year at Yale Law School, but they broke up, and since then she has not been seriously involved with anyone.

She was originally named Mary Catherine for her paternal grandmother, who had emigrated from Ireland at the turn of the century. But the old woman died a few months later, and the baby, at her mother's insistence, came to be called Katharine, as Mary Catherine was thought to be "too Irish."

Kathy O'Reilly has some typical Irish Catholic traits. She can be stubborn, pugnacious, and guilt-ridden. She is often feisty and spirited, and has a temper. Like many others with Irish blood, she is highly verbal, a good talker, very quick with replies.

Although her mother is of Scotch-English descent, Kathy always thinks of herself as Irish. St. Patrick's Day is as important to her as any of the major holidays. She is a tenacious fighter who never gives up. It does not take much to provoke her, and she has a sharp tongue.

At Vassar she was an English major and thought of getting her doctorate or becoming a writer before deciding upon law school. She still loves books. Occasionally, when it is appropriate, she quotes from literature. The authors are often Irish: Yeats, Shaw, Joyce, Beckett.

Along with Sam she is the most interested in seeing the partnership succeed. If it fails, then her path will probably lead to a law firm where she will be a woman among senior lawyers who are mostly men. At Greenbaum, O'Reilly & Stephens she is the equal of Sam and Bob. Kathy is a Democrat, although not as liberal as Sam. Politically, as well as in name, she is in the middle of the three partners.

Kathy is continually intrigued by the moral and ethical considerations that arise in their work. They are all bright, but she has the best legal mind of the three. Kathy spends more time in the law library than Sam or Bob. Partly because of her feeling for language, she is skilled at coming up with the precise wording for a key phrase in a letter or legal document. She has the potential to become a respected judge who writes memorable opinions.

Kathy has a good sense of humor. She is usually cheerful and in good spirits. But she has a dark, brooding side to her personality that she conceals. Kathy is the most complex and also the most isolated of the three. Sometimes she is depressed for no apparent reason. In a typical Irish way she seems to be always wrestling with her soul. She drinks either white wine or Scotch, occasionally too much. At times there is a sadness about her, as though no matter what happens she will never be truly happy and fulfilled.

Although Kathy O'Reilly is from an affluent background and went to the best schools, she is not at all pretentious. On the contrary she is a down-to-earth person who is well aware of her father's origins. Several times she has visited the working-class neighborhood where he was born and raised. Kathy could have spent her high school and college summers at the country club her parents belonged to. But she always worked, either as a camp counselor or a waitress or a tennis instructor.

She spent her junior year in Paris and speaks French fairly well. It is useful in communicating with some of the foreign-born clients who speak little English. In the office she dresses as casually as Sam or Bob. She likes cats and brought one to the office, a large striped tabby that roams around at will.

Kathy has no interest in team sports, but follows tennis, especially the women players. She belongs to a health club and frequently goes there after work. Although anyone would think she has a good figure, she is ten pounds heavier than she would like to be.

Robert Stephens is called Bob or even Bobby by everyone who knows him. He grew up in Guilford, Connecticut, a small town about ten miles east of New Haven. He is less a WASP than someone with no apparent ethnic background at all, someone who could be from the Midwest or California. Bob is from a typical middle-class American family, the second of three children.

At Guilford High School he was a star athlete and went to Yale on an athletic scholarship. He played football and basketball, but was best at track, as a sprinter and pole vaulter. Bob is tall, big-shouldered, moves gracefully, and is still very much an athlete. He is unaggressive and almost gentle towards people. But when words and patience have failed, he is the one who ejects the occasional crazies and troublemakers from the office.

Bob Stephens is one of those young men who seem to have everything; looks, brains, personality. Needless to say, he is very attractive to women. Of the three he is the most likeable, the most charming, the most normal and well-adjusted. If he had wanted to be, he could have been class president in high school and perhaps even at Yale. There is almost no limit to how far Bob could go, but he is remarkably unambitious. He is that rare person who is content with his life.

He secures the majority of the business. Whereas Sam can make people nervous, and Kathy asks difficult questions, Bob is a natural salesman, smiling and reassuring. He is the best with potential clients who are doubtful about the firm. Bob likes all kinds of people and is genuinely interested in their problems. He is a good listener and never interrupts when someone is talking.

Bob was a history major at Yale and history continues to be his great love. It was a difficult decision for him to choose law school over further study in history. When he is reading with his glasses on, he looks almost scholarly. From Bob, when it is appropriate, we sometimes hear historical anecdotes that have a bearing on one of their cases.

Part of the reason he joined the partnership is because of the casual lifestyle of the office. Not only was he bored with his last summer job, which was in a law firm in Hartford, but it was the hottest and most humid summer in years, and he hated having to wear a suit every day. He still dislikes dressing up for court. But when he does, he looks as good as any young lawyer in the city.

Bob Stephens is an excellent speaker. If he were only more interested in politics, he would be an ideal candidate for public office in Connecticut. It is easy to imagine him being backed by party leaders in the New Haven area, and then being elected to the state legislature, the U. S. Congress, and possibly even higher.

Bob is the least committed to the venture. If any of the three decides to leave for something else, he will probably be the one. He is periodically courted by one of the senior partners of a major law firm, and the money is very tempting. But Bob shudders at the thought of working for such a firm. He would regard it as a kind of death.

Partly because of his background in history, reading about the rise and fall of social, economic, and political movements over the years, he has never been interested in politics. He has the detachment of the historian. But as a result of his experiences in New York City, and the influence of his two partners, Bob is learning and changing and becoming politically aware. His development is one of the themes of the series.

Bob Stephens is fond of his home town and often visits his family on weekends. They are all solidly Republican in the New England tradition. His father, once a fine athlete himself, is the track coach and a physical education instructor at Guilford High School. His mother is a housewife who has returned to teaching now that her children are grown. His older sister is married and lives nearby, and his younger sister is a student at the University of Connecticut.

Bob has lived in New York City for only a year. He is basically a trusting person with little street sense. He is not naive, but has lived in a small town for most of his life. He speaks no foreign languages and has never been out of the United States. Much of the humor associated with him comes from his frequent amazement at life in the city, especially among the lower levels.

Bob is enjoying himself working with Sam and Kathy. The stimulating neighborhood, the unusual people, and the fast-paced activity of the city are all new to him. The partnership is clearly a way station in his life. But his morale is high, he is having more fun than any of them, and he shows no indication of moving on.

Bob shares an apartment with another man on East 27th Street near Lexington Avenue. He follows sports and often comments to the others when reading the newspaper in the office. He trains with weights and plays squash to keep in shape. Bob drinks beer, the preferred drink of most athletes. Although he is sometimes pursued by women, he is not very interested in them. He has confided to Sam and his roommate that most of the time he would rather be at home reading a good book of history.

Joseph Acocella is the landlord of the building on East Ninth Street. He is a fair and decent man, rather kindly, not at all the stereotype of the "bad" landlord. He is stocky, white-haired, about sixty years old, and likes to wear cardigan sweaters. He has four grown children and several grandchildren. He lives with his wife in a pleasant section of Queens.

Mr. Acocella uses the other storefront as his office, where he manages the five buildings he owns in the neighborhood. He also sells insurance and is a notary public. He is not a lawyer, but has been to court many times. He is very knowledgeable about the legal aspects of the real estate business.

His parents were immigrants from Italy and he grew up in the Italian neighborhood that is centered at First Avenue and Elev-

303

enth Street. He knows hundreds of people who live nearby, some of them since childhood. Over the years, by working hard and saving his money, he gradually acquired the five buildings.

Like other landlords in the area, because they often have large amounts of money, Joseph Acocella has a license to carry a gun. It is a .38-caliber revolver with a short barrel, the kind that cops carry when they are off duty. He usually keeps it in his desk. Sometimes he carries it around the first of the month, when rents are due; and also when he visits his worst building, which is on Avenue C.

Mr. Acocella has provided them with a few clients. Many landlords will not rent to lawyers, but he has known and liked Sam and his girlfriend since the time they first rented the storefront. From Mr. Acocella, when he drops into the office, we occasionally hear the landlord's side of tenant disputes, including horror stories of what tenants have done. He is good with repairs, but stingy with the heat. Bob does not mind, and Sam is used to it, but Kathy often complains about the chill and puts on a sweater.

Julia is the secretary who works part time in the office, five afternoons a week. She does typing and office work and answers the telephone. Julia is Chinese, nineteen years old, grew up in the neighborhood, lives with her parents on East Fifth Street, and is a student at New York University. She is bright and pretty, very personable, smiles often, wears glasses, and has long black hair.

Although they would not care if she wore jeans and a sweatshirt, Julia is usually better dressed than Sam, Kathy, or Bob. She always wears a white blouse and a skirt. Julia wants to go to law school and asks a lot of questions. Her curiosity is useful for the exposition. She does the translating for the occasional Chinese who come into the office, usually with tenant problems.

Bernard Greenbaum is Sam's uncle and has been a lawyer in general practice for many years. He has an office in an old building at 32 Union Square. It is one of those rundown New York office buildings where tiny businesses of every conceivable description are located.

Sam and just about everyone else calls him Bernie. It is partly because of his influence that Sam went to law school. They often talk on the telephone or in a coffeeshop on Union Square. They have a warm relationship and he gives Sam valuable advice in all areas. Bernie is an important character because of the exposition he provides. He would love to have Sam go into partnership with him, but Sam wants to be independent of his family, and also work with members of his own generation.

Bernard Greenbaum respects what he is doing. When he was a young lawyer he was very much like Sam, and even more political. The Union Square area has a long history of radical politics. If Bernie is genuinely helpful, partly it is because he hopes that Sam will eventually change his mind and go into partnership with him. He has told Sam that he could have all the time off he wanted to work in politics. Meanwhile his nephew is undergoing valuable training at the expense of another firm.

Bernie lives with his family in Massapequa, on Long Island. Sam and his girlfriend sometimes visit him on summer weekends and then go swimming at Jones Beach. Bernie has sent a few clients to his nephew's firm, people he didn't have the time or inclination to represent. He has been a lawyer in New York City for a long time and knows the ropes. Sam's partners often hear, "Bernie says . . ."

Clara Miller is the accountant for Greenbaum, O'Reilly & Stephens. She is a peppy, energetic woman, rather short, who always wears a business suit. She is a widow in her early fifties with a grown daughter. She took over her husband's firm when he died. Clara comes periodically to the office, works on the books, and shakes her head. Her visits are not happy ones, for hers is the voice of financial reality.

The three partners call her Clara, but Julia calls her Mrs. Miller. She thinks there are too many clients who have not paid their bills, and also too much *pro bono* work. She constantly urges them to take on more remunerative cases, and to run the firm in a more businesslike manner. Clara wants them to raise their hourly rate, which is very low. But because of their lack of experience, and the no-frills aspect of the firm, they feel it is only fair to charge low fees.

Clara wants the retainer to be a standard policy, and has accused them of chickening out when the time comes to ask for it. Being widowed early, with a child to support, and having to survive as a woman in a competitive field dominated by men, has made her somewhat hard. Clara has a strange power over the three partners.

In her presence they become somewhat intimidated and act almost like college students. She would never admit it, but she has taken a maternal interest in the firm.

Angela Fiorelli, who is Sam's girlfriend, shares the loft on Mercer Street with him. She is an actress and two years younger than he is. Angela also grew up in the Midwood section of Brooklyn, and she and Sam have known each other since the drama club in high school.

Like many young actresses in New York City, she works part time as a waitress, currently in a plant-filled bar/restaurant in Soho. She has referred several of her friends, who are cooks, bartenders, and waitresses, to the firm. From Angela and her co-workers the series has access to the bar and restaurant world in New York, which is a large one. Most of the people she works with also do something else. In addition to being in the theater, they are students, artists, writers, dancers, musicians, photographers, etc.

Angela is a talented and beautiful young woman. She has as good a chance to make it as any actress in New York City. She loves movies as much as theater, and often goes with Sam to repertory cinemas. It was Angela who found the storefront. She was the first to talk with Mr. Acocella, and they hit it off right away, partly for ethnic reasons and also because he has a daughter who is about her age.

William O'Reilly is Kathy's father and a senior partner in a Wall Street law firm. He is a handsome, distinguished-looking man, solid and imposing, who usually wears a dark three-piece suit. He sometimes has lunch with his daughter in the Wall Street area, or they meet for a drink near Grand Central before he takes the train to Rye.

On the outside Mr. O'Reilly is charming and affable. He is a self-made man. He grew up in a large, rather poor family in the North Bronx, attended a Catholic high school, then worked his way through Fordham University and later Columbia Law School. His first job as a young lawyer was with a Wall Street firm. Except for three years in Washington during the Eisenhower years, he has never left the area.

William O'Reilly waited until he was thirty-five to marry. She was from a socially prominent New York family, the daughter of an investment banker. Kathy was the first of their three children. His wife is a very pleasant, considerate woman who mostly takes care of their house, the children, and their social life. He married well; in every way she was an ideal choice for him.

William O'Reilly is smart and tough, and has worked hard all his life. He has risen to a position of wealth and influence, and in a few years may be appointed to a judgeship. Many important and powerful people are among his friends. He has long been active in the Republican Party in New York State, starting in the sixties when Nelson Rockefeller first ran for governor.

William O'Reilly has always been a strong influence on Kathy. She is his eldest child, his only daughter, and they basically have a good relationship. But he has his own ideas about how she should build a career in law, and he strongly disapproves of the storefront venture. With his extensive contacts, possibly calling a political debt, he could set her up with a job that would be the envy of any young lawyer.

Mr. O'Reilly is a formidable man who knows how to use power. But he learned long ago, when his daughter was still a child, not to put too much pressure on her. In her own way she is just as strong as he is, and will make him regret it.

The three partners all look good when they dress up for court. Kathy is especially attractive, for her father is keen on appearances and has been very generous in providing her with clothes. He is rather proud of his daughter. He likes to be seen with her in the Wall Street restaurants where they have lunch. Her partners have wondered, somewhat enviously, if one of the reasons she does well in court is because she is such a fine-looking young woman.

Frieda, who is 82 years old, is Sam's grandmother. She was born in Vienna of Russian parents and came to the United States in 1920. She now lives in the Brighton Beach area of Brooklyn, which has a high proportion of senior citizens. Sam has dinner with her every Friday night and looks forward to it. She is alert, humorous, spirited, very much like her grandson, and they have sparkling conversations.

Frieda has a trace of a German accent. Although she has lived in the United States for most of her life, she is still very much a

European, with the values and standards of her native Vienna. She had little formal education but has always read good books and knows quite a lot about classical music. She speaks five languages. Frieda has a rich background and is a remarkably cultured person. Yet she is also one of those nondescript elderly women who sit in the sun on benches along the boardwalk in Brighton Beach.

From Frieda we hear tales of her friends and what it is like to be old and living on a fixed income in New York City. Sam is always interested in the recollections of her childhood, which took place in Vienna before World War I. She also relates stories of her parents about life in czarist Russia. Frieda gives Sam much support and thinks the law firm is a wonderful idea.

The area she lives in has recently become a center for Russian emigrés, and Sam has taken her to some of the restaurants along Brighton Beach Avenue. He often brings a friend when he visits Frieda, sometimes his girlfriend or one of his partners, for she likes to meet and talk with young people. The old woman always holds up her part of the conversation very well.

Michael Stankiewicz is a New York City policeman. He is an honest, experienced cop with over ten years on the force. He lives with his wife and children on Staten Island, but grew up in the building on East Ninth Street. Mike was a typical neighborhood kid. He attended St. Stanislaus, the nearby Polish Catholic school. His parents still live in the building and he visits them several times a week.

Mike is assigned to the 20th Precinct on the Upper West Side, which also happens to be the precinct in which Kathy lives. He has come to know the three partners and often drops in when he is visiting his parents. Mike is amused by the naiveté of the young lawyers and finds pleasure in educating them. He is either in uniform or in civilian clothes, and sometimes there is another policeman with him.

From Mike we get inside information about his old neighborhood, which he knows well. We get anecdotes about a cop's work on the Upper West Side. We get descriptions of the policeman's point of view, and of what really happens in the criminal justice system in New York City. Mike is court-wise and gives accurate predictions of what the judges and prosecutors will do. He and his friends frequently use police slang, which then has to be explained.

Susan is Kathy's roommate. She met Kathy in the street when they were both carrying copies of the *Village Voice* and looking for apartments. They exchanged information, liked each other, and took a break to have coffee. Later they decided to pool their rent money and look for an apartment to share.

Susan is about the same age as Kathy, although she looks younger. She is slim, wears glasses, has long blonde hair, is a little shorter than her roommate, and has a fresh, pleasing Midwestern accent. She grew up in Nebraska and then majored in journalism at the University of Chicago.

Susan works as an assistant editor at a magazine. She does freelance journalism on the side, mostly articles for other magazines. She has a good voice and a friendly, outgoing personality, and is attempting to break into broadcast journalism.

Susan has started in noncommercial radio. She learned to edit tape and has done a few interviews and news stories. Sometimes she is seen with a cassette recorder, the kind used by professional journalists. Eventually she hopes to move into commercial radio and then television.

Through Susan, who is happy and enthusiastic about her work, the series has access to the media world of New York City: magazines, newspapers, radio, and television. She studies the newest medium, which provides opportunities to present television-within-television.

She and Kathy have become good friends. On weekends they sometimes go to the O'Reilly house in Rye, where a pool and tennis court are in the back. They belong to the same health club and often meet there and talk while exercising. They swim, play racquetball, use the sauna, and are sometimes at adjoining Nautilus machines.

Susan has no boyfriend but goes out with different men from time to time. She and Kathy, who is in the same situation, confide in each other. They talk not only about the various men, but also about the experience of being a single woman in New York City.

Eddie is the superintendent of the building on East Ninth Street. He came to the United States from Puerto Rico with his parents when he was a child. His full name is Eduardo Rodriguez, but everyone calls him Eddie, even his friends who speak only Spanish.

Eddie grew up on the Lower East Side and went to Seward Park High School until he dropped out. He is bilingual. He speaks English rapidly and well, with only a slight accent. Like most Hispanics in New York City, he has two identities and is a product of two cultures and societies. He is Eddie the super in Manhattan who is completely Americanized, and also Eduardo Rodriguez who is from a Spanish-speaking island in the Caribbean.

Eddie is in the office whenever something needs to be fixed. He has become friendly with Julia and the three partners and has brought them some Hispanic clients, including himself. So far he has built improvements in the office instead of paying legal fees. Eddie lives upstairs in one of the apartments with his wife and two children. The oldest is his eight-year-old daughter, an appealing child who sometimes looks into the office when she comes home from school.

Eddie has worked for Mr. Acocella for almost ten years. He receives a rent-free apartment and a small salary in return for being the super. His main job is driving a taxi, and the yellow cab is frequently seen outside the office. Eddie grew up on the streets and knows how to survive in New York City. He is hilarious when he describes the best route to a place, speaking rapidly and using taxi lingo.

Turner is Bob's roommate in the apartment on East 27th Street. He is an intern at Bellevue Hospital, a few blocks away. Turner grew up in Fort Worth and attended the University of Texas. He then spent four years in Baltimore, where he graduated from the medical school of Johns Hopkins University. He has a warm, friendly, down-home West Texas accent, although it has been modified by his years in the East.

Turner is a good storyteller and frequently captivates Bob and others with anecdotes about Texas, medical school, and Bellevue. He is a little homesick and speaks of Texas, especially Austin and Fort Worth, as though it were a paradise. Turner goes on and on about barbecue, Pearl beer, Mexican food, the friendliness of the people, the beauty of Texas women, etc. etc.

He has even less street sense than Bob and is also amazed by what he sees and by what happens to him in New York City. In contrast to Bob he is very interested in women. Sometimes he gets his reluctant roommate to go out together with nurses from Bellevue.

Through Turner the series has access to the world of medicine and a famed hospital: the morgue, the free clinics, the emergency room, the psychiatric ward, and so on. From him we get all the medical terms and exposition that are needed. Turner plans to write a book about the experience of being an intern at Bellevue. He often relates the day's events into a cassette recorder, sometimes while Bob is having dinner.

The mailman is black, about thirty years old, and a native New Yorker; the local city councilwoman is a blend of the real-life Miriam Friedlander and Ruth Messinger; the district attorney is based upon the tough-talking Burton Roberts, who is now a judge but was once the Bronx D.A.; a tenant activist is like the late Esther Rand; and a law professor seen in flashbacks is reminiscent of John Houseman.

The judges are remarkably fair and even-handed, although an occasional nasty one appears. Principal villains are the opposing lawyers, some of them creeps, who we see and hear in the courtrooms and the hallways outside. These lawyers are also unkind on the telephone and in letters read aloud in the office. Included among the villains are a few lying, dishonest clients who deceive the three partners.

Many locations in and outside New York City have already been mentioned. The possibilities in the city are endless, with its streets, airports, ferries, subways, prisons, landmarks, and everything else. In the neighborhood of the office, locations not already mentioned are the local police precinct, a few blocks away, called "Fort Apache South" by the cops; Mothers Soundstages on East Fifth Street, where Angela has shot a few TV commercials; and the Second Avenue Deli on the corner of East Tenth Street, a typical New York delicatessen with the usual old, grumpy, wise-cracking waiters.

Other locations in the neighborhood, besides those found in any city, include a branch of the New York Public Library on Second Avenue near Ninth Street; the intersection of St. Mark's Place and

311

Second Avenue, the crossroads of the East Village; Tompkins Square Park, less than two blocks away; the Hell's Angels club on East Third Street; the counters of the cheap Polish restaurants on First Avenue; the rundown bars that cater to middle-aged Slavic men during the day and young punk rockers at night; and the row of fourteen Indian restaurants on East Sixth Street.

nominated by Marvin Cohen and Conjunctions

UNDER ANOTHER NAME

by DORIS LESSING

from GRANTA

I HAD BEEN THINKING about writing a pseudonymous novel for years. Like, I am sure, most writers. How many do? It is in the nature of things that we don't know. But I intended from the start to come clean, only wanted to make a little experiment.

The Diary of a Good Neighbour got written for several reasons. One: I wanted to be reviewed on merit, as a new writer, without the benefit of a 'name': to get free from that cage of associations and labels that every established writer has to learn to live inside. It is easy to predict what reviewers will say. Mind you, the labels change. Mine have been—starting with *The Grass is Singing:* she is a writer about the colour bar (obsolete term for racism), about communism, feminism, mysticism; she writes space fiction, science fiction. Each label has served for a few years.

Two: I wanted to cheer up young writers—who often have such a hard time of it—by illustrating that certain attitudes and processes they have to submit to are mechanical, and have nothing to do with them personally or with their kind or degree of talent.

Another reason, frankly if faintly malicious. Some reviewers complained they hated my Canopus series: Why didn't I write realistically, the way I used to do—preferably *The Golden Notebook* over again. These reviewers were sent *The Diary of a Good Neighbour,* but not one recognized me. Some people think it is reasonable that an avowed devotee of a writer's work should only be able to recognize it when packaged and signed; others, not.

Again, when I began writing my Canopus series, I was surprised to find I had been set free to write in ways I had not used before. I wondered if there would be a similar liberation if I were to write in the first person as a different character. Of course, all writers become different characters all the time, as we write about them: all our characters are inside us somewhere. (This can be a terrifying thought.) But a whole book would be a different matter, mean activating one of the gallery of people who inhabit every one of us, strengthening him or her, setting him or her free to develop. And it did turn out that as Jane Somers I wrote in ways that Doris Lessing cannot. It was more than a question of using the odd turn of phrase or an adjective to suggest a woman journalist who is also a successful romantic novelist: Jane Somers knew nothing about a kind of dryness, like a conscience, that monitors Doris Lessing, whatever she writes and in whatever style. After all, there are many different styles or tones of voice in the Canopus series—not to mention *Briefing for a Descent into Hell* and *Memoirs of a Survivor*—and sometimes in the same book.

Some may think this is a detached way to write about Doris Lessing, as if I were not she. It is the name I am detached about. After all, it is the third name I've had: the first, Tayler, being my father's; the second, Wisdom (now try that one on for size!), my first husband's; and the third my second husband's. Of course there was McVeagh, my mother's name, but am I Scottish or Irish? As for Doris, it was the doctor's suggestion, he who delivered me, my mother being convinced to the last possible moment that I was a boy. Born six hours earlier, I would have been Horatia, for Nelson's Day. What could that have done for me? I sometimes wonder what my real name is: surely I must have one?

Jane Somers also developed from my reflections about what my mother would be like if she lived now: that practical, efficient, energetic woman, who was by temperament conservative, a little sentimental, and only with difficulty (and a lot of practice) able to understand weakness and failure—though she was always kind. No, Jane Somers is not my mother, but thoughts of women like my mother fed Jane Somers.

I and my agent, Jonathan Clowes, decided that it would be fair to submit *The Diary of a Good Neighbour* to my main publishers first. In Britain these are Jonathan Cape and Granada. Cape (not its chairman, Tom Maschler) turned it down forthwith. Granada kept it some time, were undecided, but said it was too depressing

314

to publish: in these fallen days, major and prestigious publishers can see nothing wrong in refusing a novel in which they see merit because it might not sell. Not thus, once, were serious literary publishers. I saw the readers' reports and was reminded how patronized and put-down beginning writers are.

Michael Joseph, who accepted my first novel all those years ago, has now twice published me as a new writer. On accepting *The Diary of a Good Neighbour,* the editor there said it reminded her of Doris Lessing, and she was taken into our confidence, and entered with relish into the spirit of the thing. The redoubtable Bob Gottlieb of Knopf in New York said at once, 'Who do you think you are kidding?'—or words to that effect. Interesting that these two great publishing firms, crammed with people and the possibilities of a leak, were able to keep the secret as long as they wanted: it was dear friends who, swearing their amazing and tested reliability, could not stand the strain.

Three European publishers bought *The Diary of a Good Neighbour:* in France, Germany, and Holland. My French publisher rang up to say he had bought this book, had I perhaps helped Jane Somers who reminded him of me?

This surely brings us back to the question: What is it that these three editors—one in England, one in the United States, and one in France—recognized? After all, Jane Somers's style is different from Lessing's. Every novel or story, by any writer, has a characteristic note or tone of voice—a style, consistent and peculiar to itself. But behind this must sound another note, independent of style. What is this underlying tone or voice, and where does it originate in the author? It seems to me we are listening to, responding to, the essence of a writer here, a ground-note.

The Diary of a Good Neighbour was published in 1983. We—that is, agent, publishers and I—believed the reviewers would guess at once. But not one did. A few people, not all reviewers, liked the novel. It was mostly women in women's magazines who reviewed it, because Jane Somers was described on the dust jacket as a well-known woman journalist (it was enough, apparently, to say it for people to believe it). This neatly highlights the major problem of publishing: how to bring the book to the attention of readers. The trigger here was the phrase *woman journalists:* some potential reviewers, male, were put off by it. It is this situation—bringing a book to the attention of readers—that has given rise to all these new promotional schemes in Britain: the Ten Best Young Novelists, Thirteen Best Novels, the razzmatazz prizes, and so on. The problem can only exist, it seems to me, because so many books are being published. If there were only a few, there would be no difficulty. Ever more loudly shrill the voices, trying to get attention: this is the best novel since *Gone with the Wind, War and Peace* and *The Naked and the Dead!* Overkill earns diminishing returns and numbed readers return to former habits, such as relying on intuition and the recommendation of friends. Jane Somers's first novel (first serious novel—of course she had written those romantic novels which were not reviewed at all but sold very well!) was noticed, and got a few nice, little reviews. In short, it was reviewed as new novels are. And that could easily have been that. Novels, even good ones, are being published all the time and have what publishers call 'a shelf-life' (like groceries) of a few months. Once they used the phrase as a joke, sending themselves up, but now they use it straight. 'The shelf-life of books is getting shorter,' you'll hear them say, 'it's down to a few weeks now.' As if it all had nothing to do with them. And it hasn't: the mechanisms for selling dominate their practices—the tail wags the dog. A first novel can be remaindered and go out of print and vanish as if it had never existed, if unlucky enough not to win a prize or in some way attract a spotlight, such as the admiration of a well-known writer who cries (see above), 'This is the greatest novel since *Tom Jones*.' Or, accommodating to the times, 'More exciting than *Dallas!*'

The American publisher was asked why more had not been done to promote *The Diary of a Good Neighbour*—which in the opinion of the inquirer, a literary critic, was a good novel—but the reply was that there was nothing to promote, no 'personality', no photograph, no story. In other words, to sell a book, to bring it attention, you need more than the book itself. This means that writers spend more time 'promoting' their work, because readers are now thoroughly conditioned to respond to the personality of the author. A publisher friend was heard recently to groan: 'Look what we've done! It's all our fault! We started it, not knowing where it would end! Twenty years ago we sold books; now we have to sell authors.' As for us, the authors, we are continually amazed that it is not the year or so of hard slog we put into a book and the simple fact that it is there—an expression of ourselves at our best and most intelligent—that persuade readers to buy the book: no, for that you need the television appearance. Many writers who resisted at the start have thought it all over, have understood that this, now, is how the machinery works, and have decided that if we have become part of a publisher's sales department, whether it is acknowledged or not, then we will do the job as well as we can. It is remarkable how certain publishers wince and suffer when writers insist on using the right words to describe what is happening. In very bad taste, the publishers think it is, to talk in this way. Nevertheless, you are pressured to do interviews, television and so on, but you are conscious that the more you agree, the more you are earning his or her contempt. (But, looking back, it seems to me that men publishers are more guilty of this hypocrisy than women.)

If Jane Somers had only written one serious novel, which sold, as first novels do—2,800 copies in the States, 1,600 in Britain—by now it would be remaindered and pulped, and she would be cherishing half-a-dozen fan letters. But she wrote a second. Surely this time people must see who the real author is? But, no.

Predictably, people who had liked the first book were disappointed by the second. And vice versa. Never mind about the problems of publishers: the main problem of some writers is that most reviewers and readers want you to go on writing the same book.

By now, the results of friends' indiscretions meant that some people in the trade knew who Jane Somers was and—I am touched by this—clearly decided it was my right to be anonymous if I wished. Some, too, seemed inclined retrospectively to find merit.

One of my aims has more than succeeded. It seems I am like Barbara Pym! The books are fastidious, well written, well crafted. Stylish. Unsparing, unsentimental and deeply felt. Funny, too. On the other hand they are sentimental, mawkish. Mere soap opera. Trendy.

I am going to miss Jane Somers.

nominated by Carolyn Forché

RAIN COUNTRY

by JOHN HAINES

from NEW ENGLAND REVIEW AND BREAD LOAF QUARTERLY

Earth. Nothing more.
And let that be enough for you.
                    Pedro Salinas

I

The woods are sodden,
and the last leaves
tarnish and fall.

Thirty-one years ago
this rainy autumn
we walked home from the lake,
Campbell and Peg and I,
over the shrouded Dome,
the Delta wind in our faces,
home through the drenched
and yellowing woodland.

Bone-chilled but with singing
hearts we struck our fire
from the stripped bark
and dry, shaved aspen;
and while the stove iron
murmured and cracked
and our wet wool steamed,
we crossed again
the fire-kill of timber
in the saddle of Deadwood.

Down the windfall slope,
by alder thicket, and now
by voice alone, to drink
from the lake at evening.

A mile and seven days
beyond the grayling pool
at Deep Creek, the promised
hunt told of a steepness
in the coming dusk.

II

Light in the aspen wood
on Campbell's hill,
a fog trail clearing below,
as evenly the fall distance
stretched the summer sun.

Our faces strayed together
in the cold north window—
night, and the late cup
steaming before us . . .
Campbell, his passion
tamed by the tumbling years,
an old voice retelling.

As if a wind had stopped us
listening on the trail,
we turned to a sound
the earth made that morning—
a heavy rumble in the grey
hills toward Fairbanks;
our mountain shivered
underfoot, and all
the birds were still.

III

Shadows blur in the rain—
they are whispering straw
and talking leaves.

I see what does not exist,
hear voices that cannot speak
through the packed
earth that fills them:

Loma, in the third year
of the war, firing at night
from his pillow
for someone to waken.

Campbell, drawing a noose
in the dust at his feet:
"Creation was seven days—
no more, no less . . ."
Noah and the flooded earth
were clouded in his mind.

And Knute, who turned
from his radio one August
afternoon, impassioned
and astonished:
                    "Is that
the government? I ask you—
is *that* the government?"

Bitter Melvin, who nailed
his warning above the doorway:

Pleese don't shoot
the beevers
They are my friends.

IV

And all the stammering folly
aimed toward us
from the rigged pavilions—
malign dictations, insane
pride of the fox-eyed men
who align the earth
to a tax-bitten dream
of metal and smoke—

all drank of the silence
to which we turned:

one more yoke at the spring,
another birch rick balanced,
chilled odor and touch
of the killed meat quartered
and racked in the shade.

It was thirty-one years ago
this rainy autumn.

Of the fire we built to warm us,
and the singing heart
driven to darkness
in the time-bitten earth—

only a forest rumor
whispers through broken straw
and trodden leaves
how late in a far summer
three friends came home,
walking the soaked ground
of an ancient love.

V

Much rain has fallen. Fog
drifts in the spruce boughs,
heavy with alder smoke,
denser than I remember.

Campbell is gone, in old age
struck down one early winter,
and Peg in her slim youth
long since become a stranger.
The high, round hill of Buckeye
stands whitened and cold.

I am not old, not yet, though
like a wind-turned birch
spared by the axe,

I claim this clearing
in the one country I know.

Remembering, fitting names
to a rain-soaked map:
Gold Run, Minton, Tenderfoot,
McCoy. Here Melvin killed
his grizzly, there Wilkins
built his forge. All
that we knew, and everything
but for me forgotten.

VI

I write this down
in the brown ink of leaves,
of the changed pastoral
deepening to mist on my page.

I see in the shadow-pool
beneath my hand a mile
and thirty years beyond
this rain-driven autumn.

All that we loved: a fire
long dampened, the quenched
whispering down of faded
straw and yellowing leaves.

The names, and the voices
within them, speak now for
the slow rust of things
that are muttered in sleep.

There is ice on the water
I look through, the steep
rain turning to snow.

nominated by Amy Clampitt, Cleopatra Mathis
and New England Review And Bread Loaf Quarterly

WHERE WE ARE

by STEPHEN DOBYNS

from BLUEFISH

After Bede

A man tears a chunk of bread off the brown loaf,
then wipes the gravy from his plate. Around him
at the long table, friends fill their mouths
with duck and roast pork, fill their cups from
pitchers of wine. Hearing a high twittering, the man

looks to see a bird—black with a white patch
beneath its beak—flying the length of the hall,
having flown in by a window over the door. As straight
as a taut string, the bird flies beneath the roofbeams,
as firelight flings its shadow against the ceiling.

The man pauses—one hand holds the bread, the other
rests upon the table—and watches the bird, perhaps
a swift, fly toward a window at the far end of the room.
He begins to point it out to his friends, but one is
telling hunting stories, as another describes the best way

to butcher a pig. The man shoves the bread in his mouth,
then slaps his hand down hard on the thigh of the woman
seated beside him, squeezes his fingers to feel the firm
muscles and tendons beneath the fabric of her dress.
A huge dog snores on the stone hearth by the fire.

From the window comes the clicking of pine needles
blown against the glass by an October wind. A half moon
hurries along behind scattered clouds, while the forest

of black spruce and bare maple and birch surrounds
the long hall the way a single rock can be surrounded

by a river. This is where we are in history—to think
the table will remain full; to think the forest will
remain where we have pushed it; to think our bubble of
good fortune will save us from the night—a bird flies in
from the dark, flits across a lighted hall and disappears.

nominated by Michael Blumenthal, Raymond Carver,
Tess Gallagher, and Ellen Bryant Voigt

from THE CRIPPLE LIBERATION FRONT MARCHING BAND BLUES

by LORENZO WILSON MILAM

from MHO & MHO WORKS

MY SISTER! My teacher! In 1952, she had two weeks advance knowledge of the theory and practice of the wasting disease. I want you to see her. She is my companion-in-arms.

No goddess, nor villain. A child of twenty-nine. Two years of college. Presented to society in late 1943. A woman of great sport and warmth.

She likes sailing, and tennis. She is a good swimmer, with a broad fine stroke in the school of the Australian Crawl. She loves cooking, and from time to time, I would hear her in the kitchen, humming tunelessly to herself.

Of all the unlikely people, of all the unlikely people to kiss with the grey disease: who would have guessed? As of the second of September, she is laid in the hospital bed by poliomyelitis. By the sixth of September, they have laid her in an iron lung so that she can continue to breathe. And on the 29th of December, of the same year, they lay her in the grave.

She has never thought about the functioning of her body. She has no idea in the world how her various muscles combine in their workings with bone in a magic way to carry her through the range of motion: the complex interface of muscle and bone and nerves, the action and reaction of dendrons, axons, neurones, cytons that makes it possible for her to climb into a sailboat and spend a day racing before the wind on the St. Johns River. I am sure that the knowledge of *how it is done* never comes to her. Nor the importance of it. It never occurs to her. At least, not until late summer 1952.

She is a *naïf* who spends twenty-nine years of her life harming no one and loving, to the depths she is able, a few close family members and a husband. She is an innocent, slightly freckled child who plays a fair game of tennis, and who trails her red hair behind her like a fire.

She contracts polio in late August and in the intense stage, it moves slowly over the entire field of her body. When the fever departs, she has one muscle remaining: in her left foot. Because of the loss of her breathing apparatus, she is fitted with a machine that breathes for her. "Whoosh" it goes, fifteen times a minute, nine hundred times an hour.

She cannot scratch her knee should it itch. She cannot bring food to her own mouth. She cannot brush back her fine red hair. She cannot wash nor wipe herself. She cannot reach out to hold another's hands.

In her respirator, she is flat on her back. She is turned over every hour or so to prevent the development of bedsores which can become malignant and score the body all the way to white bone.

The regularity of the bellows punctuates her every moment, asleep or awake. "Whoosh." "Whoosh." A submarine: she is lying in a submarine. Warm. Protected. With lightbulbs, festooning the iron lung, like a newly constructed building, or a Christmas tree. A submarine with portholes all along the side, so you can peer in and see where the muscles have disappeared from bone.

She my sister, the originator and founder of all this pain, is now quite thin. Bones show beneath flesh, a picture out of Dachau. A woman's once graceful body now has knobby knees, knobby elbows, celery root. The hip bones jut up from a wasted stomach. The entire skeletal frame is pushing to get out, to get born, to be done with this painful flesh.

Her eyes are quite large now. Her face so shrunken and drawn that the eyes start out as if she were some night creature, startled in her submarine body. "Whoosh." She views you, the room, the world, upside down through a mirror. People stand outside her new breathing machine, up near the head, and wonder what to say. If they stand, she looks at their legs (legs that move!) If they sit, she sees their faces backwards. Friends' faces are turned around, turned obverse.

She who never thought seriously about sickness, nor her body, nor death, is thinking on them now, thinking hard on them. And she wonders what to say to the reversed faces of her old friends who cannot imagine *who cannot imagine* what it is like to be in the pale tan submarine, with all the dials and meters, and the bellows that go "whoosh" fifteen times a minute, nine hundred times an hour.

And if they talk, and they do talk, and if she replies, and she does reply, her words are turned wispy, hard-to-hear, for the talking mechanism is dependent on lungs and air, and her lungs have been deprived of power to push air and words.

And when she talks, and she talks so that you can barely hear her, she talks on the exhale, because she cannot talk on the inhale (one does not fight the submarine), which means that her sentences are interrupted fifteen times each minute, for the breathing machine to make her breathe, which makes conversations with her quite leisurely, long pauses in the sentences, and everyone learns to be patient, very patient, with this new woman in her new submarine, who has become very patient.

Very, very patient. Doesn't demand too much, really. Can't demand too much. Except that you feed her when hungry (she is not very hungry) and bathe her when dirty (she is not very dirty, doesn't play in the mud too much) and dry off that place near the corner of her eyes when sad (she is sad very much because she doesn't know what has happened to her, nor why) and be with her when she thinks on the things that are gone now, like body and arms and legs and motion which are gone now, so soon now, things that she loved, gone so soon now, like sailing and tennis and running into the surf at the beach on the Atlantic Coast, and most of all, the ability, that important ability to scratch her knee, when it begins to itch, or turn over in her sleep, which she doesn't do very much any more, sleep that is, because of the noise, and confusion, and the strange change that has come over her body, which with the six nurses and orderlies and nurse's aides and the eight doctors and technicians and physical therapists, which with

327

all these people working at her body, somehow doesn't seem to be her body any more at all, at all.

They give her a mirror, over her face, turned at a forty-five degree angle, attached to the submarine, the submarine that pumps away, with its engine pumping away. They give her a mirror so that she can see the world, so she doesn't have to look at the ceiling, the light green institutional ceiling, with the flies, and the single naked light bulb. She is given a mirror, her own mirror, so that she can watch the world go by outside her door, there in her hospital room. She doesn't know if her room has a view out the window, because she isn't turned that way, but rather, turned so that she can see up and down the hall, see the nurses and orderlies and doctors, who come in to do things to her body, her new body, a body which has come up with such new experiences of pain, of new pain. She never thought she would be capable of surviving such pain. She never thought she would, my sister didn't, but she did. For awhile, for awhile.

They bring in a television set, into her room, and she becomes a fan of baseball, watching baseball through her mirror, on the new-fangled television set. She never cared for baseball before, before all this happened. She cared for sailing, and tennis and some golf, from time to time (she was very good at the long stroke, in the first, fourth, and eighth holes at Timuquana Country Club) but she never really cared for baseball, at least not until now, but the afternoon nurse, Miss Butts, likes baseball, so they watch it together, and my sister can watch the Dodgers (whom she never heard of before) playing the Pirates (whom she never heard of before) and she watches the occasional home run in the mirror, when the batter hits the ball, and takes off, and runs to third base, then to second, then to first, and finally to home. It is comforting, in a funny sort of way, to know that people still play, think of, watch, write on, report on, worry about something like baseball.

They never taught her very much about life, and the body, and muscles and things, before this. When she was at Stephens College, they taught her dance, and music, and a smattering of literature courses, and some math, and a little chemistry. But they never taught her about the catheter stuck into her urinary tract, which stays there to drain the piss that won't come out on its own, and how urine crystals grow, so that when they pull the catheter out, it is like they are ripping out the whole of her insides, her entire urethra shredded, to ribbons, by these crystals, that come out of her, and no pain-killers, they give her no pain-killers, because of the fact that this is a disease of the nervous system, and it might affect the regeneration of nerves. They taught her some math, and a little chemistry, and how to dance, at Stephens College, but they never taught her the dimensions of pain, which she never ever thought she could bear, never, in a thousand years, but she does, she does, even though she never thought she could.

They taught her how to diagram sentences: and they taught her about Mozart, and Beethoven. They showed her the difference between the Samba and the Rumba, and between the Waltz and the Foxtrot, she remembers her teacher played "Bésame Mucho" over and over again, so they could learn the Samba—but they never taught her about her lungs, the beautiful rich red alveoli, that lose the ability to aspirate themselves, so that one night, they think she is clogging up, suffocating, the doctor comes, with all the lights, and slices into the pink flesh, at the base of her neck, the blood jets up all over, and she can see the reflection of her neck in the mirror of his glasses, as he cuts into her neck (no anesthetics permitted because they affect the dark grey nerves nestled in the aitch of the spinal column, and polio got there first) the blood goes all over his smock, a drop of her blood even flecks his glasses, and of a sudden no air comes through nostrils or mouth, and she is sure she is suffocating, the very breath has been cut out of her, and her doctor punches a three inch silver tube down into her lungs, so that every two hours they can pump out the mucous, that collects in her lungs; they never taught her what it feels like to breathe through a little silver navel in her throat, never taught her about the feel of mucous being pumped from her lungs. They never taught her about the kiss of the trachea, the silver kiss, at the base of the neck, the kiss of this silver circle, the silver circle of the moon.

She was quite good at chemistry, my sister was: quite good. She got special honorable mention, at graduation, from Stephens College, there in Central Missouri. What she remembers most about Stephens is the spring evenings, when the smell of hay would drift into the classrooms, make her feel so alive, in the rich fecundity of Central Missouri, the rich hayfields, and the people moving so slowly, on a spring day, through the fields, those rich fields of hay. Or in the fall, when the moon would peer up over the fields come hush by midnight: the moon growing a silver medallion, hanging there in the sky, the sky so black, the moon so white-dust silver. They gave her a silver medallion, for her chemistry, she was surprisingly good at it, not so good at literature, she never cared for Dickens nor Jane Austen, but she was so good at H_2SO_4, and NaCl, and MnO_2 that they gave her a special ribbon, with a silver moon on it, which she hung on her neck, which hung where the new silver moon of the tracheotomy hangs now, her badge, the badge of a job well done, a job well done, in the new education on the nature of the body, and its diseases, and the way the body will try to kill off its own, because of the diseases, and the deterioration of the kidney, bladder, lungs, heart, mind, under the sweet kiss of the disease, under the sweet new kiss of the disease.

My sister: the new student! The student of the body, and a student of disease, and perhaps even a student of sainthood: Sainthood. The questions of the nuns and priests and ministers of all religions of all times. If a tree falls in the forest, and no one is around, and no one hears it, was there really a sound? Or, can God create a rock, such a huge rock that He Himself cannot lift it. Or, can God create a disease, such a painful awful burning disease, of the nervous system, that invades the tender spinal chord, and scars the nerves therein so completely, with such pain and destruction of the self, that one can wish not to live any more. To live no more.

My sister. An innocent saint. For slightly less than four months, from 2 September 1952 to 29 December 1952, she will have ample time to work on her sainthood. She will have 2,832 hours to recall growing up in the sun of Florida, her shadow a black hole on the burning white sands of the beach.

169,920 minutes: she will have almost a hundred and seventy thousand minutes to remember running for a fast lob on the white-line tennis courts at the Timuquana Country Club. She will have over ten million seconds, there in her new submarine, to remember that for twenty-nine years she had a constant companion, namely her body. A companion which asked little and gave much and, of a sudden in the early fall of that year, turned a dead weight like a tree which has had the life leeched out of it. So dead, so weighted, that she must ask the good nurse to scratch her forehead, move a leg, adjust the hair, or brush away the wetness that forms of its own accord at the corner of her blue-gray eyes, just below those beautiful ruddy lashes, that match her beautiful ruddy skin—turning quite pale now.

The body ceases to function as a body, and commences to try to kill itself off. Bladder infection, kidney stones, phlegm accretion in the lungs, bedsores, respiratory dysfunction, depression. Over the next three months and twenty-seven days, my sister's body, the body which has been so kind all these years, will turn enemy and try to sabotage every machine (from within and without) which makes it possible for her to survive. Her body will attempt to murder her.

And shortly before dawn, nineteen hundred and fifty-two years after the Birth of Our Lord and Savior, two days before the end of that dark year, at 4:47 in the morning, in some anonymous respiration center in North Carolina, where she has been sent for reëducation of what is left of her body, in the company of some one hundred other machine-bound patients, just as the first winter dawn is beginning to crack the still and snowy Chapel Hill sky, my sister will awaken for the last time to find her lungs clogged with the suppurating thickness of pneumonia.

There is to be a battle, a short one. A creature is squatting on her chest, trying to keep air from its proper place in her lungs. It is a silent and a lonely battle. There is no crying out. She is alone, and thinking "This is not happening to me," and for some unexplainable reason she remembers a spectacular day from last summer, with the sun coming down over the water, a spectacular day on the St. Johns River running before the wind in a White Star sailboat. She remembers the wind in her hair, and her body riding, riding on the swells from the great dark Atlantic near the jetties, and that great flowing expansive feeling of having all of life before one, of having the wind and the river and the freedom to ride them and be alive, so full of the freedom of being alive at the very edge of the river, just before it merges with the great wide dark deep Atlantic Ocean before her.

"This is not happening to me," she thinks. She cannot believe a termination of self and being in this huge room of clanking machines on a snow-dawn in North Carolina. "This is not happening to me," she thinks, but she is wrong. She is drowning in the liquids of her own body, and there is no way she can call out, to tell the nurse of her dying.

331

My sister! My sister. She is quite alone as the sun breaks through the grey waste outside. She tries to breathe in, cannot, and suddenly there is no spirit in her. My sister. Eyes, mouth, heart, single moving muscle in foot cease. There is no more warmth within or without, beyond the artificial heater placed inside the submarine which, as of now, has discharged its last patient.

The iron maiden continues to pump dead lungs for over an hour before the night nurse discovers the drowned creature, grey froth on blue lips. My sister, who never did anyone any harm, who only wished joy for those around her, now lies ice and bone, the good spirit fled from her.

nominated by Mho & Mho Works

HOT DAY ON THE GOLD COAST

fiction by BOB SHACOCHIS

from THE BLACK WARRIOR REVIEW

IT'S STEAMY HOT and the radio's loud. Fifties stuff: *shoop shoop, dee doo, waa-oo, my babee left me.* I once knew the words and sang along in a wine-cooled voice. The blues and the bop dribble my heart between them like a basketball. Here's a ballad of love. Here love is lost and much missed. A saxophone player squirts his high-rising juice out of the box.

The house is blistered white, with gables and gingerbreadish scrollwork milled by some Victorian craftsman gone deftly baroque. It is jungled-up and bug-eaten and can't be seen from the street, a residence that offers no clue to my uptown breeding. We have plenty of privacy here.

The sun has hopped off the ocean and nuzzles through the canopy of ficus leaves to brighten our breakfast on the porch stoop. For me a sweet, stringy mango and a domestic beer suffice, while Tericka picks through a bowl of protein capsules and vitamins. The kid rolls around on a blanket in the grass with a bottle in her mouth.

"Tericka," I say.

"Yes?" she says.

"I feel pretty good."

Tericka was born and raised in Titusville, Florida, the Space Coast. She is nineteen, has a tattoo and a baby. Not my baby. The father's an astronaut but I'm not supposed to know which one. She receives love letters on NASA stationary signed *Ace, Forever*. I lay awake at night counting nosecones like silver sheep. Our man must be one of the newly chosen, still nameless and faceless to the world at large, a Faustian hero in waiting. Tericka won't say; it's been classified. Oh, him, she says dismissively, and smiles wide. When a flame is struck the child displays mothlike tendencies.

The tattoo is of a small rocketship, orbiting her left breast.

We sit side by side on the top step. Elbows on her knees, Tericka's orange bikini top gulps air and my attention is fixed there. On a morning as pleasant as this, I can't take my eyes from it—the rocket, the trace of orbitry, the round atmosphere where perhaps gravity grows, the distant planet, darkish red and volcanic. For the moment all I can think of is that she is very proud of her motherly tits. These are tits like tropical mountains. The Ela Kapuua in Oahu. The Pitons of St. Lucia. (I prefer this imagery to the celestial surfaces.) These are breasts that hold no grudge against the natural world.

My own anatomy suggests the need for tuning. The stomach sags, the spine wants to bend, the lungs do penance for various sins. My hips are still very firm and boyish, I think, but there has been much amiss in this temple of flesh for one year too many. The soul has made contingency plans in case of sudden emergency. For my sake and for Tericka's peace of mind I voice a resolution, which as a gentleman I will stick by.

I will jog.

"Oh lord," she snorts. "Starting when?"

"Starting now."

Her tone has kicked a small dent in my vanity, but given further reason to honor the commitment to tighten the belly and build the biceps. Flood the brain with baptismal oxygen, add to the expectancy of life.

"You're not going to run in your underwear, are you?"

Already I am doing preliminary exercises to alert unused musculature. I touch the toes, stretch the hams. Perhaps I should fall on my knees and pray for safe passage. "Of course," I answer with the haughtiness of a pro. "Everybody does."

"Oh no they don't," she says. "You'll flop out the way those boxers are cut. Let me get you your bathing suit."

"No," I say. "These colors just beg for speed." My shorts are sky blue with a trim of firey red.

334

"I'd better get you a safety pin then."

I do not protest since she has considerable knowledge of the pitch and yaw of various missilery. She fastens my unstitched fly and gently hefts my thinly protected balls.

"Don't hurt yourself, Weber," she warns.

"I will be a better man for all this," I tell her.

"You'll be a better man if you can think of a less boring way to keep in shape."

"Ah, Tericka," I admonish her. "This sport has swept the nation. Millions of citizens can't be wrong."

"Yes they can," she says firmly. "You'll find out."

I crouch in the starting position. She opens the front gate for me and I fly past her under the arch of yellow allamanda, out of our palmed and fruited shady seclusion and onto the street. I turn down the avenue headed east, toward the coast where I shall take a northward route to the Palm Beaches. The sun is all over me and gee it's hot. The pavement burns through the thin soles of my tennis shoes but I am too much in motion to turn back. Movement and pace are the key now. Cramps threaten the instep but I sprint onward.

The seedy residential blocks of Lake Worth disappear behind me. The voices of many nationalities sweep out of the doorways of pastel bungalows. Finnish. German. French Canadian. Cuban Spanish. Jamaican. The drawling, spitting, tongue flopping gobbes of indigenous Floridian humanoids. *Whoim da fuckhell smayshup mah baym-boo bong I'll killem!* Old people everywhere. Dangerous drifters by the dozens. Bohemians and bikers and the lumpen proletariat enjoying themselves in the sun.

Past the all-night shuffleboard courts, lights blink and the barrier tilts down across the railroad tracks. The best I can do is run in place, high-stepping like a halfback, while the engineer spitefully blasts the locomotive's horn. The noise is ferocious. The ground shakes, rumbling under the weight of orange juice being rushed north. I am anxious to be on my way. Beside me, an older woman with sunwrinkled face and hair white-blonde glares at me from behind the wheel of her stupendously long car. The window slides down electrically and she speaks to me words I cannot hear over the roar of the boxcars.

"What?" I shout, beginning to huff just slightly.

She shakes her head impatiently and purses her lips. I learned

335

long ago to ignore the wealthy matrons of the land until introduced by someone trustworthy, because they are righteous, narrow-minded, and sometimes cruel. The caboose thunders by and leaves behind a rare moment of silence, soon violated by the driver.

"Young man, I know you won't mind me telling you this, but you should be in jail." Her voice is refined but conversational. She only wants to assure me that I belong somewhere.

"Thank you," I say, praying for the guard to rise so I can get away from such an awful person.

"You're quite welcome."

There is a note of satisfaction in her voice. I believe I have impressed her with my unexpected gentility. The window returns, the lights cease flashing, the road is clear. The car flows forward with the current of traffic, an unmasted clipper ship, drifting I hope toward some catastrophe with the blessings of my middle finger.

On the flats of my toes, I weave a way through gangs of consumers in the downtown district. Everyone is sunburnt, sundressed, or Bermuda shorted. Pink faces of *turistas* bob up and down on a sea of fluorescent polyester. I hurdle an occasional poodle that barks into my path, and jump out of the way of roller skaters. Past the butcher, the baker, and adult bookstore. One entire block smells of spices and fresh coffee. The sidewalk opens up after La Scala Ristorante and my stride becomes less restrained, full of confidence. Bryant Park is empty except for a lone gull feeder and a quiet audience of royal palms. The bridge across the intercoastal is the first station of my itinerary, and I come onto it feeling that I have miles and miles left in me. Maybe I'm not so bad off after all.

The water below is aquamarine and sparkling. Along the railing all the grandfathers are lined up fishing and I love the tranquil sight of them. Perhaps the best thing my old man ever did for me when I was a kid was take me with him to the jetties and teach me the finer points of cast and reel, the subtle tricks of bait and lure. Until he struck it rich, purchased a yacht, and forgot about me until my mother refreshed his memory during the course of litigation.

These fellows here are landmarks, as consistent as the warm weather, patient, gentle sportsmen until the big one strikes. I know most of them from my walks to and from the beach with

Tericka and child. All of them turn to see what they have never seen before.

"What's the hurry, Weber?"

"Running in the heat? You should be lucky you don't drop dead."

"Shame. Put some pants on."

Sam, a retired driveway salesman from upstate New York, trots alongside me for a moment. "A school of blues, Weber," he says. "Right underneath me, hitting on anything. Rubin caught one with a candy wrapper on his hook. And me, right there. I didn't getta one, I'm telling you. Maybe I shoulda said a Hail Mary or something. Holy cow, look at that. Watch out!"

Directly ahead of us the aging mass of Guido the Gorilla, a former soccer player for the national team of Italy, blocks my route. His pole is bent double and he has stepped back almost into the highway to struggle with it. The nylon line slashes left and right. His face sweats with ecstasy.

"Yank him up! Yank him up!" Sam cries. "It's a record-breaker!"

I sidestep behind Guido off the curb just as he gives his pole a tremendous jerk. The rod nearly slices my ear off as it whips by and is snapped in two by an oncoming car, popping out a headlight with a bang. But the force of Guido's effort has saved his catch. A huge, banquet-size fish sails across the railing of the bridge. It writhes through the air like a gleaming piece of shrapnel, tail twisting and evil-eyed. Over the head of Guido and into traffic, it bounces off the hood of one car which will now need repair. Airborne again, the fish smashes through the window of a delivery van which keeps going after severe swerving. Chased by Guido the Gorilla, caterwauling down the road, retired but not to be cheated. That Guido's in good shape for a man his age.

Over my shoulder, I see that Sam has thrown his arms into the air to exalt his recent vision of the almighty Pisces. "Wow!" he shouts hoarsely. "Weber wait, where are you going? Come back."

Where I am going I think is obvious, so there is nothing to say. Besides, I feel a bit knackered and at this point it is essential not to disrupt the breathing pattern.

"Weber, come back. It's against the law."

But by now I am on the drawbridge section of the span, the highest point on the bridge. To the left and right the back bay separates the mainland from the barrier island, a skinny piece of real estate known as the Palm Beaches, a place known to the more discriminating European families as the only new world locale with acceptable standards. It is true that certain Americans have declared their aristocracy here.

From my vantage point, the ocean is in view, glittering through the palms and Australian pines. The sight of the sea invigorates me like no other, my blood jumps from the smell of its primordial salt. Out there beyond the steely horizon is everything else in the world. Although my lungs hurt, there is in me a desire to run forever. I suppose I have encountered that zone in all sports where the metabolic interfaces with *mysterium tremendum*. A few of my steps fall through time and for an instant I am eternal. Even though the police car slowly tailing me reinforces the uncertainty of my well-being that I think Sam was hinting at.

On the downslope to dry land, the cruiser stalks me like a barracuda. Something is of course wrong but I'll be damned if I know what it is. Out of the corner of my eye I check the immaculate blue uniform of the driver, his humorless mouth, the angry lines of his cheekbones, the eyes entombed in black sunglasses. In a paradise of tanned bodies and bleached hair, his face in unsunned. Trepidation adds a little boost to my stride. As an entrepreneur involved in a very lucrative importation, a business that has in fact kept the Gold Coast golden, neither I nor my banker can afford to talk to this man.

As I leave the bridge my first footfall is acknowledged by a shriek of sirens. There is an amplified rustle, and then a tinny, raspy voice which addresses me publicly. "All right, sport. Hold it right there."

I don't even look at him but keep running obstinately across A1A, the coastal highway, and into Casino Park where the one-way drive loops up around the parking area, then back along the beach, past the pier and the shops, and exits again where I enter, Because the lane is filled with cars headed out, the police car can't follow me. The cruiser accelerates into the circular drive that will eventually bring him back to me, but even with lights spinning he is slowed by the ubiquitous winter traffic. Not running but racing, I head for the pier to lose myself in the crowd out there. I am panting out of control by the time my feet touch the first brown boards. The wood feels soft and loamy after the gravel in the street. The smell of creosote is as snappy as spirits of ammonia. I am safe among the fishermen but in need of counsel.

338

I keep moving, trying to regain control of my lungs. Hyperventilation helps restore a dreamy sense of proportion to the day. There must be hundreds of anglers out here elbowing each other for a spot along the rail. Down below the ocean is transparent; trash sways back and forth on the bottom.

In a white guayabera, linen pants and a panama hat, my friend Bert stands pensively down at the end of the pier, six lines out into deep water. He has years of seniority in this prime spot. Out here on the pier from seven to ten every morning, Bert has become an expert on the weather, salt-water fishing, human behavior, pipe tobacco, and smuggling. He has invested heavily into many local operations. He owns three banks. A courier brings him daily market reports at nine with coffee and croissants. He is my banker and I rely on him. Once again I need his advice.

"Bert," I say.

Bert does not turn around but remains leaning over the pier railing, examining the water.

"Weber, is that you? Why are you gasping? Even if it isn't you, be quiet. There's a cobia down there. I can feel him, I know what he's thinking. He's playing with me, Weber."

I have tried not to hear the siren as it circled the drive, but now the wail is unavoidable. The sound approaches the pier entrance and then stops.

"I think the police are after me," I whisper.

Bert wants to know why.

"I don't know why," I answer, my voice escalating. "Everything's airtight, Bert. I have the happiest people in the world working for me. I don't get it. Here I am out jogging and I get a tail on me and then bam, as soon as I set foot on A1A he gooses the siren. Bert?"

Reluctantly, Bert stops watching the water and turns to look at me with his calm, green eyes. He is a little man, thin, and mostly bald. His face is smooth and benign, strangely unweathered, boyish and intelligent. A real charmer, a sweetheart—all the trademarks of a successful crook. He gives me the once over and shakes his head compassionately. I am instantly on guard. Bert's compassion in this sequence is usually a prelude to disaster.

"What is it, Bert? What have I done?"

He sucks professorily on his burl pipe. "Weber," he says. "You remember Jimmy Jamaica, don't you? He got in on the ground floor back in the Sixties. Set it up perfectly. Perfectly. Took care of

339

everybody, never stepped on toes. One day he forgot to pay for a pack of Lifesavers in the drug store. Walked out with them in his hand and they grabbed him. He panicked. One thing led to another and that was that. Remember that fellow named Sundown from Gainesville? He could wheel and deal with the best of them but he lost everything because he shot his neighbor's dog when it wouldn't stop yapping. Alfredo the Ass down in Coconut Grove? Same thing. Same damn thing.

"Carelessness, Weber. People forget that a good businessman is one hundred per cent business, no matter what he's doing."

"For God's sake, Bert," I plead. "I was only trying to stay healthy."

"Of course, Weber. Of course. And from the looks of that belly of yours I'd say you have the right idea. Good for you, Weber. Discipline is important."

"Bert, there he is."

"Who? Ah, you mean your officer. There he is, all right."

"Bert?" I am ready to grab Bert and shake the serenity out of him.

"My assumption is, Weber, that this guy wants to arrest you for jogging without a shirt on, jogging on a north-south road, and jogging in what looks to be your underwear. All of these things are illegal in the Palm Beaches. I advise you to get the fuck away from me and jump. Call my secretary on Monday morning and let me know how things turned out. Goodbye, Weber."

I am overwhelmed by my responsibility. Jimmy Jamaica supported everybody in the Keys and kept a third world economy on its feet. Sundown pumped money into progressive political campaigns all over the country. After they locked up Alfredo the Ass, the sharks took over and people started getting killed. If I go down, Bert might end up with me, and if Bert goes, Statia goes, and golden dominoes are going to fall all over the place.

My knees are weakening. How did the structure wear so thin that the stock market would twitch if somebody got busted for jogging in Palm Beach? Perhaps this is the time to stand in full force and virtue. Give my attorneys something they can sink their teeth into. "Your honor, the bare chest of an athlete, we contend, is not unsightly. There is no more fundamental right than the right to feel good." Oh boy, am I in trouble. The cop is about fifty yards away and I can hear him blasting farts like a galloping horse.

340

"Jump where, Bert?"

He doesn't want to talk to me but he sees that I am not jumping so he mumbles to me out of the side of his mouth as he casually reels in one of his lines.

"Jump into the water, dummy. Swim out to the black cigarette laying off the reef with those fishing boats. Better hurry, Weber. Your friend is about ten steps behind you."

I am up on the railing poised like a cliff diver. Hands grab me by the waist and squeeze into me, trying to hold on. I try to pry the fingers back but they are gripping me with a maniac's resolve. I push off into space. The hands stay with me for about a second but then slip down and tear away. My impact with the water hurts; it knocks the breath out of me. I plunge deep, waiting for the release of gravity, and when it comes I feel in control again and kick slowly to the surface. Thirty feet above me there's the cop, waving my boxer shorts at me. Man, I wish Bert would get over there and talk him out of shooting me.

I am a man who rarely regrets his actions, but right now I'm a little disappointed with the way the morning has developed. My muscles ache, energy seems in short supply, the policeman may not stand for this sort of resistance, and here, from the surface of the ocean, that black cigarette looks miles away bouncing in the white-capped distance. What the hell, I tell myself. What the hell. I roll in the emerald water and breaststroke eastward. Tericka, these strokes should be for you.

Like a seal, I duck under crashing waves and pop sleekly up in the calm foam of their passing. The tide is crawling away from land and I am riding its cushion like a victorious athlete raised on the hands of his teammates. It's best to forget about bullets spitting into the water around me, or Bert's big fish nipping off the piece of bait that's waving between my sore thighs. It's best just to stroke, pull, and kick ahead through the dazzling blue and concentrate on this new challenge.

I glide across dark clumps of turtle grass and out over fields of sand bright blue with refraction. At least here a half-mile from shore there is no one to intrude on one's autonomy. Beyond the reef, the fishing boats swing and jerk like white kites against their anchors. Mackerel must be running, dolphin migrating. The coral heads are mottled rose and amber beneath me. The surge is strong and I have about had it but still I frogkick into deeper, more sinister water where death can flash up from infinity and take a big bite. The ominous black hull of the oceangoing powerboat lures me onward, my dark salvation.

On board the cigarette, I am relieved to see two fellows gauging my progress. One extends a long gaff out to me. I reach for the crook of the pole but it thrusts beyond my hand and twists to hook into the back of my neck. Maybe I am not wanted here. The violence in the motion stops at the surface of my skin. I cannot raise my head but gaze instead into the sheen of the black fiberglass and my reflection sliding by. The desperation of my image startles me absolutely cold. I didn't know, I murmur to myself. There is seaweed in my moustache. There is a familiar cracker accent calling down from above.

"Webah, is that you?"

In my exhaustion, all I can think of is Chuck Berry. Maybelline? Honey, is that you?

"Yes!" I scream it. My voice takes what juice I have left. "You tried to kill me!"

"Now, Webah, don't be like that. I didn't know it was you."

A wave slaps me and my mouth fills with salty water. I sputter and cough and begin to drift away from the boat. A strong hand locks into my hair but I feel no pain. A rope is somehow looped under my arms and I am hauled up over the gunnel and flipped on deck. I land sprawling next to a colossal blue marlin, easily five times my size. Its eye is as big as my fist. Blood has puddled around the torn beak.

"Goddamn, Webah. You're naked, boy."

I can say nothing, only sympathize with the fish. Leo Stubbs, the best diesel mechanic on the Gold Coast and a former employee of mine, crouches down beside me and helps me to sit up.

"Webah," he says. "I know there ain't no sense in askin' what the hell you were doin' bare-assed a mile offshore. Things happen to workin' men. But Webah, my man here and me's on a business trip, ya know, and this is my man's boat, and he wants you to catch your breath and leave."

"Leave to go where, Leo?"

Leo suffers the telling of his message. Loyalty and friendship are not in excess in Leo's life, but here they have crossed tracks. His weathereaten eyes appeal to me for understanding and he lowers his voice.

342

"Come on, Webah. My man the captain here is a fuckin' renegade, a regular shitball Ernest Hemingway. You won't believe what he done. Webah, I'm sorry I don't have time to be more hospitable, but you gonna have to go over the side and swim to that drift boat passin' by. Let's get together tomorrow and have us a clambake or somethin', drink some ten dollah bourbon."

I look at Leo's man to try to get a feeling for the situation. He is up in the bow lackadaisically casting a silver spoon over the reef. He's dressed in a white cotton tee-shirt and seersucker pants, unstained by salt or sweat. His face is bright red but clamped shut by wraparound shades and a stiff blue captain's hat. In his back hip pocket is a conspicuous bulge and anybody would know this is intentional, for there's more heat per capita in Miami and the Gold Coast than anywhere north of Bogota.

"Been fishing, eh?" I asked Leo.

"Oh brother, have we ever. You said it," Leo says, rolling his eyes.

"Square grouper, is it?" I ask. Square grouper is a very popular catch these days in south Florida. It stacks up neatly in the cargo hold and is the only fish I know of that stinks sweet.

"No, Webah. Wrong."

Leo has seen too much sunlight. He is a perpetual squinter. His hands, the hands of a marine mechanic, lead a rough and reckless life. They are everywhere scarred, the fingers crooked, the nails smashed off. They tell me Leo is the one man I would want with me on a boat, but he's a loner and won't stay put.

"Shit, Leo," I tell him. "We worked together, we survived a hurricane together. You even fell in love with my wife, didn't you, and now you're telling me—"

"I'm not lying, Webah."

I look at his hands, the course of the palms black with grease, and shake my head sadly.

"And Statia ain't your wife no more."

"Nobody takes a boat like this out fishing. You picked up the marlin at dockside in the Bahamas. Come on, Leo. This is me, Weber."

"No, Webah, you ain't gonna believe this. It's black gold we got. My man Captain Shitball here has himself forty-six Haitians down below sittin' on each other's feet. We picked them up in Freeport last night and each of them handed over six hundred bucks to the

Captain. I don't know where people like that get that kind of money."

Something is wrong here. A big boat like this one crosses the Gulf Stream in an hour, one thousand horsepower boiling the sea astern. Live cargo is off-loaded on the golden beaches in the dark morning hours. Leo and this man should have been at the night deposit window of the bank hours ago.

"Webah," Leo says, "my man here is insane. As soon as we're out of the harbor last night he rigs up a trawl line and sets it and we take it real slow 'cause we got time to kill. Then about twelve miles out the clothespin snaps off and the line rings through the reel. My man goes berserk. I tell him cut the fuckin' line and let's go. He pulls this runty piss-ant pistol on me and says, 'No, I want the fish.' Well, hell, that big marlin swam us up to Abaco and then back down toward Eleuthra and this way and that way. At five this morning I could still see the lights on Bimini.

"Finally he lands the son of a bitch and struts around like a *commandante*. I turned the boat west and let her fly but the time we got here the sun's up twenty degrees and we're down to the last sip of gas. Damn the man! Webah, this is the truth. We're just waitin' for nightfall."

This is not where I want to be. Nothing looks more suspicious to the Coast Guard than a cigarette, especialy one this size, laying offshore all day long.

"Leo," I say. "Give me a pair of pants or a bathing suit and I'll be on my way."

"Can't do that, Webah. Only got what I have on."

"Hell, give me your underpants then."

"Ain't wearin' any."

"What about the captain?"

"I'll ask."

My strength is returning. I am prepared for the swim to a nearby boat but I am, when possible, a man of standards myself, and would prefer not to impose my nakedness any further. I try a shaky push-up on the hot deck. Leo's conversation with his man is very short.

"Captain Shitball says go below and take what you need from off the cargo and then beat it. Come on, I'll show you the way."

I follow Leo's taut little body into the cockpit and down a ladder into a spotless, ultra-modern galley. Beyond this there's only a

344

bulkhead, teak from beam to beam, and Leo unlatches a door into the forward hold and opens it to the escaping darkness and the smell of poverty. I step through the passageway and can hear teeth chattering nervously, stomachs gurgling, one or two babies crying.

"Leo," I say. "This isn't the business for you."

Leo ignores me. My eyes adjust and I can make out the round, black faces framing the neon glow of eyes and teeth. The air is low on oxygen but satiated with hope. Several women giggle and I instinctively cover my genitals with folded hands.

"Welcome to America," I say.

"Izt Meeami?" a girl's voice sings.

"*Oui oui*," Leo answers, though it sounds like *whey whey*. "My mammy soon foof come-go yeah yeah, y'all dig that?"

The people nod their heads understandingly, joyously.

"Leo," I said. "You're a pig, telling these people you'd take them to Miami. Give me some money, man."

"What for?"

'I'm going to buy myself a pair of pants.'

"Webah," he says impatiently, but I won't let him go on.

"Just lend me the money," I tell him, "and leave it at that."

"All I got is hundreds," he says, digging into his cut-offs. I pluck a bill from the tangled bundle he reveals.

"That'll do." I tuck the money into the shirt pocket of a man in front of me and motion for him to take off his pants. He gives me a nice smile and obliges. Most probably the captain prohibited his cargo from carrying luggage, so I am not surprised to see that the man has a second pair of short pants underneath his outer ones. I have enough foresight to ask him also for the Salvation Army suit jacket that matches the pants. I shake the man's hand and the deal is complete.

"Webah, you're crazy to give a hundred bucks to a nigrah that don't even speak English."

I don't want to argue with Leo. It was a discussion much like this one that lost me the best mechanic I know of on water. (Webah, you're crazy to walk away from a woman like Statia.) I shrug and begin to step into my recently purchased trousers, blue serge circa Korean War era. Two things happen.

As if it had a nervous system for chills to run through, the boat gives a silent shake, a sequence of twitches, and then a roar crescendoes behind us. Like a horse rearing suddenly up, the bow of the boat rises, the stern punches into the water. My ankles are tied by the trousers I am struggling with and I pitch backwards through the passageway and crash into the galley. Leo tumbles after me, banging his elbow into my mouth with such force that I want to cry. We are two grains of salt buried by a rain of pepper. By the time I am able to breathe freely and move again, Leo has somehow clambered up on deck and now is back down in the galley, pushing Haitians out of the way and furiously searching the cupboards, throwing things around. He looks like a man who has just been electrocuted and enjoyed the volts.

"Leo!" I shout.

Leo has found a jar of instant coffee and from the way he's gulping the dry brown granules you'd think he had a cold beer in his hand.

"Lord, lord, lord," he says. "Marine Patrol comin' outa Boynton Inlet. Lights, siren, a big show. Shitball's borrowin' time."

Leo is grinning, he's having a good experience. My mouth, I realize, is bloody. My ribs feel cracked. Leo throws more condiments off the shelves, finds a baby food jar with a half-inch of powder in the bottom. He dumps its contents on a countertop and begins frantically chopping at the crystals with his buck knife.

"Wanna line, boy?" he asks, talking fast. "Fortify yourself for the ride. Come on now, blow summa this snow and grab a handful of vitamins there in that jar." He looks away from his project to nod toward a mason jar filled with a tropical flora of pills. In his haste he chops into the hump of his thumb. He jerks his hand away to keep the blood from spilling into the cocaine. He holds the deep gash up for me to inspect. His eyes are all squinty.

"How's that for a pain threshhold, Webah? I don't feel a damn thing."

I take a pinch of the coke and rub it across my busted lips. Hoisting myself up the ladder, I reel through the hatchway into the cockpit, gripping desperately for any handhold that will keep me from catapulting out of the boat as we hop and skip over the ocean at tremendous speed. Captain S is at the wheel, as indifferent as any midweek commuter. I'll bet catching that marlin made the worms in his heart glow. The lights of law and order are shrinking far astern.

"How many horsepower you got in this thing?" I yell idiotically. I cannot hear my own voice, but a hand cups my ear. Leo has joined us, his wound bandaged with grey duct tape.

346

"Damn impolite!" he screams. His mouth is cold on my sunburnt ear.

"WHAT?"

"Damn impolite question. After a thousand, it ain't nobody's business!"

I turn to grimace at the bouncing, jolted face but his eyes cut me away. Here's a man whose sureness and certainty are proportionate to the degree of chaos he is able to sniff out. Tericka says the same of me but she's wrong. I am satisfied enough keeping capitalism and myself healthy. I am satisfied by the girl, the tits, the baby, the house, the mango and grapefruit trees, the weather, the music, and the money. I am a gentle man, for God's sake.

Our smokey wake is as tempestuous as a squall line on the surface of the water. The Moorish towers of the Breakers Hotel rise ten degrees off our port side. We are no more than a quarter-mile out. Amid the flying spray, the crashing and pounding, the extreme noise, something within this fiberglass behemoth slips, and the kinetic clutch of our motion relaxes a second. The air stutters but then the roar continues.

"All right, goddammit," Leo is shouting. "That's it. That's all she wrote. Son of a bitch, put her on the beach, man."

Leo's man the captain, one gets the feeling, is dozing behind his sunglasses. The air cracks and stammers. *Vaa vaa vaa va va*. The passengers that have come up on deck crouch like Muslims at prayer. Leo shoves the captain aside and spins the wheel to port. The cigarette arcs and slams broadside through the water. The force of the maneuver sends several Haitans crashing through the lifeline, which they grab and dangle from like eels. Just as we regain our forward momentum, an unnatural silence implodes down into us. We are out of gas.

Captain Shitball *has* pulled his pistol and he waves it at Leo. This sort of behavior depresses the hell out of me. I try to make myself small, but the captain says in a high Latin accent, "Keep those folks here away from my feesh."

We have enough glide left in us to coast within fifty yards of the shore where up above the concrete breakwater, in the glassed bays of the Breakers dining room, I can see the faces of the aristocracy turn with concern from their *fois gras* and Chateauneuf du Pape.

To the north and south red lights are flashing out beyond the reef and you know the sirens are blasting even if you can't hear them yet. I tell Leo goodbye, and Leo's man thanks for the ride.

347

"Miami!" Leo announces. "Miami. End of the line." He begins to throw the Haitians overboard. They are shrieking and wailing hysterically. For some of these immigrants in the past, this point has truly been the end of the line, but the water here seems shallow enough to stand in, I dive over the side and freestyle as fast as I can toward the beach. Leo follows close behind. The captain has chosen to stay with his marlin, a man intent on legend.

We must seem a very peculiar aquacade to the ladies and gentlemen lining the oceanfront windows of the Hotel. Surely money is changing hands over the prospect of our individual arrivals. Small fortunes suddenly made or lost. America, I am back ashore again and ready to run.

The wet worsted of my suit chafes against me like sandpaper and I would like nothing more than to sit down in the hot sun and let everything dry up and calm down, but in a few minutes the Marine Patrol, the Coast Guard, the State Police, the local guardia, and all my friends at the DEA will be here to welcome everybody, so I must be on my way. I hurdle over Haitians and puff up the slippery steps of the breakwater, across the perfect zoysia lawn toward the circus colors of the poolside cabanas. I am thinking that this is all a rather shameful matter and that I've been made to feel embarrassingly lawless.

I think my form is pretty good as I approach the pool; the old spirit shines through. My legs still feel a bit jelly-like from the vibrations of the boat but my knees are rising respectably and I keep my elbows tucked into my side, my hands pumping out in front of me. Bikinied women on chaise lounges lean forward to check me out. A well-tanned attendant in lime-colored sportswear is striding toward me, waving his arms for me to stop. I collar him around the neck with my forearm and together we rush somewhat awkwardly into the nearest cabana. I must say this part of town brings out the worst in me. We stumble to the astroturf floor. I am holding his head down by the ears. I try to talk to him.

"I'll kill you, I'll rip these things right off your head. I'll bite your fucking nose off."

"Mister, please—!" the fellow says. There is terror in his preparatory blue eyes. I am not behaving properly, I see.

"Excuse me, I'm overwrought," I say apologetically and roll off, still holding on to one ear so I don't lose him. "I was out jogging and ran into some trouble. Understand?"

He nods his head very quickly. After all, he is a young man who has been trained to be of service to people who have everything and still want more.

"Mrs. Gerald Silverhartz," I say. "Statia Silverhartz." His eyes widen appropriately. "Do you know who she is?" He nods his fair head vigorously after I let go of his ear.

"This is a private, personal matter. Understand?"

Again, a satisfying nod.

"Ms. Silverhartz and I are business associates and I need to talk to her. Find her, please. Tell her Weber needs her. She'll come. And, of course, if you'll see to it that I am not disturbed while I wait, Ms. Silverhartz and I will express our gratitude in generous ways. Okay?"

"Okay." More than a nod now. Genuine enthusiasm. I am pleased by his resilience and help the lad to his feet.

"And look," I say cheerfully. "Could you send in a sandwich and a beer for me? I've worked up quite an appetite this morning."

I stand behind the door while he opens it to leave, but still I can see through the crack at the hinges that the Haitians are discovering Palm Beach's most exclusive hotel. Welcome to America, I say to myself. Good luck. The first of many uniformed men bounds out of the bushes and draws his gun on a black woman with a scarf wrapped around her head.

I slam the door quickly and sit back in a rattan chair to await dear Statia, the woman who once made my heart sweat: my former beauty, lean and restless, hard-mouthed and cat-faced. The first time I ever saw her, almost twenty years ago, was on the cover of the Shiny Sheet stacked inside the pink vending machines along Royal Poinciana Way. She was a debutante, she was coming out, she was bending over a table signing the Social Register. A presidential candidate had his hand on her hip. She was lovely. Three weeks later I was in bed with her learning the game I've Got A Secret Place. I never knew for sure if we were right for each other, or if our relationship was simply a prerequisite for growing up.

What I do know is that we were married once and pissed away a fortune. Which under her guidance we promptly recovered. By age twenty-six she was sneezing blood into the finest oriental silk. By twenty-seven her septum was reinforced with stainless steel plating. By age twenty-eight we acknowledged our hatred for each

349

other; at thirty she wed Gerald Silverhartz, well-known bauxite tycoon and international powerbroker. Now, six years later, we are still in business together and the hatred's gone, replaced by a quiet, honest affection. That's best, because I don't want her out of my life. She is someone to look at and say, we're alike, you and I. Hell-bent, the both of us, and yet heaven does its best to stay on our side.

From Statia I inherited Tericka. On the surface, the acquisition was another convoluted, hushed, little-said-much-implied business deal. Statia sent a messenger across the bay one day ten months ago with a monogramed note:*Weber-Please house mother and child for a day or two until we can put them on one of our boats to the islands. Signed, Stash.* Tericka stepped out of the limousine, looking very girlish, very fragile, in a flowered dress and straw espadrilles. The baby was asleep in her arms. Stash had managed to put one of the new astronauts on the payroll to deliver from Florida to Houston a special something for a special someone. Tericka was a clause in this unwritten contract. Which said, I imagine, get her and the kid out of my life. I let them in reluctantly. After three days, I couldn't let go, and nobody came to retrieve them.

I began to worry that perhaps the attendant fellow is right this moment turning me in to a roomful of arguing Pinkertons. A knock on the door makes my adrenalin zing, my heart fly about like a loose bird inside me. Nothing matters more here than tone of voice. Statia was the first to teach me this.

"What is it, damn it?" I shout curtly.

"Room service, sir. Roast beef and Guinness."

"Is the roast beef bloody rare?"

"Yes sir."

"Horseradish?"

"Uh, yes sir."

I pull the door open so that I'm hidden behind it. "Push in the service," I say, "and that will be all." I grab the silver cart and wheel it in, taking a quick bite of the sandwich, which I must instantly spit out because my mouth hurts so much. What I see outside stops me from closing the door fully. The Haitians are all queued up, cowering before a force of lawmen. One old man is weeping, pulling a few dirty dollars out of his ragged pants and throwing the money on the ground. In front of my cabana, several

350

of the local citizenry review the situation. Perhaps they hope for a good price on a gardener or yardman. Goddamn it, where is Statia? I haven't seen her for weeks. For all I know she's still in New York, or God knows where, allowing the clergy of commerce to worship her. Leo, I see, has been nabbed and handcuffed. He is set down in a lawnchair and doesn't hesitate to call the bartender for a cocktail.

I withdraw back into my appointed room, resigned to my skewed fate. Statia could be anywhere, could be receiving the dry old tongue of a Trade Commissioner at this very moment. My attendant taps on the door and enters carrying a telephone which he plugs into a wall jack. "Sir," he says respectfully. "I haven't had much luck locating your party. Would you care to use the telephone?" I must tell him I am too distressed to push the buttons properly and he must do it for me. For a half hour I call out numbers, the boy dials and makes the necessary inquiries, without success. My resolve for good health dissipates with each click of the receiver and I experience a terrific urge for vice. Nothing to do but send the attendant for cigars and vodka, and when he leaves I rise from the rattan chair where I've been sulking and stab out the numbers of Gerald's private beeper. In but a few minutes he rings me back.

"Silverhartz here, what is it?"

"Gerald, this is Weber and—."

"Goodbye Weber."

"Gerald don't hang up I have the stink of scandal and grievous harm on my breath today."

"One of your many stinks. How did you get this number?"

"I must see Statia. She must come rescue me at the Breakers."

"Heh-heh, that's a good one."

"Gerald, you are a flaccid old kraut and of limited interest to me. I hope you have enough socked away to survive the economic ruin that shall now descend on your house. You won't have a penny left to pay the young boys you bugger on your jaunts to Martinique. Goodbye, asshole."

I pitch the receiver back to its cradle and congratulate myself on gaining Mr. Silverhartz's avaricious attention. He is a bully, a pigoid, a charge-ahead pomposity but not so much a fool to keep Statia away from me if he suspects his ass is in any manner endangered by my indiscretions. I am furnished with cigars and

351

clear liquor and send the attendant out to the drive to escort Statia to my little cage when she arrives.

The room is well-fouled with tarry smoke, my blood rushes through my heart vents and valves like the Volga by the time I hear the familiar gravel of her voice pelt the ears of the crowd outside my louvered window.

"Get out of my way, please. I said *move*." Ah, the charm of authority on the lips of a self-possessed and desirable woman.

Skillfully elbowing a bewildered cop from her path, she points at Leo in his lounge chair, the mechanic double-fistedly gulping a tall pink drink, and says to a man in a grey business suit, "Rubin, you're making a mistake arresting that citizen. My lawyers will be glad to explain." The man sneers back at her but everyone knows Leo is home free. Nobody suffers the lock-up in Palm Beach until deserted by the local money-lenders.

She breezes past this scenario, nodding her head appropriately as the poolside attendant points out my cabana to her. Even at this distance she projects invulnerability, even to me, and I know better. I tuck my hands glumly into the pockets of my damp trousers. She enters the room looking eternally young and ready for sport, dressed as she is in a snappy short white tennis skirt and sleeveless jersey. She is full of energy, terrifyingly confident, though her mouth has found the reproach she so commonly employs on me these days.

"I was over at the Fays when Gerald rang, *livid*, let me tell you," she says as she closes the door behind her, and then, "Oh my, what happened to you?"

I smile sheepishly, shrug my shoulders, feel the unwanted scratchy beginnings of the affection I have for the lady. She looks good, though perhaps a bit overwintered from the recent business trip to the cold offices of New York. Her thick dark hair is drawn back from her bony face and held with a peach-colored ribbon. Her lower lip is naturally swollen, a fat slice of fruit. Her eyes are aggressively green. I have remained loyal to all this yet others have remarked that her features suffer from too many fast starts and stops.

"Statia, sorry to bother you but I'm in a jam."

She stands off from me, taking account of my condition. "Ee-yuck," she says, "that suit looks horrible on you." She clucks out ·

mild disappointment. "And who hit you in the mouth? It's all bloody, let me see." From somewhere in her skirt she has extracted a crumpy wad of kleenex and dabs at my lips. She sticks a finger in my mouth and tenderly probes. I try to explain.

"I waa yawging," I say.

"Weber," she says sympathetically. "Your front tooth here is broken. Jesus, doesn't it hurt?" She removes her finger quickly from my mouth.

"It just throbs," I say, unwilling to examine the damage myself or to think much about it.

"What in the world were you doing?"

"I was jogging."

Her geometric eyebrows furrow and she looks at me suspiciously. "You were jogging!? My goodness, how did you end up with Leo and those poor Haitians and enough cops for a baseball game? No, don't tell me Weber," she says, exasperated with me, testing her forehead with the back of her hand as if I had just sent a fever into her. "I'd rather not know."

"Well, I think you should know," I say. "I want you to know I was not behaving frivolously."

"No," she says, growling. "I definitely do not want to hear about it. Let's just clean you up and get you out of here."

"Statia, dear," I say, since I must match her hauteur, "don't dare patronize a fellow cheerist. We are special comforts to one another. A matching set of bookends on the literature of indulgence and immoderation."

She blinks deliberately slow and says, "Where's that boy with my mineral water? I asked him to bring me mineral water. Idoona Fay and I were playing doubles against John and Yoko and I'm thirsty. Idoona's selling them the McLean estate. You'd never believe it, but she's really quite good with a racquet."

This chatter, I know from experience, is a way of punishing me and my trivial concerns. She keeps on until she gets her water, and with her throat freshly doused she turns on me.

"What has gotten into you lately, Weber? Where's the class and the dash gone? That tumbledown shack you live in with that child and her baby. It's just too perverse, even for me. And now this escapade with Leo. And oh what a fool you were to telephone Gerald and threaten him."

"I panicked," I admit.

"I'll say. He's furious, he wants you disappeared."

"I worry about you, Statia," I say, trying to make a joke out of it yet unable to prevent a certain amount of righteousness from my voice. "Is there life after Gerald Silverhartz and unrestrained decadence?"

"How dare you?" she hisses back. "I'm a happy woman, Weber, and you know it. I am hard-working and loved. I am not idle or world-weary like you. Go back to where you belong with your teenybopper. And I should tell you that we've closed the Space Shuttle deal with Tericka's bum from outer space, so if you were ever motivated by certain business-wise obligations, you are free of them now."

"For your information," I say, "I love Tericka, I like the baby. You always checked into the headache clinic whenever I tried to talk to you about kids." I surprise myself because I've never said this aloud before. It sounds good to me.

"Oh Weber," Statia says. "You make me feel old and tired. But I'm happy for you, really. In fact, I'm relieved, although it all sounds painfully mature for a fellow like you."

I suppose I could bite down on that but I don't. Her voice has been icy, but she steps away from me with just a brush of melancholy across her mouth. We were most ourselves when we were in bed or bickering, and we both ran like hell from each other when we figured this out.

Statia picks up the receiver and dials, doing what she does best—business in extravagant fashion. I watch her, thinking, I'm glad I stopped *needing* you, I'm glad we're still friends. Statia, you're a woman, you're good looking, you're awfully rich, your life is sinfully exciting. I try to add all these facts up, try to attach some great meaning to the gilded patterns, the exaggerated blessings, of your life. I can't do it, for you or for me. We have strong hearts and a certain arrogant commitment to excellence of one sort or another, whether we are outlaws or saints of the new world. And we never gave up anything without a fight, including our marriage. When we were so much younger, down on our luck, very scruffy but destined to rise again, a salesman in a used car lot condescended to our few dollars that we hoped would buy an old VW bug. I want to smack him, I said to Statia then. Oh shit, Weber, forget it, she said. He's not tall enough to look down his nose at us.

354

You know what I mean? Why do you have this need to apologize or attack?

Within minutes Statia has orchestrated a dignified ending to my day. She phones her tailor, her prosthodontist, her chauffeur. She puts her cool hands on my neck and kisses my cheek. I hug her tightly, this woman who is now a goddamn institution. "Goodbye, Weber," she says. "I've got to get back. Let's get together Monday or Tuesday with Bert. Wear something nice." She smiles warmly, showing a neat line of teeth, and is gone.

I feel better. By tearing the roast beef sandwich into little bites I am able to chew it on one side of my mouth. I suck vodka gingerly from its chilled bottle, light a second cigar to keep me company now that I'm alone again. The tailor comes first and leaves me wearing satin racing shorts with a chamois crotch, expensive running shoes, a cotton pullover, and sunglasses capable of concealing the most public of identities. The prosthodontist arrives shortly thereafter and fits me with a gold cap he selects from a small leather boxful of them. "It's only temporary," he says. "Of course, many gentlemen today are finding that a golden smile is also a sound investment." For some reason this amuses him and he cackles. "Think it over," he says, handing me a script for codeine.

Like clockwork, Statia's chauffeur Raans enters the cabana and waits quietly at parade rest until the doctor leaves. When we are alone, he whips off his cap and bows. "Boy oh boy, Weber," he says. "You're looking slick."

Indeed I am in awe of myself, that simple exercise can provide such change. "Don't you find it a little queer, Raans," I say, "that Statia and I share this phoenix quality, that the second we start to smell like shit you can bet roses will be delivered?"

"Ah yes, you bet. You bet," Raans says, amiable Raans, so happy to be a handsome Scandanavian in cockstruck Palm Beach. "Where can I take you? The beach? Your broker's? Down to Hialeah to watch the ponies?"

"Just home."

We walk out side by side, assured and unapproachable. The Haitians are being whisked away in paddy wagons. Leo is gone but I doubt he will be forgotten because too many of the gentry depend on him to keep their intrigues running smoothly. Stash's Silver Cloud is parked close by. Raans holds the door for me as I slip onto the expensive leather seats occupied already by two affenpinschers. Raans gets behind the wheel and soon we are southbound on Ocean Boulevard, across the causeway and not far from my neighborhood.

"Raans, stop," I say. "I want to get out."

"Okay, Weber."

I spring out of the car and onto the sidewalk, marvelling at how comfortable the new shoes are on my feet. Every muscle is sore but the pain fades as I pick up speed, press ahead to find the limit.

nominated by Elizabeth Inness-Brown and Barbara Grossman

PIER

by D. C. BERRY

from POETRY

for Chuck E. Lewis

This dead fish was once a muscle twitch
in the waves slamming the ocean door.
All neck like a broom or an existentialist,
it was homelessly at home wherever it swept

like the strippers in New Orleans
writhing all night or the saints
writhing all day in St. Louis Cathedral,
same glass frenzy for centuries,

never running loose, no more running loose
than this door jamb the ocean slams at no address,
this dead fish with more ribs
than a noose.

Pier, I say, where bound,
pier stilting toward the next breaker.

nominated by Elizabeth Inness-Brown

THE MEAL

by SUZANNE E. BERGER

from LEGACIES (Alice James Books)

They have washed their faces until they are pale,
their homework is beautifully complete.
They wait for the adults to lean towards each other.
The hands of the children are oval
and smooth as pine-nuts.

The girls have braided and rebraided their hair,
and tied ribbons without a single mistake.
The boy has put away his coin collection.
They are waiting for the mother to straighten her lipstick,
and for the father to speak.

They gather around the table, carefully
as constellations waiting to be named.
Their minds shift and ready, like dunes.
It is so quiet, all waiting stars and dunes.

Their forks move across their plates without scraping,
they wait for the milk and the gravy
at the table with its forgotten spices.
They are waiting for a happiness to lift their eyes,
like sudden light flaring in the trees outside.

The white miles of the meal continue,
the figures still travel across a screen:
the father carving the Sunday roast,
her mouth uneven as a torn hibiscus,
their braids still gleaming in the silence.

nominated by Celia Gilbert

WHY I'M IN FAVOR OF A NUCLEAR FREEZE

by CHRISTOPHER BUCKLEY

from TELESCOPE

Because we were 18 and still wonderful in our bodies,
because Harry's father owned a ranch and we had
nothing better to do one Saturday, we went hunting
doves among the high oaks and almost wholly quiet air . . .
Traipsing the hills and deer paths for an hour,
we were ready when the first ones swooped—
and we took them down in smoke much like the planes
in the war films of our regimented youth.
                                        Some were dead
and some knocked cold, and because he knew how
and I just couldn't, Harry went to each of them and,
with thumb and forefinger, almost tenderly, squeezed
the last air out of their slight necks.
                                        Our jackets grew
heavy with birds and for a while we sat in the shade
thinking we were someone, talking a bit of girls—
who would "go", who wouldn't, how love would probably
always be beyond our reach . . . We even talked of the nuns
who terrified us with God and damnation. We both recalled
that first prize in art, the one pinned to the cork board
in front of class, was a sweet blond girl's drawing
of the fires and coals, the tortured souls of Purgatory.
Harry said he feared eternity until he was 17, and,

360

if he ever had kids, the last place they would go would be
a parochial school.
                         On our way to the car, having forgotten
which way the safety was off or on, I accidently discharged
my borrowed 12 gauge, twice actually—one would have been
     Harry's
head if he were behind me, the other my foot, inches to the
     right.
We were almost back when something moved in the raw, dry
     grass,
and without thinking, and on the first twitch of two tall ears,
we together blew the ever-loving-Jesus out of a jack rabbit
until we couldn't tell fur from dust from blood . . .
                                         Harry has
a family, two children as lovely as any will ever be—
he hasn't hunted in years . . . and that once was enough for me.
Anymore, a good day offers a moment's praise for the lizards
daring the road I run along, or it offers a dusk in which
yellow meadow larks scrounge fields in the grey autumn light . . .
Harry and I are friends now almost 30 years, and the last time
we had dinner, I thought about that rabbit, not the doves
which we swore we would cook and eat, but that rabbit—
why the hell had we killed it so cold-heartedly? And I saw
that it was simply because we had the guns, because we could . . .

nominated by Sherod Santos

SARAH COLE: A TYPE OF LOVE STORY

fiction by RUSSELL BANKS

from THE MISSOURI REVIEW

To BEGIN, then, here is a scene in which I am the man and my friend Sarah Cole is the woman. I don't mind describing it now, because I'm a decade older and don't look the same now as I did then, and Sarah is dead. That is to say, on hearing this story you might think me vain if I looked the same now as I did then, because I must tell you that I was extremely handsome then. And if Sarah were not dead, you'd think I were cruel, for I must tell you that Sarah was very homely. In fact, she was the homeliest woman I have ever known. Personally, I mean. I've *seen* a few women who were more unattractive than Sarah, but they were clearly freaks of nature or had been badly injured or had been victimized by some grotesque, disfiguring disease. Sarah, however, was quite normal, and I knew her well, because for three and a half months we were lovers.

Here is the scene. You can put it in the present, even though it took place ten years ago, because nothing that matters to the story depends on when it took place, and you can put it in Concord, New Hampshire, even though that is indeed where it took place, because it doesn't matter where it took place, so it might as well be Concord, New Hampshire, a place I happen to know well and can therefore describe with sufficient detail to make the story believable. Around six o'clock on a Wednesday evening in late May a man enters a bar. The place, a cocktail lounge at street level with a restaurant upstairs, is decorated with hanging plants and unfinished wood paneling, butcherblock tables and captain's chairs, with a half dozen darkened, thickly upholstered booths along one wall. Three or four men between the ages of twenty-five and thirty-five are drinking at the bar, and they, like the man who has just entered, wear three piece suits and loosened neckties. They are probably lawyers, young, unmarried lawyers gossiping with their brethren over martinis so as to postpone arriving home alone at their whitewashed townhouse apartments, where they will fix their evening meals in radar ranges and, afterwards, while their tv's chuckle quietly in front of them, sit on their couches and do a little extra work for tomorrow. They are, for the most part, honorable, educated, hard-working, shallow, and moderately unhappy young men. Our man, call him Ronald, Ron, in most ways is like these men, except that he is unusually good-looking, and that makes him a little less unhappy than they. Ron is effortlessly attractive, a genetic wonder, tall, slender, symmetrical, and clean. His flaws, a small mole on the left corner of his square but not-too-prominent chin, a slight excess of blond hair on the tops of his tanned hands, and somewhat underdeveloped buttocks, insofar as they keep him from resembling too closely a men's store mannequin, only contribute to his beauty, for he is beautiful, the way we usually think of a woman as being beautiful. And he is nice, too, the consequence, perhaps, of his seeming not to know how beautiful he is, to men as well as women, to young people, even children, as well as old, to attractive people, who realize immediately that he is so much more attractive than they as not to be competitive with them, as well as unattractive people, who see him and gain thereby a comforting perspective on those they have heretofore envied for their good looks.

Ron takes a seat at the bar, unfolds the evening paper in front of him, and before he can start reading, the bartender asks to help him, calling him "Sir," even though Ron has come into this bar numerous times at this time of day, especially since his divorce last fall. Ron got divorced because, after three years of marriage, his wife had chosen to pursue the career that his had interrupted, that of a fashion designer, which meant that she had to live in New York City while he had to continue to live in New Hampshire, where his career had got its start. They agreed to live apart until he could continue his career near New York City, but after a few months, between conjugal visits, he started sleeping with other women, and she started sleeping with other men, and that was that. "No big deal," he explained to friends, who liked both Ron and his wife, even though he was slightly more beautiful than she. "We really were too young when we got married, college sweethearts. But we're still best friends," he assured them. They understood. Most of Ron's friends were divorced by then too.

Ron orders a scotch and soda, with a twist, and goes back to reading his paper. When his drink comes, before he takes a sip of it, he first carefully finishes reading an article about the recent reappearance of coyotes in northern New Hampshire and Vermont. He lights a cigarette. He goes on reading. He takes a second sip of his drink. Everyone in the room, the three or four men scattered along the bar, the tall, thin bartender, and several people in the booths at the back, watches him do these ordinary things.

He has got to the classified section, is perhaps searching for someone willing to come in once a week and clean his apartment, when the woman who will turn out to be Sarah Cole leaves a booth in the back and approaches him. She comes up from the side and sits next to him. She's wearing heavy, tan cowboy boots and a dark brown, suede cowboy hat, lumpy jeans and a yellow tee shirt that clings to her arms, breasts, and round belly like the skin of a sausage. Though he will later learn that she is thirty-eight years old, she looks older by about ten years, which makes her look about twenty years older than he actually is. (It's difficult to guess accurately how old Ron is, he looks anywhere from a mature twenty-five to a youthful forty, so his actual age doesn't seem to matter.)

"It's not bad here at the bar," she says, looking around. "More light, anyhow. Whatcha readin'?" she asks brightly, planting both elbows on the bar.

Ron looks up from his paper with a slight smile on his lips, sees the face of a woman homelier than any he has ever seen or imagined before, and goes on smiling lightly. He feels himself falling into her tiny, slightly crossed, dark brown eyes, pulls himself back, and studies for a few seconds her mottled, pocked complexion, bulbous nose, loose mouth, twisted and gapped teeth, and heavy but receding chin. He casts a glance over her thatch of dun-colored hair and along her neck and throat, where acne burns against gray skin, and returns to her eyes, and again feels himself falling into her.

"What did you say?" he asks.

She knocks a mentholated cigarette from her pack, and Ron swiftly lights it. Blowing smoke from her large, wing-shaped nostrils, she speaks again. Her voice is thick and nasal, a chocolate-colored voice. "I asked you whatcha readin', but I can see now." She belts out a single, loud laugh. "The paper!"

Ron laughs, too. "The paper! *The Concord Monitor!*" He is not hallucinating, he clearly sees what is before him and admits—no, he asserts—to himself that he is speaking to the most unattractive woman he has ever seen, a fact which fascinates him, as if instead he were speaking to the most beautiful woman he has ever seen or perhaps ever will see, so he treasures the moment, attempts to hold it as if it were a golden ball, a disproportionately heavy object which—if he doesn't hold it lightly and with precision and firm-ness—will slip from his hand and roll across the lawn to the lip of the well and down, down to the bottom of the well, lost to him forever. It will be merely a memory, something to speak of wistfully and with wonder as over the years the image fades and comes in the end to exist only in the telling. His mind and body waken from their sleepy self-absorption, and all his attention focuses on the woman, Sarah Cole, her ugly face, like a wart hog's, her thick, rapid voice, her dumpy, off-center wreck of a body, and to keep this moment here before him, he begins to ask questions of her, he buys her a drink, he smiles, until soon it seems, even to him, that he is taking her and her life, its vicissitudes and woe, quite seriously.

He learns her name, of course, and she volunteers the informa-tion that she spoke to him on a dare from one of the two women still sitting in the booth behind her. She turns on her stool and smiles brazenly, triumphantly, at her friends, two women, also homely (though nowhere as homely as she) and dressed, like her, in cowboy boots, hats and jeans. One of the women, a blond with an underslung jaw and wearing heavy eye makeup, flips a little wave at her, and as if embarrassed, she and the other woman at the booth turn back to their drinks and sip fiercely at straws.

Sarah returns to Ron and goes on telling him what he wants to know, about her job at the Rumford Press, about her divorced husband who was a bastard and stupid and "sick," she says, as if filling suddenly with sympathy for the man. She tells Ron about her three children, the youngest, a girl, in junior high school and boy-crazy, the other two, boys, in high school and almost never at home anymore. She speaks of her children with genuine tenderness and concern, and Ron is touched. He can see with what pleasure and pain she speaks of her children; he watches her tiny eyes light up and water over when he asks their names.

"You're a nice woman," he informs her.

She smiles, looks at her empty glass. "No. No, I'm not. But you're a nice man, to tell me that."

Ron, with a gesture, asks the bartender to refill Sarah's glass. She is drinking white Russians. Perhaps she has been drinking them for an hour or two, for she seems very relaxed, more relaxed than women usually do when they come up and without introduction or invitation speak to him.

She asks him about himself, his job, his divorce, how long he has lived in Concord, but he finds that he is not at all interested in telling her about himself. He wants to know about her, even though what she has to tell him about herself is predictable and ordinary and the way she tells it unadorned and clichéd. He wonders about her husband. What kind of man would fall in love with Sarah Cole?

2

That scene, at Osgood's Lounge in Concord, ended with Ron's departure, alone, after having bought Sarah's second drink, and Sarah's return to her friends in the booth. I don't know what she told them, but it's not hard to imagine. The three women were not close friends, merely fellow workers at Rumford Press, where they stood at the end of a long conveyor belt day after day packing *TV Guides* into cartons. They all hated their jobs, and frequently after work, when they worked the day shift, they would put on their cowboy hats and boots, which they kept all day in their lockers, and stop for a drink or two on their way home. This had been their first visit to Osgood's, a place that, prior to this, they had avoided out of a sneering belief that no one went there but lawyers and insurance men. It had been Sarah who had asked the others why that should keep them away, and when they had no answer for her, the three had decided to stop at Osgood's. Ron was right, they had been there over an hour when he came in, and Sarah was a little drunk. "We'll hafta come in here again," she said to her friends, her voice rising slightly.

Which they did, that Friday, and once again Ron appeared with his evening newspaper. He put his briefcase down next to his stool and ordered a drink and proceeded to read the front page, slowly deliberately, clearly a weary, unhurried, solitary man. He did not notice the three women in cowboy hats and boots in the booth in back, but they saw him, and after a few minutes Sarah was once again at his side.

"Hi."

He turned, saw her, and instantly regained the moment he had lost when, the previous night, once outside the bar, he had forgotten about the ugliest woman he had ever seen. She seemed even more grotesque to him now than before, which made the moment all the more precious to him, and so once again he held the moment as if in his hands and began to speak with her, to ask questions, to offer his opinions and solicit hers.

I said earlier that I am the man in this story and my friend Sarah Cole, now dead, is the woman. I think back to that night, the second time I had seen Sarah, and I tremble, not with fear but in shame. My concern then, when I was first becoming involved with Sarah, was merely with the moment, holding onto it, grasping it wholly as if its beginning did not grow out of some other prior moment in her life and my life separately and at the same time did not lead into future moments in our separate lives. She talked more easily than she had the night before, and I listened as eagerly and carefully as I had before, again, with the same motives, to keep her in front of me, to draw her forward from the context of her life and place her, as if she were an object, into the context of mine. I did not know how cruel this was. When you have never done a thing before and that thing is not simply and clearly right or wrong, you frequently do not know if it is a cruel thing, you just go ahead and do it, and maybe later you'll be able to determine whether you acted cruelly. That way you'll know if it was right or wrong of you to have done it in the first place.

While we drank, Sarah told me that she hated her ex-husband because of the way he treated the children. "It's not so much the money," she said, nervously wagging her booted feet from her perch on the high barstool. "I mean, I get by, barely, but I get them fed and clothed on my own okay. It's because he won't even write them a letter or anything. He won't call them on the phone, all he calls for is to bitch at me because I'm trying to get the state to take him to court so I can get some of the money he's s'posed to be paying for child support. And he won't even think to talk to the kids when he calls. Won't even ask about them."

"He sounds like a bastard," I said.

"He is, he is," she said. "I don't know why I married him. Or stayed married. Fourteen years, for Christ's sake. He put a spell over me or something. I don't know," she said with a note of wistfulness in her voice. "He wasn't what you'd call good-looking."

After her second drink, she decided she had to leave. Her children were at home, it was Friday night and she liked to make sure she ate supper with them and knew where they were going and who they were with when they went out on their dates. "No dates on schoolnights," she said to me. "I mean, you gotta have rules, you know."

I agreed, and we left together, everyone in the place following us with his or her gaze. I was aware of that, I knew what they were thinking, and I didn't care, because I was simply walking her to her car.

It was a cool evening, dusk settling onto the lot like a gray blanket. Her car, a huge, dark green Buick sedan at least ten years old, was battered, scratched, and almost beyond use. She reached for the door handle on the driver's side and yanked. Nothing. The door wouldn't open. She tried again. Then I tried. Still nothing.

Then I saw it, a V-shaped dent in the left front fender creasing the fender where the door joined it, binding the metal of the door against the metal of the fender in a large crimp that held the door fast. "Someone must've backed into you while you were inside," I said to her.

She came forward and studied the crimp for a few seconds, and when she looked back at me, she was weeping. "Jesus, Jesus, Jesus!" she wailed, her large, frog-like mouth wide open and wet with spit, her red tongue flopping loosely over gapped teeth. "I can't pay for this! I *can't!*" Her face was red, and even in the dusky light I could see it puff out with weeping, her tiny eyes seeming almost to disappear behind wet cheeks. Her shoulders slumped, and her hands fell limply to her sides.

Placing my briefcase on the ground, I reached out to her and put my arms around her body and held her close to me, while she cried wetly into my shoulder. After a few seconds, she started pulling herself back together and her weeping got reduced to sniffling. Her cowboy hat had been pushed back and now clung to her head at a precarious, absurdly jaunty angle. She took a step away from me and said, "I'll get in the other side."

"Okay," I said almost in a whisper. "That's fine."

Slowly, she walked around the front of the huge, ugly vehicle and opened the door on the passenger's side and slid awkwardly across the seat until she had positioned herself behind the steering wheel. Then she started the motor, which came to life with a roar. The muffler was shot. Without saying another word to me, or even waving, she dropped the car into reverse gear and backed it loudly out of the parking space and headed out the lot to the street.

I turned and started for my car, when I happened to glance toward the door of the bar, and there, staring after me, were the bartender, the two women who had come in with Sarah, and two of the men who had been sitting at the bar. They were lawyers, and I knew them slightly. They were grinning at me. I grinned back and got into my car, and then, without looking at them again, I left the place and drove straight to my apartment.

3

One night several weeks later, Ron meets Sarah at Osgood's, and after buying her three white Russians and drinking three scotches himself, he takes her back to his apartment in his car—a Datsun fastback coupe that she says she admires—for the sole purpose of making love to her.

I'm still the man in this story, and Sarah is still the woman, but I'm telling it this way because what I have to tell you now confuses me, embarrasses me, and makes me sad, and consequently, I'm likely to tell it falsely. I'm likely to cover the truth by making Sarah a better woman than she actually was, while making myself appear worse than I actually was or am; or else I'll do the opposite, make Sarah worse than she was and me better. The truth is, I was pretty, extremely so, and she was not, extremely so, and I knew it and she knew it. She walked out the door of Osgood's determined to make love to a man much prettier than any she had seen up close before,

369

and I walked out determined to make love to a woman much homelier than any I had made love to before. We were, in a sense, equals.

No, that's not exactly true. (You see? This is why I have to tell the story the way I'm telling it.) I'm not at all sure she feels as Ron does. That is to say, perhaps she genuinely likes the man, in spite of his being the most physically attractive man she has ever known. Perhaps she is more aware of her homeliness than of his beauty, just as he is more aware of her homeliness than of his beauty, for Ron, despite what I may have implied, does not think of himself as especially beautiful. He merely knows that other people think of him that way. As I said before, he is a nice man.

Ron unlocks the door to his apartment, walks in ahead of her, and flicks on the lamp beside the couch. It's a small, single bedroom, modern apartment, one of thirty identical apartments in a large brick building on the heights just east of downtown Concord. Sarah stands nervously at the door, peering in.

"Come in, come in," he says.

She steps timidly in and closes the door behind her. She removes her cowboy hat, then quickly puts it back on, crosses the livingroom, and plops down in a blond easychair, seeming to shrink in its hug out of sight to safety. Ron, behind her, at the entry to the kitchen, places one hand on her shoulder, and she stiffens. He removes his hand.

"Would you like a drink?"

"No . . . I guess not," she says, staring straight ahead at the wall opposite where a large framed photograph of a bicyclist advertises in French the Tour de France. Around a corner, in an alcove off the living room, a silver-gray ten-speed bicycle leans casually against the wall, glistening and poised, slender as a thoroughbred race-horse.

"I don't know," she says. Ron is in the kitchen now, making himself a drink. "I don't know . . . I don't know."

"What? Change your mind? I can make a white Russian for you. Vodka, cream, kahlua, and ice, right?"

Sarah tries to cross her legs, but she is sitting too low in the chair and her legs are too thick at the thigh, so she ends, after a struggle, with one leg in the air and the other twisted on its side. She looks as if she has fallen from a great height.

Ron steps out from the kitchen, peers over the back of the chair, and watches her untangle herself, then ducks back into the kitchen. After a few seconds, he returns. "Seriously. Want me to fix you a white Russian?"

"No."

Ron, again from behind, places one hand onto Sarah's shoulder, and this time she does not stiffen, though she does not exactly relax, either. She sits there, a block of wood, staring straight ahead.

"Are you scared?" he asks gently. Then he adds, "*I* am."

"Well, no, I'm not scared." She remains silent for a moment. "You're scared? Of what?" She turns to face him but avoid his eyes.

"Well . . . I don't do this all the time, you know. Bring home a woman I . . .," he trails off.

"Picked up in a bar."

"No. I mean, I like you, Sarah, I really do. And I didn't just pick you up in a bar, you know that. We've gotten to be friends, you and me."

"You want to sleep with me?" she asks, still not meeting his steady gaze.

"Yes." He seems to mean it. He does not take a gulp or even a sip from his drink. He just says, "Yes," straight out, and cleanly, not too quickly, either, and not after a hesitant delay. A simple statement of a simple fact. The man wants to make love to the woman. She asked him, and he told her. What could be simpler?

"Do you want to sleep with *me?*" he asks.

She turns around in the chair, faces the wall again, and says in a low voice, "Sure I do, but . . . it's hard to explain."

"What? But what?" Placing his glass down on the table between the chair and the sofa, he puts both hands on her shoulders and lightly kneads them. He knows he can be discouraged from pursuing this, but he is not sure how easily. Having got this far without bumping against obstacles (except the ones he has placed in his way himself), he is not sure what it will take to turn him back. He does not know, therefore, how assertive or how seductive he should be with her. He suspects that he can be stopped very easily, so he is reluctant to give her a chance to try. He goes on kneading her doughy shoulders.

"You and me . . . we're real different." She glances at the bicycle in the corner.

"A man . . . and a woman," he says.

371

"No, not that. I mean, different. That's all. Real different. More than you . . . you're nice, but you don't know what I mean, and that's one of the things that makes you so nice. But we're different. Listen," she says, "I gotta go. I gotta leave now."

The man removes his hands and retrieves his glass, takes a sip, and watches her over the rim of the glass, as, not without difficulty, she rises from the chair and moves swiftly toward the door. She stops at the door, squares her hat on her head, and glances back at him.

"We can be friends. Okay?"

"Okay. Friends."

"I'll see you again down at Osgood's, right?"

"Oh, yeah, sure."

"Good. See you," she says, opening the door.

The door closes. The man walks around the sofa, snaps on the television set, and sits down in front of it. He picks up a *TV Guide* from the coffee table and flips through it, stops, runs a finger down the listings, stops, puts down the magazine and changes the channel. He does not once connect the magazine in his hand to the woman who has just left his apartment, even though he knows she spends her days packing *TV Guides* into cartons that get shipped to warehouses in distant parts of New England. He'll think of the connection some other night, but by then the connection will be merely sentimental. It'll be too late for him to understand what she meant by "different."

4

But that's not the point of my story. Certainly it's an aspect of the story, the political aspect, if you want, but it's not the reason I'm trying to tell the story in the first place. I'm trying to tell the story so that I can understand what happened between me and Sarah Cole that summer and early autumn ten years ago. To say we were lovers says very little about what happened; to say we were friends says even less. No, if I'm to understand the whole thing, I have to say the whole thing, for, in the end, what I need to know is whether what happened between me and Sarah Cole was right or wrong. Character is fate, which suggests that if a man can know and then to some degree control his character, he can know and to that same degree control his fate.

372

But let me go on with my story. The next time Sarah and I were together we were at her apartment in the south end of Concord, a second floor flat in a tenement building on Perley Street. I had stayed away from Osgood's for several weeks, deliberately trying to avoid running into Sarah there, though I never quite put it that way to myself. I found excuses and generated interests in and reasons for going elsewhere after work. Yet I was obsessed with Sarah by then, obsessed with the idea of making love to her, which, because it was not an actual *desire* to make love to her, was an unusually complex obsession. Passion without desire, if it gets expressed, may in fact be a kind of rape, and perhaps I sensed the danger that lay behind my obsession and for that reason went out of my way to avoid meeting Sarah again.

Yet I did meet her, inadvertently, of course. After picking up shirts at the cleaner's on South Main and Perley Streets, I'd gone down Perley on my way to South State and the post office. It was a Saturday morning, and this trip on my bicycle was part of my regular Saturday routine. I did not remember that Sarah lived on Perley Street, although she had told me several times in a com-plaining way—it's a rough neighborhood, packed dirt yards, shabby apartment buildings, the carcasses of old, half-stripped cars on cinderblocks in the driveways, broken red and yellow plastic tricycles on the cracked sidewalks—but as soon as I saw her, I remembered. It was too late to avoid meeting her. I was riding my bike, wearing shorts and tee shirt, the package containing my folded and starched shirts hooked to the carrier behind me, and she was walking toward me along the sidewalk, lugging two large bags of groceries. She saw me, and I stopped. We talked, and I offered to carry her groceries for her. I took the bags while she led the bike, handling it carefully, as if she were afraid she might break it.

At the stoop we came to a halt. The wooden steps were cluttered with half-opened garbage bags spilling egg shells, coffee grounds, and old food wrappers to the walkway. "I can't get the people downstairs to take care of their garbage," she explained. She leaned the bike against the bannister and reached for her gro-ceries.

"I'll carry them up for you," I said. I directed her to loop the chain lock from the bike to the bannister rail and snap it shut and told her to bring my shirts up with her.

373

"Maybe you'd like a beer?" she said as she opened the door to the darkened hallway. Narrow stairs disappeared in front of me into heavy, damp darkness, and the air smelled like old newspapers.

"Sure," I said and followed her up.

"Sorry there's no light. I can't get them to fix it."

"No matter. I can see you and follow along," I said, and even in the dim light of the hall I could see the large, dark blue veins that cascaded thickly down the backs of her legs. She wore tight, white-duck bermuda shorts, rubber shower sandals, and a pink sleeveless sweater. I pictured her in the cashier's line at the supermarket. I would have been behind her, a stranger, and on seeing her, I would have turned away and studied the covers of the magazines, *TV Guide, People, The National Enquirer,* for there was nothing of interest in her appearance that in the hard light of day would not have slightly embarrassed me. Yet here I was inviting myself into her home, eagerly staring at the backs of her ravaged legs, her sad, tasteless clothing, her poverty. I was not detached, however, was not staring at her with scientific curiosity, and because of my passion, did not feel or believe that what I was doing was perverse. I felt warmed by her presence and was flirtatious and bold, a little pushy, even.

Picture this. The man, tanned, limber, wearing red jogging shorts, Italian leather sandals, a clinging net tee shirt of Scandinavian design and manufacture, enters the apartment behind the woman, whose dough colored skin, thick, short body, and homely, uncomfortable face all try, but fail, to hide themselves. She waves him toward the table in the kitchen, where he sets down the bags and looks good-naturedly around the room. "What about the beer you bribed me with?" he asks. The apartment is dark and cluttered with old, oversized furniture, yard sale and second-hand stuff bought originally for a large house in the country or a spacious apartment on a boulevard forty or fifty years ago, passed down from antique dealer to used furniture store to yard sale to thrift shop, where it finally gets purchased by Sarah Cole and gets lugged over to Perley Street and shoved up the narrow stairs, she and her children grunting and sweating in the darkness of the hallway—overstuffed armchairs and couch, huge, ungainly dressers, upholstered rocking chairs, and in the kitchen, an old maple desk for a table, a half dozen heavy oak diningroom chairs, a high, glass-fronted cabinet, all peeling, stained, chipped and squatting heavily on a dark green linoleum floor.

The place is neat and arranged in a more or less orderly way, however, and the man seems comfortable there. He strolls from the kitchen to the livingroom and peeks into the three small bedrooms that branch off a hallway behind the livingroom. "Nice place!" he calls to the woman. He is studying the framed pictures of her three children arranged like an altar atop the buffet. "Nice looking kids!" he calls out. They are. Blond, round-faced, clean, and utterly ordinary-looking, their pleasant faces glance, as instructed, slightly off camera and down to the right, as if they are trying to remember the name of the capital of Montana.

When he returns to the kitchen, the woman is putting away her groceries, her back to him. "Where's that beer you bribed me with?" he asks again. He takes a position against the doorframe, his weight on one hip, like a dancer resting. "You sure are quiet today, Sarah," he says in a low voice. "Everything okay?"

Silently, she turns away from the grocery bags, crosses the room to the man, reaches up to him, and holding him by the head, kisses his mouth, rolls her torso against his, drops her hands to his hips and yanks him tightly to her, and goes on kissing him, eyes closed, working her face furiously against his. The man places his hands on her shoulders and pulls away, and they face each other, wide-eyed, as if amazed and frightened. The man drops his hands, and the woman lets go of his hips. Then, after a few seconds, the man silently turns, goes to the door, and leaves. The last thing he sees as he closes the door behind him is the woman standing in the kitchen doorframe, her face looking down and slightly to one side, wearing the same pleasant expression on her face as her children in their photographs, trying to remember the capital of Montana.

5

Sarah appeared at my apartment door the following morning, a Sunday, cool and rainy. She had brought me the package of freshly laundered shirts I'd left in her kitchen, and when I opened the door to her, she simply held the package out to me as if it were a penitent's gift. She wore a yellow rain slicker and cap and looked

375

more like a disconsolate schoolgirl facing an angry teacher than a grown woman dropping a package off at a friend's apartment. After all, she had nothing to be ashamed of.

I invited her inside, and she accepted my invitation. I had been reading the Sunday *New York Times* on the couch and drinking coffee, lounging through the gray morning in bathrobe and pajamas. I told her to take off her wet raincoat and hat and hang them in the closet by the door and started for the kitchen to get her a cup of coffee, when I stopped, turned, and looked at her. She closed the closet door on her yellow raincoat and hat, turned around, and faced me.

What else can I do? I must describe it. I remember that moment of ten years ago as if it occurred ten minutes ago, the package of shirts on the table behind her, the newspapers scattered over the couch and floor, the sound of windblown rain washing the sides of the building outside, and the silence of the room, as we stood across from one another and watched, while we each simultaneously removed our own clothing, my robe, her blouse and skirt, my pajama top, her slip and bra, my pajama bottom, her underpants, until we were both standing naked in the harsh, gray light, two naked members of the same species, a male and a female, the male somewhat younger and less scarred than the female, the female somewhat less delicately constructed than the male, both individuals pale-skinned with dark thatches of hair in the area of their genitals, both individuals standing slackly, as if a great, protracted tension between them had at last been released.

We made love that morning in my bed for long hours that drifted easily into afternoon. And we talked, as people usually do when they spend half a day or half a night in bed together. I told her of my past, named and described the people I had loved and had loved me, my ex-wife in New York, my brother in the Air Force, my father and mother in their condominium in Florida, and I told her of my ambitions and dreams and even confessed some of my fears. She listened patiently and intelligently throughout and talked much less than I. She had already told me many of these things about herself, and perhaps whatever she had to say to me now lay on the next inner circle of intimacy or else could not be spoken of at all.

During the next few weeks we met and made love often and

always at my apartment. On arriving home from work, I would phone her, or if not, she would phone me, and after a few feints and dodges, one would suggest to the other that we get together tonight, and a half hour later she'd be at my door. Our love-making was passionate, skillful, kindly, and deeply satisfying. We didn't often speak of it to one another or brag about it, the way some couples do when they are surprised by the ease with which they have become contented lovers. We did occasionally joke and tease each other, however, playfully acknowledging that the only thing we did together was make love but that we did it so frequently there was no time for anything else.

Then one hot night, a Saturday in August, we were lying in bed atop the tangled sheets, smoking cigarettes and chatting idly, and Sarah suggested that we go out for a drink.

"Now?"

"Sure. It's early. What time is it?"

I scanned the digital clock next to the bed. "Nine-forty-nine."

"There. See?"

"That's not so early. You usually go home by eleven, you know. It's almost ten."

"No, it's only a little after nine. Depends on how you look at things. Besides, Ron, it's Saturday night. Don't you want to go out and dance or something? Or is this the only thing you know how to do?" she teased and poked me in the ribs. "You know how to dance? You like to dance?"

"Yeah, sure . . . sure, but not tonight. It's too hot. And I'm tired."

But she persisted, happily pointing out that an air-conditioned bar would be cooler than my apartment, and we didn't have to go to a dance bar, we could go to Osgood's. "As a compromise," she said.

I suggested a place called the El Rancho, a restaurant with a large, dark cocktail lounge and dance bar located several miles from town on the old Portsmouth highway. Around nine the restaurant closed and the bar became something of a roadhouse, with a small country-western houseband and a clientel drawn from the four or five villages that adjoined Concord on the north and east. I had eaten at the restaurant once but had never gone to the bar, and I didn't know anyone who had.

377

Sarah was silent for a moment. Then she lit a cigarette and drew the sheet over her naked body. "You don't want anybody to know about us, do you? Do you?"

"That's not it . . . I just don't like gossip, and I work with a lot of people who show up sometimes at Osgood's. On a Saturday night especially."

"No," she said firmly. "You're ashamed of being seen with me. You'll sleep with me, but you won't go out in public with me."

"That's not true, Sarah."

She was silent again. Relieved, I reached across her to the bedtable and got my cigarettes and lighter.

"You owe me, Ron," she said suddenly, as I passed over her. "You owe me."

"What?" I lay back, lit a cigarette, and covered my body with the sheet.

"I said, 'You owe me.' "

"I don't know what you're talking about, Sarah. I just don't like a lot of gossip going around, that's all. I like keeping my private life private, that's all. I don't *owe* you anything."

"Friendship you owe me. And respect. Friendship and respect. A person can't do what you've done with me without owing them friendship and respect."

"Sarah, I really don't know what you're talking about," I said. "I am your friend, you know that. And I respect you. I really do."

"You really think so, don't you?"

"Yes."

She said nothing for several long moments. Then she sighed and in a low, almost inaudible voice said, "Then you'll have to go out in public with me. I don't care about Osgood's or the people you work with, we don't have to go there or see any of them," she said. "But you're gonna have to go to places like the El Rancho with me, and a few other places I know, too, where there's people *I* work with, people *I* know, and maybe we'll even go to a couple of parties, because *I* get invited to parties sometimes, you know. I have friends, and I have some family, too, and you're gonna have to meet my family. My kids think I'm just going around bar-hopping when I'm over here with you, and I don't like that, so you're gonna have to meet them so I can tell them where I am when I'm not at home nights. And sometimes you're gonna come over and spend the evening at my place!" Her voice had risen as she heard her

378

demands and felt their rightness until now she was almost shouting at me. "You *owe* that to me. Or else you're a bad man. It's that simple."

It was.

7

The handsome man is over-dressed. He is wearing a navy blue blazer, taupe shirt open at the throat, white slacks, white loafers. Everyone else, including the homely woman with the handsome man, is dressed appropriately, dressed, that is, like everyone else—jeans and cowboy boots, blouses or cowboy shirts or tee shirts with catchy sayings printed across the front, and many of the women are wearing cowboy hats pushed back and tied under their chins. The man doesn't know anyone at the bar or, if they're at a party, in the room, but the woman knows most of the people there, and she gladly introduces him. The men grin and shake his hand, slap him on his jacketed shoulder, ask him where he works, what's his line, after which they lapse into silence. The women flirt briefly with their faces, but they lapse into silence even before the men do. The woman with the man in the blazer does most of the talking for everyone. She talks for the man in the blazer, for the men standing around the refrigerator, or if they're at a bar, for the other men at the table, and for the other women, too. She chats and rambles aimlessly through loud monologues, laughs uproariously at trivial jokes, and drinks too much, until soon she is drunk, thick-tongued, clumsy, and the man has to say her goodbyes and ease her out the door to his car and drive her home to her apartment on Perley Street.

This happens twice in one week, and then three times the next—at the El Rancho, at the Ox Bow in Northwood, at Rita's and Jimmy's apartment on Thorndike Street, out in Warner at Betsy Beeler's new house, and, the last time, at a cottage on Lake Sunapee rented by some kids in shipping at Rumford Press. Ron no longer calls Sarah when he gets home from work; he waits for her call, and sometimes, when he knows it's she, he doesn't answer the phone. Usually, he lets it ring five or six times, and then he reaches down and picks up the receiver. He has taken his jacket and vest off and loosened his tie and is about to put supper, frozen manicotti, into the radar range.

"Hello?"

"Hi."

"How're you doing?"

"Okay, I guess. A little tired."

"Still hung-over?"

"No. Not really. Just tired. I hate Mondays."

"You have fun last night?"

"Well, yeah, sorta. It's nice out there, at the lake. Listen," she says, brightening. *"Whyn't you come over here tonight? The kids're all going out later, but if you come over before eight, you can meet them. They really want to meet you."*

"You told them about me?"

"Sure. Long time ago. I'm not supposed to tell my own kids?"

Ron is silent.

"You don't want to come over here tonight. You don't want to meet my kids. No, you don't want my kids to meet you, that's it."

"No, no, it's just . . . I've got a lot of work to do . . ."

"We should talk," she announces in a flat voice.

"Yes," he says, "we should talk."

They agree that she will meet him at his apartment, and they'll talk, and they say goodbye and hang up.

While Ron is heating his supper and then eating alone at his kitchen table and Sarah is feeding her children, perhaps I should admit, since we are nearing the end of my story, that I don't actually know that Sarah Cole is dead. A few years ago I happened to run into one of her friends from the press, a blond woman with an underslung jaw. Her name, she reminded me, was Glenda, she had seen me at Osgood's a couple of times and we had met at the El Rancho once when I had gone there with Sarah. I was amazed that she could remember me and a little embarrassed that I did not recognize her at all, and she laughed at that and said, "You haven't changed much, mister!" I pretended to recognize her, but I think she knew she was a stranger to me. We were standing outside the Sears store on South Main Street, where I had gone to buy paint. I had recently remarried, and my wife and I were redecorating my apartment.

"Whatever happened to Sarah?" I asked Glenda. "Is she still down at the press?"

"Jeez, no! She left a long time ago. Way back. I heard she went

380

back with her ex-husband. I can't remember his name. Something Cole."

I asked her if she was sure of that, and she said no, she had only heard it around the bars and down at the press, but she had assumed it was true. People said Sarah had moved back with her ex-husband and was living in a trailer in a park near Hooksett, and the whole family had moved down to Florida that winter because he was out of work. He was a carpenter, she said.

"I thought he was mean to her. I thought he beat her up and everything. I thought she hated him," I said.

"Oh, well, yeah, he was a bastard, all right. I met him a couple of times, and I didn't like him. Short, ugly, and mean when he got drunk. But you know what they say."

"What do they say?"

"Oh, you know, about water seeking its own level."

"Sarah wasn't mean when she was drunk."

The woman laughed. "Naw, but she sure was short and ugly!"

I said nothing.

"Hey, don't get me wrong, I liked Sarah. But you and her . . . well, you sure made a funny-looking couple. She probably didn't feel so self-conscious and all with her husband," the woman said seriously. "I mean, with you . . . all tall and blond, and poor old Sarah . . . I mean, the way them kids in the press room used to kid her about her looks, it was embarrassing just to hear it."

"Well . . . I loved her," I said.

The woman raised her plucked eyebrows in disbelief. She smiled. "Sure, you did, honey," she said, and she patted me on the arm. "Sure, you did." Then she let the smile drift off her face, turned and walked away.

When someone you have loved dies, you accept the fact of his or her death, but then the person goes on living in your memory, dreams and reveries. You have imaginary conversations with him or her, you see something striking and remind yourself to tell your loved one about it and then get brought up short by the knowledge of the fact of his or her death, and at night, in your sleep, the dead person visits you. With Sarah, none of that happened. When she was gone from my life, she was gone absolutely, as if she had never existed in the first place. It was only later, when I could think of her as dead and could come out and say it, my friend Sarah Cole is

381

dead, that I was able to tell this story, for that is when she began to enter my memories, my dreams, and my reveries. In that way I learned that I truly did love her, and now I have begun to grieve over her death, to wish her alive again, so that I can say to her the things I could not know or say when she was alive, when I did not know that I loved her.

8

The woman arrives at Ron's apartment around eight. He hears her car, because of the broken muffler, blat and rumble into the parking lot below, and he crosses quickly from the kitchen and peers out the livingroom window and, as if through a telescope, watches her shove herself across the seat to the passenger's side to get out of the car, then walk slowly in the dusky light toward the apartment building. It's a warm evening, and she's wearing her white bermuda shorts, pink sleeveless sweater, and shower sandals. Ron hates those clothes. He hates the way the shorts cut into her flesh at the crotch and thigh, hates the large, dark caves below her arms that get exposed by the sweater, hates the flapping noise made by the sandals.

Shortly, there is a soft knock at his door. He opens it, turns away and crosses to the kitchen, where he turns back, lights a cigarette, and watches her. She closes the door. He offers her a drink, which she declines, and somewhat formally, he invites her to sit down. She sits carefully on the sofa, in the middle, with her feet close together on the floor, as if she were being interviewed for a job. Then he comes around and sits in the easy chair, relaxed, one leg slung over the other at the knee, as if he were interviewing her for the job.

"Well," he says, "you wanted to talk."

"Yes. But now you're mad at me. I can see that. I didn't do anything, Ron."

"I'm not mad at you."

They are silent for a moment. Ron goes on smoking his cigarette.

Finally, she sighs and says, "You don't want to see me anymore, do you?"

He waits a few seconds and answers, "Yes. That's right." Getting up from the chair, he walks to the silver-gray bicycle and stands before it, running a fingertip along the slender cross-bar from the saddle to the chrome plated handlebars.

"You're a son of a bitch," she says in a low voice. "You're worse than my ex-husband." Then she smiles meanly, almost sneers, and soon he realizes that she is telling him that she won't leave. He's stuck with her, she informs him with cold precision. "You think I'm just so much meat, and all you got to do is call up the butcher shop and cancel your order. Well, now you're going to find out different. You *can't* cancel your order. I'm not meat, I'm not one of your pretty little girlfriends who come running when you want them and go away when you get tired of them. I'm *different*. I got nothing to lose, Ron. Nothing. You're stuck with me, Ron."

He continues stroking his bicycle. "No, I'm not."

She sits back in the couch and crosses her legs at the ankles. "I think I *will* have that drink you offered."

"Look, Sarah, it would be better if you go now."

"No," she says flatly. "You offered me a drink when I came in. Nothing's changed since I've been here. Not for me, and not for you. I'd like that drink you offered," she says haughtily.

Ron turns away from the bicycle and takes a step toward her. His face has stiffened into a mask. "Enough is enough," he says through clenched teeth. "I've given you enough."

"Fix me a drink, will you, honey?" she says with a phony smile.

Ron orders her to leave.

She refuses.

He grabs her by the arm and yanks her to her feet.

She starts crying lightly. She stands there and looks up into his face and weeps, but she does not move toward the door, so he pushes her. She regains her balance and goes on weeping.

He stands back and places his fists on his hips and looks at her. "Go on and leave, you ugly bitch," he says to her, and as he says the words, as one by one they leave his mouth, she's transformed into the most beautiful woman he has ever seen. He says the words again, almost tenderly. "Leave, you ugly bitch." Her hair is golden, her brown eyes deep and sad, her mouth full and affection-ate, her tears the tears of love and loss, and her pleading, out-stretched arms, her entire body, the arms and body of a devoted woman's cruelly rejected love. A third time he says the words. "Leave me, you disgusting, ugly bitch." She is wrapped in an envelope of golden light, a warm, dense haze that she seems to have stepped into, as into a carriage. And then she is gone, and he is alone again.

He looks around the room, as if searching for her. Sitting down in the easy chair, he places his face in his hands. It's not as if she has died; it's as if he has killed her.

nominated by The Missouri Review

MUTE

by WESLEY McNAIR

from POETRY

Once, on the last ice-hauling,
the sled went through the surface
of the frozen pond,
pulling the son under
the thrashing hooves
of horses. Listening for him

after all her tears was perhaps
what drew the mother
into that silence. Long afternoons
she sat with the daughter,
speaking in the sign language
they invented together,
going deaf to the world.

How, exactly, did they touch
their mouths? What was the thought
of the old man on the porch
growing so drunk by nightfall
he could not hear
mosquitoes in his ears?

There is so much no one remembers
about the farm where sound,
even the bawling of the unmilked cows,
came to a stop. Even the man's name,

which neighbors must have spoken
passing by in twilight, on their way
to forgetting it forever.

nominated by Richard Eberhart, Donald Hall and Cleopatra Mathis

THE OBJECTS OF IMMORTALITY

by PATTIANN ROGERS

from AMELIA

If I could bestow immortality,
I'd do it liberally—on the aim of the hummingbird,
The sea nettle and the dispersing skeletons of cottonweed
In the wind, on the night heron hatchling and the night heron
Still bound in the blue-green darkness of its egg,
On the thrice-banded crab spider and on every low shrub
And tall teasel stem of its most perfect places.

I would ask that the turquoise skimmer, hovering
Over backwater moss, stay forever, without faltering,
Without disappearing, head half-eaten on the mud, one wing
Under pine rubbish, one floating downstream, nudged
And spit away by foraging darters.

And for that determination to survive,
Evident as the vibration of the manta ray beneath sand,
As the tight concentration of each trout lily petal
On its stem, as the barbed body curled in the brain
Of the burrowing echidna, for that intensity
Which is not simply the part of the bittern's gold eye
Most easily identified and remembered but the entire
Bittern itself, for that bird-shaped realization
Of effective pressure against oblivion, I would make
My own eternal assertion: Let that pressure endure.

And maybe this immortality can come to pass
Because continuous life, even granted to every firefly

387

And firebeetle and fireworm on earth, to the glowing clouds
Of every deep-sea squirt, to all electric eels, phosphorescent
Fishes and scaley bright-bulbed extensions of the black
Ocean bottoms, to all luminous fungi and all torch-carrying
Creatures, to the lost light and reflective rock
Of every star in the summer sky, everlasting life,
Even granted to all of these multiplied a million times,
Could scarcely perturb or bother anyone truly understanding
The needs of infinity.

nominated by Amelia

FOR STARR ATKINSON, WHO DESIGNED BOOKS

by JARED CARTER

from FUGUE STATE (Barnwood Press)

Oldest of words, of sounds: star.
Everything of that name perishes.
The sun will reclaim each planet,
The galaxy collapse, light itself
Siphon down into a last darkness.

From you I learned how images balance
In the white space of each page,
How pages unfold like leaves,
How light and dark interpenetrate,
How what we do will not be noticed.

Light from those stars coming deep
From space, reaching our own eyes
In darkness, at the top of a hill;
Words on a page keeping the old sounds,
The ones worth saying another time.

nominated by Heather McHugh

BOHEMIA REVISITED: MALCOLM COWLEY, JACK KEROUAC AND *ON THE ROAD*

by ADAM GUSSOW

from THE GEORGIA REVIEW

All my editors since Malcolm Cowley have had instructions to leave my prose exactly as I wrote it. In the days of Malcolm Cowley, with *On the Road* and *The Dharma Bums*, I had no power to stand by my style for better or worse. When Malcolm Cowley made endless revisions and inserted thousands of needless commas, like, say, Cheyenne, Wyoming (why not just say Cheyenne Wyoming and let it go at that, for instance), why, I spent $500 making the complete restitution of the *Bums* manuscript and got a bill from Viking Press called 'Revisions.' Ha ho ho. And so you asked about how do I work with an editor. . . .

—Jack Kerouac in interview (1974)[1]

Jack and his memory are very, very unfair to me. Blaming me for putting in or taking out commas and caps and what-not in *On the Road*. I didn't really give a damn about that. . . . I wasn't worried about the prose. It seemed to me that in the original draft the story kept swinging back and forth across the United States like a pendulum.

—Malcolm Cowley in interview (1978)[2]

1. Ted Berrigan, "The Art of Fiction XLI: Jack Kerouac," from *Writers at Work: The Paris Review Interviews,* Fourth Series, reprinted in The Viking Critical Library Edition of *On the Road* by Jack Kerouac, ed. Scott Donaldson (New York: Penguin Books, 1979), p. 540 (hereafter cited as *VC*).
2. Barry Gifford and Lawrence Lee, *Jack's Book: An Oral Biography of Jack Kerouac* (1978; rpt. New York: Penguin Books, 1979), p. 206.

WHAT IS AN EDITOR? is the title of a book by Dorothy Commins about her late husband Saxe, who edited works by Faulkner and O'Neill. It's also an irksome question: What exactly *does* a literary editor do? Commins' memoir and A. Scott Berg's recent biography of Maxwell Perkins have added considerably to our understanding of the various roles editors play in the lives of writers, but the subject of literary editorship remains largely ignored by literary scholars. The editor's reasons for deciding to publish a particular manuscript are generally thought to be irrelevant to our understanding of the published work, and the editor's textual manipulations—to judge from the current low regard for Perkins among scholars of Thomas Wolfe—are frequently thought to be pernicious. In Malcolm Cowley's case, the work of an important literary editor has been neglected for a second reason: the editor is far better known as a poet, critic, and literary historian. Cowley's long and distinguished editorial career with The Viking Press, which began in the 1940's, has been slighted by virtually all of his scholars, most of whom prefer to construe Cowley—depending on their ideological bias—as either a sage chronicler of the Lost Generation or an unreconstructed Stalinist hack.[3]

It comes as a surprise, then, to recall that Cowley (who at age eighty-five still serves as editorial advisor to Viking) was responsible twenty-seven years ago for editing and publishing Jack Ke-

3. Lewis Simpson's two articles in *The Sewanee Review*—"Malcolm Cowley and the American Writer," 84 (1976), 221-47, and "Cowley's Odyssey: Literature and Faith in the Thirties," 89 (1981), 520-39—respectively exemplify the "chronicler" and the "fellow traveler" approaches to Cowley's career, although Simpson is more sympathetic to the latter phase than most. Joseph Epstein has voiced the typical Tory line; "Nearly every one of the printed literary opinions of Malcolm Cowley . . . needs to be fumigated for possible political motive" ("The Literary Life Today," *The New Criterion, I* [September 1982], 13)—a position espoused even more virulently by Kenneth S. Lynn in *The Airline to Seattle* (Chicago: Univ. of Chicago Press, 1983). In "Malcolm Cowley and Literary New York," *The Virginia Quarterly Review*, 58 (1982), 575-93, David F. Shi documents Cowley's political humiliation during the 1930's but makes no mention whatever of his subsequent role as an editorial advisor at Viking. A similar blindness to Cowley's editorial career is manifested by John Aldridge *In Search of Heresy* (New York: McGraw-Hill, 1956), where he states that "[Cowley's] experience of active emotional participation in the literary life apparently came to an end with the period which he documented in *Exile's Return.* . . . What happens now in literature clearly seems to him to be happening to other people and no longer to himself or his friends" (pp. 172-73). Hans Bak's retrospective survey, "Malcolm Cowley: The Critic and his Generation," *Dutch Quarterly Review of Anglo-American Letters*, 9 (1979), 261-83, paints an admirably balanced portrait of Cowley's career, but touches only briefly on his role as editor-critic.

rouac's still-controversial novel, *On the Road*. Cowley himself has never written a word about his relationship with Kerouac. Kerouac's biographers, writing from the other side, have for the most part been content to let Kerouac's spoken and written disparagements of Cowley stand as gospel truth. No one has bothered to ask what the chronicler of the Lost Generation saw in a work that had been turned down by four other top literary editors in New York, and no one has wondered what the chronicler of the Beat Generation might have gained from the five-year association. The answer in each case is surprising.

In the 1950's Malcolm Cowley was one of America's most influential and widely read critics. From 1953, when he first saw an early draft of *On the Road,* through 1957, when the novel was finally published, Cowley was committing himself in periodicals such as *Harper's* and *The New Republic* to a series of propositions about what good literature was and why so little of it was currently being written. When he made his famous "Invitation to Innovators" in *Saturday Review* in 1954, he was able to cite Kerouac's as-yet unpublished narrative in defense of several of his critical principles, but in a number of other ways Kerouac served him as an object lesson in the writer's trade. Six previously undiscovered letters from Kerouac to Cowley have recently turned up in the Viking files, along with Cowley's original reader's reports for *On the Road* and *Doctor Sax* and carbons of his editorial letters to Kerouac. These new documents make clear for the first time just how vital a role Cowley in turn played in Kerouac's peripatetic career.[4]

*

The publication history of *On the Road* begins in controversy. According to Kerouac's biographer Dennis McNally, Kerouac sat down at his typewriter one day early in April 1951, cranked in a long roll of artpaper sheets Scotch-taped together, and by April 25th had pounded out *On the Road* in one unbroken 175,000-word paragraph. Kerouac insists in "Origins of the Beat Generation" that

4. Letters from Jack Kerouac to Malcolm Cowley referred to in the text are on file at The Viking Press in New York. Also on file are Cowley's reader reports for *On the Road* and *Doctor Sax,* carbons of his cited letters to Kerouac, Allen Ginsberg, and Sterling Lord, and Ginsberg's letters to Cowley.

he wrote the book in May, not April; McNally says that the May draft, on teletype paper, was the second. Critic Tim Hunt argues that Kerouac began his *Road* book in 1948 and had written five primary versions by 1952, while Kerouac's first biographer, Ann Charters, asserts that the book was "rewritten and revised countless times."[5]

All accounts agree on one point, however: from the beginning, in *whatever* draft, *On the Road* received precious little editorial sympathy. In May 1951 Kerouac submitted the teletype draft to Robert Giroux, then an editor at Harcourt Brace. Giroux, who had published Kerouac's first novel *The Town and the City*, "was deaf to Jack's explanations of a breakthrough and shocked by the form of *On the Road*," according to Kerouac biographers Gifford and Lee; "[he] recoiled simply at the look of the thing" (p. 158). Kerouac's friend John Clellon Holmes gave the manuscript to his literary agent, Rae Everett. She returned it, McNally reports, "with a great deal of carping criticism" (p. 135).

"The Beats," as John Tytell observes in *Naked Angels: The Lives and Literature of the Beat Generation*, "saw themselves as outcasts, exiles within a hostile culture . . . rejected artists writing anonymously for themselves."[6] At no point until the very end of his career did Kerouac feel more rejected than during the early 1950's. When he had given up an athletic scholarship and withdrawn from Columbia in 1944 to become a writer, his father Leo had angrily disowned him; but he had gained fatherly approval and the beginnings of a literary reputation when Giroux published *The Town and the City* in 1950. Now, having written what seemed to him clearly his best work to that point, he was being denied both approval and success. For consolation he turned to the same friends who had served as subject matter for his fiction, particularly Allen Ginsberg. Ginsberg had also had a troubled relationship with his father—a poet and college English professor of conservative tastes who strongly disapproved of his son's experiments with freer

---

5. Dennis McNally, *Desolate Angel: Jack Kerouac, The Beat Generation, and America* (New York: Random House, 1979), pp. 134-35. Jack Kerouac, "The Origins of the Beat Generation," *Playboy* (June 1959), reprinted in *VC*, p. 363. Tim Hunt, *Kerouac's Crooked Road: Development of a Fiction* (Hamden, Conn.: Archon Books, 1981), p. xvii. Ann Charters, *Kerouac: A Biography* (San Francisco: Straight Arrow Press, 1975), p. 207.

6. John Tytell, *Naked Angels: The Lives and Literature of the Beat Generation* (New York: McGraw-Hill, 1976), pp. 4-5.

poetic forms—and during this period the two young rejected artists exchanged countless long impassioned letters in which they vilified the older literary men who had rejected them. In 1954, Seymour Lawrence at Little, Brown was to turn down *On the Road* with the usual complaints about lack of craftsmanship, and Mark Van Doren, a poet-critic and Columbia professor whom Jack admired deeply, would dismiss his newest work, *Doctor Sax*, as "monotonous and probably without meaning in the end" (McNally, p. 184). Kerouac was furious: Mark Van Doren, he wrote to Ginsberg, was a worthless little poet, a poor copy of Whitman. Seymour Lawrence he dismissed with a four-letter word.[7] Yet while Ginsberg could share Kerouac's feelings of rejection up to a point, as early as 1952 he had begun to win the approval of a significant literary father, William Carlos Williams. Kerouac, as late as 1953, had no one.

In March of 1953, Kerouac first met Malcolm Cowley. Several months earlier, Cowley had been sent a copy of *On the Road* by Phyllis Jackson, Kerouac's agent at the time. "I think it came into Viking marked for my attention," Cowley remembered in a recent letter to me. "I was surprised, impressed, and talked about it at a Tuesday editorial meeting. But others read it and turned thumbs down." In March, as a way of returning Kerouac's manuscript, Cowley took the neglected young writer out to lunch. On July 3rd, Ginsberg, who had replaced Jackson as Kerouac's agent, wrote to Cowley telling him that Kerouac was working on another version of *On the Road* and asking him whether he was interested in seeing it. On 14th July 1953 Cowley responded with a letter that seems in retrospect even more astonishing than it must have seemed at the time to the two young Beats:

> You are right in thinking that I am interested in Kerouac and his work. He seems to me the most interesting writer who is not being published today—and I think it is important that he should be published, or he will run the danger of losing that sense of the audience, which is part of a writer's equipment. But the only manuscript of

7. Jack Kerouac, letter to Allen Ginsberg dated May 1954. All letters from Kerouac to Ginsberg are on deposit in the Rare Manuscripts Reading Room in Butler Library at Columbia University.

his that I have read with a chance of immediate book publication is the first version of ON THE ROAD. As much of the second version as I saw contained some impressively good writing, but no story whatsoever.

Cowley's complaint about the lack of "story" in *On the Road* would return to plague Kerouac throughout his relationship with the stubborn editor. But Cowley's evident admiration for Kerouac's writing and his concern for Kerouac's career stand in striking contrast to the editorial neglect Kerouac had received to this point. *On the Road*, clearly, is at the heart of the matter: how do we explain Cowley's unabashedly favorable response to a work that had thus far produced little more than anger and incomprehension in other leading editorial minds of the day? The answer lies, among other places, deep in Cowley's own literary past.

"Since most critics had never experienced anything like the *Road*," argues Dennis McNally, "they denied its existence as art and proclaimed it a 'Beat Generation' tract of rebellion, then pilloried it as immoral" (p. 240). This is true—up to a point—but Cowley was a critic with the soul of a storyteller. He had not merely experienced something like *On the Road* but had created, in *Exile's Return*, a road narrative about his own rebellious, "lost" generation. Published in 1934 (and revised for republication just two years before Cowley first read Kerouac's novel), *Exile's Return* is Cowley's first-person account of the exploits of a group of rootless and high-spirited young Americans during the decade following the Great War. Like *On the Road*, *Exile's Return* moves back and forth nervously along an East-West axis: Paris-New York in Cowley's case, New York-San Francisco in Kerouac's. Like *On the Road* it swerves south several times for pilgrimages to spiritual fathers and for binges facilitated by favorable foreign exchange rates. These structural parallels are less important, however, than the common sensibility that had produced them—one that Cowley could not possibly have failed to perceive. Coming of age in two different postwar worlds, both Cowley and Kerouac had been driven to write honest reports about their own uprooted lives and in so doing had helped define (Cowley more retrospectively than Kerouac) two radically new generations. Both men—and both generations—had rebelled against inherited values and taken to the road in pursuit of a separate peace. In Malcolm Cowley and

Jack Kerouac, it might fairly be said, the Lost Generation and the Beat Generation were meeting for the first time—and discovering in each other an unexpected resemblance.

The connection between the Lost and the Beat Generations has never been clearly articulated, and in fact several critics have attempted to prove that no such connection exists. John Clellon Holmes, defender of the Beats and author of the Beat classic *Go*, wrote in 1958 that

> instead of cynicism and apathy which accompanies the end of ideals, and which gave the Lost Generation a certain poetic, autumnal quality, the Beat Generation is altogether too vigorous, too intent, too indefatigable, too curious to suit its elders. (*VC*, p. 371)

And in the same year Norman Podhoretz, who clearly felt himself—in his late twenties—to be one of those threatened elders, insisted that Kerouac's

> tremendous emphasis on emotional intensity, this notion that to be hopped-up is the most desirable of all human conditions, lies at the heart of the Beat Generation and distinguishes it radically from the Bohemianism of the past. . . . [The ideals of 1920's Bohemia] were intelligence, cultivation, spiritual refinement. (*VC*, p. 345)

In *Exile's Return*, however, Cowley had described the Lost Generation and Greenwich Village bohemia in terms that differ markedly from those of Holmes and Podhoretz. True Villagers, according to Cowley, subscribed to an unwritten code that included such ideals as self-expression, paganism, living for the moment, and salvation by self-imposed exile. But he went on to make an important distinction between bohemians who had settled in the Village before 1917 and those belonging to the so-called Lost Generation who had just arrived from France or college. "The truth is that 'we,' the newcomers to the village, were not bohemians," he wrote. "We might act like pagans, we might live for the moment, but we tried not to be self-conscious about it." Cowley's Lost Generation, then, was clearly not the "poetic" and "spiritually refined" crowd conjured up by Holmes and Podhoretz but a group of young men as "vigorous" and "hopped-up" as the Beats themselves. The one ideal they did share wholeheartedly with the older, self-conscious bohemians, said Cowley, was "the idea of salvation by exile": "Life in this country [had become] joyless and colorless, universally standardized, tawdry, uncreative," and the only sane response was to *go*—to the Village, to Europe, to rural Connecticut. Perpetual flight from a hostile postwar world, sustained by a free-living but tightly knit community—here, clearly is the spiritual link between Cowley's Lost Generation and Kerouac's rebellious Beats.[8]

That Cowley found in Kerouac a way of reconnecting with his own past is hinted at by his statement to an interviewer:

> I remember one night Jack and I went out on the town. I wanted him to show me the new dives in Greenwich Village with which I was totally unfamiliar, not having been a Villager for twenty years. And he took me down. (Gifford and Lee, p. 187)

What Cowley saw in Kerouac and Kerouac's novel, I suggest, was the sort of impatient young man in love with life and language that Cowley had been when he was Kerouac's age. "[T]he only people for me are the mad ones, the ones who are mad to live, mad to talk, mad to be saved, desirous of everything at the same time, the ones who never yawn or say a commonplace thing, but burn, burn, burn," Sal Paradise had cried at the beginning of *On the Road*, and his words—Kerouac's self-portrait, as it were—are, surprisingly enough, an apt description of young Malcolm Cowley. For Cowley writes in *Exile's Return* of taking the morning train into Paris after snapping himself awake with a quart of café au lait, and how

> all this hurry and loss of sleep were a stimulant like cocaine. . . . faster, faster, there was always something waiting that might be forever missed unless you ham-

8. Malcolm Cowley, *Exile's Return: A Literary Odyssey of the 1920's* (1934; rev. ed. New York: The Viking Press, 1951), pp. 60-73. In a recent letter to the author, Cowley confirmed the author's hypothesis: "At the time [I first read *On the Road*] I had just published . . . the revised edition of *Exile's Return*. You are right: that helps explain why I was impressed by Kerouac's account of a new generation."

mered on the glass and told the [taxi] driver to go faster. Paris was a great machine for stimulating the nerves and sharpening the senses. Paintings and music, street noises, shops, flower markets, modes, poems, ideas, everything seemed to lead toward a half-sensual, half-intellectual swoon. (p. 135)

But if the Dada-inspired freneticism of Cowley's early years and his experiments with lyrical prose made him sympathetic with Kerouac's attempts to capture the texture of postwar life among the young, I suspect that he was struck still more forcibly by something else: Kerouac's vision of a rootless generation bound by spoken language into a self-sustaining community.

Cowley had been trying to recover precisely such a communal life since the days of *Exile's Return*, when he first formulated his myth of diasporactive exile as a way of explaining the Lost Generation. His own life and the lives of his friends, he wrote in that book, had been marked by "a long process of deracination," a progressive destruction of all ties to place and to human community: "[O]ur whole training was involuntarily directed toward destroying whatever roots we had in the soil, toward eradicating our local and regional peculiarities, toward making us homeless citizens of the world" (p. 28). *Exile's Return,* in which Cowley depicts his generation's scattering, is full of descriptions of provisional communities held together by one unending dialogue. "[O]n Sunday nights [in the Village] there were poker games played for imaginary stakes and interrupted from moment to moment by gossip, jokes, plans," he wrote. "[E]verything in those days was an excuse for talking." (p. 50). Kerouac's sense of homelessness was no less keen than Cowley's; John Clellon Holmes has called him "the seeker after continuity who, no matter how rootless his life may seem, has always known that our anguish is uprootedness" (*VC*, p. 593). And it is a striking aspect of *On the Road* that while *written* literature per se plays only a small role in the lives of the Beats, *oral* literature—the recounted story—literally holds their lives together. "[W]e headed for Mexico, telling our stories," cries Sal Paradise, "O sad American night! All the way from Amarillo to Childress, Dean and I pounded plot after plot of books we'd read into Stan, who asked for it because he wanted to know. . . . Stan talked and talked; Dean had wound him up the night before and now he was never going to stop" (pp. 269-70). In "What Writers Are and Why," an essay published in 1954, Cowley characterized writers as "[people who] tell stories that become the myths of the tribe." This broad-minded conception of the writer's role and the communal function of language, I suggest, made it possible for Cowley to value the mad storytellers portrayed by Kerouac—indeed, to value Kerouac himself—in a way that other editors and critics evidently could not.

Norman Podhoretz was perhaps the best known of those unsympathetic critics in 1958 when he remarked in "The Know-Nothing Bohemians" that

> the unveiling of the Beat Generation was greeted with a certain relief by many people who had been disturbed by the notorious respectability and "maturity" of postwar writing. This was more like it—restless, rebellious, confused youth living it up instead of thin, balding, buttoned-down instructors of English composing ironic verses with one hand while changing the baby's diapers with the other. (VC, p. 343)

It is a fascinating point of literary history that Cowley, the editor responsible for bringing *On the Road* into print, was also the critic who worked hardest during the 1950's to foster precisely the sort of dissatisfaction with "mature" postwar fiction that might lead the public to greet Kerouac's book with relief. During his years as literary editor at *The New Republic*—a mantle he inherited from Edmund Wilson—he had established himself as one of the foremost civic critics in America: he addressed his weekly column not to a select academic audience, but to a community of general readers and working writers. In 1946 he had used his dual role as editor/critic in singular fashion to resurrect William Faulkner from near-total obscurity, persuading The Viking Press to publish *The Portable Faulkner* and writing the groundbreaking introductory essay. But the "Mississippi flood" of Faulkner studies that subsequently poured out of the academies, although gratifying to Cowley, seemed to him a distressing sign of the increasingly academic temper of the age. In 1953 and 1954 he wrote a series of polemical essays for general-interest magazines on "the literary situation," most of which were republished late in 1954 in a book by that name. It was in March of 1953, near the beginning of this project, that he first read *On the Road*.

What becomes clear when we read Cowley's essays of the period is the extraordinary degree to which Kerouac's novel met the specifications Cowley was demanding of contemporary fiction. In "A Tidy Room in Bedlam: Notes on the 'New' Fiction," published in *Harper's* in April 1953, Cowley criticized the work of Truman Capote, Paul Bowles, and others:

> [T]hey are all "serious" new writers, they are trying to produce works of art in accordance with the best literary standards, and they would like to be admired by the critics who write for Kenyon, Sewanee, Hudson, and other quarterly reviews. . . . [They give us] novels like highly polished objets d'art, not really designed to be read, but rather to be displayed like framed diplomas.

In his "Invitation to Innovators," published the following year in *Saturday Review*, Cowley complained that young novelists were content to imitate

> the asthmatic, comma-dotted style of [Henry James's] later years—as if [they] were tired expatriates who had to pause for breath after speaking two or three words, instead of being young stay-at-homes bursting with energy. . . . [T]he [novel] form might decongeal and, instead of novels like funerary monuments, we might have loosely conceived narratives that carried one or many heroes through a variety of adventures.

That the young stay-at-home Kerouac was on Cowley's mind as he delivered this exhortation goes without saying: earlier in the article he had referred to "John Kerouac's unpublished long narrative" as "the best record of [the] lives of the Beat Generation."

But if Cowley had a number of reasons for thinking so highly of *On the Road*, The Viking Press did not. "[I] got a couple more readings for it," he told an interviewer, "but no, they wouldn't publish. It was very much a matter on my mind. I thought, here is something new. Here is something that ought to get to people. A way has to be prepared for it" (Gifford and Lee, p. 187). Cowley had been rejected by Viking's conservative editorial board in similar fashion when he first proposed *The Portable Faulkner*. He had responded by writing a long essay on Faulkner's work and then doing what he called "beefing" it—publishing it in sections in several different magazines, using his independent critical voice to give Faulkner's name enough public currency so that Viking was finally forced to take a second look. He used a variation on that strategy to pave the way for *On the Road*. Not only did he praise Kerouac's fiction in print, but he convinced a reluctant Kerouac that "beefing" his novel was the surest way of persuading Viking to publish it. When Cowley wrote Kerouac in the summer of 1954 to ask if he might send an excerpt of the book to Arabelle Porter at *New World Writing*, Seymour Lawrence at Little, Brown had just rejected the book. Kerouac raged at Lawrence in a letter to Allen Ginsberg dated 30 July, but he praised Cowley repeatedly, invoking his name like a mantra. He willingly gave Cowley the go-ahead. On August 6th he received word from Miss Porter that "Jazz Excerpts" had been accepted, and he wrote a short, ecstatic letter of gratitude to Cowley. He had begun to lose heart, he said, but this gave him a lift toward further effort.

The lift was short-lived. By Christmas, E. P. Dutton had turned down *On the Road*, and Joe Fox, Editor-in-Chief at Alfred Knopf, sent it back with a comment that Kerouac characterized in a letter to Ginsberg as "contemptuous." Kerouac grew increasingly desperate during the early months of 1955, his intense need for the approval of his literary elders counterbalanced by his disgust with a publishing world that refused to recognize his genius on its own terms. In May 1955 he described to Ginsberg a nightmare he had recently had in which "he is seized with convulsions in front of two men in a synagogue lined with books. Screaming maniacally, flopping about epileptically, [he] grovels as the men calmly observe him, neither surprised nor frightened but detached" (Tytell, p. 77).

Cowley was the one bright light in Kerouac's literary life during this period. Yet as both a fatherly partisan of *On the Road* and a detached critic of Kerouac's subsequent writings, he ended up serving as a lightning rod for Kerouac's powerful insecurities and frustrations. In his interview with Gifford and Lee, Cowley hinted at the curious pressures to which his relationship with Kerouac had subjected him:

I was seeing Jack and seeing Allen Ginsberg and giving advice from time to time. I think Allen had the idea that perhaps I could act as a sort of elderly grandfather for the Beats, which idea did not appeal to me. (p. 188)

Ginsberg, self-appointed literary agent for the neglected Beats, had been trying without success to interest Cowley in the work of William Burroughs and Gregory Corso—"two writers," remarked Cowley in a recent letter, "for whom I did not feel enthusiasm."[9] Kerouac was another matter: Cowley continued to treat the author of that still-unpublished long narrative like the promising young writer Kerouac felt himself to be. In May of 1955 the two men lunched in New York, and although Cowley rejected a nonfiction guide entitled *Buddha Tells Us*, he said he would try to do something with *Doctor Sax*; Kerouac defended him ardently in two subsequent letters to Ginsberg. Then, late in June, Kerouac returned to New York with twenty-seven pages of a novel-in-progress and had a second lunch with Cowley that took on, when he later described it to Ginsberg, an intense and mingled significance. He bragged that Cowley had gotten drunk with him in Greenwich Village and had promised to get him a grant from the American Academy of Arts and Letters. Buoyed by this prospect, he had asked Cowley to convince Viking to advance him $25 a month for a year or so; he wanted to return to Mexico, live in a stone hut, and finish his novel. But Cowley, Kerouac said, had rejected the proposal—had told him bluntly that the new script smacked too much of Thomas Wolfe—and Kerouac complained

9. Several years later, however, Cowley was to feel considerable enthusiasm for another young writer, Ken Kesey. The two men first met in 1958 at Stanford: Kesey was a creative-writing student and Cowley—as he had been three years earlier, while editing *On the Road*—was a visiting instructor. Cowley told Kesey that his manuscript for *One Flew Over the Cuckoo's Nest* contained some of the most powerful writing he'd ever seen; he helped Kesey revise the novel and later persuaded Viking to publish it. A pivotal late-Beat/early-hippie figure, Kesey seems to have struck Cowley much as Kerouac did, as an avatar of the Lost Generation. By the winter of 1961, wrote Cowley, "[Kesey] had become the man whom other young rebels [at Stanford] tried to imitate, almost like Hemingway in Montparnasse during the 1920's" (quoted by Stephen Tanner, *Ken Kesey* [Boston: Twayne, 1983], p. 21). Doubtless Cowley was also struck by uncanny parallels between Kesey and Kerouac. Kesey was also an athlete (a champion wrestler), a road-hungry picaro (eventually becoming the ringleader of the Merry Pranksters in 1964), and a firm believer in drug-induced literary inspiration.

mildly that Cowley sometimes seemed insensitive to the pain of young Beat poets.

*

On 12 July 1955, Cowley wrote to Kerouac's new agent, Sterling Lord, and asked to have another look at *On the Road*. Viking had recently hired Keith Jennison, a young editor who was familiar with Kerouac's work, and when he read the manuscript he quickly became convinced that Cowley was right in wanting to publish it. But although Jennison's name subsequently began to turn up in Kerouac's letters to Ginsberg, Cowley remained Kerouac's principal connection with Viking. For a variety of reasons, including Kerouac's unstable personality and a fundamental difference in literary values, the editorial process became one long exercise in frustration.

The first thing Cowley did after securing Jennison's backing was to write Kerouac a letter describing the obstacles that would have to be surmounted if *On the Road* were to be published. According to Viking's attorneys, said Cowley, the present manuscript was both libelous and obscene. Cowley himself wasn't bothered by Kerouac's over-honest language, but he did feel that the narrative had structural problems and he later described the editorial suggestions he had made:

> I thought there should be some changes to make it more of a continuous narrative. It had swung back and forth between East Coast and West Coast like a huge pendulum. I thought that some of the trips should be telescoped. . . . All the changes I suggested were big ones, mostly omissions. I said why don't you boil down these two or three trips and keep the mood of the content. (Charters, p. 217)

Cowley's intent, clearly, was to have Kerouac rearrange his narrative of lived experience into something more closely resembling a "story," while retaining the sense of life of the original. That narrative literature should tell stories had been a near-sacred principle for Cowley throughout his career. In "The Limits of the Novel," published in *The New Republic* in 1956, he framed the principle publicly:

403

> [A novel is] a long but unified story, designed to be read
> at more than one sitting, that deals with a group of
> lifelike characters in a plausible situation and leads to a
> change in their relationship. . . . [O]n pain of early death
> for his book, [the author] must create a mood of expect-
> ancy.

And on 24 February 1957 he sent back Kerouac's latest manu-
script, *Desolation Angels,* with the same principle disguised as
editorial advice:

> The book doesn't have any plot—it's just Duluoz alone
> on the mountain. . . . One character, really. A book, a
> novel doesn't get started until one character gets mixed
> up with other people, gets into conflicts with them—and
> it ends when the conflicts are resolved, the situation
> changed.

When Kerouac received Cowley's initial suggestions for editorial
changes in *On the Road,* he was too happy with the prospects of
seeing his novel in print to argue. In a letter dated 20 September
1955 he agreed to work with Cowley on the twin problems of libel
and obscenity, and he said that he was ready to assist Cowley in
rearranging the narrative as the editor saw fit. He was never to
speak this generously to Cowley again. In fact, he was later to turn
on him, much as Thomas Wolfe had turned on Maxwell Perkins,
bitterly criticizing him for damaging the structure and texture of
his novel. His charges were later picked up and transformed into
myth by Allen Ginsberg, who bemoaned

> the sadness that [*On the Road*] was never published in
> its most exciting form—its original discovery—but
> hacked and punctuated and broken—the rhythms and
> swing of it broken—by presumptuous literary critics in
> publishing houses. (Tytell, p. 158)

The true source of Cowley's dispute with Kerouac lay not so much
in Cowley's insistence on *story,* but in a second, more fundamental
principle: his insistence on *craft.* Perhaps it was inevitable that an
editor who once confessed, "I hate to write and love to revise"

would end up at loggerheads with an impatient young writer whose own poetic was summed up in a manifesto entitled "Essentials of Spontaneous Prose." The irony of the conflict is that the two men were in far greater accord on the matter than they were subsequently willing to admit. A combination of pride, stubbornness, and sheer happenstance led them to force each other into extreme positions.

Kerouac, despite his later insistence that the writer remove all "literary, grammatical, and syntactical inhibition," felt no qualms about revising his own early drafts of *On the Road* prior to submission.[10] What he opposed, as Tim Hunt has pointed out, was others' cutting material out of his manuscript. Even so, his Whitmanesque aesthetic of spontaneity—

> tap from yourself the song of yourself, *blow!—now!—your* way is your only way—"good"—or "bad"—always honest, ("ludicrous"), spontaneous, "confessional," interesting because not "crafted" (*VC*, p. 532)—

was formulated explicitly only *after* the publication of *On the Road*, when he had an image of uncompromising artistry to protect. And although Cowley had always insisted that art should be "crafted," he was anything but a rigid formalist: he regarded inspiration and radical experimentation as equally crucial components of the artistic process. In fact, he described Whitman's composition of "Song of Myself" in his 1959 introduction to that poem in terms that might equally well have expressed his vision of *On the Road*: "It . . . bears the marks of having been conceived as a whole and written in one prolonged burst of inspiration, but its unity is also the result of conscious art, as can be seen from Whitman's corrections in the early manuscripts." Yet in later years, thrown on the defensive by Kerouac's attacks, Cowley cynically disparaged the idea that inspiration was the only source of Kerouac's art:

> Well, Jack did something that he would never admit to later. He did a good deal of revision, and it was very

10. Jack Kerouac, "Belief and Technique for Modern Prose" (1959), reprinted in *A Casebook of the Beat*, ed. Thomas Parkinson, (New York: Thomas Y. Crowell, 1961), p. 67.

good revision. Oh, he would never, never admit to that, because it was his feeling that the stuff ought to come out like toothpaste from a tube and not be changed, and that every word that passed from his typewriter was holy. On the contrary, he revised, and revised well. (Gifford and Lee, p. 206)

In light of Norman Podhoretz's complaint that *On the Road* is "patently autobiographical in content. . . .Nothing that happens has any dramatic reason for happening"—a criticism echoed even by some of Kerouac's admirers—it would seem hard to fault Cowley on principle for having pressured Kerouac to bring out the "story" in his narrative. But what revisions actually were made? Kerouac later bragged to Ginsberg that the "revision" he gave to Viking was substantially unchanged: he had simply "purged all material not directly related to Cassady, and had accepted . . . Cowley's suggestion to fuse the various trips for the sake of focus" (Tytell, p. 158). Yet in a letter he wrote to Ginsberg on 21 July 1957, shortly before publication, Kerouac made a fascinating assertion: Don't be upset, he told Ginsberg, by the passage Cowley wanted put in on page six about your "intellectualism." A reader who turns to that page in a hardcover copy of *On the Road* comes upon the following passage:

In those days [Dean Moriarty]really didn't know what he was talking about; that is to say, he was a young jailkid all hung-up on the wonderful possibilities of becoming a real intellectual, and he liked to talk in the tone and using the words, but in a jumbled way, that he had heard from "real intellectuals"—although, mind you, he wasn't so naïve as that in all other things and it took him just a few months with Carlo Marx [Ginsberg] to become completely *in there* with all the terms and jargon.

Podhoretz undoubtedly had this passage in mind when he accused the Beat Generation of "an anti-intellectualism so bitter that it makes the ordinary American's hatred of eggheads seem positively benign." That the tone of Kerouac's jibe is obviously lighthearted rather than bitter is less to the point, however, than Kerouac's suggestion that the jibe may not have been his idea at all. The

406

circumstantial evidence for Cowley's involvement is tantalizing. In "Some Dangers to American Writing," an essay published in *The New Republic* (22 November 1954), Cowley had lamented the fact that American authors were increasingly taking refuge in the universities:

> [L]earning [is] emphasized [by these writers] at the expense of invention and imagination. The scholar-writer turns his attention to the past. . . . He begins to talk—as the sociologists and some of the new critics already do—in the narrow jargon of his craft.

Like Hemingway, Cummings, and other members of his generation, whose first-hand experience of the Great War had radically disillusioned them with the patriotic "jargon" of the time—"glory," "honor," and so forth—Cowley had long had an instinctive distaste for mystifying, obfuscating abstractions. He found university-affiliated intellectuals inclined as a class to use such abstractions, such "narrow jargon," as a way of gaining prestige—of getting "completely *in there*"—and as a way of avoiding clear thought on the pressing problems of the day. "Today's 'intellectuals,'" he observed in *The New Republic* during the period in which he was editing *On the Road*, "are narrower in scope than their predecessors, more compartmented in their specialties. . . . This is a time of analysts and psychoanalysts, not bold synthetic thinkers."[11] If conclusive proof that Cowley persuaded Kerouac to add the passage mocking the "terms and jargon" of "real intellectuals" is lacking, it seems clear at the very least that Kerouac found in the civic critic a sensibility uniquely responsive to his own low regard for the systematic mind divorced from life.

Despite such shared attitudes, however, Kerouac's nascent editorial relationship with Cowley began to sour almost as soon as it had begun—and for a thoroughly mundane reason. Cowley had received an appointment to teach creative writing during the winter quarter at Stanford, and on 8 November 1955 he wrote to Kerouac at Allen Ginsberg's place in Berkeley, where Jack was spending the fall, telling him that he and Mrs. Cowley would be in Palo Alto by January 2nd. "Of course I plan to see you then if you

---

11. "Who Are the Intellectuals," *The New Republic*, 25 February 1957, pp. 14-16.

are still in San Francisco," he told him. But Kerouac, itinerant as always, was in Rocky Mount, North Carolina by the time Cowley's letter reached Ginsberg's Milvia Street apartment. Kerouac traveled up to New York after Christmas, expecting to work with Cowley on revisions of *On the Road,* and when he discovered his editor's absence he felt abandoned. By the time he made it back to California in April of 1956, the quarter at Stanford was over and Cowley had returned to New York. Angry and insecure, Kerouac decided to exploit what seemed to him a legitimate grievance with the way Cowley had treated him. On 9 May he wrote the editor and proposed a new project: an historical novel about the Zapotec Indians of Mexico, complete with Kerouacian descriptions of their legendary sex orgies. All Cowley had to do, insisted Kerouac, was write to the Mexican patron that Kerouac had lined up and assure him that he, Cowley, would be interested in publishing such a work—subject, of course, to the approval of the Viking editorial board. Kerouac followed this demand by complaining that he was penniless and ragged, and that Cowley had broken his heart by neglecting him. He begged for some kind of news.

Cowley responded immediately. He apologized for the delay with *On the Road*—he had been loaded down with "rush jobs" after returning from Stanford—and he sent Kerouac a copy of the letter he had written to Kerouac's patron. "I don't think it is the book you should be writing at this moment," he told him. "But if Mr. Garver is willing to stake you to grub and lodging, I approve of that part of the operation." Kerouac was to remind Cowley repeatedly of a truth the editor knew from his own early days as a freelance critic, that "money is the central problem of a young writer's life."[12] That July, in fact, Kerouac wrote him threatening to withdraw his book unless Cowley came through with a firm contract and an advance. Cowley could do little to hasten the editorial process at Viking, but he did manage to "beef" two more sections of the script—one of them to his old friend George Plimpton at *Paris Review*. And he used his influence at the National Institute of Arts and Letters to secure Kerouac a $300 grant. Delighted, Kerouac wrote Ginsberg that Cowley had assisted the "helpless angels" (Tytell, p. 78).

12. Malcolm Cowley,—*And I worked at the Writer's Trade: Chapters of Literary History 1918-1978* (New York: The Viking Press, 1978), p. 57.

In mid-December 1956, almost four years after Cowley had first read *On the Road* in an early draft, Viking accepted Kerouac's novel for publication. Libel remained a problem—Viking's attorneys didn't clear the manuscript until late in March—but with Keith Jennison's help Cowley had managed to persuade Viking's editors that the book was a sound investment. As Cowley's in-house acceptance report makes clear, the crafty editor preferred not to let the editorial board know the degree to which he had helped change their minds:

> [W]hile we held on to [the manuscript], prevented from working on it by other projects that might take less time, Kerouac began amassing quite a reputation. The episode of the Mexican girl was printed in *Paris Review*, a jazz passage was used to lead off one issue of *New World Writing*, and a Mexican cathouse episode was accepted by *New Directions*, so that more of a groundwork seemed to be laid for publication of the book.

The truth was that Cowley had "beefed" all three excerpts for Kerouac. Confident in the literary value of the book, he had used his contacts in the publishing world and his own critical essays to help build Kerouac's reputation. *On the Road*, he said in his clear-sighted acceptance report, "is real, honest, fascinating, everything for kicks, the voice of a new age."

> The book, I prophesy, will get mixed but *interested* reviews, it will have a good sale (perhaps a very good one), and I don't think there is any doubt that it will be reprinted as a paperback. Moreover it will stand for a long time as the honest record of another way of life.

Contrary to popular myth, Kerouac never complained about having to change the names of his friends in *On the Road* and otherwise cooperating with demands made by Viking's libel lawyers. But he felt increasingly testy about the whole idea of editorial changes. On 4 July 1957, with book publication only two months away, Kerouac sent Cowley a copy of his essay "October in the Railroad Earth," from the latest issue of *Evergreen Review*. Here, he kidded Cowley, was spontaneous prose as it should be, untouched by editorial hands. He added a biblical postscript:

"Take no thought beforehand what ye shall speak, neither do ye premeditate; but whatsoever shall be given to you in that hour, that speak ye; for it is not ye that speak, but the Holy Ghost."

Underneath the note, in case Cowley had missed his point, he typed the words "spontaneous prose." Cowley took the bait, responding on July 16th:

That's a fine quotation from Mark 13.11. If the Holy Ghost is speaking through you, fine, fine, let him speak. Sometimes he turns out to be the devil masquerading as the Holy Ghost, and that's all right too. Sometimes he turns out to be Simple Simon, and then you have to cut what he says. A good writer uses his subconscious mind and his conscious mind, one after the other, and uses them both as hard as they can be used.

Looking to the future, Cowley also told Kerouac he thought *Doctor Sax* was "the best of the present manuscripts," and he suggested that Kerouac lengthen it by writing in some new scenes about his boyhood.

Kerouac received Cowley's letter on July 21st, along with a boxful of advance copies of his book. Because of time constraints he had never been sent any galley proofs, and he now discovered, much to his chagrin, that additional cuts and changes had been made in the story without his approval. The record does not reveal what changes were made and who made them, although Cowley insisted in a recent letter to me that he hadn't seen the additional changes and that those which Kerouac complained about were made by an in-house editor with whom Cowley had been working on the book. Kerouac was in no doubt about the culprit, however; he dashed off a quick, angry letter to Allen Ginsberg. "Crafty Cowley" had asked him to write more scenes for *Doctor Sax*, he told Ginsberg, and he was sure that the editor would yank the fantasy section out of *Sax* without his permission, just as he had

410

yanked material out of *On the Road*. At least *On the Road*, he grumbled, was "undecimatable," unlike *Sax*. In any case, he was planning to leave tomorrow for Mexico City, where he would write those new scenes for *Sax* in his long-yearned-for stone hut. He would arrive, he said, with $33 in his pocket, and he told Ginsberg he was planning to write despairing letters to Cowley asking for money.

The next day he wrote Cowley from Mexico City. The long letter was an exercise in pure duplicity. He told Cowley he thought the edition of *On the Road* was excellent and he praised the "few cuts" Cowley had made—now it would fit into pocket editions, and anyway the story was "well-nigh undecimatable." Then, just as he had promised Ginsberg, he pleaded with Cowley to send him money. He had only $33 in his pocket, the advance for *On the Road* had been small, and Malcolm—he called him Malcolm six times—would *have* to send him $80 or $100 more. He was trying, he said, to write the new scenes Cowley had requested by recreating the conditions under which the bulk of *Doctor Sax* had been written; he mentioned an adobe hut and candlelight, but said nothing about his nonstop consumption of marijuana. He ended by telling Cowley that he was completely at his mercy.

The ploy worked: Cowley quickly arranged through Kerouac's agent, Sterling Lord, to have money cabled to Jack in Mexico. "Good luck on your Mexican venture," Cowley wrote him on July 23rd. "I am looking forward to reading the expanded version of *Doctor Sax*, and I hope that the new chapters will fit perfectly into what you have written already." Kerouac received the money and wrote the new chapters, but a bad case of the flu sent him staggering home to his mother's house in Florida. After his nightmarish month in Mexico, and with publication less than two weeks away, the accumulated tensions of his relationship with Cowley and literary New York burst through the surface. On August 20th he wrote a despairing letter to his friend Alan Anson. He was so sick and tired of the self-satisfied silence of wise men that he could kill them, he said. God save us, he added—in an obvious reference to Cowley—from the wise man puffing on his pipe. Two weeks later a new wise man, Gilbert Millstein of *The New York Times*, praised *On the Road* lavishly in a widely read review, and Kerouac was literally an overnight success. Except for two glancing references, he never again mentioned Cowley in his letters.

After the extraordinary popularity of *On the Road* had become apparent, Viking asked Kerouac to write another story about his friends. Kerouac's disputes with the editors at Viking over editorial changes in that book, *The Dharma Bums*, have long since passed into myth, particularly his bitter accusations about Malcolm Cowley. In fact, the editorial files at Viking confirm what Cowley himself repeatedly insisted: the editing was handled by two other editors, while Cowley (who was out of the office for most of the year) had nothing to do with the manuscript. What has never been explained, however—and what the files also help clear up—is why Cowley stopped working with Kerouac shortly after *On the Road* had been published.

Doctor Sax was the pivotal point in the relationship. During the glory days of September 1957, with *On the Road* exploding all around them and *The Dharma Bums* still off in the future, the editors at Viking had hurriedly evaluated the manuscripts Kerouac had written since composing *On the Road* in an effort to find one with comparable commercial potential. Cowley naturally wondered about *Doctor Sax*, since he had liked the first version he had read and Kerouac had recently written those new chapters in Mexico. Sterling Lord sent over the expanded script, along with several other recently completed stories. On 17 September Cowley wrote a startling memo to Keith Jennison and Helen Taylor:

> I agree with HKT [Helen K. Taylor] that DOCTOR SAX is impossible, at least as it stands—it's an exercise in self-abuse. Seems to me that I must have read it first in another version, much more public, much easier to read.
>
> Furthermore, Jack's Mexican story, TRISTESSA, is even more (if possible) impossible. It raises the question whether Jack has been completely ruined as a publishable writer by Allan Ginsburg [sic] and his exercises in automatic or self-abusive writing.
>
> I don't think he *has* been ruined and will continue my efforts to get something publishable out of him.

412

Although Cowley was deeply disturbed by the solipsism and formlessness—the lack of conscious "craft"—that marked this new version of *Doctor Sax*, he continued to believe, at least briefly, that Kerouac was not "ruined," and he made a final attempt to get the kind of writing he wanted out of him. On 8 October he sent Sterling Lord a blunt note that made it clear how he felt:

> I told him [Kerouac], roughly speaking, that any book he did for us would be fine, so long as it was a story and was about people.

Kerouac pounded out the story as requested—it became *The Dharma Bums*—but the pressure of sudden popularity, the trivialization of himself and his fellow Beats into "Beatniks" at the hands of highbrow critics and mass media opportunists, drove him even more quickly than Cowley could have predicted into drunken retreat. He surfaced long enough during the final unhappy decade of his life to write several more books, the best of which, *Big Sur*, being an unflinchingly honest account of the price he had paid for his drug-primed visionary gift. By that point, however, Cowley had quietly withdrawn—like a father who leaves his son to fight the battles in which fathers have no place.

nominated by Frederick Busch

A POEM WITH NO ENDING

by PHILIP LEVINE

from THE PARIS REVIEW

So many poems begin where they
should end, and never end.
Mine never end, they run on
book after book, complaining
to the moon that heaven is wrong
or dull, no place at all to be.
I believe all this. I believe
that ducks take wing only
in stories and then to return
the gift of flight to the winds.
If you knew how I came to be
seven years old and how thick
and blond my hair was, falling
about my shoulders like the leaves
of the slender eucalyptus
that now blesses my driveway
and shades my pale blue Falcon,
if you could see me pulling
wagon loads of stones across
the tufted fields and placing
them to build myself and my brother
a humped mound of earth where
flowers might rise as from a grave,

414

you might understand the last spring
before war turned toward our house
and entered before dawn, a pale
stranger that hovered over each bed
and touched the soft, unguarded faces
leaving bruises so faint
years would pass before they darkened
and finally burned. Now I can sit
calmly over coffee and recover
each season, how the rains swelled
the streets, how at night I mumbled
a prayer because the weight
of snow was too great to bear
as I heard it softly packing
down the roof, how I waited
for hours for some small breeze
to rise from the river dreaming
beside me, and none came, and morning
was so much mist rising
and the long moaning of ore boats
returning the way they'd come,
only now freighted with the earth
someone would carve and cook.
That is the poem I called "Boyhood"
and placed between the smeared pages
of your morning paper. White itself,
it fell on the white tablecloth
and meant so little you turned
it over and wrote a column
of figures you never added up.
You capped your gold fountain pen
and snapped your fingers to remind
yourself of some small, lost event.
My poem remained long after you'd
gone, face down, unread, not even
misunderstood, until it passed,
like its subject, into the literatures
of silence, though hardly first
among them, for there have always
been the tales the water told

the cup and the words the wind
sang to the windows in those houses
we abandoned after the roads
whispered all night in our ears.

I passed the old house and saw
even from the front that four trees
were gone, and beside the drive
a wire cage held nothing. Once
I stopped and rang the bell.
A woman said, No! before I asked,
and I heard a child say, Who
is he? and I turned away
from so many years and drove off.
Tomorrow my train will leave
the tunnel and rise above this town
and slowly clatter beside block
after block of buildings that fall
open like so many stunned faces
with nothing to hide. The cold odor
of smoke rises and the steeped smell
of wood that will not hold our words.
Once I saw the back of a closet
that burst unto sky, and I imagined
opening a familiar door and stepping
into a little room without limits.
I rose into a blue sky as undefined
as winter and as cold. I said, Oh my!
and held myself together with a wish!
No, that wasn't childhood, that
was something else, something
that ended in a single day and left
no residue of happiness I could
reach again if I took the first turn
to the left and eyes closed walked
a hundred and one steps and spoke
the right words.
                    I sit for days
staring at the dusty window
and no word comes to tell me what I

left behind. Still, I regret nothing,
not the little speeches I wrote
to the moon on the warm spring nights
I searched for someone other
than myself and came home empty
at sun-up among bird calls
and the faint prattle of rain.
I do not regret my hands
changing before me, mottling
like the first eggs I found
in the fields of junked cars,
nor my breath that still comes
and comes no matter what I command
and the words that go out
and fall short. I can hear
my heart beating, slowly,
I can feel the blood sliding
behind my eyes, so I close them
first on a known darkness and then
on a red crown forming as from
a dark sea, and I am beginning
once more to rise into the shape
of someone I can be, a man
no different from my father
but slower and wiser. What could be
better than to waken as a man?

I began as you did, smaller
than the wren who circled three times
and flew back into the darkness
before sleep. I was born
of the promise that each night
made and each day broke, out
of the cat's sullen wish to remain
useless and proud and the sunlight's
to find a closed face to waken.
Out of just that and no more.
The tiny stories my grandpa
told in which dogs walked upright
and the dead laughed. I was born

417

of these and his pocket of keys,
his dresser drawers of black socks
and white shirts, his homilies
of blood and water, all he never
gave me and all he did. Small
and dying he opened his eyes
unto a certain day, unto
stale water and old shoes,
and he never prayed. I could say
that was the finished poem and gather
my few things into a dark suitcase
and go quietly into the streets and wait.
It will be Sunday, and no one will pass.
In the long shadows of the warehouses
it's cool and pleasant. A piece of paper
skips by, but I don't bend to it
or tip my hat.

                  I hear the shouts
of children at play. Sunday afternoon
in August of '36, and the darkness
falls between us on the little island
where we came year after year
to celebrate the week. First I can't
see you, my brother, but I can hear
your labored breathing beside me,
and then my legs vanish, and then
my hands, and I am only a presence
in long grass. Then I am grass
blowing in a field all night, giving
and taking so many green gifts
of the earth and touching everything.
I never wakened from that evening.
The island still rides the river
between two countries. The playground—
yellowed and shrunken—, the rotunda
falling in upon itself, the old
huddled at separate tables and staring
off into the life they've come to.
In this place and at this time,

which is not time, I could take
the long road back and find it all.
I could even find myself. (Writing
this, I know it's not true.)

On Monday morning across the way
the trucks load up with parcels
of everything. This is New York City
in mid-May of 1981, and I am too old
to live that life again, packing
the van with frozen fish, household
goods, oriental vegetables, wristwatches,
weightless cartons of radium. That was
thirty years ago in another town,
and I still recall the mixture
of weariness and excitement as I beheld
the little mound of what was mine
to take into the world. (They had given
me a cap with a shining badge
and a huge revolver to guard
"the valuables." I hid them both
under the seat.) On the near West Side
in a two-room walk-up apartment
a dazed couple sat waiting for weeks
for a foot locker full of clothes
and kitchen utensils. They stood back
when I entered, pretending to be busy,
and they tried to keep me there,
but they had nothing to say. They were
neither young nor old, and I couldn't
then imagine their days in which little
or nothing was done, days on which it
seemed important to smoke before
dressing and not to go out until
late afternoon. I couldn't imagine
who they were and why they'd come
from all the small far-off places
to be homeless where I was homeless.
In another house an old man summoned
me to a high room. There before us

419

was a massive steamer trunk full
of books he could take back home
to Germany now he could return.
Tolstoi, Balzac, Goethe, all
in the original. Oh yes, I knew
the names, and he called down
to his wife, how wonderful!
This boy knows the names. He brought
the top down carefully, turned the key,
and stepped back, waiting for me
to carry it down three flights
by myself and offered me money
when I couldn't budge it, as though
I'd been pretending. This boy,
this American, in his pressed
work clothes, surely he could do it,
surely there was a way, if only
I would try. I left him shaking
his great head and passed his wife
on the stairs, a little brown mouse
of a woman laughing at such folly.

The memory of rain falling slowly
into the dark streets and the smell
of a new season rising above
the trucks parked in silent rows.
Even without earth or snow melting
or new grass rising into moonlight,
the year is turning, and the streets
can feel it. I dreamed this,
or I lived it for a moment, waking
in the night to no bird song
or wind pull, waking to no one
beside me asking for water
or a child calling from another room.
Awake now for a second or a lifetime,
I'm once again stepping out onto
the tiny veranda above the railyards
of Sevilla. In the room next door
a soldier has dressed a chair

with his uniform and leaned his rifle
against the glass door. A woman's clothes
are scattered on the floor. I look away.
Christmas, 1965. The halls of this hotel
are filled with sleeping peasants.
Each of my three sons is alone
in a narrow room with no windows,
asleep in a darkness beyond darkness,
and I feel their loneliness and fear.
Below the window, the lights
of the railyard flash this way
and that, and an old engine is firing up.
Distant voices speak out, but I can't
understand their words. I am falling
toward sleep again. For a moment
I feel my arms spread wide to enclose
everyone within these walls whitewashed
over and over, my own sons, my woman,
and all the other sons and daughters
stretched out or curled up in bad beds
or on bare floors, their heads
pillowed on their own hard arms
their cheeks darkened by cheap newsprint.
There is a song, bird song or wind song,
or the song old rooms sing when no one
is awake to hear. For a moment I
almost catch the melody we make
with bare walls, old iron sagging beds,
and scarred floors. There is one
deep full note for each of us.
This is the first night of my life
I know we are music.

                    Across the world
in the high mountains of the West,
I had gone one Sunday
with my youngest son, Teddy.
We parked the car and climbed
from the road's end over a rise
of young pines and then descended

421

slowly for a mile or more
through a meadow of wild flowers
still blooming in July. The yellow
ones that reached to his shoulders
stained my legs with pollen.
As we walked he spoke of animals
with the gift of speech. Bears,
he told me, were especially fond
of young people, and the mother bears
were known for coming into towns
like ours to steal boys and girls
and bring them back up here and teach
them hunting, and the children
grew into animals and forgot
their homes and their brothers.
A slight rise, and we entered
a thick forest. The air was still
and damp, and there was no longer
any trail. Soon I lost my way.
In a small clearing we stopped
to have our sandwiches, and I cooled
the soda pop in a stream whose rushing
we'd heard from far off. His head
pillowed on his jacket, he lay out,
eyes closed, the long dark lashes
quivering in sunlight, the cheeks
brown and smooth. When I awoke
he was throwing rocks as large
as he could manage into the stream
where they banged down a stairway
of stone and came to rest. The sun
had shifted, the shadows fell
across our faces, and it was cooler.
He was building a house, he said,
below the water, dark now, and boiling.
I bet him he couldn't lead us back
the way we'd come through the dark
bear woods and across the great plain
and up and down these hills.
A dollar? he said. Yes. And talking

all the way, he took the lead,
switching a fallen branch before him
to dub this little tree as friend
or a tall weed as enemy, stopping once
to uproot a purple wildflower for me.

I reenter a day in a late summer,
the heat going from the streets
and the cramped downriver flats, a day
of departures and farewells, for I
too am going, packing my box
of books and my typewriter and heading
West this time. So it seems
that all of us are on the move,
giving up these jobs that gave us
just enough and took all we had.
Going back to the little hollows
we'd come away from when the land
gave out or going back
to the survivors left in Alabama
or farther back to the villages
of Greece and Italy. From all
of these people I take a drink,
a pastry, and a coin to insure
a safe voyage, and we shake hands
around the battered kitchen tables.
Sometimes the old ones turn away
before I leave and cry without sound
or sometimes a man touches
his wife, but more often each stands
alone and silent in the old pain.

How many lives were torn apart
in those years? How many young men
went off as ours did but never
came back. It was still dark when we
drove into the great harbor and found
the ship to Sweden and said goodbye
not knowing what it was we said.
We saw him climb the gangplank

loaded down with duffle bags
and a guitar he scarcely played.
We turned back to the city
unable to face each other,
unable to face the coming day.
The sun shone on trams and markets,
and until late afternoon I tramped
the streets no longer looking for
the face I sought in childhood,
for now that face was mine, and I
was old enough to know
that my son would not suddenly
turn a corner and be mine
as I was my father's son.
A woman came out of a bar
screaming at her man, and he
hurried silently beside me
and darted quickly down an alley.
When I turned the woman's face
was smeared with tears. She shook
a finger at me and damned me
in her tongue. That night I
slept alone and dreamed of finding
my way back to the house where I
was born. It was quiet when I
entered, for no one has risen yet,
and I climbed the steps to my room
where nothing stirred in all
the rooms beneath me. I slept
fully dressed, stretched out
on a tiny bed, a boy's bed,
and in that dream more vivid
than the waking from it, the rooms
were one and I was home at last.

To get west you go east.
You leave in the dark
by car and drive until you
can't and sleep by the road

for an hour or a moment.
If the windshield is crystalled
when you waken you know
the days will be getting
colder and shorter. If you
wake soaked with sweat
then the year is turning
toward summer. None of
it matters at all, the towns
you travel through, plunging
down hills and over the cobbles
and the twisting tight passageways
and breaking for the open fields,
the apple orchards and the barns
rotting and fallen, none of it
matters to you. No one
you know dreams these houses
or hides here from the rain.
When the long day turns
to dark and you're nowhere
you've ever been before, you
keep going, and the magic eyes
that gleam by the roadside
are those of animals come
down from the invisible hills.
Yes, they have something to tell
or something to give you
from the world you've lost.
If you stopped the car and let
the engine idle and walked
slowly toward them, one hand
held out in greeting, you
would find only a fence post
bullet-scarred and deckled with
red-eyed reflectors. None
of it matters, so just keep going,
forward or back, until you've
found the place or the place
doesn't matter. They were only

animals come down to stand
in silent formation by a road
you traveled.

          Early March.
The cold beach deserted. My kids
home in a bare house, bundled up
and listening to rock music
pirated from England. My wife
waiting for me in the bar, alone
for an hour over her sherry, and none
of us knows why I have to pace
back and forth on this flat
and birdless stretch of gleaming sand
while the violent air shouts
out its rags of speech. I recall
the calm warm sea of Florida
30 years ago, and my brother
and I staring out in the hope
that someone known and loved
would return out of air and water
and no more, a miracle a kid
could half-believe, could see
as something everyday and possible.
Later I slept alone and dreamed
of the home I never had and wakened
in the dark. A silver light sprayed
across the bed, and the little
rented room ticked toward dawn.
I did not rise. I did not go
to the window and address
the moon. I did not cry
or cry out against the hour
or the loneliness that still
was mine, for I had grown
into the man I am, and I
knew better. A sudden voice
calls out my name or a name
I think is mine. I turn.
The waves have darkened; the sky's

426

descending all around me. I read
once that the sea would come
to be the color of heaven.
They would be two seas tied
together, and between the two
a third, the sea of my own heart.
I read and believed nothing.
This little beach at the end
of the world is anywhere, and I
stand in a stillness that will last
forever or until the first light
breaks beyond these waters. Don't
be scared, the book said, don't flee
as wave after wave the breakers rise
in darkness toward their ghostly crests,
for he has set a limit to the sea
and he is at your side. The sea
and I breathe in and out as one.
Maybe this is done at last
or for now, this search for what
is never here. Maybe all that
ancient namesake sang is true.
The voice I hear now is
my own night voice, going out
and coming back in an old chant
that calms me, that calms
—for all I know—the waves
still lost out there.

nominated by Louis Gallo, Dan Masterson,
Sharon Olds, Robert Phillips and David Wojahn

DEATH'S MIDWIVES

fiction by MARGARETA EKSTRÖM

from THE ONTARIO REVIEW

NOT UNTIL SHE LOST HER HAIR did she begin to cry. It fell out in tufts, she held handfuls of it. Bewildered, she ran her hand over the top of her head, feeling its familiar shape. Her ears resisted the pressure of her hand, folded resiliently. Her forehead was damp, her nose pointed. I'm going bald, she thought. Then she began to cry.

She was sixty-four years old and couldn't remember crying for twenty years. Not like this, she thought, when she sat up at last and turned her tear-drenched pillow to the cool side. These were tears not of anger but of total surrender, tears from the very deepest roots of grief. Tears that involved her entire body, leaving her thinner and weaker, ravaged and fragile. Anything could happen to her now. She was defenseless, shaken by forces stronger than those she called upon in moments of anger, indignation, occasional hysteria.

After a brief nap she stared up at the gray ceiling. There was a crack that resembled the Gulf of Finland, a damp spot that was Leningrad. She was around forty and had just come home from a trip there. Museums had unravelled their corridors for her and displayed their paintings. She was only forty and the painful lump in her abdomen was, of course, the child. When she turned her head she had the same view now as she had had then: the tall, candy-pink buildings and beyond them the park, with chestnuts in bloom, green clouds of elm, and maples bursting into leaf, so clear she thought she could smell them. But she had lost the scents long ago. Something was growing and pressing: was she going to give birth through her ear?

The walls were calm and receptive. She has asked to have the picture removed: two red tulips in a clay pot and a black book coquettishly angled in the bottom right-hand corner. Sometimes she looked for the hole where the hook had been. When she had laboriously hunted out her glasses she could see it easily and it became a hook for her to hang her thoughts on. As long as I can see the hole, she would think, imagining how she would fix her eyes on that black spot in her hour of need, finally to be swallowed up by that minute tunnel and enclosed in the wall. Like so many others who began as small floundering bodies and ended up as one single thin trembling sigh, swallowed up by these walls.

"What about some hair tonic for me?" she asked, when the day nurse came in. But she didn't get the joke, unfortunately, and hesitated for one awful moment between a sympathetic smile, astonishment, and something bordering on accusation. All this visibly crossed her familiar, rosy face. The girl was too young. Wouldn't she be frightened later, when the time came?

Finally she pulled herself together and said, "I'll be glad to ask the doctor if you like, Mrs. Malm."

"Never mind. I can do it myself," she said wearily. Her playful urge had passed. First so many lies, and now these ice-cold showers of truth, truth, truth. She could bear no more. It was too late to be stoic.

She hadn't touched her body for a long time now. All she remembered was fruitless rubbing and tickling, hours of work and not even an echo of pleasure. Only the stubborn effort to make something happen so the dry, leathery lips would moisten once more, to feel a smile spread through her diaphragm.

Now she thought of her vagina as an empty inkwell, long-forgotten in an uninhabited cottage. If a penpoint were dipped into it, it would splay, screeching apart against the shiny walls and in the rust colored residue in the corners.

But in moments of anguish she sometimes wound a strand of her thinning hair around her index finger and bit the knuckles of her other hand, as she had done in childhood. The next day the marks, some white and some red and inflamed, spoke the depth of her fear.

"It's all part of the picture," the bold midwife had said, pressing on her stomach. That was her standard expression, her theme song: "It's all part of the picture." The swollen varicose veins, the heartburn, the waters breaking too soon, the literally unbearable pain were all part of the picture. And in the end even the floundering baby boy, dangled by one leg with screams and vernix and umbilical cord and his little red sex was all part of the picture. Part of the picture was laughter and tears of joy, and the newly bathed infant whimpering beside her, with glittering eyes that charmed her for life.

At the time she had felt more as if she were being born than giving birth. Shut in the tunnel with no going back, that was what she had been. When the pain strained her to the utmost, folding her like a jackknife, and urine sprayed all over the starched hospital gown as she squeezed the container which should have held it with hands that no longer obeyed her, she glanced across at the window. Five flights. A jump.

This time she was in the other wing on the same floor. But the thought of walking over and testing the strength of her fingers on the window latches nauseated her. She wanted to save her strength. She wanted to stay. Despite the pain. Her mind mocked her poor logic, her instinct for self-preservation, and the mocking laugh became a grimace. There was little room for intellect in this sorrowful business. Just as little as there had been when he was being pressed out of her, cut free to look at her at last.

With a few shrewd little movements she managed to reach her handbag and hunt out her diary. After the page where she had noted down the name of the hospital, six weeks ago, there was nothing but blank pages. She had never been very strong on documentation, and now it seemed entirely superfluous. One of the pockets contained her farewell letter to her son. Sometimes she took it out and read it. It made her smile because it was to him, though perhaps she should have cried because she would probably never see him again. She altered a word, added something, something silly that would make him laugh. She remembered her endless love letters to his father, the joy she had taken in writing them and in reading them time and again before mailing them. The joy of expression and awareness. The sense that everything between them had been crystal clear, that there was no need to be on her guard, to interpret looks and gestures. Then, after this enormous, overwhelming effort, there had been a gradual decline, a dilution, a neutralization which seized them both, like a mutual case of consumption. By then, their son was eighteen and there was no need to pretend. They glided apart and their love was lost to both their memories. She tried to remember what it had felt like, but all she could recover was her certainty of his friendship, respect perhaps, and their independence, as complete as if they had been born in different centuries. It was not indifference. They kept in touch. They cared. But nothing mattered any more.

The nurses came and went. The farce of the rounds was pared down to a bare minimum. Most of the time they left her alone. Sometimes she asked for sleeping pills and they gave her a few at a time, overestimating her desire to take a shortcut.

Sometimes one of the nurse's aides was in the mood to talk. She would tell her all about her neighbors who did not remove their clogs indoors, foreign families who bought the wrong things at the supermarket, children who complained about their mothers going off to work. And she listened, propped up by two pillows, trying to smile. One girl named Brita lent her a turquoise chiffon scarf to cover her hair. "You look nice!" the girl beamed, but not even the compliment could make her take her mirror out of her handbag.

In pregnancy, too, she had been transformed into an inner being with no external façade. Everything was taking place inside her, in her veins, her womb, her head. She had closed her eyes to keep out the world, mumbling to the midwife: "I'm sorry. I hope you don't mind my not looking." She had wanted to concentrate on what was taking place inside her body, on the child fighting its difficult battle in the narrow tunnel.

Suddenly the oxygen mask was pressed over her mouth, and someone lifted her head: "Breathe deeply! Breathe deeply! Even deeper!"

When she protested no, no she didn't want any help, they told her it was for the baby's sake, not hers. They had fooled her with it recently. She had breathed deeply, thinking of the baby, but they had wheeled her into intensive care, where she awoke full of needles and tubes. Of course, she thought, I must really have known that it wasn't for the baby's sake now, not now—he's over twenty now, he doesn't need my oxygen or my blood. But she had simply obeyed and breathed deeply.

She turned back the pages of her diary. There it was. She had

431

made a mark there with her thumbnail. That was when she had simply obeyed and breathed deeply. If she had not, she wouldn't be here now and her thumbnail would be a speck of ash which annoyingly landed on a white sheet hung out to dry in the neighborhood of the south cemetery.

Not much had happened since then. They had wheeled her back to her room, where her blood count had continued to fall. She knew that because she felt a kind of lethargy more profound than any tiredness she had known in her life. A dullness. An indifference. I'm turning to stone, she thought. The molecules are moving more slowly, forming new constellations. The leap through the window is an impossibility, and even the thought will be soon.

She read *Memoirs of Hadrian* and wondered if Marguerite Yourcenar were still alive or, if not, what her death had been like. When she was younger she had been curious about death. She had never seen a relative die. Never seen the victim of an accident. The bloodstained man in the tobacconist's shop on Tegnér Street might have been dying, but she had had her little boy in the car and had hurried away to spare him the sight—and herself the awkward questions.

She knew nothing of what lay ahead of her, as little as she had known of childbirth the last time she had lain here. A friend had given her a record of relaxation exercises the day before she had gone into labor, that was all. Breathe deeply. Relax. Don't tense up. Make every limb heavy and relaxed. Perhaps she should have listened to it again this time.

She remembered the turbulent waves of contractions. How, as at sea, you could see them approaching from afar, inexorably. She had forced herself to let go, be dull and indifferent, allowing the pain to wash over her, as over a stranger. And she had felt it work, felt everything open up, felt the child come closer to his life. Never before had she been so close to death. Not her own death, not a personal one. But so close to the border between life and death. She had thought quite clearly, now I know more about death than before, while lying there creating life.

The midwives had come and gone. Some went to lunch. Others worked only part time. One nurse's aide had talked about her children's new teacher, about the pleasure of seeing children interact. The real pleasure was when you had two. She had thought about having two men. She had done that once, and before the complications had become too great, it had been a real pleasure. Unusually pleasant. But she hadn't bothered much about how they had interacted.

Right now she thought no more about bodies than necessary. She was pleased to be able to urinate without a catheter. But her saliva had dried up. A damp washcloth at the corners of her mouth and a sip of orange juice to rinse with occasionally and then to spit out obediently. "Like a wine taster," she had tried to say to the consulting physician, but her tongue would not obey her, so she kept it to herself. What did they need her jokes for? Did she really care about making a good impression? Stalwart to the bitter end. You can't imagine how funny she could be, even when she knew she hadn't long to live!

"I can tell you've been here before," said the nurse in the basement room where they had shaved her pubic hair, given her an enema and taken a blood sample that night. She hadn't, of course, but she felt proud to be so bright and composed, so cooperative.

Would she have cried and moaned if she had given birth alone, in a ditch? And now—if she were on a mountain ledge, the victim of a plane crash, with only death and a void ahead . . . what would she do? What gestures and expressions, what screams and curses would she rain down on the grass and the stones and the distant clouds?

The woolly gray clouds arranged themselves like iron filings above the earth, each so full of microscopic iron particles that it was forced to follow the magnetic pattern of the earth. She remembered reading a scientific version of the creation story, and her enormous joy over those poetic facts. Perhaps the rolling rhythm of the earth altered when all the trees in the northern hemisphere burst into leaf at once, increasing the wind resistance. Perhaps its speed increased again in the autumn when there were nothing but bare branches.

This was better than Isis and Osiris, better than Ask and Embla and Ygdrasil—or were both equally far from the truth—the same saga in different costumes?

When she had still been part of life, she had complained each time a day passed without new knowledge, a new idea. Now she wondered dully what the point of it was. More dully than anxiously. A repugnant lethargy. Now even what was feasible became

433

impossible, desire was cut off at the roots. She tried to remember her child and his father, the bodies she had loved most. Straight shoulders, angular joints, firm jaws, looks of warmth and light. But they seemed unreal. More unreal than the brown medicine bottle and the small rainbow of colored pill containers you could make into long, flexible chains to use as noisemakers when there was nothing good on the radio.

How long would it last? And death as relief—what doesn't exist cannot relieve—and from what?

"I have lived a good life, better than almost any other life I know of, and better than I ever could have hoped for when I was your age," she had written in the letter. But perhaps he would be able to read between the lines that however good it had been, it now seemed terribly irrelevant, the copulation which had created his little body irrelevant, the bearing down irrelevant when he was finally pressed out of her and into life and air and breathing.

No, not that. Having given birth to him, having managed to get him out whole—that would never feel irrelevant. That was where her scepticism ended and she became a common vixen, a natural she-bear, a true-bred female cat. The baby was in her womb and had to come out. The baby had to be licked. The baby needed milk, caresses and warmth, and to lie as close to her as if he were still in the darkness of her womb. That was beyond relevance and irrelevance. It was. It was Being. And she cherished this beloved prejudice and she smoothed down its fur. Sometimes she took out his picture—the one when he was twelve—sexlessly beautiful and mischievous—and held it long in her hand, hoping she could die that way.

She was in the tunnel and there was no return. But they did not put her on a high steel bed with stirrups, and no one listened to the baby's heart with a stethoscope and said comfortingly: "I'll stay here with you until it's over."

Until it's over. Then she would be two people. It had never occurred to her that she might die in childbirth. The child kicked, wanted to come out. She had protected it for nine months, and she would not desert it in the final nine hours. Yet she had never been closer to death, for it was across that boundary the child must travel in order to live. Now it was her turn. And she asked Brita, the girl, what time her shift was over. "At six, as usual," she answered. "See you in the morning."

434

In the morning? No, oh, no. Was it going to take all that time? But her body wanted it to take all that time, preferably even more.

Now, as then, flowers arrived from her friends. Flowers from the child's father. They glowed in colorful splendor and wilted. And she was glowing with fever, and wilting at the same time. They were alike: cut off from their natural root systems, fed on cold fluids pumped right into their circulatory systems. She saw the tulips stand straight, their stems gorged with water from the vase, knowing they would die. The lilac leaves did not bother to pretend, but their multipetalled blossoms with the sweet drop of nectar in the center bloomed one by one, and she asked the cleaning lady to hand her a few—yes, to pick them—so that she could suck the tiny stems as she had in the summers long ago. She would have liked to ask the consulting physician to blow on a lilac leaf, but he probably wouldn't have known how, and doctors were easily enough embarrassed anyway. She, too, was embarrassed. Confused and shy. How would she meet her death?

She had also felt shy with her little one, newly bathed and swaddled, lying in her arms. She had grimaced ironically at his father and said: "He looks like a baby-powder ad!" She had been wheeled through endless corridors, the little one sleeping in his cocoon in her arms, his wrinkled cheek so close that she could not resist stroking it. It was all so new. And her breasts, which had lain so flat in the bra cups and rested in the hands of young men, were suddenly transformed into troughs for her piglet to slurp from. She had loved nursing him and would certainly have gone on for a year if the threat of DDT hadn't become so acute that mothers were warned not to nurse.

I will fall asleep, she thought. And when I wake up it will be over. Nothing works any more, hardly even the pain. The pain has died before me. Like the scents, the sounds, the sights. I've been left behind. I am last in my own funeral procession.

Until the older night nurse sat down close beside her and said: "Now I'll stay until . . ."

That was it. Some midwives left before life came. Others stayed and held their vigil. Now I will stay until you die, one body says to the other. Then one will get up and smooth her hair and go home to the morning chores, the shopping, the lovemaking, the weeding, the lending library and the envelopes of grocery receipts and the other will stay. Quite still. Entirely alone.

435

Then she began to talk. In a weak voice, she tried to explain and elucidate. Like a child asking for a better mark, a longer summer vacation. But the stout woman in her forties took out her knitting, and the light shone on her brown hair where an occasional gray strand gleamed.

She tried to read in the pale glow of the night light: "Even water is a pleasure which, since my illness began, I must enjoy sparingly. But even when I am struggling with death and it is mixed with my last bitter medicine, I shall try to feel its fresh tastelessness on my lips."

But the book fell from her hands and she could no longer think— book. A harsh light fell on her closed gray eyelids. Someone removed her turquoise scarf and she whimpered, as if in her sleep. "*Memoirs of Hadrian*," said a hard, educated voice, and she realized they were putting her belongings away. Entirely naked and nearly bald she would suffer the final contractions.

"A hand to hold when you die," echoed his drunken voice. He had been nineteen and, like her, had just finished high school. They had been hugging and drinking on the couch in her student room and he had executed a death-defying balancing act outside the window in her honor.

No, no hand to hold. She had not wanted the father to be there when the baby was born. "I'd rather be alone with the pain. Then you can come and share the pleasure. No—no—no, it's not for your sake. I am the one who has to go through it. I want to be alone."

Suddenly the bed was so wet. But when she said, "My water!" the stupid nurse just brought her a glass of water. She searched for words, for memories, for signs that would be understood. She was so new at this, so bewildered and belittled. She felt a moment of bitter joy: today had brought some new knowledge, a new idea.

"There, there, keep calm!" And a broad warm hand patted her cheek, stroked the back of her hand.

Now, as then, she was their lawful prey. She remembered strange women patting her big, hard, pregnant belly. She brought back wonderful memories for them. What was the knitter who sat beside her now, and who had reached the armhole, thinking?

"Is he all right?"

"Oh, yes, just keep calm, you're doing fine. I can feel eight inches of head here. You're dilated beautifully." A kind Finn dipped his fingers deep into her and reported from the life on the other side of birth.

She had hoped that he would remember, and send Virginia stocks and snapdragons. But a bouquet of them arrived from her colleagues at the university instead. What did they have to do with the birth?

"Red nose. Golden mouth. Fleet foot. Sweet lark. Mamma's little Oedi-puss." And she had promised to marry him soon, as soon as he was a tiny bit bigger. And at the age of three months when he had fallen asleep on her stomach in a wide, sagging bed in England, she had fallen asleep too and dreamed he was inside her, but just with his little tiny penis, and it was a sweet, light union, far distant from incest and pornography. And yet she had never told anyone about it.

The peculiar knitter stuck her needles into her one by one, knit one, purl one, and the knits had thorns. She turned slowly onto her side, but some new tubes stopped her there. A voice in a loudspeaker echoed, and footsteps ran. Footsteps ran off with young bodies, away from her immobility.

At last she made her way up to the surface. She had dived too deeply from the cliff, into the black waters. Her mother and father smiled at her from out of a blue beach robe and the scent of the sun on the stones and tanned skin came to her nose. Her whole body was shivering, and blue with gooseflesh. They had to rub her warm, but could not stop her shaking.

Then she was suddenly in a yard. The book on her lap was *Memoirs of Hadrian*. An oak spread its foliage over her head like a parasol. She could hear his voice through an open window. It chattered and babbled, interpreting and explaining. And he couldn't say his s's. She laboriously stretched her neck and looked diagonally upwards. The sun was shining through the window. The chestnuts on the horizon bowed to an imperceptible breeze. She couldn't smell them from here. The knitter had fallen asleep over her needles. The light angled glaringly off the sterile hospital medicine stand. But all she saw was the sun bouncing through the nursery window, and his voice babbled on, and as she stretched to see his face, the sun struck her with its double-edged axe.

Like dust humming in the wind and music on a keyboard of cotton. Whispers and shuffles, wheeling and covering. Tubes

437

disconnected and clothing removed before the rigor mortis sets in. Like shadow theater, this whole thousand-headed hospital that descends slowly into the darkness of a new day, while a beam of light laughs in a window and a child talks and talks of life.

—TRANSLATED FROM THE SWEDISH BY LINDA SCHENCK

nominated by Paul Bowles

SEASON'S GREETINGS

by LEONARD NATHAN

from CEDAR ROCK

Waiting for the signal to change
in her favor, she saw him again
between sweeps of the windshield wiper,
the same man on the same corner
last Christmas, remembered now
because he was so wrong for seeing
this time of year in this part of town
where furs and jewels stared back
at one another in show windows
that he passed unseeing and unseen
in a peacoat blotched and misshapen by age
and rain, himself blotched and misshapen
under a black stocking cap,
in one hand a brown paper parcel
tied with string, and now suddenly,
she was anxious—no, fearful,
because if life, her life anyway,
meant something (and she wasn't sure
it did), meetings as odd as this
might have some purpose, a sort
of repetition to make a point
she knew she wasn't getting yet
and didn't want to because now
she wasn't just fearful, but guilty as well,
and felt the petty cash in her purse
turn to ashes, the gifts piled

in the back seat became a reason
to look away ashamed, and then
it came to her—a vision—to her
who always saw in things mere things:
there was a box wrapped prettily
in shiny red foil, and in it,
she knew, was the future, its top torn open
to reveal a little room
with a cot, one rickety chair,
an old cardtable, on it,
a dish and cup, both plastic,
and three black wire coat hangers
hung in a closet otherwise empty
and the smudged window stared blindly out
on smoky brick—the right place
to meditate on soup kitchens
or on the intensive care unit,
but it was the honking behind her that woke her
to this world where the man, whatever
he meant, had crossed before her, his eyes
ahead, his heavy face neutral
as worn stone that asked nothing
on its way into the darkened air,
and she saw she had the green light
to move, still shaken, to where
she must to get on home to the tree
the children had put up for her,
the grandchildren were now trimming,
and eased into quieter streets,
feeling boxed inside steel
and black traffic, driven below
by a power she never understood,
and feeling—well, sort of—followed,
and, glancing in the rear-view mirror,
smiled at her little panic, but drove
faster, recalling that this was the time
for exchanging gifts and she had given
that man (somewhere behind her) her guilt
(as if he needed that) so now

it was his turn, and she drove faster,
wondering with a cold thrill just what
he'd picked for her, and slowed down
when she saw ahead through rainy dark
another vision—her lucky day!:
Under the tree, almost buried
in glittering golds and greens and reds
a brown paper parcel tied with string,
with her name on it, to be opened
the morning of Jesus' nativity,
and what it contained to be held up
in shaky fingers to her breast
(where her heart now worked unwilling
as a windshield wiper) to find,
of course, it was a perfect fit,
a garment made for her alone
centuries ago, and the man would be there
nodding in the corner, unseen
by the others—not really a man,
a thing older than humans, older
than Christmas, as though a stone or log
could, with terrible effort, take
our shape to tell us something, something
we had to know but didn't want to
because there was no remedy for it,
not even children (it was much older
than love), and she thought of all that ruin
of beautiful torn wrapping paper,
the afterbirth of giving, and saw
also she was simply home, parked
in the driveway, sitting motionless
to stare at the fragile strings of light
melting in the drops that ran
across the glass, and it was then
she put her head down on the wheel
and cried softly because she knew
the reasons for crying and knew too
that if nothing was saved of all the works
of joy, nothing would stop wanting

to be reborn, which made life
a kind of defiance. Yes. Well, then,
drying her eyes, she was ready now
to go in, ready to receive
whatever the children thought she wanted.

nominated by Naomi Shihab Nye and Gary Soto

VESPER SPARROWS

by DEBORAH DIGGES

from ANTAEUS

I love to watch them sheathe themselves mid-air,
shut wings and ride the light's poor spine

to earth, to touch down in gutters, in the rainbowed
urine of suicides, just outside Bellevue's walls.

From in there the ransacked cadavers are carried
up the East River to Potter's Field

as if they were an inheritance,
gleaned of savable parts,

their diseases jarred and labeled, or incinerated,
the ashes of metastisized vision

professing the virus that lives beyond the flesh,
in air . . .

       The first time I saw the inside of anything
alive, a downed bird opened cleanly

under my heel. I knelt
to watch the spectral innards shine and quicken,

the heart-whir magnify.
And though I can't say now what kind of bird it was,

443

nor the season, spring or autumn, what
dangerous transition,

I have identified so many times that sudden
earnest spasm of the throat in children,

or in the jaundiced faces of the dying,
the lower eye-lids straining upward.

Fear needs its metaphors.
I've read small helplessnesses make us maternal.

Even the sparrows feel it
nesting this evening in traffic lights.

They must have remembered, long enough to mate,
woods they've never seen,

but woods inbred, somehow, up the long light of instinct,
the streaked siennas of a forest floor

born now into the city,
the oak umbers, and the white tuft

of tail feathers, like a milkweed meadow
in which their song, as Burroughs heard it,

could be distinguished:
come-come-where-where-all-together-

down-the-hill . . .
here, where every history is forfeited,

where the same names of the different dead greet
each other and commingle

above the hospital's heaps of garbage.
From the ward windows, fingerprinted,

from the iron-grated ledges,
hundreds flock down for the last feed of the day

and carry off into the charitable dusk what
cannot be digested.

nominated by Stanley Plumly

WILDERNESS

by VERN RUTSALA

from BROWN JOURNAL OF THE ARTS

We invented these trees and mountains, that long gash
of gulley tumbling toward the lake.
By main force we brought each rock into being,
each of a different size and shape, each carved
into its dim life by us. We squinted that mica
from nothingness through our eyelashes and pulled
each giant fir from the ground with tweezers—
each beginning thinner than a hair but we
nursed them up with curiosity and the weak strength
of our thin fingers. Before we came
none of this was here—all the ferns and brush
were made with pinking shears. We shoveled
every lake and compelled water
to bear the fruit of fish. With our pens we drew
the creeks and nudged bear and deer from deep shadows.
None of this was here before we came.
We invented these trees and mountains,
conjured each pebble and boulder, shaped
those rough peaks with our hands, nursed those great trees
up and up from the near nothingness
of hairs. A whiskbroom and moonlight
made cougar and wildcat, dry sticks and dust
the snake and mole, with rain and mud we made
beaver, wood chips formed eagle and hawk we whittled
so fast! We needed all this, you see,
not for you but for us. We needed

a wilderness but had found none. Which is why
we invented this lovely one just here
between Thompson and Brazee in Northeast Portland.
Our love, you see, demanded such a setting.

nominated by Maura Stanton

RONDO

by LINDA GREGG

from SONORA REVIEW

When Saskia lay down that night, she was wet
under the chin and she might die. She was weak
and her teeth showed. One foot touched the other
and should not. She didn't push against me
with her feet. She didn't eat my hair.

My feet were bare when I saw her dead.
My blanket was still warm when I took her down
the wooden steps to the grass and the fig tree
and buried her in the ground.
My spirit was a fountain from all the air,
from the giving and the taking. I was on my hands
and knees putting what I love over the body.
A leaf fell on her from the tree.

I hold on to so many things. When I lived on the island,
I climbed the vacant mountain again and again
to put pomegranate on the rocks where Aphrodite
had been. My friend Michiko sat gentle at her table
under the tree on the other mountain and did not live
long after she left. I hold my mother, the earth and cows.
We go by boat, bicycle, by owl to get beyond ourselves,
beyond this world. To include the other, and fail.
Or get only a little. I carry ashes across this snow
and dump them on the place that will sink down

when the whiteness is gone. Some of the ashes blow
a small distance, making a stain. I remember
the woman in Kurosawa's film after they lost the battle
with something on her back looking for people
she knew by their absence—as the planet was found
because of the force of the invisible.

I sat in Portsmouth square after Saskia,
watching the Chinese man talk crazy to me as long
as I faced him. Between him and the row of pines
(with poplars behind), a man sat on the concrete shaking
as Saskia did, marring the lotus he was making.
The trees are fine, I thought, even though they don't shine.

So I went at random into a store directly behind me.
A man came forward and said, what do you want?
What do you have? I said. I sell things
for the living and the dead, he answered. And I said,
I want to buy those things. Two women at the rear
were eating soup, sucking the crab shells. I bought
a pink dress made of paper with pomegranates on it.
Paper things of red with green and black and yellow.
I bought money for the ghosts and the spirits,
remembering the fig leaf falling that morning
just before I covered her with dirt. A day I touched
life twice. One real, one of paper. One for myself,
one for both realms which want to touch.

That was the religious part. But Saskia was dead and Saskia
might die. By fear and memory. Her hands felt small,
like balls on sticks under the blanket. She might die
and that softness go away. Nothing to be done.
The fog comes in. Can we let memory suffice? Is it possible
to keep the body about itself? Hands holding dirt.
The poplar trees not shining behind the dark pines.
The man on the concrete shivering. The custard pie I ate
after which cost sixty cents in the Chinese coffee shop.
Custard and coffee and memory and presence. The spirit

449

of her soft fur and the body hardened by death.
Myself who isn't anything stopped yet. Who must learn
    everything
over because she is another with my memory. Taken away.
Mostly lost. The geranium I put on her, paper heart,
paper fish, lots of mint. Five-fingered fern
and the fig leaf that fell by itself.
My heart vacant. My position like a rabbit.
My eyes vacant, blurring her in the light.

nominated by David Wojahn

TO FUTURE ELEANORS

by ELEANOR ROSS TAYLOR

from *New and Selected Poems* (Stuart Wright, Publisher)

How will you
cut off from Zions,
　fall on your knees among the lions?

What if you
cut off from hymns
　confound worksong with anthem

Cut off from Scripture
　find sense suspect
　and worship
　　incoherence—
　distrust the laces
　and adore the tangled thread?

What of you
　without a holy thing,
　but every sacrilege
　of the sacrileged class?

Godsave your unsuspecting fists
grasping the fiery ladder bare,
your forehead
fighting a wordless solitaire.

Without some future language
how can I ask you?
If I could ask in Euphorese,
Moonskrit, in Ecolow. . . .

What will you do with
Grandma's savings—
those relics atticked
in your head
of effort, vision?

On pain of death, scratch pictures
in the dust
            as she did—
I fear my after-thirst.

nominated by Barbara Thompson

OUTSTANDING WRITERS

(The editors also wish to mention the following important works published by small presses last year. Listing is alphabetical by author's last name.)

FICTION

When This Van is Rockin' Don't Bother Knockin' — Keith Abbott (Coffee House)
Autoclysms — Michael Anania (Thunder's Mouth Press)
from The Heart of the Order — Tony Ardizzone (TriQuarterly)
Inventory — Lynne Barrett (Minnesota Review)
Two — R. Bartkowech (Center Press)
Winter Journey — Charles Baxter (Black Warrior Review)
Triptych 2 — Madison Smartt Bell (Crescent Review)
Saving the Boat People — Joe David Bellamy (Ontario Review)
The Salamander Kind — Hal Bennett (Callaloo)
Dr. H. A. Monynihan — Lucia Berlin (Tombouctou Books)
The Films of R. Nixon — Kenneth Bernard (Fiction International)
A Dream of Fair Women — Gina Berriault (Kenyon Review)
Massachusetts 1932 — Paul Bowles (Conjunctions)
Two Minute Hero — P. M. Brandt (Croton Review)
The Darktown Strutters — Wesley Brown (Phoebe)
Crowe Bovey's Burning-Cold — Carolyn Chute (Agni Review)
A Field of Corn — Carolyn Chute (Ohio Review)
Bodies of the Rich — John J. Clayton (University of Illinois Press)
Billy Will's Song — Daniel Curley (Quarterly West)
Breaking Over — R. C. Day (NER/BLQ)
The Fugitive — R. C. Day (Kenyon Review)

Berkie — Susan M. Dodd (University of Iowa Press)
Land Where My Fathers Died — Andre Dubus (Antaeus)
Saving the Dead — Kurt Duecker (Shenandoah)
All Set About With Fever Trees — Pam Durban (Georgia Review)
The Biggest, Most Perfect Bubble in the Whole World — Joan Eades (North Dakota Review)
A Daughter's Heart — Susan Engberg (Wisconsin Academy Review)
The Plunge of the Brave — Louise Erdrich (NER/BLQ)
Harry, Sylvia & Sylvia and So On — Welch Everman (Grand Street)
Like A Hully-Gully But Not So Slow — Anne Finger (13th Moon)
Inside The Body of a Green Apple Tree — Leon Forrest (Iowa Review)
Everybody's Got A Hungry Heart — K. C. Frederick (Quarterly West)
Fruit of the Month — Abby Frucht (Ontario Review)
Culp — William H. Gass (Grand Street)
TV — Brad Gooch (Sea Horse Press)
Island Lives — Jaimy Gordon (Sun)
Embarrassment — Donald Hall (Ploughshares)
The Hospital Story — James Baker Hall (Shenandoah)
Breaking and Entering — James Hannah (Crazyhorse)
from All The Dark and Beautiful Warriors — Lorraine Hansberry (TriQuarterly)
The Day The Kites Went Away — George Hitchcock (Quarry West)
Ain't No Indians in Hell — Linda Hogan (13th Moon)
Moths — Mary Hood (Kenyon Review)
The Day Satchel Paige and the Pittsburgh Crawfords Came to Hertford, N.C. — Bill Howard (Spitball)
Only the Little Bone — David Huddle (NER/BLQ)
A Room At Oberc's — Bruce Hunsberger (Seattle Review)
Fragment of An Ancient Face — Aaron Jacobs (Agada)
The Mango Community — Josephine Jacobsen (Ontario Review)
Broken Glass — Harold Jaffe (Minnesota Review)
John Crow — Harold Jaffe (Fiction International)
Starring — Cori Jones (Fiction Network)
Infinite Variety — Rodney Jones (TriQuarterly)
Home Again — Paul Kafka (Shenandoah)

454

The Woman Who Talked to Horses — Leon Rooke (Yale Review)
Heat — William Pitt Root (Montana Review)
Instruments of Seduction — Norman Rush (Paris Review)
Splittin' a Dime — Alfred Schwaid (Chicago Review)
At Sea — S. M. Schwartz (Sequoia)
Trespass — Sandra Scofield (Ploughshares)
No Place To Be On Christmas — Janet Beeler Shaw (Story Quarterly)
Approximations — Mona Simpson (Ploughshares)
The Colonel's Daughter — Rose Tremain (Grand Street)
Lu-lu — Joy Williams (Grand Street)
The Axe, The Axe, The Axe — Eric Wilson (Massachusetts Review)
Impressions — Rudy Wilson (Paris Review)
Sister — Tobias Wolff (Ploughshares)
T.V. Guide — Allen Woodman (Carolina Quarterly)
from Seduction by Light — Al Young (Quilt)

NONFICTION

Family — Walter Abish (Antaeus)
I Bow to Chin Shengt'an — Joel Agee (Virginia Center for Creative Arts)
Durations — David Antin (Formations)
The Caretaker's Daughter — Dudley Bailey (Prairie Schooner)
Last Pictures — John Berger (Threepenny Review)
From Harriet Monroe to AQ: Selected Women's Literary Journals (1912-1972) — Mary Biggs (13th Moon)
Growing Old — David Bradley (Virginia Center for Creative Arts)
The Uses of Biography — David Bromwich (Yale Review)
Literatures of Milieux — Algis Budrys (Missouri Reiview)
Memories of North Pennsylvania — Frederick Buell (NER/BLQ)
A Possibly Momentary Declaration in Favor of William Butler Yeats and Charles Ellsworth Russell — Hayden Carruth (Conjunctions)
The Question of Voice — Denis Donoghue (Antaeus)
The Great Chain of Quantum Being: What The Physicists Are Telling Us — Louis Gallo (Missouri Review)
The Death of the Author — William H. Gass (Salmagundi)
The Habitations of the Word — William H. Gass (Kenyon Review)

POETRY

OUTSTANDING SMALL PRESSES

(These presses made or received nominations for this edition of *The Pushcart Prize*. See the *International Directory of Little Magazines and Small Presses*, Dustbooks, Box 1056, Paradise, CA 95969, for subscription rates, manuscript requirements and a complete international listing of small presses.)

Abbetira Publications, P.O. Box 30001, San Bernardino, CA 92413
Adler Publishing Co., P.O. Box 9342, Rochester, NY 14604
Agada, 2020 Essex St., Berkeley, CA 94703
The Agni Review, P.O. Box 229, Cambridge, MA 02138
Ahnene Publications, Box 456, Maxville, Ontario, CAN. K0C 1T0
Ahsahta Press, English Dept., Boise State Univ., Boise, ID 83725
AKLM Publications, 42 Lake St., Wakefield, MA 01880
Alaska Quarterly Review, English Dept., Univ. of Alaska/Anchorage, 3221 Providence, Anchorage, AK 99508
Alcatraz Editions, 354 Hoover Rd., Santa Cruz, CA 95065
Alexandrian Press, 1070 Aratradero Rd., P.O. Box 10080, Palo Alto, CA 94303
Ali Baba Press, 163 Candy Circle, Winterville, GA 30683
Alice James Books, 128 Mt. Auburn St., Cambridge, MA 02138
Amelia, P.O. Box 2385, Bakersfield, CA 93303
American-Canadian Publishers, Inc. Drawer 2078, Portales, NM 88130
American Poetry Review, 1616 Walnut St., Philadelphia, PA 19103
The American Scholar, 1811 Q St., NW, Washington, DC 20009

American Studies Press, Inc., 13511 Palmwood La., Tampa, FL 33624

Andrew Mountain Press, P.O. Box 14363, Hartford, CT 06114

Anhinga Press, P.O. Box 10423, Tallahassee, FL 32302

Another Chicago Magazine, Box 11223, Chicago, IL 60611

Antaeus, 18 West 30th St., New York, NY 10001

The Antioch Review, P.O. Box 148, Yellow Springs, OH 45387

The Apalachee Quarterly, P.O. Box 20106, Tallahassee, FL 32304

Arkansas Technical University, School of Liberal & Fine Arts, Russelville, AR 72801

Armenian General Benevolent Union, 585 Saddle River Rd., Saddle Brook, NJ 07662

Artemis, P.O. Box 945, Roanoke, VA 24005

Ascent, 100 English Bldg., Univ. of Illinois, Urbana, IL 61801

Asphodel, 613 Howard Ave., Pitman, NJ 08071

Atticus Press, P.O. Box 34044, San Diego, CA 92103

August House, Inc., 1010 West Third St., Little Rock, AR 72201

BOA Editions, 92 Park Ave., Brockport, NY 14420

Bad Henry Review, P.O. Box 45, Van Brent Sta., Brooklyn, NY 11215

bamboo ridge press, 990 Hahaione St., Honolulu, HI 96825

Banana Productions, P.O. Box 3655, Vancouver, B.C., CAN V6B 3Y8

The Barnwood Press, River House, RR2, Box 11C, Daleville, IN 47334

Barrington Press, 22669 Nadine Circle, Torrance, CA 90505

Basal Books, 726 Lafayette Ave., Cincinnati, OH 45220

Beginning, 1530 Bladensburg Rd., Ottumwa, IA 52501

Bellingham Review, 412 N. State St., Bellingham, WA 98225

Beloit Poetry Journal, RFD 2, Box 154, Ellsworth, ME 04605

Berkeley Poets Workshop & Press, P.O. Box 459, Berkeley, CA 94701

Berkeley Works, 2206 M. L. King Way, #C, Berkeley, CA 94704

Between C & D, 255 E. 7th St., New York, NY 10009

Beyond Baroque Foundation, P.O. Box 806, Venice, CA 90291

The Beiler Press, P.O. Box 3856, St. Paul, MN 55165

Big Foot Press, 7 Suffolk Lane, East Islip, NY 11730

Bilingual Review Press, Graduate School, SUNY, Binghamton, NY 13901

BITS Press, English Dept., Case Western Res. Univ., Cleveland, OH 44106

Black American Literature Forum, Indiana State Univ., Terre Haute, IN 47809

Black Buzzard Press, 4705 South 8th Rd., Arlington, VA 22204

Black Ice Press, 6022 Sunnyview NE, Salem, OR 97305

Black Sparrow Press, P.O. Box 3993, Santa Barbara, CA 93130

Black Swan Books, P.O. Box 327, Redding Ridge, CT 06876

Black Warrior Review, P.O. Box 2936, University, AL 35486

Blackwells Press, 2925B Freedom Blvd., Watsonville, CA 95076

Blast, (see Black Sparrow Press)

Blue Cloud Quarterly, Blue Cloud Abbey, Marvin, SD 57251

Blue Moon & Confluence Press, College of Arts & Sc., Spalding Hall, Lewiston, ID 83501

Blue Unicorn, 22 Avon Rd., Kensington, CA 94707

Bluefish, P.O. Box 1601, Southampton, NY 11968

Blueline, Blue Mountain Lake, NY 12812

Bomb Magazine, P.O. Box 178, Prince Sta., New York, NY 10012

Bombshelter Press, 642½ Orange St., Los Angeles, CA 90048

Books of a Feather, P.O. Box 3095, Terminal Annex, Los Angeles, CA 90051

Brightwaters Press, Inc., 235 Park Ave., SO, New York, NY 10003

The Broken Stone, P.O. Box 246, Reynoldsburg, OH 43068

Brooklyn Review, English Dept., Brooklyn College, Brooklyn, NY 11210

Brushfire, 118 W. Palm Lane, Phoenix, AZ 85003

CabArt/CabPress, 1000 W. Huron, Apt. 5B, Ann Arbor, MI 48103

Cache Review, 4805 E. 29th, Tucson, AZ 85711

Cafe Solo, 7975 San Marcos Ave., Atascadero, CA 93422

California Quarterly, Univ. of California, Davis, CA 95616

Callaloo, English Dept., Univ. of Kentucky, Lexington, KY 40506

Calliope, Creative Writing, Roger Williams College, Bristol, RI 02809

Calliope's Corner, P.O. Box 110647, Anchorage, AK 99511

Calyx, P.O. Box B, Corvallis, OR 97339

Cambridge Poetry Magazine, 602 King's College, Cambridge, CB2 1ST, England

Canadian Literature, Univ. of British Columbia, 213-2021-W. Mall, Vancouver, BC, CAN V6T 1W6

The Cape Rock, SEMO State Univ., Cape Girardeau, MO 63701

Caribbean Review, Florida Internat'l University, Tamiami Trail, Miami, FL 33199

Carolina Quarterly, Greenlaw Hall 066-A, Univ. of N.C., Chapel Hill, NC 27514

Carolina Wren Press, 300 Barclay Rd., Chapel Hill, NC 27514

Cedar Rock Press, 1121 Madeline, New Braunfels, TX 78130

The Centennial Review, 110 Morill Hall, Michigan St. Univ., East Lansing, MI 48824

Center Press, P.O. Box 387, Ranches of Taos, NM 87557

Central Park, P.O. Box 1446, New York, NY 10023

Chariton Review, Northeast Missouri St. Univ., Kirksville, MO 63501

Charnel House, P.O. Box 281, Sta. S, Toronto, CAN M5M 4L7

Chattahoochee Review, DeKalb Community College, Dunwoody, GA 30338

Chelsea, Box 5880, Grand Central Sta., New York, NY 10163

Chiaroscuro, 108 N. Plain St., Ithaca, NY 14850

Chicago Review, Univ. of Chicago, Faculty Exchange, Box C, Chicago, IL 60637

The Chicot Press, Box 21988, Baton Rouge, LA 70893

Cincinnati Poetry Review, Univ. of Cincinnati, Cincinnati, OH 45221

City Miner Books, P.O. Box 176, Berkeley, CA 94701

Cleveland St, University Poetry Center, 1983 E. 24th St., Cleveland, OH 44115

Clockwatch, (see Driftwood Publications)

Coelacanth Publications, 55A Bluecoat, Irvine, CA 92714

Coffee House Press, 213 E. 4th St., St. Paul, MN 55101

cold-drill, Boise St. University, 1910 University Dr., Boise, ID 83725

Confluence Press, Inc., Spalding Hall, L-C Campus, Lewiston, ID 83501

Confrontation, C. W. Post of Long Island Univ., Greenvale, NY 11548

Conjunctions, 33 West 9th St., New York, NY 10011

Copper Canyon Press, P.O. Box 271, Port Townsend, WA 98368

Cornfield Review, Ohio State Univ., 1465 Mt. Vernon Ave., Marion, OH 43302

Cotton Lane Press, 2 Cotton Lane, Augusta, GA 30902

Cottonwood Arts Foundation, P.O. Box 2731, Norman, OK 73070

Cottonwood Review, Box J, Kansas Union, Univ. of Kansas, Lawrence, KS 66044

Coydog Review, 203 Halton Lane, Watsonville, CA 95076

Coyote Love Press, 27 Deering St., Portland, ME 04101

Crawl Out Your Window, 4641 Park Blvd., San Diego, CA 92116

Crazyhorse, University of Arkansas, Little Rock, AR 72204

Creeping Bent, 433 W. Market St., Bethlehem, PA 18018

The Crescent Review, P.O. Box 15065, Winston-Salem, NC 27103

Croissant & Company, P.O. Box 282, Athens, OH 45701

Cross-Canada Writers Quarterly, Box 277, Sta. F, Toronto, Ont. M4Y 2L7, CAN

Crosscurrents, 2200 Glastonbury Rd., Westlake Village, CA 91361

Croton Review, 340 Grand St., Croton-on-Hudson, NY 10520

Cumberland Poetry Review, P.O. Box 120128, Acklen Sta., Nashville, TN 37212

Curbstone Press, 321 Jackson St., Willimantic, CT 06226

CutBank, University of Montana, Missoula, MT 59812

Dawn Valley Press, P.O. Box 58, New Wilmington, PA 16142

Dawnwood Press, Two Park Ave., Suite 2650, New York, NY 10016

Denver Quarterly, Univ. of Denver, Denver, CO 80208

Descant, P.O. Box 314, Sta. P, Toronto, Ontario, CAN M5S 2S8

Descant, English Dept., TCU, Fort Worth, TX 76129

Dimension, Box 26673, Austin, TX 78755

Dog Ear Press, P.O. Box 143, So. Harpswell, ME 04079

Dolphin Moon, P.O. Box 22262, Baltimore, MD 21203

Domesday Books, P.O. Box 734, Peter Stuyvesant Sta., New York, NY 10009

Dooryard Press, P.O. Box 221, Story, WY 82842

Dragon Gate, Inc., 508 Lincoln St., Port Townsend, WA 98368

Driftwood Publications, 737 Penbrook Way, Hartland, WI 53029

Duck Soup, English Dept., North Lake College, 5001 N. MacArthur Blvd., Irving, TX 75038

Duir Press, 919 Sutter, #9, San Francisco, CA 94109

Ron Dultz Publishing, P.O. Box 985, Reseda, CA 91335

Earth's Daughters, P.O. Box 41, Central Park Sta., Buffalo, NY 14215

Electrum, 2222 Silk Tree, Tustin, CA 92680
Elizabeth Street Press, 240 Elizabeth St., New York, NY 10012
Epoch, Cornell University, Ithaca, NY 14853
Exile, P.O. Box 1768, Novato, CA 94948

Fabbro, English Dept., Univ. of Kentucky, 1215 Patterson Office
    Tower, Lexington, KY 40506
Fairisher Press, P.O. Box 9090, Rapid City, SD 57709
Feminist Studies, c/o Women's Studies, Univ. of Md., College
    Park, MD 20742
Fiction Collective, Inc., English Dept., Brooklyn College, Brook-
    lyn, NY 11210
Fiction International, English Dept., San Diego St. Univ., San
    Diego, CA 92182
Fiction Monthly, 545 Haight St., Suite 67, San Francisco, CA
    94117
Fiction Network, P.O. Box 5651, San Francisco, CA 94101
Field, Rice Hall, Oberlin College, Oberlin, OH 44074
The Figures, RD 3, Box 179, Great Barrington, MA 01230
Fire, P.O. Box 811, Rochester, MN 55903
Fireweed Press, P.O. Box 83970, Fairbanks, AK 99708
Floating Island Publications, P.O. Box 516, Point Reyes Station,
    CA 94956
Florida Arts Gazette Press, Inc. P.O. Box 397, Himmarshee
    Village, Fort Lauderdale, FL 33302
The Florida Review, English Dept., Univ. of Central Florida,
    Orlando, FL 32816
Flume Press, 644 Citrus Ave., Chico, CA 95926
Friction, 2130 Arapahoe Ave., Boulder, CO 80302
Frontiers, Women Studies, Univ. of Colorado, Boulder, CO 80309

Galileo Press, 15201 Wheeler Lane, Sparks, MD 21152
Gallery Works, 1465 Hammersley Ave., Bronx, NY 10469
Gargoyle/Paycock Press, P.O. Box 3567, Washington, DC 20007
Georgia Review, Univ. of Georgia, Athens, GA 30602
The Goldsmith Press, Ltd., Newbridge, Co. Kildare, Ireland
Grand Street, 50 Riverside Drive, New York, NY 10024
Granta, 44a Hobson St., Cambridge, CB1 1NL, England
Grass-Hooper Press, 4030 Connecticut St., St. Louis, MO 63116
Graywolf Press, P.O. Box 142, Port Townsend, WA 98368

Green's Magazine, P.O. Box 3236, Regina, Sask., Canada S4P 3H1

The Greensboro Review, English Dept., Univ. of N.C., Greensboro, NC 27412

Guild Press, P.O. Box 22583, Robbinsdale, MN 55422

Heirloom Books, P.O. Box 15472, Detroit, MI 48215

The Harbor Review, English Dept., Univ. of Mass., Boston, MA 02125

Helicon Nine, P.O Box 22412, Kansas City, MO 64113

Hob-Nob, 715 Dorsea Rd., Lancaster, PA 17601

Holy Cow! Press, P.O. Box 618, Minneapolis, MN 55440

Home Planet News, P.O. Box 415, Stuyvesant Sta., New York, NY 10009

Horizons, Star Route 3, Box 9A, Hermosa, SD 57744

HOW (ever), 554 Jersey, San Francisco, CA 94114

The Hudson Review, 684 Park Ave., New York, NY 10021

Illinois Writers Review, P.O. Box 562, Macomb, IL 61455

Illuminations, (see Rathasker Press)

Indiana Review, 316 N. Jordan Ave., Indiana Univ., Bloomington, IN 47405

Individual Artists of Oklahoma, P.O. Box 5036, Norman, OK 73103

Integrity Times Press, 118 Laidley St., San Francisco, CA 94131

The Iowa Review, University of Iowa, Iowa City, IA 52242

I. Reed Books, 1446 Sixth St., #D, Berkeley, CA 94710

Ironwood, P.O. Box 40907, Tucson, AZ 85717

Israel Horizons, 150 Fifth Ave., Rm. 1002, New York, NY 10011

Ithaca House, 108 N. Plain St., Ithaca, NY 14850

Jam Today, P.O. Box 249, Northfield, VT 05663

Johns Hopkins University Press, The Writing Seminars, Baltimore, MD 21218

Journal of Regional Criticism, 1025 Garner St., Box 18, Colorado Springs, CO 80905

Jump River Press, Rte. 1, Box 10, Prentice, WI 54556

Kaldron, P.O. Box 541, Halcyon, CA 93420

Kalliope, 3939 Roosevelt Blvd., Jacksonville, FL 32205

Kansas Quarterly, Kansas State Univ., Manhattan, KS 66506

Kelsey St. Press, P.O. Box 9235, Berkeley, CA 94709

Kenyon Review, Kenyon College, Gambier, OH 43022

Kinraddie Press, P.O. Box 15272, Sante Fe, NM 87506

KIO (Kick it Over) Collective, P.O. Box 5811, Sta. A, Toronto, Ont., M5W 1P2 CAN.

Labyris Press, Box 16102, Lansing, MI 48933

Lake Street Review, Box 7188, Powderhorn Sta., Minneapolis, MN 55407

Lame Johnny Press, Rte. 3, Box 9A, Hermosa, SD 57744

Laughing Bear Press, P.O. Box 36159, Denver, CO 80236

Laurel Review, W. Va. Wesleyan College, Buckhannon, W. VA 26201

Lighthouse Books, P.O. Box 882884, San Francisco, CA 94188

line, Eng. Dept., Simon Fraser Univ., Burnabu, B.C. V5A 1S6, CAN.

Lips, P.O. Box 1345, Montclair, NJ 07042

The Literary Review, Fairleigh Dickinson Univ., Madison, NJ 07940

Little Free Press, Rt. 2, Box 136, Cushing, MN 56443

The Long Story, 11 Kingston St., North Andover, MA 01845

Lost & Found Times, (see Luna Bisonte Prods.)

Lost Roads Publishers, P.O. Box 5848, Providence, RI 02903

Lotus Press, P.O. Box 21607, Detroit, MI 48221

Luna Bisonte Prods., 137 Leland Ave., Columbus, OH 43214

MSS, SUNY, Binghamton, NY 13901

Macdonald Publishers, Edgefield Rd., Loanhead, Midlothian, EH20 9SY, Scotland

The Madison Review, Eng. Dept., Univ. of Wisconsin/Madison, 600 N. Park St., Madison, WI 53715

Manna, Rt. #8, Box 368, Sanford, NC 27330

Massachusetts Review, Univ. of Mass., Amherst, MA 01002

The Maya Press, 1716 Ocean Ave., Box 181, San Francisco, CA 94112

Memphis State Review, English Dept., Memphis State Univ., Memphis, TN 38152

Merging Media, 59 Sandra Circle, A-3, Westfield, NJ 07090

Mho & Mho Works, Box 33135, San Diego, CA 92103

Micah Publications, 255 Humphrey St., Marblehead, MA 01945

Michigan Quarterly Review, Univ. of Michigan, Ann Arbor, MI 48109

Mid-American Review, Eng. Dept., Bowling Green St. Univ., Bowling Green, OH 43403

Middleburg Press, Box 166, Orange City, IA 51040

Milkweed Chronicle, Box 24303, Minneapolis, MN 55424

The Minnesota Review, English Dept., Oregon State Univ., Corvallis, OR 97331

Miriam Press, 6009 Edgewood La., Alexandria, VA 22310

Mississippi Arts & Letters, P.O. Box 3510, Hattiesburg, MS 39403

Mississippi Review, Univ. of Southern Miss., Hattiesburg, MS 39406

Mississippi Valley Review, Eng. Dept., Western Ill. Univ., Macomb, IL 61455

Missouri Review, English Dept., 231 Arts & Sc., Univ. of Missouri, Columbia, MO 65211

Modern Haiku, P.O. Box 1752, Madison, WI 53701

Momo's Press, 45 Sheridan, San Francisco, CA 94103

The Montana Review, (see Owl Creek Press)

Mothering Publications, Inc., P.O. Box 8410, Santa Fe, NM 87504

Mountain Laurel Publications, P.O. Box 1621, Harrisburg, PA 17105

Moving Parts Press, 419A Maple St., Santa Cruz, CA 95060

Mylabris Press, case postale 171, 1018 Lausanne, Switzerland

Mystery Time, P.O. Box 2377, Coeur d'Alene, ID 83814

NRG Magazine, 6735 SE 78th, Portland, OR 97206

Naked Man Press, c/o M. Smetzer, Eng. Dept., BGSU, Bowling Green, OH 43403

Nantucket Review, P.O. Box 1234, Nantucket, MA 02554

Nebo, English Dept., Arkansas Tech. Univ., Russellville, AR 72801

Negative Capability, 6116 Timberly Rd., N. Mobile, AL 36609

Never Mind the Press, 1986 Gouldin Rd., Oakland, CA 94611

New Directions, 80 Eighth Ave., New York, NY 10011

New England Review and Bread Loaf Quarterly, Box 170, Hanover, NH 03755

New England Sampler, RFD1, Box 2280, Brooks, ME 04921

New Letters, 5100 Rockhill Rd., Kansas City, MO 64110

New Oregon Review, 537 N.E. Lincoln St., Hillsboro, OR 97123

New Renaissance, 9 Heath Rd., Arlington, MA 02174

New Rivers Press, 1602 Selby Ave., St. Paul, MN 55104

The New South Writer, 828 Royal St., Suite 510, New Orleans, LA 70116

Nimrod, 2210 S. Main, Tulsa, OK 74114

The North American Review, Univ. of No. Iowa, Cedar Falls, IA 50614

North Dakota Quarterly, P.O. Box 8237, Univ. of N. Dak., Grand Forks, ND 58202

Northeast, Juniper Press, 1310 Shorewood Dr., LaCrosse, WI 54601

Northwest Review, Eng. Dept. Univ. of Oregon, Eugene, OR 97403

Northwoods Press, P.O. Box 88, South Thomaston, ME 04861

Nostoc, Box 162, Newton, MA 02168

Now it's Up to You Publications, 157 S. Logan, Denver, CO 80209

O.ARS, Box 179, Cambridge, MA 02238

The Ohio Journal, OSU Dept. of Eng., 164 W. 17th Ave., Columbus, OH 43210

The Ohio Review, Ellis Hall, Ohio University, Athens, OH 45701

Oink!, 1446 W. Jarvis, Chicago, IL 60626

The Old Red Kimono, Floyd Jr. College, P.O. Box 1864, Rome, GA 30161

The Ontario Review, 9 Honey Brook Dr., Princeton, NJ 08540

Open Places, Box 2085, Stephens College, Columbia, MO 65215

Orca Press, SR 4314 Helibut Point Road, Sitka, AK 99835

Orphic Lute, P.O. Box 2815, Newport News, VA 23602

Osiris, Box 297, Deerfield, MA 01342

Owl Creek Press, P.O. Box 2248, Missoula, MT 59806

Oyez Review, 430 S. Michigan Ave., Chicago, IL 60605

Padre Productions, P.O. Box 1275, San Luis Obispo, CA 93406

Paintbrush, Eng. Dept., Ga. Southwestern College, Americus, GA 31709

Painted Bride Quarterly, 230 Vine St., Philadelphia, PA 19106

The Pale Fire Review, 162 Academy Ave., Providence, RI 02908

Pangloss Papers, Box 18917, Los Angeles, CA 90018

The Panhandler, Eng. Dept., Univ. of W. Fla., Pensacola, FL 32514

Panjandrum Books, 11321 Iowa Ave., Ste. 1, Los Angeles, CA 90025

Paper Air, 825 Morris Rd., Blue Bell, PA 19422

Parabola, 150 Fifth Ave., New York, NY 10011

Paris Review, 45-39 171 Place, Flushing, NY 11358

Parnassus, P.O. Box 1384, Forest Park, GA 30051

Partisan Review, 121 Bay State Rd., 3/F, Boston, MA 02215

Passages North, Boniface Fine Arts Center, Escanaba, MI 49829

The Pawn Review, 2903 Windsor Rd., Austin, TX 78703

Pax, 217 Pershing Ave., San Antonio, TX 78209

Pequod Press, 344 Third Ave., Apt 3A, New York, NY 10010

Perivale Press, 13830 Erwin St., Van Nuys, CA 91401

Pessimistic Labor, c/o Grenier, 2338 McGee, Berkeley, CA

Petterle Publications, 3 Greenside Way, San Rafael, CA 94901

Phoebe, 4400 University Dr., Fairfax, VA 22030

Piccolo Press, 1303 Briar, Muncie, IN 47304

Piedmont Literary Review, P.O. Box 3656, Danville, VA 24543

Pig Iron Press, P.O. Box 237, Youngstown, OH 44501

Pillar Press, 636 Tarryton Isle, Alameda, CA 94501

Pineapple Press, Inc., P.O. Box 314, Englewood, FL 33533

Plainsong, Box U245, Western Ky. Univ. Bowling Green, KY 42101

Planet Detroit, 8214 St. Marys, Detroit, MI 48228

Ploughshares, Box 529, Cambridge, MA 02139

Plover Press, P.O. Box 874883, Wasilla, AK 99687

Poet & Critic, Iowa St. Univ., 203 Ross Hall, Ames, IA 50011

Poet Lore, 4000 Albemarle St., NW., Washington, DC 20016

Poetic Justice, 8220 Rayford Dr., Los Angeles, CA 90045

Poetics Journal, 2639 Russell St., Berkeley, CA 94705

Poetry, Box 4348, Chicago, IL 60680

Poetry/LA, P.O. Box 84271, Los Angeles, CA 90073

The Poetry Miscellany, English Dept., Univ. of Tenn., Chattanooga, TN 37402

Poetry Newsletter, Eng. Dept., Temple Univ., Philadelphia, PA 19122

Poetry Northwest, Univ. of Washington, Seattle, WA 98105

Poetry Now, 3118 K St., Eureka, CA 95501

The Poetry Review, 15 Gramercy Park, New York, NY 10003

Point Riders Press, (see Cottonwood Arts Foundation)

Poly Tone Press, 16027 Sunbrust St., Sepulveda, CA 91343

Pooka Press, 2000 E. Roger Rd., #E9, Tucson, AZ 85719

Prairie Schooner, 201 Andrews, Univ. of Neb., Lincoln, NE 68588

Precisely, P.O. Box 73, Canal St., New York, NY 10013

Prescott Street Press, P.O. Box 40312, Portland, OR 97240

Press Porcepic, 235-560 Johnson St., Victoria, B.C. V8W 3C6 CAN

The Priapus Press, 37 Lombardy Dr., Berkhamstead, Herts, England

Prickly Pear, 3350 E. Pima St., Tucson, AZ 85716

Primavera, Univ. of Chicago, 1212 E. 59th St., Chicago, IL 60637

Priority Press, P.O. Box 30152, Dallas, TX 75230

Progressive Platter, P.O. Box 638, Kenmore Sta., Boston, MA 02215

Prospect Hill, 216 Wendover Rd., Baltimore, MD 21218

Pulp, c/o H. Sage, 720 Greenwich St., New York, NY 10014

Pulpsmith, 5 Beekman St., New York, NY 10038

Pym-Randall Press, 73 Cohasset St., Roslindale, MA 02131

Quarterly West, Univ. of Utah, Salt Lake City, UT 84112

Quarterly Review of Literature, 26 Haslet Ave., Princeton, NJ 08540

Quilt, 1446 Sixth St., Suite D, Berkeley, CA 94710

Quorum Editions, Ten North Mill, Cranbury, NJ 08512

Raccoon Books, 323 Hodges St., Memphis, TN 38111

Random Weirdness, 6092 N. Newburg Ave., Chicago, IL 60631

rara avis Magazine, (see Books of a Feather)

Raritan, 165 College Ave., New Brunswick, NJ 08903

Rat & Mole Press, P.O. Box 111, Amherst, MA 01004

Rathasker Press, 1712 Henderson St., Columbia, SC 29201

Reader's Choice, 88 Otter Crescent, Toronto, Ont. M5N 2W8 CAN

Real Fiction, 298 9th Ave., San Francisco, CA 94118

The Reaper, 8600 University Blvd. Evansville, IN 47712

Reflect, 3306 Argonne Ave., Norfolk, VA 23509

The Review of Contemporary Fiction, 1817 79th Ave., Elmwood Park, IL 60635

Rhyme Time, P.O. Box 2377, Coeur d'Alene, ID 83814

Rhino, 3915 Foster St., Evanston, IL 60203

Ridge Review, P.O. Box 90, Mendocino, CA 95460

River Styx, 7420 Cornell St., St. Louis, MO 63130

Rolling Stock, Campus Box 226, Univ. of Colorado, Boulder, CO 80309

Rowan Tree Press, 124 Chestnut St., Boston, MA 02108

Rubes Publications, 14447 Titus St., Panorama City, CA 91402

Ruddy Duck Press, 4429 Gibraltar Dr., Fremont, CA 94536

SZ Press, 321 W. 94th St., New York, NY 10025

Salmagundi, Skidmore College, Saratoga Springs, NY 12866

Saltillo Press, 607 Gregory, El Paso, TX 79902

Samisdat, Box 129, Richford, VT 05476

San Fernando Poetry Journal, 18301 Halsted St., Northridge, CA 91325

Santa Barbara Press, 1129 State St., Suite H, Santa Barbara, CA 93101

Score, 2625 Ivy Dr., #9, Oakland, CA 94606

Sea Fog Press, Inc., P.O. Box 210056, San Francisco, CA 94121

The Seal Press, 312 S. Washington, Seattle, WA 98104

The Seattle Review, Padelford Hall, GN-30, Univ. of Wash., Seattle, WA 98195

Second Chance Press/Permanent Press, RD2, Noyac Rd., Sag Harbor, NY 11963

Second Coming Press, P.O. Box 31249, San Francisco, CA 94131

Seneca Review, Hobart & William Smith Colleges, Geneva, NY 14456

Sequoia, Storke Publications Bldg., Stanford, CA 94305

Serpent & Eagle Press, 1 Dietz St., Oneonta, NY 13820

Sewanee Review, Univ. of the South, Sewanee, TN 37375

Shadow Press, P.O. Box 8803, Minneapolis, MN 55408

Shankpainter, Fine Arts Center, Provincetown, MA

Shearwater Press, Box 417, Wellfleet, MA 02667

Sheet, P.O. Box 3667, Oak Park, IL 50303

Shenandoah, Box 722, Lexington, VA 24450

Shepherd Publishers, 100 Sheriff's Pl., Williamsburg, VA 23185

Silver Wings, P.O. Box 5201, Mission Hills, CA 91345

Silverfish Review, Box 3541, Eugene, OR 97403

Slipstream, Box 2071, New Market Sta., Niagara Falls, NY 14301

The Small Pond Magazine, P.O. Box 664, Stratford, CT 06497

Snowy Egret, 205 S. Ninth St., Williamsburg, KY 40769

Sojourner, 143 Albany St., Cambridge, MA 02139

Sonora Review, Univ. of Arizona, Tucson, AZ 85721

South Carolina Review, English Dept., Clemson Univ., Clemson, SC 29631

Southern Humanities Review, 9088 Haley Center, Auburn Univ., Auburn, AL 36830

Southern Poetry Review, English Dept., Univ. of N.C., Charlotte, NC 28223

The Southern Review, 43 Allen Hall, Louisiana St. Univ., Baton Rouge, LA 70803

Southern Writers Guild, (see The New South Writer)

Southwest Review, Southern Methodist Univ., Box 4374, Dallas, TX 75275

Space And Time, 138 W. 70th St., Apt. 4B, New York, NY 10023

The Spirit that Moves us Press, P.O. Box 1585, Iowa City, IA 52244

Spitball, (The Literary Baseball Magazine), 1721 Scott Blvd., Covington, KY 41011

Spuyten Duyvil, 520 Cathedral Pkwy., #5C, New York, NY 10025

State Street Press, 67 State St., Pittsford, NY 14534

Stories, 14 Beacon St., Boston, MA 02108

Story Quarterly, P.O. Box 1416, Northbrook, IL 60062

Sulfur, 852 S. Bedford St., Los Angeles, CA 90035

Sun Dog, English Dept., 406 Williams Bldg., Fla. State Univ., Tallahassee, FL 32306

Sunstone Press, P.O. Box 2321, Sante Fe, NM 87501

Swallow's Tale Magazine, P.O. Box 4328, Tallahassee, FL 32315

Tamarack Editions, 128 Benedict Ave., Syracuse, NY 13210

Tamarisk, 319 S. Juniper St., Philadelphia, PA 19107

Tanam Press, 40 White St., New York, NY 10013

Tar River Poetry, East Carolina Univ., Greenville, NC 27834

Telescope, Box 16129, Baltimore, MD 21218

Ten Mile River Press, 2155 Eastman Lane, Petaluma, CA 94952

Tendril, Box 512, Green Harbor, MA 02041

Third Eye, 189 Kelvin Dr., Buffalo, NY 14223

The Third Wind, P.O. Box 8277, Boston, MA 02114

13th Moon, Box 309, Cathedral Sta., New York, NY 10025

Threepenny Review, P.O. Box 9131, Berkeley, CA 94709

Threshold Books, RD 3, Box 1350, Putney, VT 05346

Thunder City Press, P.O. Box 600574, Houston, TX 77260
Thunder's Mouth Press, Box 780, New York, NY 10025
Tightrope, 72 Colonial Village, Amherst, MA 01002
Tilted Planet Press, P.O. Box 8646, Austin, TX 78712
Tombouctou Books, Box 265, Bolinas, CA 94924
Tooth of Time Books, 634 E. Garcia, Sante Fe, NM 87501
Touchstone, P.O. Box 42331, Houston, TX 77042
Trackaday, Rte. 1, Box 330, New Market, VA 22844
TriQuarterly, 1735 Benson Ave., Northwestern Univ., Evanston,
    IL 60201
Trivia, P.O. Box 606, N. Amherst, MA 01059
Trout Creek Press, 5976 Billings Rd., Parkdale, OR 97041
Turkey Press, 6746 Sueno Rd., Isla Vista, CA 93117
Tuumba Press, 2639 Russell St., Berkeley, CA 94705
2 Plus 2, (see Mylabris Press)

Universal Black Writer Magazine, P.O. Box 5, Radio City Sta.,
    New York, NY 10101
Uranus, 1537 Washburn, Beloit, WI 53511
Utopic Furnace Press, 729A Queen St. E, Toronto, CAN M4M
    1H1

VAAPR, Inc., P.O. Box 44370, Capitol Sta., Baton Rouge, LA
    70804
Vagabond Press, 1610 N. Water St., Ellensburg, WA 98926
Vanishing Cab, 827 Pacific St., Box 101, San Francisco, CA 94133
Virginia Quarterly Review, One West Range, Charlottesville, VA
    22903
Voices Israel, 38 Nehemia St., Nave Sha'anan, Haifa 32 295, Israel

Walt Whitman Quarterly Review, Univ. of Iowa, Iowa City, IA
    52242
Washington Review, Box 50132, Washington, DC 20004
Washington Writers Publishing House, 3207 Macomb St., NW.,
    Washington, DC 20016
Waves, 79 Denham Dr., Richmond Hill, Ontario, CAN L4C 6H9
West Anglia Publications, Box 2683, LaJolla, CA 92038
West Branch, Bucknell Univ., Lewisburg, PA 17837
West Coast Poetry Review, 1335 Dartmouth Dr., Reno, NV 89509

West End Press, P.O. Box 7232, Minneapolis, MN 55407

Western Humanities Review, Univ. of Utah, Salt Lake City, UT 81112

White Pine Press, 73 Putnam St., Buffalo, NY 14213

The Widener Review, Humanities Div., Widener Univ., Chester, PA 19013

Willow Springs Magazine, P.U.B. P.O. Box 1063, EWU, Cheney, WA 99004

Windfall Prophets Press, English Dept., Univ. of Wis., Whitewater, WI 53190

Wingbow Press, 2940 Seventh St., Berkeley, CA 94710

The Windless Orchard, English Dept., Indiana Univ., Fort Wayne, IN 46805

Wisconsin Academy Review, 1922 University Ave., Madison, WI 53705

Woodrose Editions, P.O. Box 2537, Madison, WI 53701

Wormwood Review, P.O. Box 8840, Stockton, CA 95208

Stuart Wright, Publisher, Box 7527, Reynolda Station, Winston-Salem, NC 27109

Writers Forum, Univ. of Colo., Colorado Springs, CO 80907

Yale Review, P.O. Box 1902A, Yale Sta., New Haven, CT 06520

Yellow Silk, P.O. Box 6374, Albany, CA 94706

Zerx Press, 400½ Laurel Ave., Upland, CA 91786

INDEX

The following is a listing in alphabetical order by author's last name of works reprinted in the first ten *Pushcart Prize* editions.

481

491

CONTRIBUTORS' NOTES

JAMES ATLAS is the author of a biography of Delmore Schwartz and is a contributing editor to *Vanity Fair*.

BO BALL has published stories in *Chicago Review, Prairie Schooner, Southern Humanites Review* and *South Carolina Review*. His fiction previously appeared in *Pushcart Prize V*.

RUSSELL BANKS' most recent novel is *Continental Drift*. He teaches at Princeton University.

SUZANNE BERGER has published two collections of poems, *These Rooms*, (Penmaen Press) and *Legacies* (Alice James).

D. C. BERRY lives in Hattiesburg, Mississippi and teaches at The University of Southern Mississippi.

T. CORAGHESSAN BOYLE's most recent book is *Greasy Lake and Other Stories* published by Viking. "The Hector Quesadilla Story" won *The Paris Review*'s John Train Humor Prize for 1984.

CHRISTOPHER BUCKLEY's recent collection of poems is *Other Lives* (Ithaca House). He lives in Santa Barbara.

CHARLES BUKOWSKI won the 1969 Wormwood Award for *Notes of A Dirty Old Man* (Essex) and his most recent book is *War All The Time* (Black Sparrow).

ANNEKE CAMPBELL worked as a midwife and received her M.F.A. degree from Indiana University. "Cranes" is her first published poem.

JARED CARTER was awarded Guggenheim and NEA fellowships and won the Walt Whitman Award in 1980 for *Work, For the Night Is Coming* (Macmillan).

AMY CLAMPITT's poetry collections include *The Kingfisher* and *What Light Was Like*, both from Knopf. She was awarded a Fellowship by the Academy of American Poets in 1984.

MARTHA COLLINS was a Bunting Fellow at Radcliffe and director of the University of Massachusetts creative writing program. Her poems have appeared in *Field, Ironwood* and elsewhere.

PETER COOLEY's poetry collections include *The Company of Strangers* (Missouri University Press), *The Room Where Summer Ends* and *Night Seasons* (Carnegie-Mellon University Press).

GERALD COSTANZO lives in Pittsburgh and is director of the creative writing program at Carnegie-Mellon University. He is editor of *Three Rivers Poetry Journal* and author of *Wage the Improbable Happiness* (1982).

MALCOLM COWLEY's most recent publication is *The Flower and The Leaf*, just out from Viking.

DEBORAH DIGGES' poems have appeared in *American Poetry Review, Antaeus, Georgia Review* and elsewhere. She lives in Iowa City.

STEPHEN DOBYNS new poetry collection is *Black Dog, Red Dog* (Holt).

SHARON DOUBIAGO is the author of *Hard Country*, an epic poem (West End Press) and is a faculty member of The Napa Valley Poetry Conference.

STUART DYBEK is the author of *Childhood and Other Neighbors*, a short story collection, and *Brass Knuckles*, a poetry collection.

MARGARETA EKSTRÖM is one of Sweden's outstanding short story writers. Ontario Review Press will soon publish a collection of her stories, the first in English.

JANE FLANDERS' most recent book of poems is *The Students of Snow* (University of Massachusetts Press). She teaches at New York's 92nd Street YM-YWHA.

KENNETH GANGEMI's most recent books are *The Volcanos from Puebla*, about living in Mexico, and *The Interceptor Pilot*, a novel. Marion Boyars has just reprinted in paperback his first novel, *OH*.

BARRY GOLDENSOHN teaches in the English Department of Skidmore College and is the author of several books of poetry.

LINDA GREGG received a Guggenheim Award in 1983. Her most recent books are *Alma* (Random House) and *Too Bright to See* (Graywolf).

ADAM GUSSOW's essays and reviews have appeared in *Boston Review, The Wall Street Journal* and elsewhere. He studies at Columbia and is at work on a novel, *Blues for the Lost Generation*.

JOHN HAINES is a poet and essayist who has homesteaded in Alaska for more than twenty years. His latest book is *Other Days* (Graywolf).

JANET KAUFFMAN's poetry appeared in *Pushcart Prize V*. She is the author most recently of a collection of short stories published by Knopf, *Places In The World A Woman Could Walk*.

CRAD KILODNY claims to be the only author who not only publishes his own books but also sells them on the street as his sole occupation. He lives in Toronto.

GALWAY KINNELL's most recent collection is *Mortal Acts, Mortal Words*. He delivered "The Fundamental Project of Technology" as the 1983 Phi Beta Kappa poem at Harvard.

WILLIAM KITTREDGE's most recent book is *We Are Not In This Alone* (Graywolf Press).

CAROLYN KIZER won the 1984 Pultizer Prize in poetry. Her most recent books have been published by BOA and Copper Canyon.

AUGUST KLEINZAHLER works as a locksmith in San Francisco. Moyer-Bell has just published his most recent poetry collection, *Storm Over Hackensack*.

DORIS LESSING is the author of *The Golden Notebook* and other novels. Her essay here concerns work under the pseudonym "Jane Somers."

PHIL LEVINE is the author of *Years From Somewhere* and *Ashes* and has won both the National Book Critics Circle Award and the National Book Award. He and David Wojahn will be poetry editors for next year's Pushcart Prize.

WESLEY MCNAIR has published poetry in *The Iowa Review, The Atlantic, Ploughshares* and has won the Eunice Tietjens Award from *Poetry*. He is the author of *The Faces of Americans in 1853* (University of Missouri Press), which won the 1984 Devins Award.

SANDRA MCPHERSON is the author of the poetry collection *Patron Happiness* (Ecco) and the chapbook *Pheasant Flower* (Owl Creek). She teaches at the University of California, Davis.

LORENZO WILSON MILAM was born in Jacksonville, Florida, studied at Yale University, Haverford College, and the University of California at Berkeley. He is the author of *Sex and Broadcasting* and *The Cripple Liberation Front Marching Band Blues*, from which this is an excerpt.

MARK C. MILLER has written and lectured extensively on George Orwell and he teaches at Johns Hopkins University.

LEONARD NATHAN lives in Kensington, California. His poetry collections are *Holding Patterns*, and *Dear Blood* (University of Pittsburgh Press).

SHEILA NICKERSON lives in Juneau, Alaska. Her most recent books are *On Why The Quilt-maker Became a Dragon* (Vanessapress) and *Writers In The Public Library* (Shoestring).

TIM O'BRIEN is the author of *Going After Cacciato*, a portion of which appeared in *Pushcart Prize II*. He lives in Cambridge, Massachusetts.

BIN RAMKE teaches at the University of Denver. His first poetry collection was *The Difference Between Night and Day*, a 1978 Yale Younger Poet selection. His *White Monkeys* was published by the University of Georgia Press in 1981.

DONALD REVELL is the author of the poetry collection *From The Abandoned Cities* (Harper and Row) and teaches at The University of Denver.

ALBERTO ALVARO RIOS won the 1984 Western States Book Award in fiction for his story collection *The Iguana Killer*. He also won the Walt Whitman Award for his first collection of poems, *Whispering To Fool The Wind*.

PATTIANN ROGERS is the author of *The Expectations of Light* (Princeton University Press). Her work has appeared in many journals including *Pushcart Prize IX*.

ANTONIO BENÍTEZ ROJO is the former director of Cuba's Casa de las Americas and now teaches at Amherst. His book of short stories in Spanish, *Estatuas Sepultadas y otros relatos*, is available from Ediciones del Norte.

VERN RUTSALA is the author of *Paragraphs* (Wesleyan University Press) and *The Journey Begins* (University of Georgia Press). He lives in Portland, Oregon.

BOB SHACOCHIS has a novel forthcoming in 1986 and is the author of *Easy in The Islands*, a short story collection just out from Crown.

CHARLES SIMIC's most recent book is *Austerities* (Braziller). He lives in New Hampshire.

JIM SIMMERMAN's poetry collection *Home* (Dragon Gate Inc.) was an NEA/Pushcart Foundation "Writer's Choice" selection. His second collection is *Once Out of Nature*.

MAURA STANTON is the author of the poetry collection, *Lives of Swimmers* (University of Utah Press). She teaches at Indiana University.

ELEANOR ROSS TAYLOR lives in Charlottesville, Virginia. This poem is from her most recent collection, *New and Selected Poems* (Stuart Wright, Publisher.)

GORDON WEAVER teaches in the English Department of Oklahoma State University. He is the author of three novels and three short story collections.

GAYLE WHITTIER teaches in the creative writing department of SUNY Binghampton, New York. Her fiction has previously appeared in *Ploughshares, Masschusetts Review, Carolina Quarterly* and *Pushcart Prize VI*.

ELLEN WILBUR's first story collection was published in 1984 by Stuart Wright, Publisher. Her fiction previously appeared in *Pushcart Prize V*.